SILENCE THE ECHO

Steve,

Step into the highest vision for your life, empowered and at peace!

Alea Carroll

Silence the Echo
Copyright © Alea Carroll 2018

All rights reserved. Published in the Unites States of America by North Node Press, Washington

This book and parts thereof may not be reproduced in any form, stored in a retrieval system, or transmitted in any form by any means—electronic, mechanical, photocopying, or otherwise—without prior written permission of the publisher, North Node Press, except as provided by the United States of America copyright law.

Carroll, Alea.
Silence the Echo / Alea Carroll. – 1st ed.
1. FICTION/Fantasy/Historical. 2. FICTION/Romance/Science Fiction.
3. FICTION/Visionary and Metaphysical

Summary: At the end of the last ice age, an advanced civilization invites a cataclysmic end by its reckless pursuit of energy. Among young telepaths instructed in the science of conscious projection, Seerce and Aaron strike out on their own to find what disturbs Earth.

ISBN: 978-1-7329976-0-8
eISBN: 978-1-7329976-1-5

Printed in the U.S.A.
First Edition, December 2018
The text type is set in Minion.

Cover art and maps by Brad Luke
Interior by Bryan Tomasovich at The Publishing World

This is a work of fiction. Names, characters, places, and incidents are either a product of the author's imagination or are used fictitiously. Any similarity to actual persons, living or dead, organizations, locales, and/or events is purely coincidental.

SILENCE THE ECHO

ALEA CARROLL

North Node Press

Dedicated to my children,
Ryan and Brad,
whose creativity inspires me.

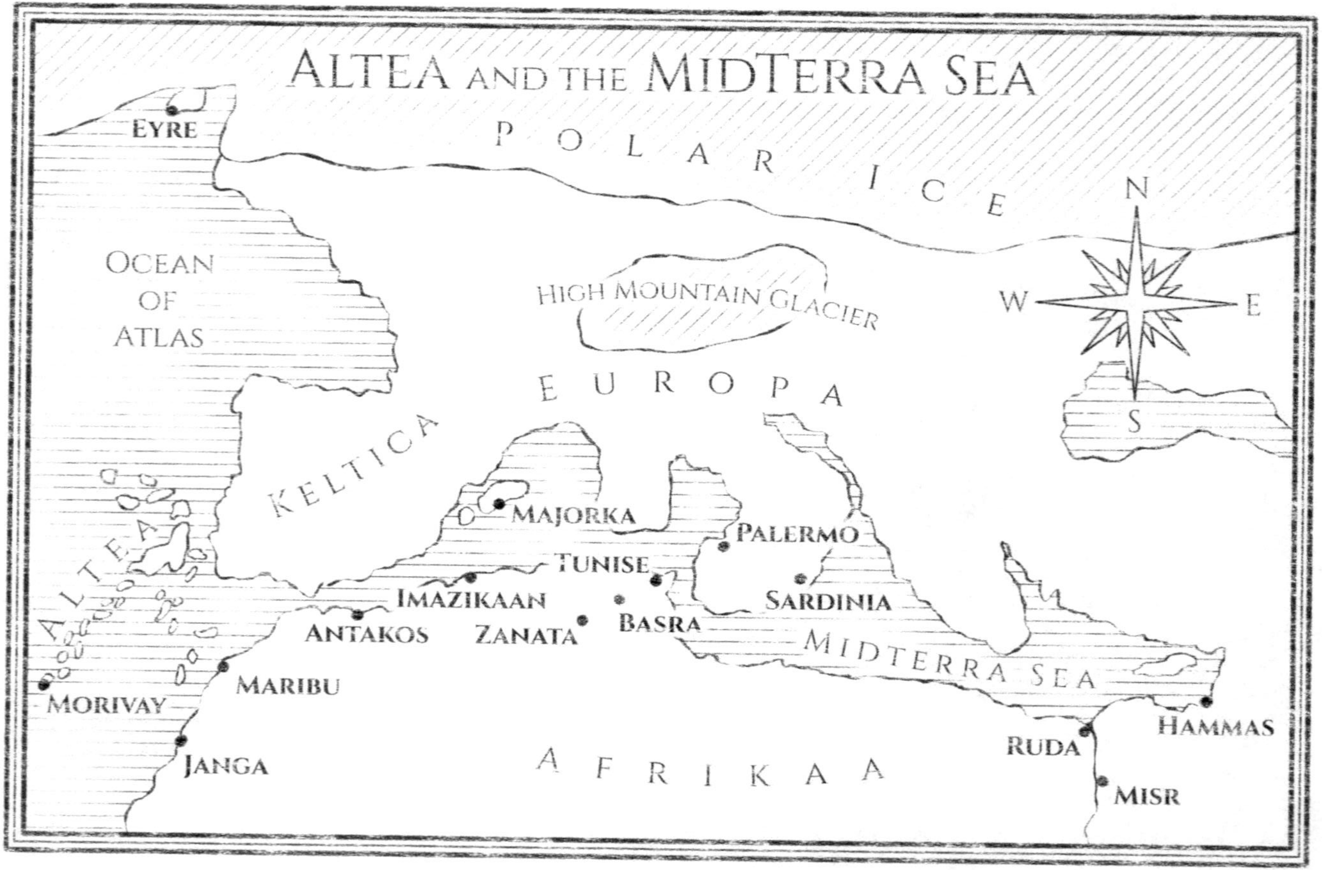
ALTEA AND THE MIDTERRA SEA
POLAR ICE
EYRE
OCEAN OF ATLAS
HIGH MOUNTAIN GLACIER
N
W
E
S
EUROPA
KELTICA
ALTEA
MAJORKA
PALERMO
TUNISE
SARDINIA
IMAZIKAAN
ANTAKOS
ZANATA
BASRA
MIDTERRA SEA
MARIBU
MORIVAY
JANGA
AFRIKAA
RUDA
HAMMAS
MISR

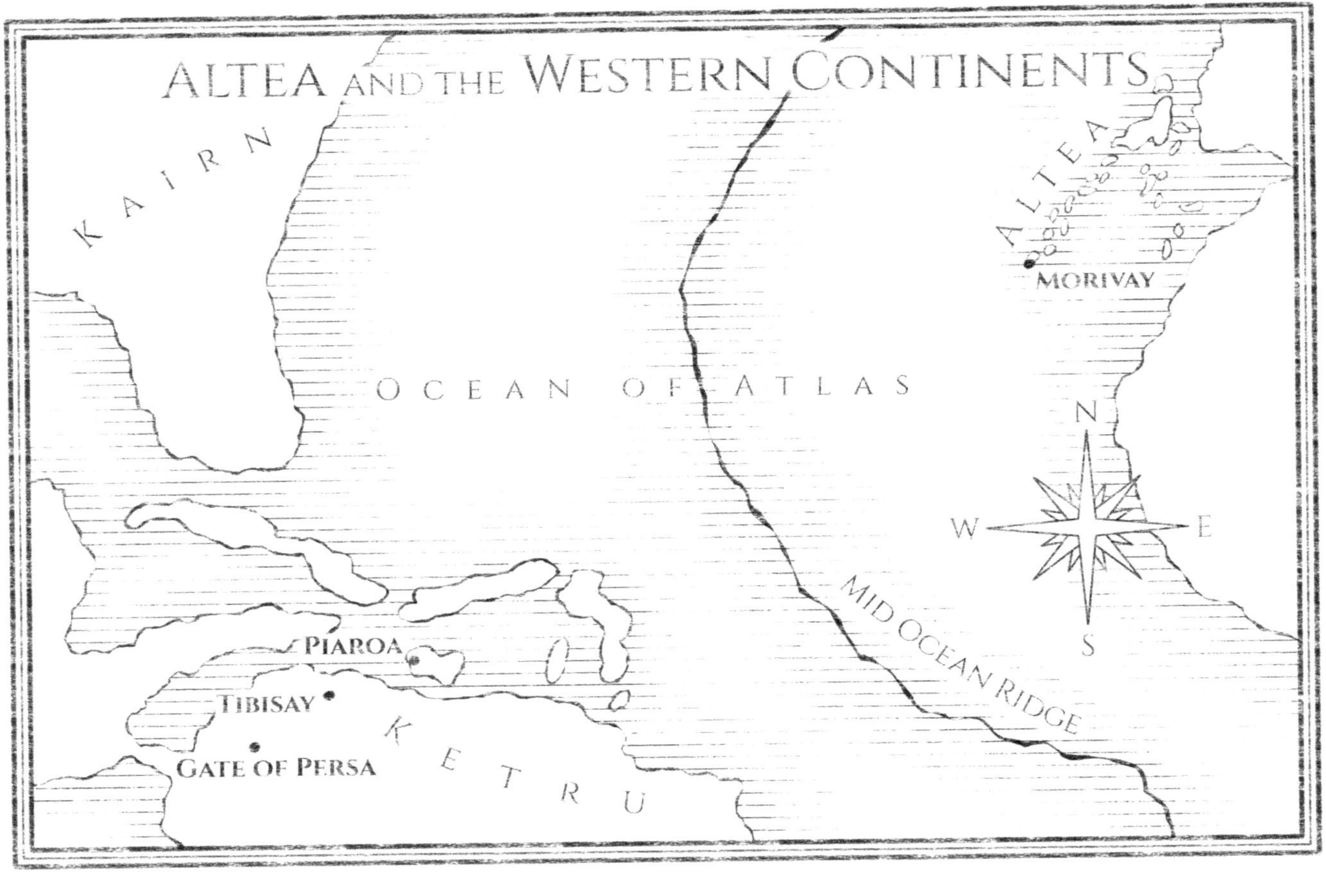

ALTEA AND THE WESTERN CONTINENTS
KAIRN
ALTEA
MORIVAY
OCEAN OF ATLAS
N
W
E
S
MID OCEAN RIDGE
PIAROA
TIBISAY
GATE OF PERSA
KETRU

PROLOGUE

The last ice age on Earth spanned forty thousand years. For much of that time, an extensive polar ice cap covered Canada and the northern tier of the United States, the British Isles and the greater part of Europe. Periodically, glaciers pushed as far south as France and steppe tundra bordered the Mediterranean Sea. Much of Earth's water was locked in a frozen state, expanding coastlines and keeping sea levels significantly lower than they are today, perhaps by as much as four hundred meters.

Running parallel to the western coasts of Portugal and Morocco was the planet's tallest undersea mountain range, its volcanic peaks exposed as islands. Warm currents from southern oceans flowed northward, moderating the climate of a large island and its trailing archipelago. Escaping frozen Europe, a race of red-haired giants found this paradise, calling it Altea.

Rain fell reliably on the windward side of the mountains. Volcanic soils were fertile and seafood was abundant. Forests provided wood for boats and quarries supplied building materials. Over tens of thousands of years, an isolated and homogenous society industrialized and mechanized, its steady progress interrupted only by an occasional eruption, earthquake, or landslide.

Around the Mediterranean Sea, small settlements came and went with the cycles of advancing and retreating glaciers. It was a struggle to raise food in that cold, dry climate, above what might be fished from shore. Across North Africa herds of goats and cattle were shepherded by nomads, rainfall there too scarce for crops.

Over thousands of years the ice sheets retreated for the last time, the melt inducing a gradual rise of the seas, overtaking low-lying islands and reducing the breadth of Altea's mainland. By then the long-lived civilization was technologically advanced. It possessed a formidable navy, the means to relocate its burgeoning population by force if necessary. What it lacked was an energy source to fuel its resettlement in new environs.

Increasing warmth and rainfall in the Mediterranean region spurred the regrowth of woodlands. Agriculture improved and food supplies stabilized. Trade replaced competition for scarce resources. But the emerging ports were no match for a willful empire in need of a new home. One by one they fell under the flag of Altea.

As the rise of the seas accelerated, violent weather raked the coasts and tremors shook the Altean nations. Something disturbed Earth.

PART I

CHAPTER 1

Suspended by no discernible means beneath the gold-gilt Temple dome, a magnificent crystal globe slowly rotated. Wisps of clouds and streaks of color crossed its surface, an occasional spark darting between it and small oval windows placed up high. Those facing west admitted the last light of this spring equinox, causing sections of the ribbed vault to brighten and glow briefly, like lightning in a distant bank of clouds. The air was damp and decidedly cool, harboring the mustiness of ancient stone.

From richly-carved foyer doors, the flagstone aisles of this theater-in-the-round declined to a marble block altar at the sunken center. From every cushioned seat of red wool the view was unobstructed. Sconces as yet unlit were the only adornment upon walls of stately, pale stone block.

Ten young people in white robes occupied the first row. Seerce scarcely breathed, stupefied at the grandeur of this seat of the Order of the Sun. What visions had been seen here, what power gathered, what influences wrought over the millennia through which the Temple of Altea had stood upon its rocky mount?

Startled by the creak of aged hinges, she turned in that direction to see three robed men walk singly and slowly down a side aisle. The first and last wore purple. Between them was an elder of great height. Proceeding to the altar, the younger men positioned themselves to either side of it. From behind it the Archaean faced the acolytes, his shoulders stooped, broad hands resting upon its highly polished surface. A cowled, brown robe hung limply about his giant bony frame. No matter that he held the highest office in the Order, this was his customary dress: wool in the cool seasons, linen for the abbreviated summers.

There was depth to the shadows beneath his copper eyes. Strands of long hair and beard, more salt than faded red, waved down his chest. At his breastbone hung an exquisite Crystal of the Sun, its pale yellow rays aglow from within. Seerce recalled cradling that mysterious jewel in one hand and stroking his beard with the other, as he and her grandmother conversed. Often had she fallen asleep in his lap.

Now he addressed the initiates in the common language of Altea, every nuance of his baritone voice made resonant by the acoustic properties of the Temple. He spoke slowly and precisely for the benefit of the foreign-tongued. "As you heard from me upon your invitation to join us, we are convinced of a drastic change to the world we know. Sooner than anticipated, this greatest of civilizations appears set to vanish from Earth, likely within your lifetimes. Our recent analysis suggests the survival of only a few widely scattered settlements, at great distances from the homeland of the Ryk, either considerably inland or at high altitudes."

A shiver coursed down Seerce's spine. Ever had Altea suffered geologic mishaps, landslides, sink holes, an occasional eruption on an outer island or the spewing of pumice and poisonous gas from a seamount. Now its densely populated main island succumbed steadily to a rising ocean. In the MidTerra Sea, storms flooded the ports and towering rogue waves had washed over several—including Tunise, where Seerce's people traded. Tremors were frequent in her desert homeland.

"We have searched for a generation among the ancient clans to find you, young people in possession of unique capabilities, grounded in traditions that honor the original agreement between Gaia and humankind. The records of all time, preserved by the Order of the Sun since the dawn of Altean civilization, must be secured. Without this repository of wisdom, catalogued over twenty millennia, any who might survive the cataclysm are condemned to begin anew without benefit of history, invention, or knowledge of the world they inherit."

Now night fell beyond the Temple walls, dimming the interior to near darkness. Slowly the sconces brightened with stored energy, but momentarily Anakron's face appeared to hover in gloom. "Still we do not know the nature of the catastrophe," he stated, "but we are certain of a drastic reduction in human presence upon the planet. Only a short time remains to transfer our records to a safe and accessible location."

Seerce was aghast. Why would the Order accept such a fate when the best minds of science and academia were pledged to its number? Surely the causes of such a disaster were identifiable and subject to intervention. With improving light, she was able to see those with whom she would live and study, of many races and traditions, each a stranger to her. Every gaze was straight ahead and unflinching. But the undercurrent of their consternation buffeted her, masked though it might be by the youthful invincibility of those seated and the placidity of these priests. Then a young man leaned forward, turning his striking emerald eyes toward her.

I share your perspective was his telepathed message.

She startled. How had he perceived her thoughts unbidden? How dare he intrude upon her ruminations!

Anakron resumed his address. "Your faculty stands with me. Tane, to my right, is Exemplar of Physics. He shall acquaint you with secrets of the universe and its dimensions. It is his responsibility to secure the records in an indestructible setting, accessible to future seekers but safe from the vagaries of time and those who would destroy wisdom out of ignorance.

"On my left is Exemplar Cyan of the Cenon Project, master of the arts of observation perfected by the first people of Earth. You will learn and practice their methods, that you may contact future leaders and teach them access to the records."

There was a stirring among the students. Was there truth to Mu mythology? Long had Seerce been intrigued by their tales of travel through time and other realms. Never had she met a descendant, if that was what these purple-robed exemplars were, with their slight statures, brown skin, and hair and eyes as dark as midnight.

Anakron remained silent for a time, gazing deeply and briefly into the eyes of each initiate. Engaging Seerce last, he telepathed, *Have you regret for your decision to join us?*

No, Petrae, she replied firmly, calling him 'grandfather' in her native language. *All the more reason to be here, though I am surprised you have kept these revelations from me.*

We agreed that your status here is equivalent to your fellows. Now they and you know, he replied, his tone uncharacteristically cool. All her life had she idolized this man, studying the subjects he brought her, following the path he outlined, living in anticipation of his next visit. There must be no perception of favoritism by her peers—this he had emphasized and she understood why. But had he meant she must undertake this rigorous training without his counsel and support? Was she to be his granddaughter no longer?

It was with considerable guilt that Seerce had left behind her familial obligations, for she was heir to the priesthood of her clan. She risked her father's forgiveness. Ever had he resented Anakron's influence, warning against the folly of joining his priesthood here in the poisonous heart of the Ryk. Now she was days of sea travel from home. For the first time, Seerce of Basra considered how gravely she may have erred.

*

May I join you?

Seerce looked up to the emerald eyes.

Surely you heard me yesterday, he telepathed. *We have commonalities.*

"Forgive me if I missed our introduction," she responded curtly in the common language, heavily accented. Setting down her cup and rising to her feet, she swung the length of her gold hair behind her. "I am called Seerce."

A bit taller than average height among non-Archaean males, he towered over her. Undaunted, she raised her right forearm in greeting, her open palm toward him.

Stepping forward to touch his right palm lightly to hers, he stooped a little. Wavy auburn hair loosed itself from behind one ear to cover a curved scar at his temple, as a fishhook might have made. Bemusement settled around his mouth. "Have I offended you?" he asked, his accent one she did not recognize.

"Among my people, telepathy is reserved for family and dearest friends," she declared. "It is never the privilege of strangers. Do you have a name?"

"I am Aaron of Eyre," he replied. "And you are Seerce of what land?"

"Basra," she answered.

"Among my people, failure to acknowledge one's birthplace is considered deceitful," he told her. The glowing emeralds danced.

"Please accept my apology," she demurred. "We have some to learn from each other. You may fetch tea and join me, Aaron of Eyre, if it suits you."

Allow me to warm yours, he suggested, reverting to telepathy, taking her mug and her scraped-clean breakfast plate with him. *You must have enjoyed the meal.* Returning from the tea table, he set down steaming vessels for each of them and took a seat across from her. *I shall conduct your tour of the campus*, he told her. *This is my second year at the Temple.*

Looking around, she saw no other white robes among the diners, nor had individual tours been mentioned by the administrator.

We shall look from windows. The weather is abominable, he remarked, as curtains of rain bounced off the stone patio outside the dining room. Somehow the floor-to-ceiling windows cleared themselves, spasmodic splashes thinning to flowing sheets, quickly restoring the view. Seerce had consumed breakfast contemplating how such a thing was possible.

"Tell me about the iron fence around the campus," she requested. "Does it keep the Order in or society out?"

He laughed at her cheekiness. *It was put up two centuries ago in an era of political upheaval, when neighboring estates were looted in an uprising of the working class. The Order's schools in Altea were closing then for lack of attendance, the relevance of classical education lost on its military technocracy. Now the priests have their audience in the conquered nations, where children must learn the common language if they hope to make something of themselves.*

"I attended the Order's academy in Tunise," Seerce interjected, persisting in her use of orality. This young man was rather stubborn.

Aaron rebutted, *All ten of us were vetted in the Order's schools or we would not be here.*

Seerce considered this as it regarded her relationship with Anakron. "Vetted?" she queried.

We initiates are the harvest of a twenty-year breeding program. It took me a while to figure that out.

"This is your own conjecture," she pronounced.

I asked among my classmates. Each of their families has a close relationship with someone high up in the Order. A headmaster, a professor, an exemplar—someone whose job it was to notice potential, or even to introduce our parents to each other that we might be conceived. Are you a half-breed? he inquired. *I have never seen anyone with hair the color of ripe wheat or eyes like sea foam.*

This Aaron certainly lacked couth to use such an insult. "My parents are of two peoples," she replied evenly. "Might the same be true of yours?" Those orbs were otherworldly, almost haunting.

No, he stated, *but I am of human parentage.*

Heat spread upward from her chest to her cheekbones as she blushed deeply.

I take no offense, he told her, but he looked away.

How would she guard her every thought around this person?

He looked back to her. *All of us were watched and coached and availed of certain opportunities. Barlas, the administrator, was a schoolmate to uncles of mine. He used to visit Eyre when I was young.*

If each initiate was sponsored, Seerce wondered, why did Anakron insist she keep their prior acquaintance undercover?

Barlas asked the same of me, Aaron said, replying to her unspoken question.

"Stop this!" she demanded. "Must you read the thoughts of everyone all the time?"

No, he told her, laughing. *You have a unique wavelength that happens to match my own.*

"I do not hear your thinking!" she countered.

Much to my advantage, I believe. Finishing the last of his short cup of tea, he suggested, *Allow me to show you the campus from its highest indoor point. There are tunnels beneath the buildings. You will not need a cloak.*

She looked up to see a white-robed initiate heading toward their table. "Forgive m-my interruption, miss," stammered this chubby boy with high color in his face, too nervous to make eye contact. "I was sent to fetch you for a meeting of the first years and a tour of the campus. P-please come with me."

Seerce excused herself and rose to follow him, taking her teacup with her, looking back just once to see the sheepish look on Aaron's face.

As she followed her classmate into a room down the hall, Kessa recounted a tale to the administrator, who laughed uproariously. Seerce had met her in the women's domicile; both their apartments were on the fourth floor. A big-boned Archaean, her spiky short hair was dyed an improbable shade of burgundy, offending her sallow complexion. The other two first years, female and male, smiled politely as Seerce took a seat across from them at the oval conference table, the handsome gentleman rising from his chair and tipping his head to her.

"Ah, Seerce," said Barlas. "Please meet Tavia and Rayn. I trust Jair has introduced himself."

"Indeed, sir," she pretended, turning to smile at Jair, as he peeked out from his mop of strawberry curls. His innocent blue eyes met hers briefly and he blushed again.

"This is your lecture room and laboratory," Barlas told the five, standing and gesturing toward the back of a long rectangular room with a second entrance from the hallway. Dressed in a brown robe such as Anakron favored, his corded belt slipped below his ample waist, though he did not seem to notice. Short grey hair fringed the sides of his pale bald head, and he kept a perpetual grin. Pointing out the windowed wall, which faced the courtyard of gardens and stone paths, he told them, "This is the ground floor of the women's domicile. The men's is across the way, and beyond that, the great Ocean of Atlas."

Seerce had spent time gazing from her apartment's broad windows at an unobstructed southwesterly view, the direction from which the storms blew. She wondered at the placement of female initiates on the uppermost floor, for they enjoyed commanding views of sky and sea. However, their sleeping lofts were topped by transparent pyramidal ceilings. The break of dawn might always wake her, though a starry night or a full moon would be a sight to behold—if the sky ever cleared.

"We follow Altean time conventions, each day and night divided by ten decans, commencing at dawn and dusk. Chronometers are above most doors," Barlas told them, "and you may instruct the one in your bedchamber, by voice or telepathy, when to wake you with a chime. Our days of rest coincide with the full, half, and new moons—when you will have no class or obligation, but delicious meals are served," he added, patting his midsection. "Unless you are told otherwise, lecture commences here at the third decan, beginning tomorrow.

"While you are free to travel the air barges of Altea, we suggest you do so in groups. Parts of the city are notorious, to be avoided by women and men alike unless you are expert in defensive arts. See me for particulars if you plan an excursion. Whenever you leave campus, you are required to check in and out at the Administration office.

"Meals are communal, though tea may be had any time until kitchen staff goes home at night. I will show you the tunnels that connect to Admin and the Healing Temple and take you through both buildings. But first, Anakron has asked that I remind you of something he discussed with each of you some time ago." Barlas chuckled, saying, "We have trouble with one particular expectation." Pausing for effect, he added, "Abstain from intimacy with your classmates. Your apartment is your own to sleep in alone."

The initiates tittered. Jair covered his face with both hands.

"Priests of this Order have relationships and liaisons," Barlas acknowledged. "Such is human nature and among the gifts of life in flesh. However, we do so quietly and unobtrusively, with utmost consideration for the work and only *after* induction. Meanwhile we are obligated to uphold the mores of your clans. You shall attain a level of maturity over the next two years, which includes forethought for the consequences of every personal choice, for yourself *and* your community. All of us once sat where you do, among vibrant young people in the prime of their lives. Attractions are inevitable. But the success of our endeavors rests upon the order we keep in our communal relationships."

Seerce had no objection. The mechanics of coitus her mother had explained, but the appeal of such she could not fathom. Having witnessed childbirth under the tutelage of her priest grandmother, she found the suffering and blood and products of conception rather horrifying. Affection she craved, but her one brief crush ended when she told her beloved she would study at the High Temple.

"Accompany me," Barlas requested, "to see a city view from the Healing Temple." They took a side door into a tunnel, sconces lighting as they approached. "On your left is the Admin tunnel." But they tread straight ahead over a stone floor, through a wide hall with a low ceiling, coming eventually to another staircase. "All aboard," he directed as the door of an adjacent lift slid open.

"You may speak your destination or send a thought to the door crystal. Your choices are one, two, three, four, or tunnel, as they are in your domiciles." On the far side of the top floor they entered a spacious lounge with several seating groups. Three sides of this room were windowed. Seerce gasped at the view of the sprawling city before them, for the rain had diminished. The mighty volcano remained enshrouded in clouds. To the south, the Ocean of Atlas tossed and rolled. "On clear days, the residence of the Autark, supreme leader of the Ryk, may be seen atop the mountain," Barlas told them. "Out here on the promontory we try to be a balancing force." He allowed the five to linger with their wonderment.

Awestruck by the sprawl of the city over and around every hill and the enclaves of the wealthy climbing up the formidable mountain, Seerce's eyes lingered on stands of tall trees and unbuildable ravines that fractured the imposed order of a mighty society. In places, mist softened the puncture of energy spires across the landscape, those which enabled floating transport barges to run between them. The face of ruin showed itself in the nearer view, where older buildings crumbled and the narrow streets channeled the morning's rain to the sea, workers with their push carts maneuvering around the deepest ruts.

The students followed Barlas back to the lift. He opened the door briefly on each floor to crowded waiting rooms for various clinics. Kessa offered a more personal tour, saying she had just left a role here. "Barlas made me give it up." She sighed theatrically. "He says every moment of our time shall be taken by study."

He smirked, telling her, "You shall thank me."

They toured the aged Administration building, which fronted the campus on the north side. For millennia it had housed staff and students, but now it was offices, storage, and guest rooms. A gymnasium took up a large portion of its first floor, shared with the kitchen and dining hall, where Barlas left them. "Unpack your belongings and arrange your living quarters this afternoon," he suggested. "Tomorrow your lives are forever changed."

*

Exemplar Tane stood at the head of the large conference table as the initiates filed in, an errant shock of straight black hair falling into his eyes. Sweeping it aside, he smiled. "I am honored to be here among you," he told the ten, both first and second-year students. "Please, take your seats." Dressed informally in a light-colored tunic and trousers, his expression was impish and a glint shone in his dark eyes. His cheekbones were prominent and his nose a bit flattened. He wore no facial hair, save longer pointed sideburns, and his brown complexion glowed with good health.

"My father and his father were researchers with the Altean Energy Authority, involved in design and maintenance of power transmission systems, those which operate hypersound air barges and the navy of the Ryk. My mother is from a line of educators. We are descendants of the Mu and quite a traditional family. My choice as eldest was to become a physics educator." He grinned and the students laughed.

"It has been my fervent wish to power society in an Earth-friendly manner. I found my place in the community of this Order. We conduct research that diverges greatly from that which Altea sponsors. You might wonder why physics is your first topic this year. I shall lay the intellectual groundwork for your travels across time and space. Methods shall be Exemplar Cyan's subject, once we have established your foundation in science."

Seerce was captivated by this promise, for sciences were her passion.

"The universe is malleable and elastic, replete with information that humankind has forgotten how to access. I shall challenge your conceptions about our physical world, for we are possessed of inner senses that allow direct perception of the greater universe. You shall learn to employ these, for they inform your Greater Mind, an entity grander than your physical being, an inhabitant of multiple planes. Your youth affords you an ability to establish such connections before your physical brain solidifies its focus upon three dimensions. You are here because your individual talents are crucial to conquering the monumental challenges before the Order.

"But intellectual prowess will not be our only pursuit, for our spirits have indeed taken physical form. May I tell you of my interest in handball?" He paused, allowing the students their bewilderment. "In the interest of maintaining my corporeal housing, I took up the sport years ago. Anakron agreed, in exchange for my professorial services, to refurbish the gymnasium as handball courts. I have a proposal for you to consider: your release from class a decan earlier each day, if you meet me to play. Or you may choose lab projects to fill that time."

The students looked at each other. Did he speak in jest?

"Exemplar Cyan and I will demonstrate the game tomorrow after class. Barlas has acquired appropriate clothing and footwear, which you may select afterward. I seek serious competition, initiates, for I am weary of playing only Cyan. What say you?"

There was an enthusiastic burst of agreement.

"An excellent choice," Tane commented. "Now to the subject at hand. The Order of the Sun distills its wisdom into Five Central Tenets to which you shall be introduced. We demand no adherence to canon and we worship no gods. We have no quarrel with any beliefs you may hold. We simply carry forward ancient observations regarding the relationship between the planet and its occupants, emissaries of a body of knowledge amassed by the Mu. A broader and deeper universe is observable and navigable by our inner senses. We have access to other realms and so shall you.

"Earth spins at an intersection of planes made manifest by higher intelligence. Physical existence here provides a unique experience in cooperation and creativity. The planet belongs to a majestic order of life with its own purposes, conventions, and companions. Humans are guests upon the physical body of Earth, whose spirit the Mu called Gaia.

"The first people of Earth emerged cognizant that they were no more and no less than other sorts of life. They joined a cooperative venture already in progress between the planet and zoological and botanical orders. Altea chooses to dominate all of these, plundering natural resources, disrupting delicate balances, and destroying species in pursuit of all that it desires. The original agreement has been forgotten. This is folly, for our host has no particular need of our presence. She follows Her own course of evolution, as the geologic record reflects.

"On the table are recording crystals and subject crystals for each of you. You may record my sessions for review. You may begin your reading of the Central Tenets now. Go where you study best, then have your lunch and return here at the seventh decan for discussion. You are dismissed."

Seerce pocketed her crystals and climbed three flights of stairs to her apartment. There she sat down on her divan to claim the recorder as her own, touching the point of the slender six-sided rock quartz, about as long as her hand was wide, to the middle bracelet of her left wrist. To record a lecture, she need only touch again to the same place. A touch to her right wrist retrieved what was stored. These were standard tools of learning in the Order's academies.

The study crystal, a prasiolite quartz, was the same shape and size, but a 'public' crystal, one instilled with static information and graphics to supplement Tane's presentations. To start the flow, she touched the point to her forehead. Closing her eyes, she saw and heard the material unfold in her mind, like dreaming or active imagining, but with sharp clarity. A touch or a release of the crystal increased or decreased the rate at which it transmitted. When satisfied with its speed, she set it in the silver crystal holder on the low table in front of her and lost herself in the First Tenet: Consciousness exists apart from physical manifestation. With heavy fog outside her windows and the pulse of rhythmic surf, she crossed spellbound into the science of the ancients.

Silence the Echo

*

Chatting with the cooks, arms crossed, leaning against the door to the kitchen, Aaron seemed to wait for her. When Seerce took her place at the end of the serving line, he moved in behind her. Then he seated himself across from her, taking a bite before he telepathed, *May I join you?*

She replied, "You may explain your deceit of yesterday, Aaron of Tours."

This he disregarded as he studied her face. *Who are your people?* he asked.

"If you consent to speak, I shall answer you," she countered. Telepathy conveyed far more than he needed to know of her.

"Agreed," he conceded reluctantly.

"My mother is Aurean, a northern race of alabaster skin, light eyes, and flaxen hair. 'Ghost people' they were called as they emerged from southern Europa among the darker-skinned of the MidTerra, in search of warmer climes. My father's ancestors wandered across the North Afrikaan savannah with their goats. The coloring of the Basrans is like that of our classmate, Rayn—olive skin, dark hair, and brown eyes." Aaron's eyes seemed to dim at the mention of the other man.

"You are beautiful," he told her. "Why do you want to be a priest?"

"We have a civilization to save," she replied.

"This one may not be worth the effort."

"Tell me of your mother," Seerce requested, for most of the old clans were matriarchal.

"She died when I was a child," he responded unemotionally, "murdered by an Altean patrol in a neighboring village. She attended a difficult birth at a dangerous time."

Seerce's throat tightened and her right hand moved to cover her heart. "The light of the Goddess upon her way," she told him, the condolence of her people.

Aaron asked, "Is your mother well?" His uncanny intuition missed nothing.

"She was gravely injured in a tidal wave over Tunise six years ago," Seerce acknowledged, "blinded as a result. But she does well at home."

"Your father objects to you being here."

Seerce sat back in her chair, flummoxed. "How do you know this?"

"I feel it," he said.

"Father equates the Order with the Ryk of Altea, which he loathes. He expects me to take the mantle of priest from his mother and serve the clan of Basra."

"My father wishes me to be priest of Eyre. Our lives run in parallel."

"Perhaps," said Seerce, picking up her spoon and tasting her soup.

"My people arrived to our north sea peninsula a century ago as fishers. The land was until then covered in ice, forbidding and useless. Now Earth warms. Draining marsh and moving rock allows for short-cycle summer crops. More people come. My father is a good leader, wise and kindhearted. Eyre remains independent but Altea presses us.

"Of late there are tremors and rockslides at home. Some of the fish are sickly and the catches smaller. Tides are high and the coast is pummeled by angry storms. At times there is a strange glow to the sea at night. Something is wrong. We fear the Ryk unleashes forces against our homeland."

"Earth often shifts in Basra," Seerce told him. "Four centuries ago, the rivers fell beneath the savannah and rainfall ceased. My people had quickly to adapt to life underground. When I was small my family narrowly escaped the collapse of one of our subterranean waterways. We continue our horticulture in stone caverns with crystal light, but the rivers clog with rockfall. Now we depend upon Altea's power grid to operate our air barges, the only means we have to get produce to market. It worries my father and my uncles endlessly."

Aaron took a sip of tea before he responded. "My clan's struggle may take precedence over my stay here. We consider unpriestly measures to get Altea off our backs. Would you like pudding?" he inquired. "I shall fetch you a bowl."

"No, thank you. I must finish here and review Tane's lecture." When he returned, they discussed the day's subject matter. Then she picked up her dishes and bid him a restful night.

Her heart hurt for Aaron's loss. Seerce still had nightmares about her mother's near-drowning. But she felt no call to share that with him. There was commonality between them, yes, but a burden seemed to accompany Aaron. She was leery of it.

CHAPTER 2

Following her classmates through the tunnel to the gym, Seerce saw tables of sports apparel set up at the entrance. Inside, Tane motioned to the students to gather around him. "We shall start by building your endurance," he told them. "Tomorrow wear a rain jacket over your gym clothing as we will warm up by walking or jogging the perimeter path around the campus. Then we shall practice particular skills you need to play the game. Kessa, leave your rings at home. Seerce, tie your hair back or you will never see the ball." The coastal humidity had turned her waist-length waves into a wild tangle. Seerce looked down, embarrassed, while Kessa held up her jeweled hands for all to see.

Donning face masks and headgear, the two professors demonstrated use of the paddle, degree of force, and footwork. Performing a series of gentle volleys, they hit the bright orange ball against two walls, the floor, and the ceiling. Pausing, Tane remarked, "Your brain gets a nice geometry workout. Watch from here while we play a standard six rounds in the backcourt."

Seerce was amazed at the speed of the game and the dexterity and endurance of the exemplars, their muscularity apparent in close-fitting navy-blue uniforms. The ball went everywhere, but consistently it was smacked back by the opponent after a single bounce.

"This may be a fate worse than physics," rued Sootchie, a second-year student with a pudgy build.

"Oh, yes," buxom Tuura agreed. "What a gift a decan of lab assignments might be."

Tane won the first set and Cyan the second. They were dripping when they finished. "Be sure you take headbands and hand towels," Tane advised, drying his face and neck. "You will need them."

Barlas assisted selection of clothing and shoes. Returning from quick showers, the professors fitted headgear. Exemplar Cyan kindly suggested that Seerce braid her hair. "Some competitors wear one braid down the back," he told her. "Your eye shield will keep it from striking your face as you pivot. Do I remember correctly that you played table ball at your academy?"

"Yes, sir. I was school champion these last two years."

"The skill sets are similar in timing, speed, and hand-eye coordination. I anticipate a serious challenge from you."

"One day, sir, I shall offer you that," she replied boldly. A glimmer of a grin pulled at the corners of his thin lips, but failed to engage the tiny crinkles at the corners of his small, dark eyes. Surely those were the result of squinting, for there were no smile lines around his mouth.

*

Seerce tried to keep her attention on Tane's subject. He was an interesting and enjoyable presenter, but her memory was full of new concepts and she was exhausted. Rayn sat across the table from her, as he had each day, seemingly absorbed in an explanation of multidimensional common ground, whereby individual consciousness might join others to become a group mind.

Her mind wandered over Rayn's beautiful person, thick hair expertly cut, his handsome face sporting a short beard and mustache. She admired his profile and the length of his black eyelashes, but it frustrated her that she perceived nothing of his inner workings. From most people she picked up nuances and generally more than that. Shifting a little in his chair, absently he placed an elbow upon the table, propping his pretty head in his palm, his focus intent upon their instructor.

Likely he was older than the other initiates, behaving more formally and carrying himself regally. On the occasion that he asked a thoughtful question, it was phrased in perfectly unaccented Altean diction, as though he was a native speaker—which he could not be, for she heard mention of his lengthy journey from the eastern MidTerra. Perhaps she stared too long. Aaron, sitting next to him, gave her a look.

Lunch, lecture, jogging, handball—Seerce finished out the day and went to eat, intending to retire early and sleep long. Jair dined alone. He looked embarrassed when she asked to join him, but he assented. Telling him not to give her seat away, she hurried to scoop up dinner before Aaron caught her.

"Jair," she said warmly as she sat down, "would you fill me in on crystal manifestation? When you spoke of it in class, I had no idea what you meant." This was partially true. She was determined to get to know other classmates.

He seemed pleased to be asked, but nerves had him. "I have forgotten your name," he confessed, the color in his face brightening.

"Seerce," she said. She repeated it slowly, "Sear-see, emphasis on the last syllable."

Coming close by the fourth try, his accent was of yet another native tongue. "Perfect," she judged. He was nearly finished with his meal, so she suggested, "I shall eat while you explain."

He nodded, appearing to relax a bit. "My father has propagated the Temple crystals for decades. When I was young, he experimented with growing round crystals. It was a long time bringing the first one into existence, but eventually the right mix of minerals in a perfect bath developed into something remarkable. Generations later, so long as one perfect crystal is left with a new batch, they all seem to figure out what they are supposed to be. It is almost magical."

Seerce smiled at his childlike wonder. "Is a morphologic field the means by which they catch the pattern?" Just then Tavia and Kessa walked up with their plates, asking to join the table. "What do you think, Jair?" Seerce teased. "Are they worthy?"

"I am sure they are," he replied, color coming again to his face.

"We are deep in conversation, ladies, about how crystals learn to be round."

Tavia's eyes lit up as she exclaimed, "Mineralogy is my subject!"

"And I wear jewels," Kessa laughed, "except when I'm playing handball."

"Have a seat," Jair invited, smiling shyly.

Rayn walked past them to sit down alone at a table in the corner. Seerce tried to meet his glances, but each time he looked away. Seldom had she seen him in the dining room. Maybe his classmates were too young to interest him. Maybe he was a loner. She knew nothing of him and that frustrated her.

*

"The Second Tenet holds that time is an illusion. When does time pass quickly?" Tane asked the ten. "Call out your responses."

"For any enjoyable activity."

"On our common day off."

"Sleeping."

"Now cite examples of time passing slowly," Tane requested.

"While in physics class," Kessa responded wickedly. Routinely she stationed herself at the end of the oval table, opposite Tane. He shook his head, smirking.

"If I am ill."

"Waiting for summer."

Tane told them, "Dreams also demonstrate the variability of time. Perhaps you recall history with your dream people, as though you have long known these characters and that world.

Meanwhile, the moon and constellations rose and set in the same period they always do, night passed in a flash, and you lived a lifetime in a dream. Your sense of time depends upon where you place your focus.

"How many of you know prior lives on Earth?" Each of the ten placed a hand upon the table. "How many of you have glimpsed a future life?" he asked. All hands were withdrawn.

"What you define as *now*," he told them, "is what you perceive in this moment. What you think of as *past* is a previous now. It is your physical brain's focus that prevents you from seeing your future. From the perspective of your Greater Mind, all your existences occur simultaneously."

Doubtful looks were exchanged between students.

"Consciousness is unbound by distance or time. The marking of time is but a method by which our physical brains order a myriad of life events. Your Greater Mind is free of time because it dwells beyond the physical. The Super Mind of the Universe organizes itself *outside of time*, reaching from all points in the future to all points in the past, gathering information that allows its intelligence to grow. *Information* is the substance of the universe.

"Listen carefully. Pulling information from the supposed future to utilize in the present may well be a universal operating procedure. If this is the natural activity of greater consciousness, then the Order's observations of the future may allow us to adjust what appears to be a collision course with the end of our civilization."

Here is an exemplar with a ray of hope for the human race, Seerce thought. Aaron looked up and smiled at her.

*

On the second communal day off, out for a run in rare sunlight, Seerce realized some improvement in her endurance. She started a second lap around the campus. Tiring quickly then in the heavy sea air, she slowed to a walk as she came by the southern tip of the promontory. The water sparkled in the brilliance of midday. Shading her eyes, she noticed Rayn on a small patio below the level of the path. Panting heavily, she stopped at the top of the stone stairs leading to where he stood. His back was to her as he looked out to sea, outfitted in his sports clothes. "Would I be bothering you?" she called breathlessly. "I was…running by…and saw you."

He turned to her with a smile upon his face. "There is no one I would like more to see," he called to her.

A small current passed through her being. "I had not known… of this patio…before now," she huffed.

He came up the steps toward her, suggesting, "Let us walk until you cool down. I finished my run a while ago, but I could not go back inside on such an afternoon." Close to his person, she saw that he was of lesser height than Aaron and a heavier build, broader in his shoulders and chest, but slender of waist and hips.

Seerce nodded. Approaching the Healing Temple, her heart rate slowed and her breath came easier. They turned around to regain a view of the undulating water and a turquoise-blue sky. "Thank you," she said. "Now I can talk."

"You glisten as the dew upon grass in springtime," Rayn teased.

"I doubt I smell as good." She giggled. He laughed with her. Shading her eyes, she saw within his richly brown irises the gold starbursts which encircled his pupils. Momentarily she was fixated. Impulsively she asked, "Why do you stare at me?"

He looked away. But returning to her eyes, he answered, "I try to be unobtrusive. You notice."

"No need to stop," she told him, "just toss a word or thought in my direction now and again. Mysterious types confound me."

Again he laughed. "I like to study the delivery of your bold pronouncements, which you soften with a smile. Your expressions are priceless, for you wear your thinking upon your face. I marvel at how genuine you are."

Playfully Seerce told him, "The height of your pedestal makes me dizzy."

"Then sit with me," he beckoned, starting down the stairs to the patio. Following him to a bench in the shade, she relished an opportunity to study him.

"You, sir, say nothing of yourself ever," she reflected, "and you hold yourself apart from the rest of us. Why? You are well-spoken and most attractive."

"You flatter me," he responded. "It was necessary in my former role to portray neutrality while observing carefully. I retain those habits."

"So you were a spy and now you hide among priests," she ventured, tongue in cheek.

Chuckling, he told her, "I negotiated trade deals for my father's merchant fleet."

"A traveling man living a singular life?" Seerce asked.

"For many years, yes."

She read more of him now, gathering that other tasks had occupied him since, upon which he did not elaborate. If she reserved her curiosity and allowed for his trust to grow, perhaps more of his story would unfold.

"Your speech harkens to the north coast of Afrikaa," he judged.

"Yes. I learned the common language in Tunise. Basra is my homeland."

"But I see Aurean influence."

"You are correct, from my mother's side. Who are your people?"

"Craftsmen and merchants, sailors and traders," he said. "We are descended from nomads along the eastern MidTerra."

Perhaps his clan was patriarchal, for he mentioned professions of men. "Do you favor physics?" she asked.

"Hardly. I must listen to the lectures over and over again. How do you fare?"

"I give it my all. Jair helps. He frames strange concepts in pictures I can fathom. You might join us for dinner some evening."

"I shall endeavor to be less of a stranger," he promised, ending their exchange by standing. "I beg your pardon, but I have a prior appointment. Thank you for seeking me out today. I enjoyed our conversation."

"As have I," Seerce replied, watching him climb the steps, disappointed to lose his company. Sitting with the cool spring breeze and the rhythm of waves against the seawall, she tried to identify what had awakened in her through the course of their exchange. It had no familiar name.

*

Tane busied himself with instruments in the back as the initiates arrived to class in twos and threes. "Bring your recording crystals to the lab," he requested, "and perch on a stool here at the counter." Their customary seating pattern disrupted at this table, Rayn slipped in next to Seerce on the far side of the square. Speaking softly, he said to her, "Salama."

"Salama ieta," she replied, returning his wish for a good morning in the language of her homeland. Enchanted that he would know a Basran greeting, she missed the exemplar's instruction for placing their crystals. Rayn's forefinger on the counter pointed to his own, set into a recession in the countertop. Embarrassed, she set hers. Then Tane began.

"To perceive beyond three dimensions, your physical brain must stand down its guard and allow your inner senses to connect directly to your Greater Mind. It resists doing this, as its prime responsibility is to interpret your physical environment and keep your person safe within it. Among humankind there are those whose brains are more broadly receptive, children in particular. If they keep the trait into adulthood, we call them daydreamers, seers, or even deranged. They are guilty only of perceiving what others generally do not.

"Be not afraid. Our practices do not induce lunacy. While your brain sleeps, your inner senses and your Greater Mind carry on an unimpeded dialogue. This is why you wake up with insights and solutions to problems that have confounded you." The students sat up straighter on their stools, intrigued.

"Let us review a few basics," Tane suggested. By his thought, apparently, he caused a holographic projection to appear over the greater portion of the table. A mad soup of colored particles organized itself into a model of the solar system. "This represents Earth's immediate neighborhood," Tane stated. "Tuura, where is Venus today?"

"At seven degrees of the Water Bearer, sir, in your fifth house." With a straight face she added, "You shall meet a worldly woman who is forbidden to you." Laughter erupted around the table.

"Ah, a fortune teller in our midst," Tane chuckled. "Here we view our solar system from a geocentric perspective, as astrologists do. Though less predictive of my social life, we might choose to look from a heliocentric perspective," he said, altering the view.

As a third view appeared, he told them, "From Pluto, Jupiter appears larger than the Sun. Old Sol is but a pinpoint of bright light in the distance. Or, we could look from the center of our galaxy"—the hologram reconfigured itself again—"outward to our quite ordinary yellow star at the end of one of its arms." Picking up a pointer, he walked around the students, stopping between Ell and Sootchie to indicate a speck just above the countertop. Then blackness filled the cube before a group of galaxies appeared. "Beyond considerable dark space are our closest galactic neighbors. Consider the increasing order of complexity in each of these systems. Do you know that consciousness is associated with complexity?"

A collective gasp escaped the students.

Allowing them to ponder, Tane dissolved the hologram and took a seat. Then he resumed, saying, "A system's ability to be influenced by its previous state, and to influence its next state, defines consciousness. Inorganic systems possess this capability.

"The Mu held that Earth is both conscious and willful. Think of the many interrelated systems we know within the planet. An

25

iron core and a molten mantle spin by rotation to produce an electromagnetic field, Her version perhaps of a nervous system, extending through solid layers and liquid oceans to an airy atmosphere. The outer reaches of that same field function as a type of skin, deflecting the harmful radiation of solar storms. Perhaps this is the means by which She feels Her companion moon, perceives the motion of Her planetary neighbors, and spies the occasional random space rock by which She might be struck. Lava is Her lifeblood, minerals Her veins, oceans and rivers and rain the moist humors of Her body, and the winds Her exhalations. These are poetic descriptions left to us by the Mu, who had neither telescope nor magnetometer, only their inner senses to know Gaia's body.

"Does Earth even notice those who crawl across Her surface, made as we are of the same substances that She is? Perhaps to Her we are no more than dust mites, too insignificant to be bothersome. Or does She consider us a part of Herself, noticeable only when what we do becomes too irritating, too sickening, or too painful to disregard? I speak particularly of powerful energy transmissions, forces that echo through Her deeper realms and her atmosphere. What damage have we done, what symptoms does She show, when She is treated as a large lump of lifeless rock?"

The faces upon the students reflected introspection, puzzlement, anger, and passion ignited. Seerce's eyes held tears as did Aaron's. "Your thoughts, please?" Tane requested.

Ell, a second year, placed his slender dark hand upon the lab table, the whites of his dark eyes luminous in his long ebony face. "Points you have made since the first day of class, sir, while framed in science, are akin to traditional spirituality taught by my tribe's shamans: the existence of greater realities, consciousness which precedes human birth and survives death, and personification of the planet."

Tane responded, "There are parallels between the Order's theorems and certain spiritual principles. Your clans are of ancient origin. It is likely that base truths are preserved in your traditional teachings and practices. The longer I study physics, the fewer differences I find between one and the other. Once, our species knew from whence we came, why we chose human form, and our obligation to live lightly upon Gaia's body."

There was silence for a moment before Tavia's caramel-colored hand appeared on the table. She asked, "How does the planet express Her will?"

"Let us assume in complex systems a will to survive," said Tane. "There have been prior mass extinctions of botanical and zoological species upon this planet. The Mu were decimated in an upwelling of the southern ocean in the other hemisphere. Were these random upsets, the dawn of new evolutionary stages, or purposeful defense against harm?"

Goose bumps rose on Seerce's arms and Aaron's hands clutched the edge of the countertop.

"A pattern of observable changes in certain systems of Earth may be found in your study crystals. Not all are human-caused. There are cycles to the brilliance of the sun and its emissions, to energy pulses originating deep in the galaxy. Earth is a member of a larger community in which She dwells. Your individuality is part of a greater consciousness in which you dwell." Glancing at the chronometer above the door, Tane suggested, "Take some time for a discussion among yourselves while I attend to another matter. We shall reconvene after lunch."

*

Seerce ran upstairs to change clothes and braid her hair, happy to jog in the drizzle. It would clear her mind of the muddle of equations Tane introduced that afternoon. She much preferred the pictures he painted to his mathematical proofs, though she was able to follow most of them.

She and Aaron paired for paddle volleys across the gym floor. He seemed a bit testy. The third time he smacked the ball to the far end of the gym, she stopped on her way to give Jair a pointer and on the way back, to chat briefly with Rayn. Then she showed Aaron some skill and let him chase the ball. Finally they settled into a rhythmic volley.

Rayn pays you attention, Aaron telepathed.

Because the gym was noisy, she assented to telepathy. *As do you, if it suits you.*

Having conveyed his notice, he changed the subject. *You told me you were named for the seercens, the Earth listeners among your mother's people. Do you hear Earth speak?*

"Not as they did. I do not know the turning of the weather nor how to tell an edible plant from one that is poisonous. I attribute the voice I hear to the spirit of a distant grandmother."

"Perhaps your intuition speaks loudly."

"Perhaps, though once it warned of tremors."

Aaron stopped in his tracks, missing the ball. "Did those occur?"

"Oh, yes, nearly immediately. My family was visiting the catacombs of my people along one of our subterranean rivers. As I touched the carving of Seah's face on the front of her tomb, a voice in my mind insisted I tell my father to take us home. We narrowly escaped rockfall in the river channel."

A whistle signaled the start of matches. Cyan called out pairs and court assignments. Seerce and Sootchie would referee the first round along with Tane and Cyan. Midway through the second match, Isla took a hard fall.

Kessa was close enough to hear her ankle pop, perhaps the sound of a fracture or a torn ligament. A tall and slender second year, Isla was overcome with pain, her lips pursed tightly, roses absent from her porcelain complexion, and tendrils of her braided black hair dripping perspiration into her eyes, which she squeezed shut. Her knee was drawn up to her chest as she lay on her side, holding her left ankle.

Rayn raced to her and knelt, helping her turn face up, allowing her head and shoulders to rest upon the tops of his thighs. Kessa got down on the floor to press the back of Isla's bent knee with one hand and a particular spot at her lower back with the other. Crouching, Aaron gently removed her shoe and stocking.

"Look at me, Isla," Aaron insisted, as Rayn mopped her brow with a towel that Cyan fetched. "Look into my eyes and breathe with me, slowly, completely…slower, deeper…there, just like that. Do your best to relax your ankle that I might infuse it with light." Encircling the affected area with his hands, he instructed, "Let it go. Let me have your ankle."

Seerce saw Isla's eyes lock to Aaron's, his taking on a warm, hypnotic glow. Some color returned to her blanched face. Kessa held her pressure points and Isla stayed with the connectivity as the others watched in silence.

"Now, Isla, I am giving back your ankle, and for good measure, your foot, too." Opening his hands, Aaron released the injured area. "Kessa, would you maintain a bit longer?" he asked.

She nodded.

"Is there pain?" he asked.

"I do not feel pain," Isla answered quietly, "but neither do I feel my leg below my knee."

"Kessa knows her anesthesia," Aaron commented. "She will direct you further."

"Now, Isla," Kessa requested, "disconnect from Aaron's mesmerizing eyes and give the same level of attention to your ankle. Know it to be well and whole. Affirm it entirely healed." Kessa watched for a while. "I shall release the nerve center at your lower back. Take a deep breath now and hold it." She withdrew her right hand from Isla's spine. "Now exhale slowly…and breathe normally. Well done.

"This time I want you to exhale slowly and completely." Pulling her left hand from behind Isla's knee, she said, "Now breathe in and continue to breathe normally." Isla's bare foot and ankle regained color. "Tell me how you feel."

Isla sighed deeply. "I am comfortable," she said, her furrowed brow relaxing, her taut lips becoming full again.

"No pain?" Kessa asked. Isla shook her head no. Rayn clasped her shoulders, and she tipped her head back to smile up at him.

"May I examine your ankle and test the feeling in your foot?" requested Kessa.

"Of course," Isla agreed, affirming that she felt Kessa's touches and squeezes with no discomfort. Aaron and Ell assisted her to sit up and then to stand on her unaffected foot while they supported her balance. Kessa continued to assess the ankle's range of motion and weight-bearing capacity. "My dear," she said, sitting back on her haunches, "you are as good as new."

The group cheered. Seerce's eyes met Aaron's. *All hail, Lord Healer*, she conveyed sincerely. He smiled at her and then looked back to the relief on Isla's face.

"I have a fine bottle of wine," Tane announced, "and if you meet me in the dining hall, we shall toast Isla's good health and the gifts of our talented colleagues."

*

Seerce invited Aaron to watch the sunset with her after dinner, for the rain clouds had scurried east, leaving only shreds to reflect vivid color. Wrapped in cloaks, they walked through the rose garden, yet to bud, and sat down upon a bench. "Thank you for your aid to our classmate," she told him sincerely. "You have an amazing gift."

"Praise to the Creatrix and my mother," Aaron told her, "for I am but an instrument. Truly it was a joint effort with Kessa, who made Isla comfortable enough that I could help." This he expressed with simple humility, something new to Seerce's picture of him.

He perceived this, of course, responding, "There is no ego when the pain of another calls me. My only wish was to relieve Isla's suffering." He looked away from Seerce.

"Oh, Aaron, I mean no disrespect! I am ignorant as to the whole of who you are. We know little of each other, for we are acquainted not even a moon. I have never heard of anyone doing what you did!"

They watched as the rays of the sun pierced the scatter of clouds near the horizon, gilding their edges in gold and yellow. Eventually he spoke again. "Then may we spend more time together, perhaps meet for a short while at the end of each day, to get to know one another?"

Seerce reacted, exclaiming, "We are in each other's presence the better part of six days out of seven, ten decans a day, and nearly every meal! I crave time alone, to reflect upon daily discoveries, to soak in a bath, to sleep as long as possible! In the course of time, we shall know each other very well, I am sure."

The breeze picked up as the sun dropped beneath the watery horizon, the last of the light cast to high cirrus clouds, tinting them pink and purple, those colors reflected by the sea. Aaron took her mug from her and set it aside. Then he reached for her hands, taking both into his.

She was shocked by his advance. But his hands were incredibly warm, almost hot. By this physical connection she perceived much more than he had yet revealed. She realized the excitability of his nervous system, the high state of alert that caused his restlessness and the emotional storms he could not temper. All this and his insatiable intellect drove his quest to unearth everything hidden. Aaron simply could not wait for what he desired in the moment. These insights were strongly undeniable, but Seerce did not know if they were hers or his.

He released his hold and she withdrew her hands to the pockets of her robe, relieved to return to the quiet order that characterized her own inner workings. She asked in a hushed tone, "Do you want me to know so much of you?"

"Yes," he told her, "this and more. But the breeze cools and you shiver. You should go inside." He walked her to the door of her building and there he kissed the top of her head. Turning in the direction of the men's domicile, he crossed the courtyard, leaving her mystified.

CHAPTER 3

"**We shall continue with the notion** of group mind," Tane told the ten, their recording crystals set in lacy silver holders upon the dark polished wood of the conference table. Lately, Seerce had followed the alignment of these. Today the oval pattern was perfect, every holder equidistant from the table's edge and its neighbor to either side. She wondered if Tane realized how his precision had rooted in his students. She suppressed a giggle at the notion. The exemplar must have heard her.

"Seerce is uncommonly cheerful this morning," he observed. "Please, share the good news with all of us."

She stood up, unabashed. "Exemplar, I request that you and my colleagues rise and take three steps back from your chairs. Give your powers of observation to the tabletop." They complied. Tane laughed uproariously.

Every few moments a classmate saw the pattern, hooting or snickering. Two required clues from their neighbors. Kessa promptly moved her crystal out of alignment, exclaiming, "We cannot have this!"

"Thank you, Seerce," Tane told her, bowing in her direction, "for noticing the evidence of an evolving group mind among you."

"With respect, sir," she said, raising her voice above the

laughter, "I suggest that the evidence supports the notion that perfectionism is contagious."

"Mine?" he asked.

"Yours," she replied.

"Then my work here is finished," he announced, heading for the door. He went out to the hall but came back in, wiping tears of laughter from his eyes. "I feel like a proud papa," he told the class. "But the subject merits further discussion. Take your seats, everyone."

Resuming his professorial demeanor, he began, "There are folk tales and fables from many cultures about diverse beings and their adventures together. One I heard in east Afrikaa concerns kindnesses repaid to a child by an ape, a lion, and a snake. Have you examples about cooperative ventures across species, through time, or with inanimate beings?"

Tuura responded, "My people maintain an awareness of our jungle community. Our elders say the elder animals speak to them. Many times we have had to move our villages, because the river was about to flood or the locusts were coming. Always we are forewarned."

Tane remarked, "An intriguing example of survival through inter-species collaboration."

Seerce cited the Khubradan ceremony of her people. "We believe our departed commune with us in our midday meditation. The living clan is far flung, in enclaves that span a vast desert. We resolve many issues by bringing them to Khubradan. Someone of the clan receives guidance, though not always immediately. Sometimes an answer comes before the question has been posed. It is as though the communion operates outside of time as we know it."

"An excellent example," Tane commented. "Anyone else?"

Jair took a turn, his cheeks brightening as he spoke. "I have been several times on test sessions for temple crystals. Priests participate so that technicians may determine best frequencies. As priests engage in speaking and telepathing, we assess whether the crystals transmit properly.

Silence the Echo

"A visitor walking in might perceive indecipherable noise, but those participating are able to focus upon their particular exchanges. It is as though the crystals keep it all straight for us, shifting wavelengths to accommodate the complexity of the transmission." He looked down.

Tane explained, "Jair's father manufactures the Order's round crystals in Palermo. What he describes may be an evolutionary advance in crystalline properties. Members of my staff are studying the phenomenon. It appears that the crystal community teaches itself new skills."

The students listened with rapt attention.

"Incredibly," he added, "we see older temple crystals adapting to the capabilities of younger generations as these are installed at the school sites."

"Are you telling us," Sootchie asked incredulously, "that these crystals have consciousness?"

"In a crystalline sort of way, it seems they do," answered Tane. "A fortunate outcome of their evolution is that Altea has nothing like them, which enhances the security of the Order's communications."

When Tane allowed a morning break, Rayn waited at the door, speaking quietly to Seerce as she neared him, "Perhaps you would join me for tea."

"I would be delighted," she responded as her heart skipped a beat. They passed Aaron standing outside in the hallway. After she and Rayn filled their cups, he led her to a window table for two. Periodically the sun won a skirmish with a cumulus cloud and a brilliant blue sky showed itself briefly. Seerce returned Rayn's gaze, watching those gold petals reflect the sunlight. Finally he said, "I believe pale celadon most aptly describes the color of your eyes."

She smiled. "Dazzling describes yours!"

He smiled, sipping carefully at his hot tea. "Khubradan is a word from my native language. For us it names a holy state achieved by self-sacrifice, one of seven gates to eternal happiness."

"I would not be surprised if our peoples branched from the same tree," Seerce told him. "You look so much like the Basrans. What do you call yourselves?"

"Tarqans," Rayn replied, "after a river to the east of Hammas."

"I am told that our ritual of Khubradan evolved from the habit of our shepherding ancestors to stop at midday, allowing their animals to drink and forage. Before taking their own refreshment, the people thanked Gaia for Her bounty and remembered their distant kin, for it was only at solar festivals that small bands came together, scattered as they were across the savannah. A few among Basrans heard telepathy from distant kin, and generally these were elders. Petitions were made with an expectation for guidance."

"Do you hear the thoughts of your distant people?" Rayn inquired.

"Only on occasion, the first time as a toddler. My clan was in Khubradan when I escaped my nap and went up to the surface. I might have succumbed to the heat of the desert noon, but a commanding voice required me to telepath my picture of the hatch door to my kin, for I could not open it. They came running, else I would not be here to tell the tale."

Rayn's eyes widened. "Whose voice did you hear?"

"I did not know at the time, but I heard it again later at the tomb of our matriarch's grandmother. Thereafter I was required to attend Khubradan, much earlier than any other child of the clan."

"Your gifts showed themselves early," he remarked with awe.

"I was born an adventuress." Seerce laughed. "It is fortunate both living and departed kin kept eyes on me. Tell me of your attributes."

"Languages are my gift and music is my passion," he told her.

Ah, now he revealed secrets. "Do you sing?" she asked, envious of any who did. Raised as a telepath, her vocal cords missed an early introduction to song.

"Yes, but I am better at playing the oud."

She did not know this instrument.

Quickly he added, "At another time I shall play for you, but I have taken too much of your attention."

"I have no wish to leave your company," she protested.

"Aaron grows impatient. I doubt he waits for me."

Seerce glanced behind her, to see Aaron scowling from a table near the entrance. As she turned back to Rayn, he rose, saying, "There will be other opportunities." Taking her hand from where it rested upon the table, he kissed the back of it. "A custom of my people," he told her before he went out the patio door.

She took a moment to delight in that man's enchantment. When finally she turned around, Aaron was gone.

*

In the lab, the hologram portrayed a rotating Earth tipped realistically on its axis. "Travels through time are among the interesting activities you shall undertake with Cyan," Tane told the initiates. "Today I provide a couple models for your brain's reference, lest it panic at the thought. Be reminded that time is a root assumption peculiar to our plane. Elsewhere there is only the spacious present.

"Suppose we wish to observe the dome of the High Temple being placed some four thousand years ago. We might utilize one of the timeless planes which intersects Earth's three dimensions. Such a plane perhaps looks like this." He caused the globe's rotation to cease and a curved, transparent yellow field of minimal thickness to intersect the Altean mainland. "We might slide in along this plane," Tane suggested.

"Or perhaps the notion makes more sense this way." The yellow plane disappeared and one end of a narrow spiral tube, purple in color, pierced the Temple's promontory, the greater portion extending into Earth's atmosphere. "The purple plane operates like the lifts in your domiciles. Move a portion of your consciousness into the tube and state the occurrence you wish to view. A door opens to the Temple grounds, depositing you among the builders and their levitational devices. I hope you can find the purple door when you are ready to come back," he told them, eliciting chuckles.

"When you travel with Cyan, you shall take your inner sensorium through one of several gates on Earth. These interchange time and sound, opening a departure point between planes for your inner traveler. The gate draws you back at a point in Earth time that you specify. How all this works we shall take up later, once you gain some travel experience with Cyan. Following the common day off, he will assume your tutelage for a moon or two, and I will rejoin you thereafter. To finish out this course, please accept the assignment of a short presentation to be delivered by each of you two days hence."

Seerce and Kessa left with their topics, riding the lift to their apartments and reserving energy for handball. The roots of Kessa's naturally ginger hair had grown out enough to make the fading burgundy dye look sickly pink. Her spikes fell like shingles across her forehead, too long to stand up. "What topic do you have, Seerce?" she asked.

"Vector Components, hardly bearable, let alone interesting. What is yours?"

"Cosmic Background Radiation," Kessa announced, bowing with a flourish, "which I shall subtitle, 'Friend or Foe?'"

Seerce giggled. When they reached their floor and the lift door closed behind them, Kessa asked seriously, "You know, do you not, that I have a stellar view of the dynamic across the conference table? There are two you hold in charmed captivity, seated next to each other."

"Oh, no!" rued Seerce. "Is it so obvious?"

"I think it is hard to miss, but surely it escapes Ell and Jair at my end of the table. Tane would never notice. But here is the pattern: You stare at Rayn when he is not aware. Aaron rolls his eyes. When you are caught up in the lecture, Rayn watches you and Aaron smirks. I see you frown at Aaron, but then he makes you laugh. If Rayn sees you smiling, he thinks you smile at him, then Aaron grins because he knows Rayn is wrong. But all your secrets are safe with me!"

The two doubled over in laughter. Eventually Seerce remarked, "All three of us will be in trouble if Cyan takes class as seriously as he does handball."

"Indeed," replied Kessa. "But if you and I trade seats, it seems unlikely the boys will turn all the way around from Cyan to flirt with you."

"You are a genius," Seerce judged.

*

Standing at the head of the classroom table, Cyan waited for the initiates to show. Arriving early, Seerce and Kessa's trade spurred a total reconfiguration of the seating pattern. The exemplar watched as students hesitated to choose chairs, intermittently returning his expressionless gaze to Seerce opposite him, soon flanked by Aaron on her left and Rayn on her right. Initially alarmed, it occurred to her that those two just made themselves equally conspicuous—which should work in her favor, as long as she disregarded Aaron's telepathy. So far he was strangely silent.

"Exemplar Tane informs me that you are prepared to deepen your understanding of the First Tenet," Cyan began solemnly, "which holds that consciousness exists apart from physical manifestation. You shall learn to project portions of your own consciousness beyond the confines of your physical body."

Similarly to Tane, he wore a V-necked wheat-colored tunic and matching trousers of loose fit, but his appearance was more conservative, black hair cut short above his small ears, thick and course enough to show no part. Heavy brows overshadowed his dark eyes. All the features of his brown face were small except the flattened broad apex of his nose. Cleanly shaven, he was neither attractive nor displeasing. Disturbingly, his eyes returned repeatedly to Seerce, who looked away.

"My distant ancestors survived a great calamity over twenty thousand years ago, ending the era of the Mu. A few mountainous islands fed and sheltered survivors. They had what was needed, but they were possessed of restless souls, a traveling people driven to wander and experience all that Earth was." Cyan spoke with precise enunciation, the mark of someone who acquired Altean later in life and worked at it. With just enough volume to be heard, his timbre was nonetheless authoritative, as though what he delivered was beyond question.

"For centuries after the destruction, they lacked materials to build boats seaworthy enough to take them much beyond their immediate surroundings. So they taught themselves to move consciousness instead. Out-of-body states became as natural as wearing the cloak of physicality. Trusted others kept watch over vacant bodies, for travel was sometimes mesmerizing enough that one might forget to return." Cyan's demeanor failed to reflect the wonder of this tale, while his eyes kept their target at the far end of the table.

"In this fashion, they continued their exploration of all life hosted by Gaia. Having only an oral tradition, travelers recounted for their companions what they found. The best of tales were committed to memory and handed down. Eventually, the Mu learned of human explorers in the opposite hemisphere, a race of giants with gliding boats, light skin, and wild red hair. A few of our learned met up with them in the Isles of Altea, teaching a few magi their Mu traditions. Their wisdom survives today within the Order of the Sun." His tone more dutiful than pleased, he stated, "I will share with you what the Mu knew of consciousness."

Mornings would be devoted to lecture and discussion, interspersed with exercises in projection. Once Cyan conducted individual interviews with the ten, he would determine a unique course of study for each to follow, afternoons to be spent on those assignments. He encouraged their continuing participation in handball, for the benefit of sound sleep which supported successful journeys. Beginning the next evening, all were to meet him daily in the Temple for sunset meditation, which he said would aid the development of a group consciousness.

Seerce recoiled at this news. Now every moment of every day would be structured! Sincerely she hoped the communal day off remained outside the exemplar's control. She watched a flash of consternation cross Cyan's eyes. Always her expressions gave her away, but had he read her thought? Aaron shifted in his seat beside her.

"Among your inner senses," he continued, his neutral mask restored, "vision is the most readily moved. The second years have some experience with remote visioning, so I ask your forbearance while the first years catch up. Together all of you will learn tandem and group observation, methods important to the work of the Order. Please follow me now to the Temple for a simple exercise. You may leave your recording crystals here."

The students rose and stood in place until Cyan exited the room. Past were the days of Tane's informality. Seerce left last, wondering if anyone else noticed his undue attention to her. At the outside door, she picked up the hem of her robe to dash after them in a sputtering rain, across the stone paths of the courtyard.

Aaron held the heavy Temple door open for her. "He hears our telepathy," he said softly. "Be careful." Seerce nodded her agreement, pausing in the foyer to sweep raindrops from her face.

As Aaron hurried to an inner door down the way, Jair opened the nearer door for her, remarking under his breath, "Not a cheery fellow, is he?" They strode swiftly down an aisle to take the last two seats at the end of the front row. The Temple Crystal rotated just above the altar, huge, sparkling with light though the day was dim.

Standing before the students, beginning at the moment Jair seated himself, Cyan told them, "Meditation quiets your brain's stringent guard upon your inner senses. Alignment with a crystalline field aids your attunement to more subtle realities. Once you learn the techniques, you may free your inner senses at will without the Crystal. But for now, its mineral order provides assurance to reluctant portions of your psyche, those that require grounding to Earth. By successful exercise of your inner senses, your brain will relax its grip, learning by experience that it yet remains in charge of your physical function.

"Our sunset meditation will assist the establishment of a common wavelength among us. Telepathy is rooted in one of our inner senses and indeed there would be no spoken language without it. All of you are telepaths, but you communicate differently according to your cultures. You will require telepathy during tandem and group observations, to coordinate your efforts and in some situations, to remain safe. So it is vital that we achieve commonality.

"Close your eyes now and imagine what you would see if you hovered above the Temple campus. Picture in detail the rooftops, the walkways and gardens, the seawall around the promontory, as if you were a bird in the sky." He gave them a good long time to do so.

Eventually they heard a tinkle of chimes. "Now," Cyan said quietly, "place yourself in a meditative state by the means you prefer. When you are perfectly relaxed, keep your physical eyes closed and send your inner vision straight up. This inner sense operates independently of your physicality, so it moves readily through the dome. It will stop at the height you find appropriate. It will convey its picture to your physical brain. By employing your imagination as your first step, you have built a connection between your seeking mind and your interested brain, which is now prepared to allow this unusual perspective. Once you are satisfied with the detail of your inner vision, open your physical eyes and sit quietly."

Seerce followed the instruction, thinking that what she saw was precisely what she had just pictured by supposition. To her great surprise, two unexpected details showed themselves: solar crystals arranged in horizontal rows atop the shallowly pitched roof of the Administration building, and a lightning rod shaped like a trident atop the Healing Temple's peak.

When everyone was finished, Cyan projected his own highly detailed full-color vision into the Crystal, where all could see it vividly. Seerce was pleased to have two matches on her first try.

"Did any of you see my likeness or those of your classmates during your experience?" Cyan asked. None had. "To do so requires the participation of another inner sense. Let us return to the classroom and begin that subject."

*

Their professors were absent from handball that afternoon. The initiates played less-than-enthusiastic doubles, worried by Cyan's stringency. Several left early. Aaron challenged Seerce to a second set. He was easily the best athlete among the men and she among the women. They played hard, discharging their frustrations, for Aaron had been the subject of Cyan's surveillance that afternoon.

What does he want from us? Seerce asked.

Control, Aaron replied. *He will not have it.*

Of everyone or just you and me?

You and I think for ourselves. But you are more interesting to him.

Why do you say that?

Because he has watched you all along.

Do you mean here in handball? Otherwise, she had not been in Cyan's company.

When you mind your game, he minds you. But he is stealthy about it.

I hope no one else notices.

Rayn does.

Hence the guard you keep to either side of me? she teased.

Yes, Aaron replied seriously.

You do not mean that.

We have no agreement, if that is what you ask. Obviously he cares for you.

She glanced over to the next court, where Rayn played Isla.

Seerce's paddle missed the ball. *Sorry,* she apologized, going after it.

He will find himself in Cyan's crosshairs before long, Aaron told her. Seerce missed again and Aaron won the match.

*

Several days hence, in the Temple for a second exercise, Cyan gave the initiates an unfamiliar location to view remotely. "On one of the Altean islands is a gold pyramid," he said. "Find it and view the inscription. Look for what is contained within the centermost chamber of the structure."

Seerce glanced at Kessa next to her, who shrugged, saying quietly, "I do not know of a gold pyramid."

Rayn to the other side of her gave Seerce a smile. "I will see you there," he whispered.

Seerce settled into her preparation. In her mind's eye, she pictured a pyramid of gold-colored stone, doubting that the structure was gold-plated. Holding her picture and relaxing into an even breathing pattern, eventually a fog seemed to lift, revealing a stepped pyramid of honey-colored limestone blocks, more square than those by which the Administration building was constructed.

She counted nine staggered rows to the top of the pyramid, crowned by a small square edifice. Moving her vision around to examine all four sides, she noted that each featured a smooth stone quadrangle upon its face, narrower at the top than the bottom, overlaying the stepped block. Perhaps decorative, these were too smooth to climb, but above each there appeared to be a door.

Seerce willed her vision upward, to see recessed spaces in shadow, not doors. Circling again, she found no visible entrance. Remembering that inner vision moved readily through physical obstacles, she sent her sight through the stone. The space within revealed a glow from the chamber below. Moving her sight nearer to the floor, she saw a spirit hovering, appearing as a blurry outline of Rayn!

I told you I would see you here, he telepathed.

She was so surprised that she suffered a moment of disorientation. *Seerce,* he said firmly, *stay with me! Part of me really is here. Remember? Cyan taught us how to add a body image so we can find each other.*

Now she saw him more clearly.

How is it that I understand you so well? she asked, surprised.

Mutual will? he guessed. *Kessa is here somewhere. I caught a glimpse of her. What do you think this is?* His filmy arm gestured to an object hovering at the center of the floor. Its glow provided the only light in the chamber. Appearing to be solid, it did not seem to be a crystal. As Seerce observed, it became more egg-shaped, whereas before it had been more round.

Did you see that? she exclaimed.

Yes, Rayn said. *It has happened several times. Its color changes, too.*

Kessa's likeness came into view. *Hey, girl, can you see me?* she asked. *Pretty strange, is it not?*

Yes, I see you and I hear you. I am mystified by this object. Have you tried communicating with it? Neither had. *Let me try.* Seerce telepathed to the object, *Good day to you. I am Seerce. My friends are Kessa and Rayn.*

There was a splash of brighter sparkle within the entity. They were astonished.

We do not know how you communicate, she said, *but we will observe for your responses.* Trails of light weaved through the glow in rhythmic patterns. *Do you have a name?* she asked. There were more pronounced sparkles and then a return to quiet patterns. *Tell us how long you have been here,* she requested, to no observable response.

It does not have much to say, Seerce concluded. *I go in search of the inscription.* She pictured in her mind's eye a recessed space, and momentarily her vision was outside looking at one. Carved in stone above it was a depiction of a human eye floating within a five-pointed star. The other three spaces bore no symbols.

When the initiates returned their knowing to the Temple, they were jubilant. All of them had found the location, the inscription, and the inhabitant. Cyan congratulated those who had seen each other. "The 'entity,' as Seerce called it, is known as a living crystal. It is a cybernetic device, one that receives, stores, and processes information about our etheric travels. It functions as a beacon when you are out of body, able to retrieve your energetic signature from another plane according to instructions that you leave with it, a safeguard against being away too long. Your physical person might suffer ill effects, dehydration or malnutrition, even death, if you do not come back to tend it.

"This device, which we call Protos, is also your guide should you become disoriented during travel. It will direct your consciousness to where you left your person."

A murmur arose from the students.

"Before you travel etherically, your energy signature must be recorded with Protos. I will assist with this when I meet each of you for your first multidimensional experience. All your etheric journeys are to begin there."

CHAPTER 4

The later sunsets of late spring required that dinner be had before meditation, so the initiates began eating together, sharing their travel experiences. The second years were full of tales, having received their instruction in remote viewing from Anakron last year. Tonight, Ell and Tuura recounted a crazy tale of an extracurricular journey the two had made together.

Suddenly a low-toned vibration stopped all conversation in the crowded dining hall. It seemed to come from the west, both heard and felt. Seerce experienced a moment of nausea before a sharp jolt shoved the floor one way and then another, as if the building had been impacted on two adjacent sides. Dinner plates slid and goblets tipped over. Voices hollered, "Earthquake!"

The students saw fellow diners dive beneath the tables for cover and followed suit. The sound of crashing dishes followed. The tremor stopped as suddenly as it started. "Stay here," Aaron told his classmates. "There may be more."

Anakron's booming voice interrupted the silence that followed. "All of us will exit now in an orderly fashion to the courtyard. Remain there until staff has searched the buildings for any injured."

Outside, campus residents huddled together for warmth in the cool evening, no wraps save their worries. A full moon skirted among white and silver clouds as they began to take on the pinks and mauves of evening. Conversation among the initiates was frenzied. For several, this was their first quake, for others, one of many.

Seerce trembled still. To Aaron she telepathed, *This was different than what we experience at home, sharper, stronger. It is the level of the water that concerns me, for it is high tide. Will such a tremor send a wave toward us?*

I doubt that one was strong enough, Aaron told her. In the growing darkness, he stood close enough to take Seerce's hand, his touch warm and assuring. Shortly, the assembled community learned there were a few minor injuries and some cracks in walls. Anakron acknowledged the likelihood of aftershocks, giving assurances that the picture windows in the newer buildings and the dining room were indestructible. Meditation was canceled, and the initiates were asked to await Anakron in the Temple foyer.

Before long, he arrived, saying, "There is something I want you to see. Please follow me." He led the students to a small room in an area past the foyer. Once all had squeezed in, a wide pocket door slid closed. "The door crystal responds to the spoken or telepathed command, 'transport,'" he told them. "When returning, say 'Temple.'"

The small room moved slowly downward. The motion stopped and then it seemed to move sideways. The initiates were wide-eyed. Again motion ceased and the door slid open. Stepping out to what appeared to be an undersea loading dock, through a row of heavily framed double windows, a submarine vessel bobbed in murky water.

"We have the means to transport one hundred twenty of us to safety," Anakron told them, "sufficient capacity to accommodate our community. I suggest that you keep a small travel bag packed and ready at your apartment door."

"Where would we go?" asked Aaron.

"In the direction of safety," the exemplar responded. "There are two ports in the MidTerra and one private estate in west Afrikaa that can accommodate this vessel. On the southwest continent, we have an arrangement with a facility not far from Tibisay. It has never been necessary to leave. We keep it for extraordinary circumstances, be they natural or political."

That concerned Seerce more than it relieved her. How long had the Order lived under threat of one or the other to make this kind of investment in a dock and a vessel?

Anakron accompanied them back to the foyer and hurried off. Like Seerce, the others were speechless. They moved in a huddle down the courtyard path, the men leaving the women outside their domicile.

*

The morning meal betrayed a level of shared anxiety, for there had been minor aftershocks through the night. Resident priests, healers, and more staff than Seerce had ever seen were in the dining hall. Every seat was taken and some stood with their cups so others could eat at the tables. Aaron headed straight for the kitchen, motioning Seerce to come with him. Obviously the staff knew him. He introduced her, and the cooks bowed their heads respectfully. She returned the gesture.

"Are your families safe?" Aaron asked them. All nodded that they were. "What is the official word?" He telepathed to Seerce that kiosks in their neighborhoods offered news by recorded voice.

"Failure of one of the thermal power stations," recited a small brown man.

"We have shattered windows," said another.

An elder woman added, "My family ran outside to escape falling plaster."

"Anakron will give us more information shortly," Aaron told them. "Come out so you may hear him." They nodded and returned to their work.

Altea feeds misinformation to the masses, thought Seerce.

Conversation ceased when Anakron strode into the dining hall. "Geology has examined the available data. At the mid-ocean ridge, there was sudden movement along a deep fault, whereby one rock face slipped past the other." He used his broad hands to demonstrate. "I am told the forces of nature are great there and this is not unusual for that location. This type of movement is followed by aftershocks, as the ocean floor resettles itself along the fault line.

"Campus buildings are situated upon bedrock, and the heavy stone construction is unlikely to shift in a quake such as we experienced last evening. In the event of tremors, take cover under something substantial. For staff who live off campus, it is best to get outside and away from older buildings quickly. May you and yours remain safe."

The priests and initiates followed Anakron to the Temple. The Crystal was at viewing height as they entered. Tane delivered a brief explanation of the technology to be demonstrated. "You will see and hear Exemplar Nova speak with us from the School of Geology, displaying graphic representations within the Crystal." Momentarily, the face of a nondescript woman appeared, her mousy hair pulled back severely. Somewhat past middle age, the shadows beneath her eyes indicated she had been up all night, but she spoke commandingly and dispassionately.

"Good day, colleagues. Geology continues to analyze data from temple crystals, which are sensitive to vibration. Unrest continues today beneath the central floor of the Ocean of Atlas in the form of hundreds of minor tremors. The epicenter of last night's quake is due west of the Altean mainland." A graphic appeared, illustrating the central seam of the ocean floor, running parallel to the ancient undersea mountain range whose peaks formed Altea's archipelago. "The region is an area of constant slow splitting, where molten material seeps upward through a relatively thin crust." Attendees leaned forward in their chairs, captivated.

"Several distinct energy waves radiate from every quake, slowing at different rates as they move through crustal structures and the deeper mantle of the planet. Last night, for the first time, we observed curvature to energy signatures in this area." A new graphic portrayed a section of ocean floor circled in blue, west of the seam, halfway to the southwest continent. "Early data indicates the crustal layer is absent here. This is an intriguing finding. We know no other place on Earth where the mantle is exposed.

"It is possible that molten material comes closer to the surface here, modifying patterns that we usually see." Nova then displayed a map of the ocean basin bordered by the shores of five surrounding continents. She overlaid the S shape of the mid-ocean ridge, marking the epicenter with a red triangle.

"We have insufficient information to provide you with accurate predictions. Generally we expect minor aftershocks for four to ten days. We shall post you on any other significant discoveries."

"Thank you, Nova," Anakron said, striding back to the altar from the seat he had taken. To the community he stated, "We shall come together as necessary to share information. You are free to begin your day." The Crystal darkened and the Temple emptied.

Seerce walked to class with Aaron. He telepathed, *Did you see the red aurora just before midnight?*

No! she exclaimed. *I have never seen the aurora.*

I woke up with one of the tremors and looked out. Shimmering red curtains hung in the sky over the sea. Seldom does the aurora appear so far south. In Eyre, we see it sometimes in the spring and fall, if the sky is clear, by our proximity to the north magnetic pole. There it shows blue or green. We see the lights in the northeastern sky, in the direction of greater darkness, not in the west.

What do you make of this?

That something is decidedly wrong, Aaron told her.

Perhaps you should let Tane know.

I have, he stated solemnly.

*

The ten lingered in the dining hall that evening, long after kitchen staff had gone home, exhausted but too unsettled to sleep. Sootchie attested that the submarine was never previously revealed, despite a similar quake last summer. "Obviously," he stated, "that wide lift and the dock have been here a long time."

"Perhaps the vessel was donated by a benefactor," Kessa said. "Or maybe the Order provides moorage in exchange for its emergency use."

"But the community, other than us, already knew the evacuation plan," Sootchie rebutted.

"So what is different this year?" asked Ell. "The same sort of tremor elicited greater concern from Geology."

"Perhaps their new findings?" Isla ventured.

"Tane recently mentioned the security of the crystal network and Anakron named politics as one reason to go hurriedly," Aaron reminded them. "Does Altea threaten the Order?" His question went unanswered.

Tavia shared her impressions. "There is something wrong out there in the deep ocean," she told them, her forehead resting in one hand as she tried to describe something indescribable. "The waves bring with them…mmm…some kind of poison or residue, as though the deep rock cries out and the waves catch those tears. Do not laugh. These are the best words I have for what I perceive."

No one laughed. Sootchie and Ell corroborated Aaron's description of the red aurora.

"Nova described some bizarre seismic signatures," Seerce reminded them.

"Are we safe to be here?" Isla questioned.

"We have the means to leave," Tuura replied. "Most Alteans do not." There were nods of assent around the table.

"Worry nets us nothing. Let us try to sleep," Ell suggested, "as best we are able."

*

Silence the Echo

Over several days, aftershocks diminished to none and familiar routines prevailed. The community anticipated two communal days off, an occasional occurrence due to the difference between the period of the full moon and seven-day cycles. Cyan requested only one commitment from the initiates over the longer holiday—a brief private interview in his office. First years would see him on the first afternoon, and second years on the next.

Ell organized an outing for the upper class on their full day off, a tradition from their prior year together. The new initiates decided on a class picnic, weather permitting, ahead of their individual appointments.

That day dawned bright, but Seerce managed to sleep long with a pillow over her head. She soaked in her bath, then plaited her washed tresses into braids, pinning these in a coil at the back of her head. Tying a pale green scarf around the coil, she knotted it at the nape of her neck. A wide cinch belt dressed up a plain long linen dress. Draping a light shawl around her shoulders, she freed the scarf to flutter behind her, intending to scout a sunny location or perhaps arrange a group of chairs in the courtyard.

As she emerged, she saw Rayn upon the stone path to the Temple. Gazing at the sea between the obelisks of the Stone Circle, he turned to her, smiling broadly. Dressed handsomely in a caftan of broad vertical stripes and linen trousers, his thick hair shone in the sunlight and he sported a more closely trimmed beard. She thought him such an attractive man.

"May I say you are as beautiful as the day?" he said, striding over to her.

"Only if I may reply in kind," she responded, returning his smile. "I had in mind to find the perfect spot for lunch."

"Perhaps on the south patio, where you and I met recently? A table with seating has been placed there. The kitchen staff is preparing a lunch basket. We can walk back to fetch it whenever it suits us."

"Then you have thought of everything!" she enthused, including, she hoped, how he might be alone with her. She strolled with him along the perimeter path.

"Your friend Aaron is an accomplished healer," Rayn remarked, as they seated themselves behind a wind screen.

His choice of subject took Seerce by surprise. "As is our friend Kessa," she responded, angling to broaden the subject, unwilling to spend Rayn's singular attention discussing Aaron.

"Indeed, but did you see Aaron's eyes as he engaged Isla? The way he enjoined her? It was as though he amplified her own recuperative powers, sped up all the processes that her body might undertake through a long period of healing. I was reminded of Tane's lecture about the absence of linear time beyond this plane. Did they move out of time? Does Aaron know how he accomplishes such miracles? It was a phenomenal act," he concluded with amazement.

Seerce prickled. "You might ask him," she replied neutrally.

"There are among healers those who suffered great losses as children," Rayn told her.

He must know of the murder of Aaron's mother, she thought. A correlation between woundedness and a healing gift was something she never considered. She relaxed some, for Rayn's purpose seemed innocuous enough.

"I do wish to know everyone better," he continued. "We have little time for personal acquaintance. For the tasks expected of us, we should know each other intimately."

Seerce misunderstood his meaning, perceiving that he proposed to know *her* intimately.

Rayn must have seen shock on her face, immediately apologizing for offending her. "Let me say instead that the ten of us must become familiar with each other's strengths and weaknesses, for there will be unknowns as we take on the Order's challenges." He watched her closely. "Having sailed with many crews, I learned to find the capabilities of my mates early in a voyage. It was preparatory practice for unanticipated trouble. Again, my apologies," he said sincerely. "I spoke too passionately."

"I misunderstood you," Seerce told him, regretting her skill with the common language. "I am sorry for my upset."

"No matter," said Rayn. He looked out to sea and up to the billowing cloud that temporarily obscured the sun. "Relax here," he suggested. "I shall pick up lunch and intercept the others, for it seems near to zenith."

"I shall," she replied.

He rose and tipped his head slightly to her. Maybe his elegant manners were customary for his former occupation. Or they might be the way of his people. He had the acumen of a successful businessman and appeal that would turn any woman's head. She was but a sheltered clan girl and she should keep her focus upon the mission. All the initiates were here for the same reason, were they not? Nothing about her association with him need feel so personal nor cause her heart to flutter as he did.

She found his attention both disconcerting and beguiling. Perhaps she imagined his interest in her. Maybe he was this way with everyone, a bit gallant, a bit intense.

Rayn returned with their classmates, a basket, and a tablecloth. Jair carried a pitcher of tea and Tavia had a tray of mugs. Kessa danced around them, a pirouette here and a twirl there. The five acknowledged their good fortune to meet on the prettiest day of spring to date. Laying out the luncheon, they served themselves.

"Who has the first interview today?" asked Seerce. "I know I am last."

Nervously Jair acknowledged he had that privilege. "Never were we told of projection at my academy. Remote viewing is interesting, but I like to work with my hands."

"You do a fine job of working your brain, Master Jair," Tavia told him, the light brown tent of her tightly curled hair motionless upon her shoulders, which convulsed with laughter. "I would have failed physics without you. Who is second?"

"That would be me," Kessa said. "We students of the Healing Temple experienced some altered states while in training. I keep a little box in my brain for what makes no sense at all. Those oddities are stored there." She laughed.

"Were you ever afraid?" asked Jair.

"I was," Kessa admitted. "But like anything else new, I had to conquer my fear. We have an experienced guide in Cyan. Who is after me?"

"I am," said Tavia. "I take my little personal journeys when I sculpt and my mind is free to wander. There are priests among my extended family, but from them I hear only of dream travel. The rest is foreign to me. We will commiserate," she told Jair, who grinned.

"Rayn, you must be fourth," Seerce said. "Have you sailed out of body?"

Missing her clever reference to his former seafaring life, he answered. "I have odd experiences at times and do not know what to call these. Sometimes in the dream before I wake, I am with a group of familiar people, in lively conversation or working on something together. When I open my eyes, I do not know them. But eventually I encounter them in waking life. And when I do, I anticipate segments of conversation before it is spoken, because I have heard it before." He paused momentarily. "Some of you seem familiar to me, our conversations as well."

Seerce wondered if this was why he observed her so closely.

"You will have no difficulty with Cyan's adventures!" remarked Kessa. "Already you travel in time."

"Thank you for the encouragement," Rayn replied. "Seerce, what of your odysseys?"

"I have none to report," she stated, omitting her vivid dream experiences. "But I will gladly study any discipline that allows Geology to find what they know of the ocean floor." Jair and Tavia applauded. Rayn looked surprised.

The five shared stories as they ate. Seerce was drawn to Tavia's innocent goodness and the light in her amber eyes. Kessa's self-deprecating humor made for hilarity. Jair could be Seerce's brother, someone whose social discomforts needed encouragement as his brilliance outshined all of theirs.

While an excellent conversationalist, cordial and most attentive, there was something that Rayn shielded from view. But the current that passed between them was unmistakable, unlike anything Seerce had ever felt.

*

Exemplar Cyan's eyes were closed and he rubbed his forehead as Seerce approached his open office door. The sun of late afternoon streamed through his west-facing office, illuminating intricately carved masks arrayed on the wall behind him, painted strikingly in black and white and red. Like one of these, his narrow lips were held almost in a grimace. On the handball court, he moved so gracefully and youthfully, but here he looked much older than he likely was—and world-weary.

She remained at his door until he opened his bleary eyes, whereupon he suggested they get iced tea from the kitchen. "Let us walk rather than sit on this beautiful afternoon. We can make this a casual conversation." The tone of his welcome surprised her, much friendlier than his usual presentation. He might even seem pleased to see her.

"I would love to be outside again," she agreed. She had left open her apartment windows for the breeze was pleasantly warm.

With glasses in hand they strolled, occasionally sitting on a bench for an exchange. In answer to his question, she told him, "I traveled out of body once, spontaneously, at a time of crisis. But etheric travel is not an activity of my people. It was Anakron's wish that I take my training here. I have honored his requests, all of them, to the best of my ability."

Cyan looked intently at her. "His love for you is profound," he stated.

She withheld tears, for it had not seemed so since she arrived to the Temple. Recovering herself by sheer will, she responded, "By all he has done for me, yes, I am sure of it." Regardless, she was taken aback by this most personal observation.

"He has been purposeful in arranging his work," Cyan told her, "to remain in proximity to you and available as you grew up."

Indeed he had been headmaster at the academy in her mother's village and later a superintendent of schools in the region. But she wondered how well Cyan knew him, for it was Anakron's friendship with her grandmother that afforded his visits to their compound. "He is a grandfather to me," she acknowledged, "and my only advisor after my mother's devastating injury. My family had to focus upon her care, grieve for my uncles, and keep the clan's business alive." She realized she was too forthcoming. "Why am I telling you all this?" she asked.

"Because it is what I need to know," he replied. "Because your ability to travel has been affected by trauma. We will resolve this as we work together."

"Oh," said Seerce.

"You are perfectly safe to travel with me and in groups. You and I will rectify the emotional trappings. Most all priests have some door that must be opened, some healing to be accomplished, before they can travel individually and freely. Many drawn to this work have risked their lives for others. We must be sure our entanglements are resolved before we venture into other realms. Otherwise, we may attract discarnate beings who wish for us to save them, too. That is not our purpose. Each soul is obligated to learn its own lessons."

"Oh," she said again.

"I meet individually with you and your fellows that I might tailor assignments to benefit each of your unique circumstances."

"It is good of you to assist us," Seerce commented, glimpsing some of the great responsibility he carried. "It must be personally challenging, if not grueling, to take us on."

"You are most perceptive. But this is my contribution to your training and to the good of the Order. It is my great honor to serve." Walking back to the kitchen in silence, they returned their empty glasses.

When Seerce took her leave, she said simply, "I am appreciative of your guidance, Exemplar." He bowed his head to her before he turned and left. Kind though he seemed to be, it concerned her that he pulled from her what she was not ready to reveal. She did not know what to think of him.

*

Availing herself of an early dinner, Seerce had in mind to take a plate back to her apartment and digest all that she had experienced today. Deep in thought as she served herself, she startled when Rayn touched her elbow.

"Will you join me for dinner?" he asked. "I am puzzled by my encounter with Cyan and wish to seek your counsel."

"Yes, of course," she replied, surfacing from her reverie. "I hope I have something helpful to say. My encounter was… strange," she told him. She followed him to a corner table in the empty dining room.

"Allow me my moment to take in your countenance," Rayn requested. "You do me so much good."

"Why do you embarrass me?" she asked.

"That is not my intention," he told her, looking deeply into her eyes.

"What *is* your intention?" she asked, willingly meeting his gaze.

"To know you well. But my work is cut out for me. You are a wellspring of surprises."

She laughed. "So are you."

He lifted his goblet of water and she lifted hers. "To life's mysteries," he toasted. Then he savored a few bites, so she picked up her fork and tested her fish.

"Cyan plans lessons for me in self-analysis and emoting. He judges my emotional self to be underdeveloped."

Seerce chortled, commenting, "As if he possesses any emotion at all."

"He tells me I am rooted in physicality. He finds me unusual among acolytes. I do not wish to violate your privacy, but is this akin to what you were told?"

Though she wanted to laugh at the insight Rayn had just provided her, she responded seriously, "I have quite the opposite problem. I am too wrapped up in emotion to be trusted to travel singly. I am confined to group travel until I do my work."

"I am grateful for your sharing," he said with relief. "I fear that I am flawed by what I do not recognize in myself. May I consult you from time to time? I would like to return the favor, if there is anything at all I may do for you."

Do you hear my telepathy? she asked.

Yes, clearly, he replied. *We heard each other on our Protos journey.*

I am relieved to know it works in the real world. Perhaps you reveal more of yourself by telepathy.

He looked puzzled.

Seerce explained, *I do not know how to take your interest. Looking deeply into me seems rather intimate*—she used the word that had shocked her earlier—*when I know so little of you. Your spoken words enchant, but they say nothing about who you are.*

Then perhaps I shall benefit by my assignments. Is it too familiar to ask what Cyan requires of you?

I do not mind you knowing, she replied. *Maybe I will feel better if I tell someone. I have buried a deep and wide emotional wound and Cyan wants to probe it. Pain awaits me. I am not pleased.*

How dare he? Rayn asked, fire in his eyes.

The same way he dares to teach you emotionality. I need it and you need it, for reasons he sees and we do not. My gut does not trust him yet, but we have no choice about these assignments. Please, keep this between you and me!

I will, of course. Promise me the same, he requested.

I do.

For a while they ate and thought and looked to each other. *You may find what you seek from me in my music,* Rayn told her. *I would like to play for you tomorrow afternoon, if it suits you.*

It does, she replied. *I look forward to meeting this oud who knows you so well. Is she a jealous mistress?*

Silence the Echo

Rayn laughed. *She is! But I have told her of you. I shall arrange a music room at the Healing Temple. Meet me at your building's door tomorrow at the seventh decan.*

CHAPTER 5

Too much sun on the day prior had turned her nose and cheeks pink. Today Seerce wore her broad-brimmed straw hat and her only other linen shift, this one pale blue with a striped scarf as a sash. She had left her long hair loose, crimped by the braids she had worn yesterday. On the patio outside the dining hall she and Kessa shared a platter of cut vegetables and a bowl of hummus, sipping iced tea. Spreading soft cheese over crusty bread, Kessa told her, "You look delicious."

"Thank you," Seerce replied, wondering if her friend might accept advice for her wardrobe. Also wearing a hat, Kessa's was heavy for the season and perspiration trickled down her neck. A shapeless chartreuse sundress over a long-sleeved blouse completed a shabby look.

Aaron emerged from the dining room with his lunch to sit down with them. "What shall I expect from Cyan's interview?" he asked the women.

"That he knows you better than you know yourself," Kessa replied.

"He saw right through me," admitted Seerce.

"Because you are transparent," Aaron joked.

Seerce wrinkled her pink nose at him.

"After that misery is accomplished, I intend to hike up the coastline a ways. Would you ladies care to accompany me?"

"I have an engagement," Seerce told him, "but I would like to go another time."

"My sunburn requires an afternoon indoors," Kessa replied.

Seerce looked up to see Rayn coming her way from the men's domicile. Dressed in a long tunic of marigold over beige trousers, he carried a pear-shaped musical instrument, honey-colored, polished and gleaming in the sunlight. Aaron's back was to him.

"Leave your dishes," Kessa said to Seerce. "I will take them in."

Patting her mouth with her napkin, Seerce thanked Kessa and wished Aaron a pleasant interview. Getting up, she met Rayn at the door, where he tipped his head to her and smiled broadly. *How is it possible that you are only more beautiful today?* he telepathed.

The sun blinds you, she teased.

They walked the cool tunnel to the lift in the Healing Temple, stopping at the deserted third floor. Rayn led her into a small south-facing room and closed the door behind them. There were but a few chairs and stands for instruments. He set his oud in one and came to join her at the window, for she never missed a chance to wonder at the restless surf, so powerful, so beautiful, so worthy of trepidation.

"Come sit," Rayn beckoned softly. "Lady Oud shall reveal my secrets." He positioned two chairs, one across from the other, Seerce's to face him and the window. Then taking the instrument gently into his arms, he showed off his lady's gourd-shaped figure of carved wood, striated in shades of amber from her full, rounded bottom to her curved and tapered top. Held upright, she looked to be precisely a half gourd, her flat, light face featuring an intricately carved circular design and a wide hexagonal sound hole. Five double strings and a thicker, single string stretched from keys over the bent crook of her short, slender neck, down her music box to a narrow bridge just above her base. Rayn cradled her, plucking at her strings, making small adjustments in their tension. With lithe, long fingers sliding along her fretless neck, he sounded notes and chords with an ivory plectrum, the expression on his face transformed to a picture of joyous concentration as he began.

Reverberations of deeply somber and richly complex chords lent a haunting quality to dirges of old and a love song Seerce recognized, then a jaunty tune, and a sailor's song. He finished with a piece so compelling, so aching, so exquisitely moving that Seerce's eyes welled. When the last resonance died away, Rayn told her, "This last one I composed for you."

She sat quietly for a long time, feeling the reverberations of her own heartstrings, for he played these as familiarly as his oud, conveying within the universality of music how deeply he felt and how well he knew that the current between them was old and powerful and it would not be denied. He showed her the precision that possessed him, the depths of his self-examinations, the manner in which his heart spoke through his hands to tell her who he truly was. Words would never portray her wonderment or the privilege she felt to know all this of him, but eventually she told Rayn in her native tongue, "I have heard the voice of your soul."

Now tears came to his eyes.

*

Standing before the altar, Cyan began, "When you send your consciousness anywhere, it arrives instantaneously, for time and distance are only constructs. Our destination today is the future Hall of Records at the Monument of Leo in Misr. Chambers have been hollowed from bedrock beneath and between the lion's front paws. Endeavor to remember that it is an energetic portion of you that travels. There is no need to claw your way through stone. Simply picture standing on the ground before him. Once oriented, you may transfer yourselves into the suite of chambers below, where I shall await you.

"To facilitate your journey, I shall assist you to enter into a light trance. You will remain conscious and aware of your surroundings here. This slight alteration of your ego's attention will allow you to travel readily and be more aware of detail at your new location.

"Now take a few cleansing breaths, get comfortable, and then maintain even, rhythmic breathing. I will give you instructions shortly."

Seerce had warned Rayn that Cyan registered the students' telepathy. So she flashed a smile down the row to him and he smiled back.

Cyan touched the chimes on the altar. In a slow, soothing cadence, he delivered the instruction: "With each breath you are drawn into a pleasant, relaxed state. As I count back from ten, you will notice that you feel even more relaxed.

"Ten. Your mind is at ease and peaceful.

"Nine. Your breathing is even and deep.

"Eight. Your gaze looks inward.

"Seven. You are drawn more deeply into a relaxed state.

"Six. Your vision is called to the Monument of Leo.

"Five. Your mind and your spirit feel only peace.

"Four. At the chimes, your inner knowing is fully present at the monument.

"Three. Your mind is calm and peaceful.

"Two. Your breathing is even and deep.

"One. Your inner vision sees the Monument of Leo."

Distantly Seerce heard chimes. As the mist cleared from her inner vision, a limestone structure loomed before her, more than twice her height. Carved in an undulating pattern, there were recessions between four prominences. Moving her vision back, she recognized a front paw of the lion. Rising up, she viewed the enormity of Leo, the height of its maned head, and its thick torso stretching some distance. The monument stood within a deep depression, apparently carved in place by quarrying the surrounding layers of limestone. Strata were clearly visible along the sides of his body. By the variable colors and thicknesses of these layers, Seerce knew the area had been a shallow sea several times in its geologic history. It was the wondrous rock layers of Basra that had made geology her favorite subject early on.

We are behind you, telepathed Rayn. She turned to see filmy representations of her classmates with him.

Let us move all the way around Leo before we go down, Tuura suggested. *Tavia, you should lead the way.*

It was Tavia's extended family of quarrymen, builders, and carvers who had worked on the monument for more than forty years. The lion's face was finely detailed, his enormous eyes indicative of wisdom, nares like upward caves within his snout, the exquisite mane artfully woven with the rays of the sun. *Those rays represent the Order,* Tavia told them. *Six of our most skilled did the mane's finishing work suspended from scaffolding.* Her classmates were incredulous. *I worked on his tail. Let me show you when we come to his right flank.*

Muscular strength was portrayed in the working of Leo's massive haunches. Placed languidly alongside the right back paw and a short distance from his torso, the tail was capped with a stone tuft of fur. Moving together high and low, the ten returned to hover between the front paws. Ell called for their descent to the chamber below.

Convening then in a high-ceilinged stone room, they found it empty but for Cyan's image glowing in iridescent blue light. *This is the color I display when I travel with you, so you may readily find me,* he told them. *I am pleased with your advancement. Tavia, have you ever been below ground here?* he asked.

No, she replied. *I knew nothing of the chambers until you told us this morning.*

The Order has been careful to shield their existence, Cyan acknowledged. *Six smaller chambers surround this one. We continue to debate what belongs here. Rayn and Tavia may be involved in developing universal symbols to be carved in stone for permanency. We must convey to future visitors how to use the records. We must also decide whether these chambers will retain entry from the surface or be accessible only by conscious projection.*

They followed Cyan through the other empty spaces, each glowing in a different color. *As you see,* he told them, *the only light available is by a temporary treatment of the stone. The glow may last centuries but not millennia. An energy source for permanent lighting is a challenge for us, as well as the accumulation of stone dust over the records.*

Seerce asked why the Order chose Altea's mascot for the monument.

Thought was given to creating what Altea would not destroy, Cyan replied. *The lion also represents the current astrological Age of Leo in the twenty-six-thousand-year cycle of the precession of Earth's axis. We hope future people might thereby deduce the era in which the monument came to be. Our ventures to the future suggest the past is soon forgotten. We have found no civilization as long-lived as Altea.*

Seerce could not help but view the Order's grand scheme through a geologist's eyes. What they anchored in bedrock today might tomorrow blow away in dust or dissolve in future seas.

At Cyan's behest, they returned their knowing to the Temple of Altea. He counted forward from one to ten and released their trances with a ring of the chimes.

*

"A smile never left your face today," Aaron observed.

Seerce gave him a quizzical look. He and she were the first to arrive for handball.

"Oh, never mind," he told her. "I think it is time we challenge Cyan and Tane to doubles, if they come today." Lately the exemplars had been absent from handball rather frequently.

"That we may be slaughtered?" she asked incredulously.

"Maybe. But our classmates do not wish to play us anymore, and we do not get better playing each other."

"I dare you to picture doubles with them as Cyan comes through the door!" Seerce challenged. "Prove your theory that he hears our thoughts."

"Oh, no," Aaron replied seriously. "He does not need to know anything else about me or you."
"He seems to miss nothing."
"Anyway, did your beau play as handsomely as he dressed for you yesterday? That instrument is exquisite."
Simply, Seerce answered, "Yes."
"He plays often with Isla and her flute. Did you know that?"
"I do now."
The others poured into the gym from their warm-up run, including the exemplars. Aaron's verbal challenge was accepted and sharp-eyed Ell agreed to referee.
You are a wild woman! Rayn telepathed to Seerce. She smiled back at him before she donned her headgear. In doubles, either teammate could return the volley. Knowing the force with which their professors hit, both students took backcourt positions. So, of course, Tane served the first volley softly. Seerce ran like lightning to return it, but not before the ball bounced out of bounds.
I will play forward, she telepathed to Aaron.
Do not announce your plans! Aaron fired back, reminding her of Cyan's reception. Angered, she slammed Cyan's return just inside a back corner of the court, bouncing it halfway across the gym.
Beautiful! Aaron enthused as they earned a point. The initiates cheered.
Ell tossed Tane a new ball, which he served against the ceiling. But Aaron caught it with his paddle before it hit the floor, angling it against a side wall. Seerce met that rebound, directing the bounce to where their opponents were not. When Aaron served, Cyan missed, earning the challengers another point.
The lead was traded several times before fatigue got the better of the younger two, whose stamina did not match that of the veteran players. Dripping wet, Aaron and Seerce bowed to each other and then to the opposing team, the initiates cheering all the while, thrilled with their colleagues' efforts.
Tane hollered, "Who else wants to play?" But there were no takers.

Silence the Echo

"We should challenge them to singles, too," Aaron said quietly to Seerce, "to learn more of their tricks."

*

It was several days later that Cyan distributed their individual assignments. Seerce set her study table to face her windows. For the moment, the sun warmed her apartment nicely, but storm clouds advanced quickly from the west. In her hands were two crystals. Touching the point of each briefly to her forehead, she determined their contents.

Directed to begin with a lecture on the development of the emotional body, she was stopped at points and reminded to place responses into the recording crystal, one reportedly tuned to 'subtle limbic energies.' The limbic system was described as a cerebral structure in charge of motivation, emotion, learning, and memory. Cyan would review the crystal's contents at individual counseling sessions each week. If needed, a referral might be made to practitioners at the Healing Temple. Seerce wondered how deeply he intended to dredge, for it was recommended that the student take breaks to rebalance emotionally. Several methods were prescribed.

Settling into the material, Seerce soon reached the point where she had to recount seeing her uncles dead and her mother badly injured. She did not want to call all that up. She avoided those memories every way she could. At the age of twelve, she was as unprepared as any child to cope with such a horrible scene. It was with trepidation that she deposited into the memory crystal her account:

> At my family's compound in Basra, I had gone to bed early that night with a headache, unusual for me. It was two days after the autumnal equinox. My family played a betting game at the kitchen table. Mother remained in Tunise due to the press of business there. Usually she came home for holidays, but as our trade ambassador, her plans were subject to change.

As I slept, I heard my mother's voice from a long way off, calling in desperation. Instantly I was transported to her side. She stood in seawater up to her knees, her nightclothes soaking wet, bleeding from her forehead. Her left arm was caught between fallen beams. I tried, but I could not move them. It was as though I had no substance or strength. Her beach house was reduced to a heap, the roof gone, and the heavens above holding only dim stars.

Looking over and under the rubble, I found my uncles in what had been the back bedroom. They were still, their limbs and bodies horribly twisted. No one answered though I shouted.

Mother laid her head against one of the timbers that caught her and closed her eyes. I saw her spirit emerge from her body and I screamed at the sight. Then she heard me. 'Child, listen to me,' her spirit said. 'Tell your father to come quickly. Tell him the sea crashed over my house. Please, Seerce, hurry!' She begged me to return to her as soon as I had.

Then I was back in my own bed. I opened my eyes to see my family packed into my little sleeping chamber. Perhaps I had screamed. What I had seen was horrifically detailed, more vivid than any of my lucid dreams.

In her Altean apartment Seerce sobbed. It was excruciating to relive the sights and emotions of that night. She hoped with all her might that depositing the nightmare into this crystal would free her of its terrifying repetitions, which this many years later still woke her from sleep every so often.

She went upstairs to her bed and wrapped herself in a blanket. Drawing in the light of healing with every breath, she did her best to recover her composure, staying cocooned until she stopped shaking. It was a long time.

*

Silence the Echo

In line for dinner, Rayn looked as spent as Seerce felt. *Your assignment affects you,* she observed.

I will struggle with this work for Cyan. But I do not wish to burden you. May we discuss anything else at dinner? He looked to her red eyes with concern. *How do you fare?*

Similarly, she answered. They sat down with Kessa and Ell, who debated what the initiate class might contribute to the community's upcoming solstice celebration. Kessa shared that Sootchie, Aaron, and she would sing.

Seerce had no idea of Aaron's voice for song. "I can wait tables," she joked.

"Wonderful!" Ell replied, saying, "I will list your contribution." He touched a crystal from his pocket to his forehead. Only Ell kept a recorder with him.

Finishing dinner with time to spare before meditation, Seerce excused herself. Rayn did also, leaving the planners engrossed in their subject. Following Seerce into the hall, he requested, *Walk with me.*

Where are we going?

To a side door I have discovered. She accompanied him through the Admin tunnel, into an alcove and out an exit she had never noticed. Narrow stone steps led up to a ground-level path, weed strewn and neglected, along the wrought iron fence. Beyond was a dirt road seldom used, bordered by woods and ferns. They were perfectly alone.

Let me hold you, Rayn requested. He pulled Seerce to his chest and she laid her head against his heart, hearing its strong, steady beat, feeling the warmth of his body and his compassion. Leftover tears dripped one by one on his robe. *I fear you are deeply hurt.*

I was once, she answered. *Now I am forced to remember. You, too?* she asked, for sorrow knows the sorrow of another.

Yes. Perhaps we require something to hold out as a reward for our penance. Accompany me on an air barge tour of the city our next free day. Let us take an outing.

She looked up to his kind expression. *I accept your medicine. Thank you.*

He released her and they picked their way along broken pavers and pebbles until they intercepted the well-kept perimeter path. Silently they walked, coming around to the High Temple in time to join evening meditation.

*

Often Seerce anticipated her outing with Rayn, procrastinating on her studies, looking through her abbreviated wardrobe, twisting and pinning her hair before her mirror. Finally she made herself go downstairs.

For a long time she sat cross-legged upon a floor cushion, breathing evenly, present only to peace. Then she picked up Cyan's crystal to recount the next installment:

> I shivered uncontrollably. My grandmother placed her hand on my forehead. Aunt Ena brought blankets. Father was at the foot of my cot, demanding to know what was wrong. At first, thoughts would not come, so I conveyed pictures. My grandmother cupped her hands over my ears. Then I remembered Mother's plea well enough to recite it.
>
> My grandmother is matriarch and she commanded my father, 'Take me and all the men on the air barge now! The women will tend to the child.' Then I dropped away from them and returned to my mother, by what means, I do not know.
>
> I told her, 'They are coming,' and asked how much she hurt.
>
> Her spirit said, 'My body is in excruciating pain, but I am not in it. Tahj and Aban have gone.' I could not see or hear my uncles' spirits, but Mama telepathed them, saying, 'I will wait for Narad. He and the men are almost here.'
>
> 'No, Mama,' I told her. 'They are just leaving Orion. It is a long way to Tunise.'
>
> 'Child, I can see them,' I heard her say. And momentarily, the air barge was there, hovering over the devastation. Her spirit

disappeared into her body, which looked to be failing, so pale and limp she was.

'Stay with me, Mama!' I cried.

'I am so very cold,' was all I could make of her telepathy.

I told her I would give her heat. I put my arms around her and set my ear to her heart, willing it to beat. I pictured everything hot that I could imagine, a steaming bath, a fire for cooking, the sun baking the desert sand. I sent all the heat I could conjure into her body.

I did not look at what the men were doing until Papa lifted Mama free. My grandmother bandaged her head and splinted her arm and dripped medicine on her tongue. The men wrapped her in blankets and laid her on the deck of the barge.

"There," Seerce told herself aloud, "it is done." Tears streamed down her cheeks. She put the crystal back in its silk pouch and looked out to the placid swells of turquoise-blue water. How could anything so lovely be so deadly?

*

"It seems you shared with no one the entirety of what you perceived the night of the tragedy. Is that correct?" Cyan asked. Seerce was in his office for her first appointment. They sat in comfortable chairs near his window, opposite each other, cups of tea on the small round table between them.

"It is," she answered.

"From knowledge you have gained since, look back and tell me what you think happened that night."

Seerce picked up her tea and sipped, organizing her thoughts before she replied. "Being asleep, I was open to my inner senses, which operate outside of time and space. Mother knew my empathic traits, as she is an empath. Some portion of her being contacted some portion of mine, for she was in grave danger.

My inner senses gave the information to my brain as a vivid nightmare. I had to wake up to get her help."

"What about your uncles' crossing?" Cyan asked. "Again, look from your present-day wisdom."

"There was nothing I could do for their broken bodies. Their spirits were yet present, consistent with what we know of death. Consciousness persists and may remain in the area of the body until it can accept its disconnection from the physical."

Cyan asked if it was disturbing to be present with the dead.

"No," Seerce answered. "My people think of our departed as near to us. We are among them every day in Khubradan."

"What about this experience still frightens you?" he inquired gently, looking deeply concerned.

This subject she had given much thought. "That the sea took my cousins' fathers and my mother's sight. That I did not do enough to help her. That deep water is a frightening force and I am not safe around it. These are the themes of my nightmares."

"Seerce, instinctively you transmitted the heat that saved your mother's life. Getting help, returning to her, keeping watch with her—your acts of bravery and devotion were more than most anyone would think to do."

"My mother is blind," Seerce repeated, starting to cry.

"Please, give yourself all credit for saving her life," Cyan insisted, "for yet she lives beloved of your father and you, of sons born since the tragedy! But tell me, how is it that you accepted study in Altea, at the shore of this great and restless ocean?"

She blinked back her tears and dabbed at her face. "From an early age, I dreamt of living on an island. Anakron told me of the Temple of Altea when I was but a child. Ever I yearned to be here. Now I am here, so I must overcome this dilemma."

"Your astute mind knows you are safe. It is your emotions that need relaxing. Allow me over our next several sessions to assist you."

"I will," she replied, "gratefully."

*

Rayn and Seerce ate an early lunch, watching the cloud cover break up and the sun emerge on what promised to be a pleasant day. She had dressed simply, as Rayn had advised, lest they attract the attention of pickpockets—a light shawl over a plain blouse and long skirt, her most comfortable shoes. Her hair was knotted at the top of her head to keep it tidy in the breeze, though tendrils had already freed themselves.

"You look positively Tunisian," she told Rayn in his unpretentious caftan, narrow-legged pants, and leather sandals. He pulled a corded sheath from inside his neckline, withdrawing a small knife, its handle inlaid with pearl. "I am prepared to defend your virtue, for men we meet shall find you ravishing," he teased her, smiling.

"Is it necessary to carry that?" she asked seriously, her eyes wide.

"In the business district, perhaps not. But we will walk a fringe neighborhood to and from the air barge station. Guards ride the barges, so I expect no trouble as we view the city from on high. However, I am always prepared."

They cleared their dishes and made a stop at the Administration office, leaving word with an assistant about their plan for the afternoon. Walking the edges of narrow dirty streets, Rayn kept his hand at her elbow, stationing himself between her and streams of workers, carts, and transports passing by, for the poor earned no day of rest. Seerce doubted anyone noticed her, but strangely dressed women stared openly at Rayn, their bright lips smiling, their painted eyes vacant.

Quickly the two crossed into a dilapidated neighborhood. Perhaps these rooming houses had been beautiful estates at one time, for some featured remnants of columns and porticos. All displayed considerable neglect. Patches of vegetables and herbs and a few large fruit trees grew in what had probably been grand gardens. Thin children of every race and age chased through the lanes. Steam and the cries of babies poured through open windows.

When they reached the air barge station, Rayn paid the duty with tokens and followed Seerce closely up the ramp. An air barge arrived soundlessly to the platform. No operator was apparent, but a uniformed guard disembarked after the departing passengers. Another guard saluted him and walked on ahead of the boarding call, which was an automated voice. Transparent view walls enclosed the wide double-decked barge with rows of seats running lengthwise, all directions visible. As they climbed spiral metal steps to the upper floor, the barge pulled away, picking up speed. Rayn placed a hand at the small of Seerce's back to steady her.

They took seats facing the city. The metal roof rattled some with the wind, the heating elements on its underside providing only a little warmth as cool breezes found their way in. Seerce pulled her shawl around her shoulders and tied it at her neck. Rayn took her cold hands in his.

"Now we may relax," he told her. She smiled, thrilled by his affection, though surprised at its public display. There were only a few other passengers on the upper deck, none paying any mind. "I give you Altea," he told her, sweeping one hand across a panoramic view of the volcano and the city, then returning it to cradle hers.

Seerce gasped. The scenes she had viewed in crystals did not portray the infamous metropolis. In places were dilapidated heaps, but next door might stand a stately tower, a fountain, or a park. Neighborhoods were apparent by narrow streets arranged in spokes, connecting with open-air markets, shops, and air barge stations at their centers. A bevy of barges sailed at a minimal height over the cityscape, higher up among the foothill communities. The Autark's palace of white stone crowned the mountain, four turrets marking the cardinal points, jutting toward wispy clouds sprayed across the blue sky. Each was topped by a broad, blood-red banner of the Ryk snapping in the wind. A huge white energy dome gleamed at the center of the complex.

The people are to remember the great power that keeps them in check, Seerce commented.

Silence the Echo

It is quite a display, Rayn agreed, then he reverted to oral language. "The port is on the other side of the mountain. I am a better guide for that area."

"How would you know the port when you have been in Altea only as long as I?"

"I went every free day to walk the market streets," he answered, "an old habit from years of trading. Now I have better things to do."

She giggled, taking back her warmed hands, sliding her forearm between the crook in his elbow and his warm body, leaning into him a bit. The easiness between them seemed natural. He smiled broadly, looking as content as she felt, with the familiar current pulsing strongly. Of late she perceived it in the lower regions of her abdomen, a warm heaviness there.

They took in the sights from the air barge, pointing and wondering, conversing all the way around the island. Rayn told her of his father's shipping enterprise. While his gift for languages and an eye for value made him an astute trader, he was young to be on his own, impressionable, witness to the dalliances of itinerant men.

"Too much, too soon," Rayn told her, shaking his head. "The closest I came to self-discipline was taking up the oud, something to amuse myself between ports. Practice gave structure to my time and music improved my standing with the crews. Otherwise I was just a kid to be tricked and teased and dared. They worked for my father and they knew I was there only because of him.

"But when I played on deck, the men came by to sing. All of them knew songs of their homelands. Grown men wept at the memories that old ballads brought back. I worked out the chording whenever one could hum or sing a melody. In ports, I visited establishments where music was played, sitting in with accomplished performers, learning better technique and more songs. I found that none were better loved by women than musicians."

Seerce laughed out loud. "So this is your magic!"

"I merely wish to illustrate the influences at work in my young life," Rayn insisted. "While my shipmates bought ale for poor women, hoping to arrange a bed for the night, I was playing music."

"Am I to feel sorry for you?" she asked.

"No," he replied. "Becomingly dressed ladies asked me to their tables at breaks and bought me expensive libations."

"I see. These are better stories of port life than my mother told me."

"Sometimes at the end of the evening, a woman would send her coachman for me, whereby I was escorted to a fine home with"—he cleared his throat—"fine accommodations. How could I refuse? You are blushing."

Seerce unlinked her arm to cover her face with her hands. Peeking at him between her fingers, she asked, "How would you get back to the ship?"

"If the man of the house was away, the coachman drove me to the dock before dawn."

"And if the man of the house happened to arrive home?"

"At the time I was also known for my distance running, oud in hand."

Seerce doubled over in a fit of laughter. Rayn, seeing this, laughed until he cried.

CHAPTER 6

"**As you conduct research** for the Order, your inner vision may be required in places where your physical person would not be safe: at the mouth of a volcano, among moving ice floes, even in the midst of hostile people. Your brain must learn to set aside its concerns for self-preservation, for your inner senses are safe wherever you send them. Today we shall attempt a view from underwater," Cyan told the initiates.

Seerce tensed.

"How should your brain direct your breathing when your inner vision is immersed in water?" Cyan asked.

Now her heart leapt into her throat. From two seats down in the Temple, Aaron leaned forward, looking to her with concern.

The exemplar assured them, "Of course, your physical body is here in the Temple breathing easily. Now I ask that you look within and around the submarine that Anakron showed you. Meditate before you begin, then prepare your brain with an imaginative preview, recalling your impressions when you first learned of its presence.

"When ready, move your inner vision to the interior of the vessel and take a tour, noticing details. Then attempt to move your vision into the water on the ocean side. View the vessel's length and features. We will share observations when you return."

Why must Cyan introduce this exercise now, when he knew Seerce's fear of water, before he had counseled her? All she could hope was to interest her inquiring mind and try to keep her anxiety in check.

Soon she viewed the enclosed space in dim greenish cabin lights. At the windowless nose there was a console and two swivel chairs. Turning her vision to the rear of the ship, she saw rows of grey upholstered seats, three to each side of a narrow center aisle. These were faced in alternating directions, so six passengers would sit as a group. There was one small oval window per seating section, and moving down the aisle, she saw the murky appearance of the sea. Either the vessel was deeply submersed or the water's surface was shaded. At the back, she spied a narrow spiral staircase descending to a lower deck.

Below were storage compartments, lavatories, and a tiny galley—but no windows. A shorter deck than the upper, a solid wall separated the walkable area from what she assumed must be the propulsion system. She passed her vision through the wall into a tightly packed space, with an array of metallic tubing and opaque white panels, set between wide octagonal crystals the length of her arm. Resting on scarce floor space was a hammered copper box, its upper surface dished out as if to hold something large and round—perhaps the Temple Crystal, thought Seerce.

From here she could have tried to pass her vision into the surrounding water, but she might better preserve her orientation if she moved outside from the front of the upper deck. By that thought, her vision went there. But she was terribly afraid to know water all around her. She panicked, her physical body gasping for breath. Immediately her inner vision rejoined it. Opening her eyes to see the altar, she willed herself to slow and deepen her breathing. Eventually her racing heart calmed and her constricted throat relaxed. Cyan's eyes met hers. Nonchalantly he looked away.

Only Aaron and Sootchie were able to transfer their faculties into the water. But everyone saw great detail within the submarine. Cyan praised their progress. Seerce felt utterly defeated.

Silence the Echo

*

The wind was intent upon bringing a new storm, blowing ferociously when Seerce went to lunch a little late, for she and Tavia had remained in the classroom to discuss Leo's limestone strata. The dining room was more crowded than usual. She was surprised to see Anakron at a long table, conversing with a group of priests she did not recognize. There were two unoccupied chairs at the table where Jair and Sootchie ate. Perhaps she would join them.

Starving in the long serving line, Seerce distracted her hunger by conversing with visitors about the miserable turn weather took each time they came to Altea. Finally she held a heaping plate in her hands. Turning, she saw Anakron motion her to an empty table, for his group had dispersed.

Setting her plate down and sensing his receptivity, she telepathed, *Is it permissible to give you a hug?*

I think so, he responded, smiling, standing to tower over her, *though these two in the corner may require an explanation.* He inclined his head toward Aaron and Rayn. It surprised Seerce to see them eating together. Anakron wrapped her in his long arms and squeezed her briefly to his waist, for the top of her head only met his sternum.

Do you know everything? she asked incredulously, looking up to his grin.

As it concerns you, yes, I believe I do. What do you think of your program?

I am pleased to be here, Petrae, she responded, using his familiar name. *How is it to run this operation?* she inquired. He did look better than he had when she arrived two moons ago.

I am perpetually busy. Now I must run to yet another meeting of minds. Is there anything you need from me? he asked.

So relieved to feel her grandfather's acknowledgment, if only briefly, she replied, *That hug took care of everything.*

Keep those boys at arm's length, he advised. *The Order needs you.* Off he went.

Mulling over that directive, Seerce took her lunch to her apartment.

*

There are strange things going on beneath the volcano, Aaron told Seerce. *Come with me tonight and I will show you.* After handball, the two sat on one of the benches in the rose garden, cooling off in the sea breeze.

For this subject, she acquiesced to telepathy, asking, *Are we breaking into the power dome? Or have you perhaps acquired a position with Altean government?*

The look on his face remained serious. *Last year one of our remote views with Anakron was over the volcano. I thought it strange that the eye of the dome was closed, when Altea had relied on the dark energy of the night sky to power the city. So I went back on my own to see what they do in there.*

What did you find?

Nothing I understood. But lately I wonder if the red aurora is a side effect of their new venture. I find nothing about this technology in Physics or Geology files.

Where might I examine those?

You need access to the Hall of Records, he told her, *which your class will get later this year. Until then, I am your source.*

My inner vision shall accompany you tonight, she agreed.

*

At the decan before midnight, Seerce met Aaron in the Temple, dim but for the faint glow of the wall sconces, the Crystal rotating above them in the dome. Momentarily the vision of each hovered over the energy dome, bodily outlines in Aaron's signature yellow, which he dimmed, and Seerce's violet.

A quadrangle with the dome at its center, the Autark's palace was constructed of huge blocks of clean white stone, light standards casting bright circles over the plaza inside its walls. Four turrets stood watch at the corners, dimly lit windows providing vantage points for the Autark's elite guard. Above the conical roof of each snapped the flag of the Ryk in a stiff breeze, emblazoned by a golden lion poised to lunge, face snarling and front paws extended to capture prey. Only the welcome entered here.

Aaron and Seerce moved their inner vision through the wall of the energy dome. Within the cavernous structure was a tangle of columns, canisters, catwalks, and platforms, dimly lit by the glow of immense tubes snaking through it. The ceiling of the dome was invisible in the darkness overhead.

Follow me down, Aaron directed. The two descended along a perimeter wall. Below the metallic jungle was a wide and thick platform of stone, perhaps a fabricated stone-metal mix, for there was sheen to it. Groups of wide tubes snaked out the bottom of this strange block, stretching far below into the gullet of the mountain. The glow within each was uneven, showing as a spiral of separate light sources.

I recognize nothing I see here, Seerce told Aaron.

Neither do I, he replied. *I did not know there were such metals or alloys as these.*

Moving down, Seerce focused her examination on the rock into which the tubes had been threaded. *These channels were cut with ultrasonic tools,* Seerce told Aaron, *dividing the stone along molecular boundaries. This is the way my clan's enclaves were carved into the bedrock of Basra. But see how the rock crumbles? There must be strong energy coursing through here.*

Are you saying the tube system weakens the rock around it?

I say that molecular-level sculpting does not result in such deterioration. There is another force or forces and this energy is suspect. Shall we try to move our vision between the tubes and the rock?

We have no idea how that might affect our beings.

We brought only our inner senses and a reflection of our bodies! Seerce argued.

Yes, but we are energy even as spirit. When we are priests, we might ask Tane about our safety, but for now we are initiates doing unauthorized fieldwork.

You are right, Seerce conceded, surprised that Aaron ever considered consequences. *What other than heat may be extracted from the depths?*

I do not know. But if this energy is electromagnetic, perhaps it is what draws the aurora southward.

They took another look above the platform but found no clues. Full of questions, the two returned their vision to the Temple, as quiet and dark as they had left it.

*

"This is heartfelt and clearly stated," Cyan told Seerce, after a quick review of her assignment. "Carry on with the next set of questions, which you will find less disconcerting. There are other topics we should discuss today.

"You have been a positive influence upon Aaron. He has ongoing work to do, but he has made a good start. He would like to explain himself to you, and I hope you will allow this."

"Of course," she replied, wondering what he meant.

"You will be pleasantly surprised," he predicted. "Rayn has his own confession to make. Try not to judge him harshly, for he is sufficiently hard on himself. You three are a powerful trio. The joining of your developed energies will be a force to behold." With that, he dismissed her.

Perhaps it was well that he and Anakron kept eyes on her. Clearly she did not understand all that was at work here.

*

Across from Seerce at breakfast, Kessa observed, "I see in your face that the struggle continues."

Exhausted by numerous concerns, Seerce replied, "So many struggles at so many levels."

"The boys?" Kessa asked.

"Oh, they are always in the mix," Seerce acknowledged. She did not know what to make of Rayn's affection toward her nor what she felt when alone with him. Aaron never stopped surprising her, though increasingly she enjoyed his competitive nature and his bent for research, similar to her own.

"Who do you love?"

Seerce sighed. "Both appeal in such different ways, but lately there is so much else to consider. Seeing what the Order has spent forty years sculpting makes our central problem real, does it not? My personal assignment from Cyan has taken all the wind from my sails. In this fishbowl where we live, I feel my every move is watched. And come to think of it, I am homesick."

"Oh, my!" Kessa exclaimed. "This may take longer than breakfast to fix." Both laughed. "But let me say something to you about what I think is happening here."

"Please," Seerce begged.

"It seems that all of us try to find allies within our little group. How is anyone as young as we are supposed to step up to the task before us? This is not what young people do! We should be out looking for love, trying on relationships, figuring how life works. Instead, the ten of us are captive here in this odd cocoon, pursuing an occupation few would ever consider, expected to play nicely and bond with strangers so very different than we are. This, my dear, is a recipe for crazy-making. I am surprised we do as well as we do."

"You make me feel no better, Kessa."

"Hear me out, sister. I give you my speculation about your two fine hunks of male energy. They and everyone here would at least like to be loved before we sacrifice ourselves to this outlandish pursuit. Maturity and strength of character are what our task requires and we are not old enough! So we look for reinforcement from our fellows.

"Handsome young men," Kessa continued, "here and everywhere, may command anything they want from admiring young women. But looks and charm have their downsides. One might manage to avoid one's personal development for some time. These boys can do their own growing up, or they can work merrily through the women around them to see who might help out. Things will go better if first they learn to love themselves."

Seerce supposed there might be truth to that statement. "You sound like the voice of experience, my friend. Who do you love?"

"Someone not at all pleased that I chose the priesthood. It is a long story that I will tell you sometime." She paused. "I count myself fortunate to have my family and friends nearby. I speak the language, I know the city, and I have learned the culture of the Order. All of this must seem so bizarre to you and our classmates, each of you alone in a very strange place."

"Thank you for that perspective. I had lost sight of just how weird all this is."

"Happy to help. Now we had better get to class."

*

"Rayn, I think these limbic recordings we do for Cyan reveal far more than we realize. And I am sure now that the faculty keeps eyes on our relationships." At Seerce's invitation, the two returned to the dining room for tea following meditation. A few resident priests sat together on the other side of the room, involved in their own conversation.

"What arouses these suspicions?" he asked worriedly.

"Anakron suggested that I keep you and Aaron at arm's length. Cyan tells me you have a confession to make."

Rayn sat back in his chair with a hand to his temple, closing his eyes. "There is more you should know about me." By his expression, she knew it would not be good news. He dropped his hand and opened his eyes to meet hers. "My weaker portions have recently been…summoned. Seerce, I am older than you by at least a decade. I lived a decadent life before I sought the priesthood. From a young age I indulged in wine, women, and song in every port where our ships called. Memorable beauties no longer have names, there were so many. I worry that I have fathered children I have never met." He paused to take in the look on her face. "You are shocked," he observed, "as you should be."

"This is not my picture of you!" she exclaimed.

"It is nothing I want you to know of me, but it is my story. I continue to try to forgive myself. That is the work Cyan has set for me." His look was forlorn. "Three years ago, I asked a priest of my people to teach me his path. No easy taskmaster, he required of me celibacy, work in the orphanage, and my resources to be given to poor women and children. He conducted the rigorous training required. Then he approached Anakron, when he visited the temple in Hammas. They must have debated my merits late into a number of evenings. Ultimately, Anakron acknowledged that my linguistic skills would benefit the Order. I am here with my failings known to him and to Cyan."

Seerce shook her head, saying nothing.

"Your close proximity, your touch, ..." he trailed off for a moment, "ignites desire I thought I had conquered."

"And in me, desire I did not know I possessed!" Seerce exclaimed. "But I will not be one of your many!"

Devastation took his features. "I am deserving of your disdain. But please allow me to explain myself."

"You may try!" she answered vehemently.

"Everything about love I must learn, because I do not know love. I know only the physical act."

Seerce simmered in silence. This subject was an affront to her.

"I was drawn to you the day we met, with the hope we might be friends, just friends. Your goodness was evident. It was helpful, actually, that you and Aaron seemed to be …attracted. If your heart was engaged, I might learn of love by your example."

Staring at him, she said nothing.

"It became a challenge, yes, to come near you with Aaron on guard. So I watched for opportunities."

"You look to the wrong woman," she told him flatly. "I know nothing of love." If she did, she might have made a place in her heart for Aaron's innocent feelings to root. He was a man of honor, devoted to Gaia and his people, blessed with a healing gift and a shrewd mind.

"You were raised by a loving family, Seerce, in a close-knit clan whose bonds of love transcend time and death. The love you know shows in your kindness, your words and actions, in your confidence and self-regard. One does not radiate what you do unless love fills the center of her being."

If only his eyes betrayed disingenuity, but they did not. He spoke the truth as he knew it. "Who raised you?" she asked, for he had yet to reveal anything of his people.

"Servants," he answered.

"Servants? Where were your parents?"

"My father pursued only wealth, and my mother had her… habits."

A picture formed in Seerce's mind of the women who sought after Rayn as a performer—wealthy and bored, starved for companionship and attention, his mother perhaps like them.

"Your affection," he continued, "which you share sweetly and trustingly—I ask that you withhold it from me. I must learn to love respectfully and emotionally and spiritually first, or I may never outgrow my infantile craving for flesh and blood to cradle me."

Ignoring this tug on her sympathies, she was furious that he had engaged her in the first place and angrier at her own naiveté. Controlling her tone, she stated emphatically, "Live your life as you please. I am here for studies, in pursuit of ideals that I hold dear. Among my people that is what women do. We are not handmaids to men. Please excuse me."

She stood up and took her cup to the kitchen, then strode out into the hall. Coming to the stairs, she gathered the length of her robe in her hands and ran up. Breathless from exertion, she willed the door of her apartment open as trickles of tears started down her cheeks. Leaning against the cool stone wall inside, she tried to catch her breath, and when she did, trudged up to her loft to fling herself across her bed, surrendering to rage and self-pity, sobbing uncontrollably.

*

A grand illusion had she made of Rayn, but there was no camouflage for her puffy bloodshot eyes when the sun rose. If she possessed a veil, she would wear it, as some women did on the streets of Altea. Seerce thought of staying in bed, missing class and handball, hiding indoors today and on tomorrow's day of rest. But she was too proud to be defeated by a man. Damn him and his pretty face, she thought. Nameless women and unknown children? The thought reignited her indignation.

Employing her grandmother's remedy, she drank a glass of water and lay down again with a cold compress over her closed eyes. She considered what she might do to make herself feel better. By the time she walked downstairs, she had a plan.

Intercepting Aaron in the serving line, she asked when she might accompany him on a hike. He looked surprised. *Tomorrow after breakfast,* he answered.

If it is a long ways, I will request a lunch be prepared for us.

He smiled. *It is. I will have water canisters for you and me.*

Thank you, she told him. *I want to challenge Cyan to a singles match today.*

Then I will challenge Tane, he replied. Together they had been practicing some of their instructors' signature moves. Excusing herself, she went to find Jair, inviting him to lunch with her just to see his grin. Then she picked up her breakfast and sat down with Isla.

"I am told you are among our musically inclined," Seerce said. "How long have you played?"

"Since I was seven," Isla replied, smiling. "My flute is my best friend."

"I stand in awe of your dedication. Kessa told me several of our colleagues will play or sing for the solstice celebration."

"Oh, many of us will," Isla told her. "There are fifteen more musicians among the residents of the Temple, and at least that many voices."

"Do you practice together?"

"As we rehearse for the solstice celebration, yes. Afterwards we shall break again into our several ensembles for musical recreation."

"Are observers allowed in your rehearsals?"

"We have had none, but I doubt anyone would object. We meet in the Music Hall on the third floor of the Healing Temple. Tell me of your interest," Isla requested.

"I do not know music at all and feel I am deprived."

Taken aback, she responded, "Oh, that is hard for me to imagine. Do join us," she encouraged. "Music soothes the soul."

That was one of Seerce's purposes.

*

Their classmates cheered Ell's announcement of the student-instructor challenges, to be played one game at a time. Seerce drew the long stick, electing to serve first. Standing behind the backcourt boundary, she fired the ball hard to the floor, bouncing it high and angling her paddle to aim it alongside the left court boundary. It traveled low, rebounding from the wall shallowly. Cyan raced up from his backcourt, but not before the second bounce. The students erupted in applause and whistles for Seerce's first point.

When Cyan served, she missed the return, but went on to score three points, with more serving tricks patterned after his. Clearly, he did not anticipate seeing these one after another from her. He turned up the heat on his returns, denying her points. Playing hardball then with his serves, Seerce had to run to cover the court, but she was fast and strategically accurate, smacking the ball to where he was not. She kept a two-point lead. When she tired, she began returning shots to the ceiling, conserving her energy, exploiting Cyan's weakness in returning those. So involved she became in working the ball's angles, she no longer heard the cheers and shouts of encouragement. To her it seemed that she played in slow motion, with time to consider options, to execute accurate strikes. Cyan came within a point of her score, but he never gained the lead.

When she realized she had won, she doubled over laughing and huffing and dripping sweat. Aaron draped a towel around her and hugged her with all his might. Then he paraded her around the court, holding her fisted hand up high, hollering "Yes!" at the top of his lungs. Finally, he let her go and she sauntered over to bow to Cyan. He returned the gesture, and then got down on his knees to bow again, his arms and hands straight out in front of him across the floor in a gesture of supplication, as the initiates roared with laughter. When he rose to his feet, with a bona fide smile on his face, he told her, "You are serious competition."

Seerce went out to get another towel and a long drink of water, while the match between Aaron and Tane was set up in another court with a dry floor. She returned to hugs and kisses on the cheek from her classmates. Surprised, because she had ceased to think about him, Rayn stepped forward to say, "Congratulations on an astonishing feat of athleticism and confidence." Though he smiled, his eyes were dull. She acknowledged him with a slight tip of her head and turned into Ell's outstretched arms to collect another hug. Nearer to the players' court, she sat down cross-legged on the floor to send what was left of her warrior will to Aaron. He fought mightily, only to lose by two points.

Tane played like lightning, she told him afterward. *You did everything in your power.*

Yes, he said, *I did. But you kicked Cyan's hindquarters to the islands of the Mu. You are one tough goddess.*

*

"May I petition for a short walk?" Seerce requested of Aaron at breakfast the next day. "I treasure this outing, but I gave my all to the game yesterday and I am exhausted."

"Me, too," Aaron replied. "A nap this afternoon might suit us. Separately, of course," he added quickly.

"Maybe together," she teased, "if we nod off after lunch."

He grinned. "I look forward to it."

Both wore a clean set of their athletic wear and shoes, topped by rain capes with hoods for the drizzle. Their food and water Aaron carried in an old leather satchel strapped to his back. Walking west to the end of the road, then north from the Temple campus, a well-worn path forked and they took the less traveled, which narrowed and threaded through a forest of mixed deciduous and evergreen trees. The contrast of new spring-green leaves against the darker firs enchanted Seerce.

"This is truly beautiful," she told Aaron. "The needles beneath our feet and the blossoms of these bushes make a heavenly scent. Never have I walked in a forest." She stopped to look up to the canopy of intersecting branches overhead. "I can scarcely see the sky or feel the rain!" she exclaimed.

Aaron smiled at her delight. "There is a bit of elevation coming up, and on the descent, a wooden bridge over a small creek."

She squealed like a child. "Oh," she said, "show me!"

"Then come along," he said, reaching for her hand. She rather liked the feel of her hand in his and let him keep it. They said nothing for a long ways, over the bridge and up another incline until they heard tumbling water.

"Coming from the desert, perhaps you have never seen a waterfall?" Aaron spoke today, which surprised her. Perceiving that thought, he added, "Because you have a lyrical voice. I like to listen to it."

"But I do not sing," she told him.

"You have not sung," he corrected. "I believe you could with training."

"Truly?" she asked, then gasped at the sight of a cascade of water pouring off a high bluff to their right, tumbling over boulders, catching briefly in a stone pool, and falling into a deep ravine below the level of the path upon which they stood. With wonder, she whispered, "Behold the goddess of the falls."

"All the goddesses are here," Aaron told her, smiling.

She smiled back, his eyes no longer strange to her but familiar, his inner workings humming softly today—no demands, no call to action, and no upset at all. His tranquility matched that of the forest and now she knew why he came here.

"Just a little ways farther to a path that descends to the wild coast," he said. "We might eat lunch there."

"I am hungry," she admitted.

He laughed and said, "I know. Your innards growl." As they emerged from the trees, a glimmer of sun peeked out above the roaring surf. "The bay is boulder-filled and therefore noisy," he told her.

Seerce was entranced by the dance of the spray and shooting jets of white water. As the sun brightened, rainbows appeared in the mists overhanging the maelstrom. "Astonishing, Aaron! Such powerful beauty!"

He let go of her hand to remove the pack from his back. "It seems our rain capes have dried," he told her. "We can sit on them for lunch. There is a place I like over there." He pointed. She followed him. Spreading their capes over adjacent boulders, they leaned their backs against them, eating voraciously, watching the tumult in the bay, hearing the cries of jealous gulls whose companions flew away with fish in their bills. Low clouds sailed by on the breeze, peeks of sun warm upon their faces.

"I have realized something I would like to share with you," Aaron said eventually.

"Please," Seerce replied.

"Unwittingly, I have tried to fit you into the hole inside me, where my mother's love used to be."

"By the Goddess, Aaron! What an insight!"

"Cyan helped me realize it. Never will I trust him, but the explanation resonates. It gives me some relief, actually, to think I might one day narrow that abyss. I did not know its name, only its emptiness." He remained clear-eyed, as though he recited fact, but he saw the tears that welled in hers. "I knew you would understand."

How many of us, Seerce wondered, grieve for our mothers?

"I do not know," he answered aloud.

"At least four of us ten, by my count," she said. Rayn's mother was incapacitated and Jair had only ever spoken of his father.

"Willingly, I shall work with a counselor at the Healing Temple."

"I salute your courage, Aaron. Cyan knows his subject, just as he knows entirely too much about all of us."

"You fascinated him yesterday. That was evident."

"I did not notice," she rued. "I minded the ball."

"He minded you."

Seerce sighed deeply.

"You need to watch yourself. Cyan's interest is more than platonic."

"Oh, Aaron! He is what, twenty years older than us? A scholar, an exemplar, a crucial player in the Order's dilemma! I am just a clan girl, a student."

"He was a clan boy once, and I doubt he has ever known anyone like you. Just be careful, please."

She changed the subject, knowing his concern was real and she should heed it. They strolled back to the campus after lunch, hand in hand, enjoying each other's company. When Seerce napped in her own bed that afternoon, it was with a measure of contentment.

CHAPTER 7

"**I trust you are ready** to vanquish your fear of water." Seerce was in Cyan's office for her regular appointment.

"I am," she said.

"There is a suggestion I would like to make to your subconscious mind. It is that you remain unconcerned, though alert, around and in water. You shall remember all that you remember now, but you will recognize that your mother's circumstances were her own and they are not yours. I will count back from ten, as I did with your class before the visit to Leo. Were you caused any adverse effects?" he asked.

"No," she reported truthfully.

"There will be none with this either. Do you wish to proceed?" She affirmed that she did.

"Relax, then. Close your eyes. Breathe deeply and completely. Inhale fully, exhale fully, slowly."

Seerce rested her back against the comfortable chair, placing her hands in her lap, closing her eyes. Attending to his reverse count, she ceased to hear him. Unaware of any time that passed, she heard Cyan call her name. Fluttering her eyelids open, she was surprised to find herself in his office, unsure why she was there. He reminded her.

Pouring tea then, Cyan inquired how Seerce had fared through her mother's recovery. She was a bit fuzzy-headed, but she remembered instilling a response to this question into Cyan's crystal. Perhaps he had not read it. Maybe those exercises were for self-realization.

"It was a lonely time for me," she admitted. "My family was caught between grieving my uncles, caring for my mother, and keeping our agribusiness alive. The Port of Tunise where we traded was destroyed by the sea wave, along with the academy where my cousins and I boarded. If it had not been for the healer that Anakron sent, my mother would not have survived.

"Kee-ay was a beautiful man from the east coast of Afrikaa, his ebony skin so dark one might think it blue-black, similar to Ell's, so strong and relentlessly cheerful. Effortlessly he lifted my mother from her cot while we changed her bedding. Every day he exercised her joints, protecting her fractured arm. He asked us about Mama's personality, her interests, and her people, that he might treat her as a most capable woman, an empath, and an Aurean.

"Father obtained the grains and seeds that Kee-ay specified, which he then pressed and sieved into extracts, adding them to the juices of vegetables and fruits. Using hollow reeds that he chose from our gardens, he dripped nutrition into my mother's mouth a few drops at a time so she would not choke. She lay unconscious for nearly two moons.

"As Kee-ay directed, all of us telepathed or spoke to Mama when we attended her. 'Tell her what you do to assist her and why,' he advised. 'But tell her also of your activities and the business of the clan. You help her brain make new connections to the areas that control her hearing and speech, feeling and movement.' It was the most challenging time of our lives, Exemplar, but we would do it all again if need be." Finally Seerce took a sip of her tea. Cyan had finished his while listening intently.

"Your will to conquer is like your mother's," he stated. "Are you ready to try a water view?"

Interestingly, Seerce felt no fear at the thought of immersing herself in water. "Yes," she answered decisively.

"There is a pool within the Healing Temple, just inside the main entrance. Direct your inner vision there and let us try a plunge."

Closing her eyes, Seerce prepared her inner vision to travel. Shortly, she saw before her a tiered fountain within a pool, water pouring from shallow bowls to cascade over sculpted copper fairies at its base. She moved her vision all around these fanciful creatures, whose wings sparkled with inlaid colored stones. Enchanted by them, she forgot her mission entirely.

Follow me down, she heard Cyan say.

Without hesitation, she took her vision into the water. There were trails of bubbles at the feet of the fairies and the silent motion of water running in ribbons of blue, twisting into darker strands below. Farther down, the water lightened again, which surprised Seerce. Curious as to why, she descended to find that the pool was actually a huge clear bowl upheld by metal latticework, supported by pillars resting upon the basement floor below. Moving down to look through the bowl, she saw another ring of copper fairies dancing around a substantial central column. People passed back and forth on the promenade below!

In her mind, she heard Cyan say, *Let us return, Seerce.* She was smiling when she opened her eyes in his office. He looked to be as delighted as she.

*

Purposefully late, Seerce waited outside the back door of the Music Hall, a jumble of discordant sounds and voices rising and falling inside. Finally there was a sharp rap-rap-rap of wood against wood. Quiet fell. A feminine voice spoke at length. Beginning softly, a melody soon took form, swelling with the addition of sounds she had never heard. Opening the door slowly, she entered into a dark narrow walkway, along a few railed steps just inside.

These bordered an ascending set of benches at the back of the performance hall. Between those and the musical company was space in the center for chairs, but none were set up.

At the front, instrumentalists were arrayed on the lower portion of a bi-level stage, vocalists behind and above them. From an elevated platform, a slender Archaean woman faced the group, the length of her cinnamon-red hair falling in waves down her back, a short pointed stick in one hand, the other marking the beat or cuing musicians. Singers stood quietly. Participants were of all ages, dressed informally, not a robe among them.

Trying to remain inconspicuous, Seerce seated herself in the first row close to the rail. Only a few seemed to notice her entrance. Kessa and Aaron smiled at her. Rayn and Isla were engrossed in playing. Many faces she recognized from the dining hall, though Sootchie and Tuura were the only others she knew.

Seerce disliked the volume, her hearing as sensitive as anyone raised to communicate soundlessly. She could not ascertain which instruments made which sounds. An elder woman's slender arms reached across an elegant harp. Others played stringed instruments with bows or mallets, some of these held upright, some flat like small tables, and one small hourglass shape resting upon a man's shoulder. There were long brass horns and hanging chimes and small drums held between knees, struck with the flat of palms. One other oud player, older than Rayn, sat next to him, his instrument worn and considerably less ornate. Rayn cradled his lady, his fingers flying, and his eyes intent upon his colleague's nimble hands.

Having dreamt of Rayn last night, Seerce awoke feeling sorry for him and ashamed of herself. Before bed she had made a cup of tea, recalling every word and tone and nuance of the evening she walked away from him. She had not met his eyes lately, though she watched him surreptitiously in the gym, distracted, pained, and clearly not himself. There had been a time when she could not read Rayn at all. Now, sitting next to him in class, his sorrow hurt her and she could not ignore it. She had no doubt of her importance to him.

Cyan had said he was sufficiently hard on himself. Then why was he forced to tell her of his shame? How much should his past matter to anyone, when he had atoned for it? What kind of a man asks a woman to withhold her affection while he learns what love is? Likely someone who is at least a worthy friend. She recalled advice that Barlas gave the first years early on. "Clear any differences that arise between yourself and another. Grudges and gossip tear the fabric of our community."

The piece ended and Rayn looked up to the conductor, his expression serious, his eyes shadowed and tormented, no trace of the joy she witnessed when he played his personal concert for her. A forced confession, the resurrection of his past, and her judgment—these changed everything between them. She must apologize for her part.

A few of the string instruments and Isla's flute opened a ballad by the singers. She was awed by the intricacies of high-pitched and low-toned voices, soft or soaring, with interludes by the instrumentalists, and the engaging beauty of Altean poetry set to music. At the end of this piece, the vocalists shifted places on stage, two back rows humming mutedly while the exquisite voices of soloists traded lead parts in front, Tuura among them. She took dramatic liberties with the melody in the last phrases, the background singers coming alive in a range of resounding harmonies. Seerce was enthralled.

She sat enchanted for six more pieces before their conductor dismissed the musical company. Aaron and Kessa hurried over to greet her, to ask what she thought and what she liked best. Standing quite close to her, Aaron reached boldly to take Seerce's hand. She squeezed it and let go, moving a half step away and turning toward his face to praise his contribution to a trio of male voices. "You, my friends, are gifted performers!" she exclaimed. "I am bedazzled by all of you. Allow me to congratulate our colleagues." With that, she hurried to intercept one or another, keeping an eye on Rayn as he replaced a string on his instrument. Seeing that he remained alone, she stepped onstage and took the chair beside him. He remained bent over his work.

"I am in awe of what all of you do individually and collectively, Rayn. In my life I have known nothing like what I heard and saw here tonight." She spoke softly so only he would hear. But he did not look up.

Leaning in she launched her apology. "I have wronged you horribly, abandoning you in your time of need. I am deeply sorry for hurting you, for adding to your hurt. You deserve better from me." His fingers stopped working. "I wish to honor your request for our friendship absent affection. Know that I will struggle because"—she took hold of her emotions lest she weep—"I remain so very fond of you and I relish your warmth and I want more of it. I did not know what to make of your early chapters, for I come from simple people, farmers and weavers, hidden in caverns beneath the desert. I am immature and selfish and stupid and…I have never felt for anyone what I feel for you."

Blinking back tears, staring at her hands, she waited to see if he would respond. If he did not, at least he knew what was in her heart. "I leave you in peace to make up your own mind about my worthiness as a friend." She stood to go.

Without looking up, he telepathed, *Will you meet me shortly in the room next door?*

I will, she replied, relief washing over her.

Take the long way around, he advised.

Doing so, she encountered Aaron at the lift, standing alone, looking annoyed, and surely waiting for her. But that would have to be tomorrow's dilemma. Thinking quickly, she asked him the whereabouts of the lavatory and he pointed. Moving past him, she called back, "Thank you. I will see you in the morning." She lingered in the lavatory.

Coming round to the small music room, she knocked softly and Rayn opened the door. The sconces were dim and the curtains open to the waxing moon among silvered clouds. "Do you prefer more light?" he inquired, closing the door.

"No," she replied, "I prefer your arms around me."

"Then perhaps our agreement commences tomorrow," he responded, taking the few steps to her, his fingers scarcely touching the tops of her shoulders, as though she might be an apparition in moonlight. She searched his eyes. Unwaveringly, he searched hers. She knew again that familiar vibration in the depths of her. He cast a tight net, this worldly man, this unbeloved child, this musical soul.

She dared to place her hands upon his chest, her fingertips at the base of his throat. She rose on tiptoe to incline her head toward his. Then his arms were all around her, his head bent toward her, his breath upon her face, the sweetest softest touch of his lips to hers. She kissed him back tenderly and he kissed her again, more urgently, pulling her close. Reaching her hands up to encircle his neck, her thumbs felt his racing pulse in the arteries beneath his jaw. Her lips yielded to his, opening to his tender penetration, her breath coming hard and her heart racing. They kissed long.

When he dropped his hands to her hips and pulled her tightly to his thighs, warmth and pressure spread through her pelvic floor. But this was uncharted territory.

Coming down from her toes, she dropped her hands to his chest and shoved, breaking his squeeze. Taking his hands from her buttocks, she moved his arms to cross his chest, laughing, and scolding, "Where is a whistle when I need one? Game over!"

"That was so wrong of me," he pronounced, breathing hard.

"Yes, it was!" she retorted. "But I have myself to thank for starting it. Now I know I play with fire. So what is our plan, Sir Rayn?" She sat down in a chair. "You go sit on the other side of the room," she directed, "on your hands. From there you may tell me if I am forgiven."

"Oh, yes, you are, love," he asserted. Then he covered his face with his hands. "Woman, you discombobulate me," he said between his fingers.

"Did you mean to call me love?" she asked incredulously.

"I meant to reserve saying so. I have no notion what is proper to say or do."

"We might learn together. But you had best speak your intentions before you commit them."

He laughed. "I have never known a woman such as you. I do know I had best follow Cyan's directives for my behavior."

"So I must keep my hands to myself?" she queried.

"And your lips and your hips and all your beautiful person, yes. You see what happens otherwise."

"I have never known the like."

"Nor me."

"That is a bald-faced lie, sir, though you wear a beard," she countered. "You play me like your oud."

"You respond as willingly, but at heights and depths and frequencies she does not sing."

Seerce sighed.

"Allow me to walk you home," he suggested, "before I think better of it."

"We shall struggle, Rayn."

"I know," he told her, opening the door.

*

Next to her, iciness possessed Aaron. Seerce did not know what she should say or do. She realized her error accepting his affection the day of their hike, forgetting his tendency to read more than she meant to convey. For her hand-holding had been the warmth and support of friendship on a day when she needed some, a shared experience in the majestic sanctuary of the forest and the thunder of the bay. Undoubtedly, she rekindled his hope of her interest. She should have thought through the consequences.

Kessa noticed, as she always did. Before Cyan came in, she telepathed to Seerce, *What have you done to these man-children? Rayn glows and Aaron froze!*

Seerce made a face and Kessa stuck her tongue out. Both of them suppressed giggles as Cyan entered, striding quickly to the front of the table and beginning with a question. "What do you know about the pyramidal ceilings above your bedchambers?"

Awakened every morning at first light, Seerce knew that as the solstice approached, the darkness of night was shorter-lived.

But often she was lulled to sleep by the patter of rain above her, and that she liked very much.

Ell answered, "The pyramids assist the warming and cooling of the domiciles."

"They do," Cyan confirmed.

Kessa ventured, "Ancient priests had a predilection for sleeping under the stars."

"The Mu did," Cyan clarified. "Altea is better known for cloud and fog than starry nights. Are you aware that your etheric bodies leave your physical selves at night? Have you had dream experiences such as seeing from a distance above Earth, or falling a long ways, or hovering around your body, trying to get back in?"

There were nods of affirmation around the table.

"These are indicators of your natural comings and goings, for your inner senses have no need of rest. In our next moon together, I will meet you in a dream state and beckon your etheric self to accompany mine. Your brain will sleep, unaware and undisturbed. At first you may not remember much when you awake, but do not concern yourselves. We plant seeds so that later you may launch from a waking state. You are quite adept now at moving your inner vision. What I describe will also become routine for you.

"The etheric body, as we call it, has no difficulty crossing any physical barrier, but the clear ceiling does allow me to assess your dream state without invading your bedchamber. I do not wish to frighten you, should you be in a transitional state or awake. Once your etheric body agrees to come with me, we shall stop at Protos and deliver instructions. Later you shall do this on your own, for reasons we have discussed.

"I will meet you for your journey the night before your scheduled session with me. You may, if you wish, share your experience in class. Otherwise, we will discuss it when I see you in my office. There is much to learn from each other and sharing is preparation for three or four of us traveling together later. I see your interest. Shall we proceed?"

Their responses were positive.

"Allow me to impart some background information. Your dream world has continuity. Unaware of any break, it exists to a vivid degree while you sleep. In the morning, you rejoin a waking life in progress. When you fall sleep, you rejoin a dream life in progress. These are parallel existences that enhance the creative quests of your Greater Mind.

"Remind yourself, as you climb into bed, to remember your travel experience. Train yourself not to move when you awake. Keep your head still and your eyes closed and give yourself a few moments to recall the night's journeys. This is a good method for remembering dreams. At first, your memories of both will be incomplete. Recollection improves with practice. You may wish to keep a recording crystal next to your bed so that you may deposit your memories before they evaporate.

"One of the purposes of sleep is to facilitate communication between your Greater Mind and your physical incarnation via your inner senses. You elected a task upon this plane and you are guided to accomplish it. You may meet up with other souls involved with this and other missions. While your physical body rests and heals, your eternal essence continues its activities. If you are open to it, your physical brain learns to accept more and more from your inner sensorium. Meanwhile, your dreams carry messages in personal symbolism. Pay attention.

"Cenon business calls me, so please begin reading the sections on etheric travel in your crystals. You will find affirmations to use at bedtime. I hope to see you in the gym this afternoon. Exercise assists deep sleep and profound dreams." He bowed his head slightly to them and left.

Seerce marveled at Cyan's friendly and encouraging introduction, making their upcoming sessions sound like fun. He might enjoy it more than walking ten of them through their sorrows, though she wondered how much sleep he would lose.

The first years pestered their more experienced colleagues with questions about their etheric travels. Tuura insisted there was nothing to it, as it was something she had done since childhood.

Across the table, Ell waved a hand dismissively at Tuura, telling her, "You had a unique if not entirely fictional upbringing." Laughter rang out.

Tuura's mirthful brown eyes crinkled in her mahogany face as she stood up to chastise Ell, tossing her head with each inflection, swinging her multiple long braids around her ample figure. Today each braid was intertwined with a different colored ribbon, contrasting fancifully with the plain white robe. "Brother, may I remind you that my people lived *upriver* of yours, and *my* elders taught *your* elders all they came to know? I thought you understood your place in my world." The students tittered.

"I was seriously uncivilized as a child of the jungle," Tuura confessed, looking around the table, talking with her hands, exaggerating her expressions. "In fact, it was not until my mama put me in the priest's school at the Port of Janga that I ever witnessed such a thing as being quiet. In the course of my very long ed-u-ca-shun, while my body was confined to the schoolroom, my spirit was out flying with the birds, running with the wolves, and laughing with the hyenas."

Snickers and giggles circled the table.

"I had a very hard time staying *in* my body. It was just so easy to get on out. The priests, well, they tried, but they could not contain me," she lamented, a pitiful look and a pouting lower lip on full display. "So they sent me here. They said I had the gift of as-tr'l trav-el-ing."

Laughter erupted again.

"So, if you are talkin' to me and you find no one home, you just come on back a little later. I get hungry and my spirit will return."

Hoots and cackles spilled out into the hall. Aaron thawed long enough to laugh out loud.

*

A few days later, Seerce awoke remembering to lay still and keep her eyes closed. A mist enshrouded her journey with Cyan. She could not see beyond it. Thinking of a window through which she might view the experience, she imagined opening that window. The mist lifted and the memory unfolded.

Where was this? A type of laboratory came into view. Several people were there. The Exemplar of Climatology introduced herself as Rika. She was dressed strangely for her high office, wearing a tiered gauze dress of bright colors such as tribal people wore, but pinned up on her head was the wiry faded red hair of an elder Archaean. Where was Cyan?

I am here, Seerce, look to your left. His form was cloaked in blue light, as she had seen him at the Monument of Leo. *Follow me,* he requested.

She turned, and suddenly they hovered far above Earth. *Look down at the Altean islands,* Cyan directed. She saw them much as Exemplar Nova had portrayed the archipelago in the Temple Crystal on the occasion of the earthquake. *Look at what lies south and east.* Off the west coast of Afrikaa was a spiraling cloud mass. With its arms and its empty center, it resembled a fuzzy galaxy.

What is that? Seerce asked.

It is a powerful cyclone, Cyan responded.

The window slammed shut. Seerce sat straight up in bed, her eyes wide open. She reached for her memory crystal and instilled the vision, grateful to recall something, but feeling just a bit unnerved. She got herself ready and hurried downstairs to breakfast.

Cyan intercepted her in the hallway. "That was an excellent first journey," he told her. "Would you be willing to recount it for the class? It makes no difference how much or how little you remember."

She agreed and came back after a quick meal to sit at the oval table alone and organize her thoughts. It was a struggle to choose Altean words descriptive enough for that incredible sojourn. When everyone was seated, Cyan gave her the floor. She stood to recount her impressions, using gestures to portray the lifting of the window, Rika's appearance, and the mass of the cyclone, which was greater in circumference than the mainland of Altea. The initiates were riveted. Finishing the tale, Seerce sat down.

"The use of the window was a most creative solution," Cyan commented. "The brain will often respond to such familiar symbols. My own recollection is this: Seerce was soundly asleep, which is the ideal, and engaged in a dream. I called her by telepathy and she turned her inner awareness to me, leaving the dream unfinished. She accompanied me to Protos, as I requested. We accomplished her introduction and I gave my instructions."

Seerce recalled none of this.

"We visited Exemplar Rika in her climatology lab at the University of Zanata. Her team monitors all the storms that roll off the Afrikaan continent, because some of them become problematic for us here in Altea. She gave us instructions on how to view the storm which her team currently monitors.

"Whereas Seerce perceived being above Earth immediately, I remember much more effort to get there." Cyan actually chuckled. "First we had quite a conversation about flying dreams, falling off swings high up in the sky, and other experiences from Seerce's dream life. She did ultimately agree to come with me."

She remembered none of that, either, but she smiled at the titters of her classmates.

"We started much nearer the ground, hovering here, just above the Temple campus. As Seerce acclimated herself, we moved higher and higher. I must say, both of us were astounded by the size, but also the beauty, of that rotating mass of energy. I had never seen such a sight. For me, as well, the storm resembled a flattened galaxy.

"We conversed about what storms symbolize to the human psyche, then stopped at Protos before returning Seerce's etheric self to her sleeping body. She resumed the dream that had been in progress when I came to her.

"Seerce, your personal recollection was exquisitely descriptive. Thank you for allowing us to see through your eyes. Would you take a few questions from your classmates?" he asked, and she did, for the better part of a decan.

At their lunch break, Seerce followed Aaron out, striding quickly to catch up to him. *Would you eat with me?* she asked. *I wish to clear the air between us.* He kept walking.

*

Arriving to the next rehearsal, Seerce was surprised to find Aaron and Rayn just outside the music hall. By their stances, she deduced an intense conversation. Seeing her, Aaron motioned emphatically for her to join them.

Rayn continued speaking, his eyes intent upon Aaron, his manner of speech rather pointed, as Seerce heard him say, "She is her own woman with no wish to choose between us. You perceive me as a risk to your place in her heart, but I am not. I accept her love for you and her friendship with you."

Aaron's eyes widened. Seerce was stunned.

"However, you must understand that I, too, have a friendship with her," Rayn told Aaron. "She has a loving spirit. She acts as she was born, a force for good. Allow her to be the woman she is. Love her that way."

Aaron turned to her, asking defiantly, "Is this true, Seerce?"

"Yes," she affirmed, incredulous at how Rayn knew her heart. "I might have told you myself." Though she doubted she could phrase her truth so eloquently.

Aaron turned back to Rayn. "I give you my apology," he said, raising his right arm in the priests' gesture of goodwill. Rayn's arm met his from elbow to open palm. Aaron turned on his heel to go inside.

"Is everything all right?" she asked Rayn.

"It might not have been. He was about to take a swing at me when Annecy stepped between us."

"Annecy?"

"Exemplar Annecy of the Healing Temple, our conductor."

"My Goddess, Rayn!" she exclaimed, the implications multiplying in her mind.

"It is handled now. I must get to my chair. Shall we take a short walk before night falls?"

"Yes," she assented. "Should I stay for this rehearsal?"

"That would express your support for Aaron. Wait for me outside the alcove of Admin. I will take Lady Oud home and meet you there." He headed for the front door and she went in the back entrance.

Several new selections were performed, but Seerce scarcely heard them, marveling at Rayn's command of conflict and worrying for Aaron's volatility, blaming herself for these upsets. Aaron might well have been dismissed from the choir, even from the initiate program, had he struck Annecy or Rayn.

At the close of practice, Aaron left quickly. Seerce chatted with Tuura and Sootchie, learning that both had joined the choir last year. Annecy was nearby when Seerce was about to leave. Perceiving the exemplar's receptivity, she walked over to introduce herself. Near to middle age with knowing copper eyes in a flawless ivory complexion, the bronzy red tint upon Annecy's lips played up her cinnamon hair. "Ah, you are Anakron's granddaughter, the young woman between our two young men. Now I understand why."

Seerce could not help but blush.

"Likely you know that Aaron grew up rough and tumble with male role models and little nurture."

"He tells me your staff assists him, Exemplar," Seerce replied. "Thank you."

"Thank you for joining us. I wish you much success with the Order."

Seerce bowed her head politely, awed by what she perceived in this woman: extraordinary kindness, faith in the intrinsic goodness of her charges, and leadership sufficient to inspire an orchestra, a choir, and no doubt the healers who worked for her. Annecy was a role model to emulate.

Remembering her promise to Rayn, she hurried to Admin, slipping out the alcove door into his waiting arms. "We are not supposed to do this," she admonished.

"It is only a hug of friendship," he replied, wrapping her tightly.

"I met Annecy," she told him.

"She is a force to behold, is she not?"

"In the most positive way, I believe."

"You are like her."

Seerce pulled back a little to look up to his eyes.

"That is a grand compliment I hope one day to deserve. How is it that you know my heart better than I do?"

"Because it shines with the clarity of a jewel in sunlight. Anyone might know if they would look or listen."

"But you should not speak on my behalf. I fight my own battles."

He smiled. "I grant you that. Tonight I missed a fist to my face. You were not there to protect me."

She giggled. Taking their stroll around the perimeter path without further touching, they watched Venus emerge as the western horizon darkened. "The goddess of love graces us," Seerce told him.

"I see her," Rayn replied. "She walks at my side."

*

In the early morning hours of the common day, Seerce was awakened by vivid lightning and tremendous claps of thunder. She went downstairs to peer out the windows. In the lantern light of the gardens, trees bent nearly to the ground with the force of the gale. Surprised to see residents outside, Seerce watched as they hauled patio furniture through double doors to a storage room between the gym and the dining hall, before the wind blew it against the windows. Donning her rain cape over her night clothes and a pair of athletic shoes for traction, she hurried down to help. Kessa was already there. "This must be the storm you and Cyan saw. It is nasty."

"Is this what happens in the summer here?" Seerce asked. Tunise had its thunderstorms in monsoon season but nothing so violent.

"At least a couple times, but lately they are much worse than when I was a child. Now they kill people."

Heavy downpours started just after dawn, arriving periodically throughout the day. Tall waves crashed over the seawall, spilling salt water through the rose garden and swamping the courtyard. In the men's domicile, the first floor flooded. Little could be done until the storm diminished. Those affected were assisted by their fellows to carry their belongings to the gym, for the Admin building was on higher ground. The displaced took vacant rooms on upper floors in the ancient building.

Class was canceled the following day. Residents and students earned sore backs and shoulders lifting and scrubbing. Working side by side with those who had weathered prior furies, Seerce heard their concerns for the rising of the sea. Salt water had been driven further into the campus than any recalled.

Kitchen staff brought news of some five hundred deaths across the islands. Flat roofs and old construction gave way in the pelting rain and heavy hailstones. The southwest coasts of many smaller islands were under water, fishing boats swept into flooded farmland or carried out to sea. Kessa said the storms were one reason Altea imported so much of its food now. "Then how long before the Ryk has to move camp?" Sootchie asked.

"Tunise fell under the Altean flag six years ago," Seerce answered, "the thirty-eighth of its forty nations. The Ryk moves as we speak."

CHAPTER 8

"**Senses of the inner spectrum** include several beyond the range of our physical senses. For instance, an etheric traveler may experience a sense of history or future for the locale visited. Generally, one may more clearly perceive inner emotions within people they observe, as well as insight into their motives." Today Cyan made random eye contact with all from his stationary position at the head of the oval table.

"For example, by projecting your inner workings to Majorka, an island of the MidTerra, you may pick up on the series of cultures and settlements there, some long past, others yet to occur, for all eras of that or any place exist simultaneously. When observers travel together, each views the experience according to the perceptual ranges of their individual sensoria. Each has her or his own instrument and we are all a little different.

"Some features of your inner senses are better developed than others. Some may be diminished, even absent but compensable—just as those with limited hearing employ other senses to determine what is said. Some people have inner senses unique to them, just as some claim sixth and seventh senses beyond the usual five of physicality."

It was Tavia's turn to recount her etheric journey with Cyan. She stayed seated, closing her eyes to recall what she described. "We came to a sailing ship unlike any I have seen. Its wooden prow was ornately carved and highly polished, arched and high." She traced its shape in the air by the sweep of her hand. "There were rows of fixed oars along its sides, unmanned for the sails were filled with wind. On deck we observed a conversation between an elder Nubian and a young sailor whose coloring was like my own. It seemed the two were acquainted by prior conversation.

"Heru was the elder and he spoke of the ancient people of Poseidon, seafarers beyond the columns of Heracles. Sandros, the younger man, did not know this place. Heru claimed a prior life in the end times, drowning when the sea swelled its boundaries and the vessel upon which he sailed capsized. He described the ancient people's abilities as godlike, saying they wreaked havoc in the weather and the seasons and the length of the day, for they were carelessly powerful. I realized he spoke of the times we live in now, and he spoke from the future.

"Sandros asked, 'Why do you tell me this, old man?' Heru answered, 'We have records of that era in the Temple of Hatshepsut, where I serve as priest. Most all people died of flood. Those who survived could not reckon when to plant their crops. Many starved. Is this tale told in your homeland?' the priest asked.

"'Sailors know tales of raucous seas,' Sandros attested. 'To return home they pay homage to the god Poseidon.' He advised Heru to visit the priests of Eleusis once they came to port.

"The next I recall was Cyan's telepathy saying we must return."

"Thank you, Tavia, for this fascinating account," Cyan told her. "Cenon observers are aware of the Temple of Hatshepsut, which arises much later in the vicinity of Misr. Tavia has an interest in future cultures of her homeland and Heru is the subject of ongoing observations by two Cenon researchers. As yet, we do not know if Hatshepsut's records are based upon our own, but that is the question to answer. The Pillars of Heracles is a future name for the channel between the Ocean of Atlas and the MidTerra Sea.

For millennia after the destruction, ships do not venture beyond the pillars. You see how fragments of history survive in legend and ritual. What questions have you?"

Rayn inquired, "How far into the future does Heru live?"

Cyan answered, "We see that every culture counts time differently, sometimes quite generally, such as 'during the reign of Neheb.' Conquered people become subject to the time-keeping of their conquerors. Accuracy is subject to a symbolic language and durable methods of preserving records. Both are lacking in many locales we visit."

"Tavia," Aaron asked, "how did you manage to recall this conversation so completely, particularly those foreign names?"

She looked to Cyan, who answered, "Tavia accepted a hypnotic suggestion from me this morning, which enabled her to bypass her brain's filter and access most of the memory."

Tavia admitted, "I recalled so little of it when I awoke this morning."

"The same is your privilege if you so choose," Cyan offered to the students.

Seerce knew what Aaron's opinion of such would be. Regardless, she had lost her fear of water by Cyan's intervention and she remained grateful.

*

As she left dinner, Aaron intercepted Seerce. *There is something I would like to share if you would walk with me up shore.* He wore a forest-green fisherman's sweater, for the evening had turned cool, the wind threatening a new storm. Fetching was that color with his emerald eyes and auburn hair.

I will, she replied, relieved to be on speaking terms. *But you have rehearsal, do you not?*

Annecy has excused me for the evening.

Allow me to change my clothes, she requested. *Rayn expects me in the music hall, so perhaps you would say to him that you and I* have other business? He and Ell are in conversation at the dinner table.

Grinning slyly, Aaron told her, *With pleasure I shall.*

Barlas's office was closed, so they left campus without official notice. "I have not been this way," Seerce remarked, as Aaron led her west on the dirt road to a tangle of greenery that blocked the ocean view. A path through it turned northward.

Aaron asked, "Do you remember Nova's description of the bald ocean floor, where the seismic energy tracked peculiarly?"

"Yes," she replied. Quickly the path became rocky and climbed steeply, but shortly they emerged from the brush to overlook a wide seawall of enormous boulders. Waves lapped noisily below. The wind had its way with Seerce's long hair. Gathering its thickness to the nape of her neck, she twisted its length to tuck under her shawl as they walked on.

"Geology finally posted their report with the coordinates of the area," Aaron told her. "I waited long for their updates to the Hall of Records."

"I am sure there are levels of review before departments send anything to the seat of the Order. This is a bureaucracy after all."

Aaron laughed. "How would you know?"

"Anakron complained of such when he was but a lowly superintendent of schools. Never repeat this to anyone!"

"I promise I will not."

"So now you know the longitude and latitude of the anomaly. What else?"

"That Altea constructs something upon the ocean floor there."

"No!" she exclaimed disbelievingly. "How does Geology know that?"

"I am not sure they do. But I have watched ships and industrial barges converge upon a spot where there is nothing more than deep blue sea. So I took my vision down through the water."

"What could you see in utter darkness?"

"Sections of the ocean floor are lit. The work is accomplished robotically, progress monitored by an occasional submersible vessel. Drilling seems to be the primary activity and it continues day and night."

"What does Altea want beneath the seafloor? Minerals? Gold? A repository for some dangerous chemical? Halfway to Tibisay is a long way to go."

"Come with me on our next day off. I want you to see in daylight just how far away this is."

"I shall."

Following the wall of boulders, they came to a narrow precipice jutting out over the sea. "This rock is most substantial, I assure you," Aaron told her, "but only wide enough to proceed singly. When I stand upon it, I feel like I fly." He took the few paces to its endpoint, turned, and shouted back to her over the tumult of the waves, "Come see if you can fly, too!"

Seerce dropped the shawl from her shoulders and double-knotted it tightly around her waist, lest the wind make a sail of it. Gathering her loose hair, she braided it deftly and tucked the length into the neckline of her dress. Then she inspected both sides of the crag to assure herself that it was indeed one contiguous rock and firmly anchored. Aaron watched her with amusement.

Before taking her first baby step, she stooped to scrutinize the uneven bare surface, satisfied that it was devoid of pebbles and slippery lichen.

Aaron extended both his hands to her. Stepping out gingerly, she reached toward him. He took only her right hand in his left, saying, "Now turn carefully into the wind and extend your other arm." Seeing that he flapped his outer arm up and down, she did the same with her left. Aaron let go of her hand and stepped a pace farther from her. Working both her wings now, she shouted over the tumultuous surf and the wind in her ears, "Now I fly!" Laughing like delighted children, they carried on until their tired shoulders could not.

*

In class, Jair and Kessa were set to give their accounts of a joint sojourn. "Tandem and group observations employ the giftedness that each observer brings," Cyan commented. "A fuller picture of any situation emerges by joint observation."

Jair was asked to begin. "I remember the three of us in front of Protos briefly," he recounted. "Then we stood before a domed building. The walls were faded yellow, as was the low stucco wall that surrounded it. Bright blue tiles covered the dome. We moved inside where there were at least a hundred people fanned out in sections from a central podium. An elder man spoke loudly and passionately, but I did not understand his speech.

"Looking around, I realized there were outer rooms, so I went to survey. In one of them was a round crystal, like our Temple Crystal. It rested on a slatted copper support. Pockmarked and scratched, it looked very old and poorly treated. I tried to communicate with it, but it gave no response, so I returned to Cyan and Kessa.

"An older boy kept looking up toward the place where we hovered. I thought maybe he perceived our colors. Everyone else looked straight ahead. I recall returning to Protos, but nothing else."

Cyan thanked him and called on Kessa.

"As we arrived to this temple, I tried to figure where on Earth we were. By the dusty haze in the air it seemed an arid land. However, there were stands of trees in the distance and a few green fields, so possibly farms bordered a river. Compared to the bright midday, the temple interior was dim and it was sparsely appointed.

"The people were of Rayn's coloring, the men with long beards and heads of thick dark hair, sitting in chairs. Women wore veils over their heads and faces, and sat on their haunches behind the men, their children on the floor with them. The speaker was a different race, pale-skinned and grey-haired. I tried to catch familiar words, but the cadence was far different than our common language. It had a clicking sound to it and a singsong lilt. I tried listening telepathically, but I could not keep up with his foreign concepts.

"It was my strong impression that females lived virtually enslaved, subject to what males ruled."

Cyan thanked her, explaining, "This is a future people in a land called Akkad, east of Rayn's homeland, far beyond the shores of the MidTerra Sea. There is a fertile river valley between spines of rugged mountains. The area becomes home to multiple subsequent civilizations. We think it an excellent locale for the work of our visiting delegations, teaching the open-minded about the Hall of Records.

"The speaker we observed is someone I have personally contacted in dreams, but he is aware of this only at a subconscious level. As a child he was trained by adepts who had access to the Order's wisdom. However, as his life advances, he espouses a much more limited theology. Here he advocated for obedience to the rule of one male god who sees and controls all.

"The young man who perceived our presence is the grandson of one of those adepts. He trains privately with that group, while maintaining the outward appearance of acquiescence to the speaker's religion. This is a theme we observe throughout the region, as prevailing beliefs come and go and recombine. Sometimes a worldview such as our own is in vogue and sometimes wisdom survives underground in the hands of a few."

Cyan explained, "Kessa seeks to determine the culture of the people and their relationship to the land. Her third inner sense enables her to detect the nuances of situations she observes. Food security is a challenge for this community and women are held to strict codes, even as to what they may eat.

"Jair's attunement to crystals has given us an intriguing clue as to how we may be able to follow paths into the future, observing what unfolds around a single crystal."

Some of these initiate journeys must be treasure troves for Cenon, thought Seerce, perhaps some recompense for Cyan's interrupted sleep. She wondered how he sustained himself, teaching day and night.

Silence the Echo

*

Aaron's remote vision met Seerce's in the living room of her apartment. *Let us stay under the cloud cover and follow the archipelago as it curves southwest.*

She kept her inner vision upon the more visible red glow he adopted for their journey. *Again we fly!* she exclaimed, as they passed irregular rocky clumps, some with a few scraggly trees or hardy bushes rooted in crevices, others painted white by the excrement of sea birds that nested there. She had no sensation of motion or air temperature, no feel of the breeze or smell of the sea, just a rapidly moving picture as they skimmed over these uninhabited islands.

Aaron imparted that they would change direction at the small port of Morivay, the southernmost tip of Altea's island chain. *Due west from there, on the other side of the mid-ocean ridge, we shall rise up to locate a ring of sea barges. Next time you may return instantly, but I want you to understand just how remote this place is. The Ryk goes to considerable trouble and expense.*

Morivay was quite small, with two docks for bigger ships and a sheltered harbor on the east side for fishing boats. This was the point of departure for the ocean journey to Tibisay Colony, where the Order had established a temple and school. Cyan mentioned this one day in class, saying he had been stationed there a number of years to study future people of that mountainous region, inland from the Ocean of Atlas.

Finding a wide circle of stationary barges, the two descended to see these packed with machinery, parts, and long lengths of hollow tubes, a few people engaged in activities upon their decks. A navy frigate pulled away as another approached. *We should assume a military application for whatever it is they build,* Aaron told her.

For the wealth they expend, I would think so, Seerce commented.

Her descent through dark water disoriented her. Direction was meaningless absent any sensations to judge it. Aaron turned his glow to bright yellow and Seerce stayed focused upon it, showing herself in orange. Eventually the darkness gave way to an odd amber glow. They came upon orbs shining as brightly as daylight, but dimmed in short distance by the black motion of deep water. These were set upon tall standards fastened to sunken barges, crowded with heavy machinery and anchored somehow to the ocean floor.

Piercingly bright spotlights up and down those standards were focused upon drillers that plunged and rose repetitively, undoubtedly sonic separators, for the stone plugs they freed were smooth-sided. These would rise from the holes to float away, but for the catch nets arrayed around the drillers. Two operated continuously, while a third rested. There was no human presence.

I wonder what will happen once these deep holes are drilled? Seerce asked.

The hollow tubes we saw at the surface are a close match by circumference, Aaron answered. *Maybe those will be slid in, like the tubes beneath the volcano.*

I wish we could retrieve rock samples to view under magnification, for the clues those would provide.

Aaron told her, *Geology's research postulates that the mantle is largely crystalline. By extreme heat and pressure at the depths, common minerals acquire characteristics they lack at the surface.*

Like what?

The capacity to transmit wavelengths of energy that the crust of Earth does not. We know that compressed quartz crystals generate a weak electric current. It is plausible that mantle crystals do the same or better.

Do you suppose that Altea intends to transmit energy through the mantle?

It certainly looks that way.

I find that horrifying, Aaron!

So do I, he replied.

*

Rayn sat upon the ledge of the fountain at the public entrance to the Healing Temple, holding a crystal vase with a single red rosebud.

"How precious!" Seerce enthused as she walked toward him from the tunnel, the lobby empty in midafternoon of the common day. "Thank you!"

Sitting with him, she admired its perfection and sniffed its heavenly scent. The tight petals had just begun to unfurl, its sepals yet standing upright. Behind them the copper fairies splashed and gurgled.

"I want to say that there is a new energy that enlivens me," Rayn told her, "greater enthusiasm, sharper focus, a brighter outlook."

Seerce looked up to his eyes, drinking in the moment.

"I mark the day I noticed. It was on the south patio prior to our class luncheon. Something traversed the space between us, reconnecting me to life. I woke up that day from a slumber where I had lived as half myself."

How poetically he speaks, she thought. "It was the day I realized how strongly you pull me," she told him.

Smiling, he continued, "Now you are woven into my thinking. I try not to impart that to Cyan's crystal, as I work through exercises for him. Yesterday he congratulated me on my progress, saying my most difficult tasks are done. It was more praise than I have heard from him."

"Be proud," Seerce encouraged. "This has been an arduous journey for you."

"Regardless, he maintains that the time we spend together weakens my resolve."

Seerce reacted. "It is little time that we are alone and we have a plan! We follow it. How well we come to know each other is none of his business!"

"Your understanding relieves me greatly. I worry for the problems I cause you."

"I can assure you," she said, looking down to the rose, "I suffer not at all."

Aware of daybreak, Seerce lay still with her eyes closed, endeavoring not to think but to see by her mind's eye and feel by her inner senses. A series of pictures came to her, of a tropical jungle and a stepped pyramid obscured by overgrowth. There appeared to be a high entrance on one side, but no means to reach it. Cyan and Rayn were present with her. Together they moved through to the interior.

Hovering in the upper reaches was a round crystal, but it was asleep. The space was empty of anything else, save vines that crept in through decaying joints between blocks of stone.

Tell me how this crystal came to be here, Cyan requested.

It is an artifact found by later people, long after the cataclysm, Rayn responded.

Who met here? he asked.

Rayn and I have both been here, Seerce told him, *to meet a priest called Itka-ke and teach other priests.*

Outwardly he was friendly to us, Rayn said, *but some were not. We scarcely escaped with our lives! But access to wisdom remains.*

Locked up in this dead crystal and well out of sight, Seerce commented. *We will have to do better than this.*

The pictures faded. There was nothing else she could remember, as she lay in bed in her Altean apartment, filled with wonder at these visions. Surprised she had slept at all, she had been as excited to travel with Rayn as he had been apprehensive. Now they were to meet with Cyan before class.

As they entered his office, he was quick to remark, "You two are interesting travel partners." He sat to one side of his office window, the raining sky indistinguishable from the sea of grey, which Seerce observed from the chair across from him. Rayn moved the middle chair closer to her as Cyan poured cups of tea on the table between them. He asked first for Seerce's recollection, which she recounted.

"Now, Rayn, if you would," he requested.

"Leaving Protos, we were instantly near a pyramid, Seerce between us. As I looked for entry, the wall before us shimmered and gave way for us to pass. The space seemed to grow larger. Upon a stone table was one of our recorder crystals in a carved wooden holder at the center. I saw wavering images of a group around this table with Seerce and me, small brown people wearing colorful headdresses and little clothing.

"That scene vanished, leaving me fearful for Seerce's life. With her etheric body hovering next to mine, I interpreted what I had seen and felt as a recollection of an earlier occurrence." Pensively he added, "I have a duty to protect her."

Seerce was shocked that he would say such a thing to Cyan.

Rayn continued. "Itka-ke-kahn told me the round crystal was found by the draining of a swamp, when these Olmekah people built a new city. It had been wrapped and kept hidden until he showed it to earlier Cenon visitors. He called for a temple to be built on the site of the crystal's discovery. A later delegation installed it.

"It seemed that Seerce was greatly admired by Itka-ke-kahn," Rayn added, "so he ordered that she be captured. I traded my Crystal of the Sun to a guard who gave me access to her. We escaped. Later I went back on my own to recover my pendant. Intently I loathed that place and wished only to leave," he concluded. Drawing a ragged breath, he placed his hand over Seerce's as it rested upon the table, by which she perceived how truly frightened he had been.

We are safe, she telepathed, *have no fear,* seeking to soothe Rayn's terror without regard for Cyan's perception. Withdrawing his hand to his lap, Rayn clenched it with the other and both hands shook.

"You need to understand how your tandem energy was perceived by the Olmekah priest," Cyan stated. "But first, allow me to give you context for this journey. The Fifth Tenet holds that probable events occur simultaneously."

The two nodded their recall of that from physics class.

"Any number of probabilities might have played out by the first delegation's visit to the future. Cenon has found that if we project ourselves *beyond* the time frame that interests us, and then look back, we may see a fuller picture. But how many probabilities are there? We cannot be certain.

"Following that particular crystal into the future allowed me to look back through a sequence of probabilities. What we saw last night might play out if the two of you are sent together to visit that future priest. It is the Cenon project's obligation, of course, to ensure the safety of the Order's members as they travel. Some are a better fit for certain missions than others. There are two lessons apparent to me by our experience last night: The Olmekah civilization does not survive overly long and you two may be endangered if you visit there together."

"Do not allow Seerce to go at all!" Rayn insisted. "Keep her safe and send me instead!"

Cyan did not react. Instead he stated coolly, "Those you met perceived the sexual dynamic between you."

Seerce's face grew hot.

"That is what created problems for you," Cyan judged. "Seerce was regarded by these priests as one of their virgin goddesses, so Rayn had to be…vanquished. Not always do we meet the well-intentioned. We do learn something by every journey. Take from this experience what you may. It shall not be discussed in class, where we are due shortly." He stood. The two preceded him out the door.

Scarcely did Seerce hear Cyan's presentation other than its conclusion. He expressed to the class his satisfaction with their attainments and his plan to finish the current subject two days hence, just ahead of the summer solstice. Thereafter, the second years would assemble their personal biographies under his tutelage, and the first years would study with Anakron.

Relief washed over Seerce and surely over Rayn.

*

Nice weather held for the celebration, though skies remained cloud-filled. As yet the breeze was gentle. Looking from her apartment window, Seerce saw chairs and benches arranged on the lawns and patios. Aaron and Sootchie set seats for the instrumentalists within the Circle of Stones. She went to help, but Ell intercepted her. *Are you good at chopping vegetables?* he asked.

Better at that than cooking, she replied.

Follow me to the kitchen, he requested.

The staff had the holiday off to be with their families. Cooks among the priests made the kitchen their own, setting out simple breakfast and lunch meals while preparing the evening's feast. Seerce was provided tools to slice and dice. She stayed longer to ferry trays and platters to rows of tables in the dining room. The sounds of instruments being tuned floated in as doors opened and closed.

A decan before sunset, residents began to gather at the perimeter of the Circle of Stones between the High Temple and the west garden. One tall obelisk aligned to sunrise at the winter solstice and one marked the sunset today, this one crowned by a wreath of roses. Shorter, wider stones marked the equinoxes. Performers took their places on the flagstone floor within the circle. Hearing introductory notes to a traditional solstice anthem, the crowd quieted to hear the orchestra play. A group of voices joined in and then a countermelody arose from another section. More instruments and harmonies joined the weaving, volume increasing with each addition. Seerce could not see the performers for the press of taller people in front of her.

There was warm applause at the song's conclusion. Walking around to the far side, Seerce was able to slip in closer. Tuura and a resident priest faced each other from opposite obelisks. With their big voices they led the lines of a traditional chant, women repeating after Tuura and the men after Edes, as she heard someone near her call him. It was an ode to the sun.

At the last word of the last line, Kessa, Sootchie, and Aaron began their a cappella harmony, a song Seerce had heard them rehearse, heartfelt and flawless. A moment of silence thereafter gave way to a burst of applause and cheers, though many blinked back tears at the words of reverence for Gaia's gift of the bounty of Earth.

Now Seerce could see Annecy, her cinnamon hair twisted and pinned at the back of her head. She wore her Crystal of the Sun pendant, as many priests did today, her slim ankle-length dress a flattering shade of amber gold, the fabric having a sheen to it. Her Archaean height was sufficient to be seen by the singers standing behind the seated orchestra. Aaron focused upon his parts and partners, but Rayn looked up between songs, his eyes searching the crowd, his smile radiant when he located Seerce.

The gathered sang along with the standards, harmonies springing up here and there. When finally the musicians broke for the feast, Seerce waited politely for Rayn to extricate himself. *You are enchanting in your summer frock,* he told her, though often she had worn it. *Do you know that I play every song for you?*

Now I do. What prompts this revelation? she inquired.

I would prefer to stroll around a solstice party with you.

Let us stroll, then, Seerce said, *right over to our meal, before you play your next set.* With all her being she wanted to link her arm through his, to be his lady for the evening. But she contented herself with the seat next to him at dinner and with watching him play, pretending her shawl was his embrace, keeping her warm as night deepened and the breeze cooled. The clouds drifted away, allowing the spill of the galaxy across a moonless Altean night.

In the second performance, the community was treated to a smorgasbord of traditional songs from cultures the musicians represented. Rayn, Isla, the violinist, and one of the hand drummers performed an ancient piece full of rhythmic pulses and haunting strings, ethereal high notes and the oud's low and complex quarter tones. Aaron joined in numerous choral arrangements as Seerce marveled at his command of such. Watching them perform, a realization worked its way into her consciousness—that Aaron challenged her intellect and delighted her child-self, while Rayn touched her heart and called her awakening womanhood. She hoped never to part with either one.

*

"I did not realize until I gave my account to Cyan, how much I feared for your safety." This Rayn told her as he walked with Seerce along the seawall north of campus. Sparkling blue ocean waves played in the warmth of the second of four free days commemorating the solstice. They sat down to watch from a stone bench along the way.

"That was just one probability," Seerce told him, "though it is well that we saw it. Let it leave you. It has no more influence over you than a bad dream."

But his apprehension was not so easily assuaged. "These feelings are new to me. I did not know how exquisitely I could feel ecstasy within love, nor abject terror at the thought of harm to you. These are strong emotions."

"You are by your own calling a passionate man."

"I am passionate for music," he told her. "What I feel for you is greater and broader and deeper than that."

There were times when Seerce's desire for him overwhelmed her, but today she was content to wonder at his transformation into a feeling man. "I choose to be unafraid," she said. "You and I can reach through any veil to find one another. In the earlier probability, I could have projected myself out of Olmekah at my will."

"You were unconscious when I found you," he told her gravely. "It is what they might have done to you in that state that terrified me."

A chill ran down Seerce's spine. "Were we there in physical form? How is that possible, Rayn? We have not been told of physical projection!"

"We are early in our studies and there is much to learn. Guard your optimism about the motives of people," he insisted, worry clouding his eyes. "You see a big picture and grand possibilities, but well I know the weaknesses of men."

"I do not intend a career with Cenon. My interest is in science, in what is happening to the planet and finding what is reparable. I hope to join Geology or Climatology."

"Your ambitions are laudable. But in the present you must be mindful of one who seeks to influence you more than you realize."

"Who?" she asked.

"Cyan," he replied.

She had her misgivings about Cyan, certainly. But his assistance she interpreted as aid for her advancement. "Why did you place your hand upon mine in his presence, Rayn? That was risky, given his prior instructions to you."

"His interest in the plans of Itka-ke-kahn I found lascivious. I wished to know his reaction to me protecting you. I wanted him to feel the strength of our connection, to understand that it flows both ways between us."

"And what did you learn by your provocative experiment?" she asked.

"That he desires you."

Seerce was aghast.

Rayn warned, "I am a man and I find a false heart in that man."

CHAPTER 9

Anakron sat with the first years, gathered round him at the head of the classroom table. Seerce was excited to learn more from this man she had loved and admired all her life, missing for so long the conversations they used to have. "Allow me to tell you of myself," he grinned, copper eyes twinkling beneath bushy grey-and-white brows, "for I know far too much of you. We should balance the scales."

The students snickered. Rayn flashed a smile across the table to Seerce.

"Like Her Most Important Self, Lady Kessa," Anakron began humorously, meeting her eyes as she pretended to glower at him, "I was born here in Altea of blue bloods, an odd circumstance for my spirit, which had then and still possesses little respect for authority."

The initiates laughed out loud.

"You can imagine where this leaves me, trying to lead an Order of independent thinkers. However, my devotion to wisdom is unshakeable. What called me to this work was the teaching of wisdom. I attended the priests' schools here in Altea, as everyone did when I grew up, two centuries ago."

Chuckles broke out. Anakron might count one hundred fifty years, Seerce thought, by the age spots across his bony hands and the way his long fingers had gnarled. But certainly he had not lived this life for two centuries.

"You have had plenty of history poured down your gullets through the course of your fine educations in our schools." He took a moment to look at each and remember their backgrounds. "Yes, that would be correct. All of you are products of our indoctrination," he jested. "Early on I taught in the academies around North Afrikaa, then for the better part of four decades I was superintendent in that region. When I took on the role of Exemplar of Education, I made it my business to reestablish the initiate program. Somehow or other I was elected chair of the Order and here we find ourselves," he said, smiling broadly.

"Of course, our priests have been careful to teach an acceptable brand of Altean history, one which keeps open the doors to our schools. For you I shall impart a different version, closer to the truth. You will notice differences. We come to the end of a long era upon Earth. There will be another only if we send truth forward."

That sobering thought hit Seerce between the eyes every time she was reminded!

"We will meet for discussion in the mornings, and you will have research to do in the afternoons. There is a set of study crystals here for each of you. I value your input and your viewpoints, so you will also prepare and teach lessons to your peers and me.

"Spending two moons together, we shall make our way through twenty millennia of Altean history more quickly than I prefer. In our final half moon, we shall focus upon the disturbing developments of the last five hundred years, which have wrought the crises we live today." He distributed their crystal sets of six different colors, each set into a narrow marble holder. "Please begin your reading immediately and I shall see you here tomorrow morning."

Seerce took her crystals upstairs, returning to the kitchen to fetch a mug of tea. Aaron came in behind her. *I have looked* up everything I can find about the Altean Energy Authority—the location of its headquarters, which divisions are in what buildings, their quest for more energy than their geothermal plants produce.

The Order has information like that in the Hall? Seerce questioned.

Apparently we have a number of researchers who once worked for the EA. What they know has found its way into science department records. The Order keeps everything it verifies.

That explains six crystals for history class, Seerce commented.

Aaron grinned. *You will love your time with Anakron. My time is fairly much my own now, since my biography is an individual project. I plan to observe some high-level meetings at the EA.*

You have some nerve, she told him admiringly. *Have you found anything at all about the volcano station or what they build on the ocean floor?*

Nothing, he told her. *I have looked in every current geology and physics subfile. Some records are off limits until our induction, though. The darkest secrets may be sequestered.*

*

It was several days later that Anakron was late to class, his expression grave as he came through the door. "Two of our physicists were out surveying this morning. They found the pyramid around Protos imploded. We do not know if the living crystal was destroyed or captured. All the energy signatures of priests and students are in that device, if it survives."

Worried looks surrounded the table.

"Never have we held much concern for monitoring by the Ryk. We conduct all sorts of investigations, of course, by unobtrusive means. Tane is reviewing the failsafe protocols built into Protos. The other gates will be checked for signs of intrusion. Until further notice, there will be no etheric travel and your physical persons are to remain upon the campus grounds."

By Seerce's reckoning, Anakron harbored no personal alarm for this development. It was his nature to trust those he led and clearly the Exemplar of Physics was the priest for this job. Returning to his subject, he elicited what the students had learned of Altea's geophysical landscape in the time of its earliest inhabitants.

Jair spoke of the eruption of a super volcano in the area of his homeland, Palermo, upon a peninsula of the north central MidTerra. "Geology called it the greatest eruption in our part of the world these last two hundred millennia!" Jair exclaimed. "Pumice rained over southern Europa and eastward beyond the MidTerra's shores. Volcanic ash was carried by the winds all around the mid-latitudes, diminishing sunlight for years to come, even here in Altea."

Tavia commented, "Whereas the climate had warmed somewhat in the interglacial period of that time, it cooled again precipitously. The ice crept southward over southern Europa and the sea levels diminished, expanding the continent's coastlines, Altea's as well."

"What effects would you extrapolate for human activity?" asked Anakron.

She answered, "That people, fauna, and flora for some distance around the volcano died from poisonous gases, rockfall, and magma flow."

"Ash clouds from such an explosion," Seerce added, "would have mixed into high prevailing winds. Diminished sunlight must have impacted the food supply, even at great distances from the volcano."

"Sunlight grows the small foodstuffs of the sea," Rayn reasoned, "so likely the catches in the MidTerra declined. If fisher people were driven farther from home, perhaps they made it all the way to Altea."

"A logical theory," Anakron judged. "Indeed, those who arrived on Altea's mainland had been frozen out of Europa's southwest peninsula, at that time called Keltika, where the red people fished along the western coastline. The low sea level exposed mountaintops between there and here. It is likely they island-hopped to the Altean mainland. Witness the irony. Now the ocean rises and the children of the Kelts seek a new homeland."

This is what Seerce loved about the way Anakron taught, painting with broad strokes through time, illuminating cause and effect, requiring the consideration of nuances in any examination of a bigger picture. It was he who made of her a global thinker with a penchant for detail.

*

Having composed a presentation on the Reign of Xerxes III in Altea's First Age, Seerce climbed into bed late. Through the course of her schooling she had learned to complete projects at least a day ahead of due dates. Sleeping on the almost-finished product always generated a few new insights. One more day allowed her to incorporate those.

But she was a bit late for breakfast, whereupon she learned the community had been summoned to the Temple. She grabbed a roll and a bunch of grapes, consuming them on the way, tagging along with Aaron and Rayn, who had waited for her. The three found seats together in a high row.

Tane addressed the assembled. "Members of my team found the housing for Protos destroyed early yesterday morning. We could not tell if fragments of the living crystal were in the debris and we chose not to investigate personally. My department has reviewed the records for the development, installation, and maintenance of Protos. The device has never been disturbed through ten millennia of its existence.

"The structure around it, however, has been replaced three times. Its original home was a temple. Over centuries, most of the Island of Timnos has succumbed to the sea and the population has dwindled to none. We have known the day would come when we would have to disconnect Protos from its energy source. There is an alternate device in development and we shall commence testing it.

"As Protos lost power, what it knew was locked into its crystalline structure and cannot be recovered as data. If the device was captured, perpetrators will learn nothing from it. Our only remaining concern is whether the device was accessed by others while it was yet living. We cannot say with certainty whether our energy signatures and destinations are of use to anyone outside the Order."

Does he imply, Seerce asked Aaron, *that signatures and destinations are of use within the Order? That comings and goings are perhaps monitored?*

That is my assumption, he replied.

"Etheric travel may be accomplished via the gate near Tibisay," Tane continued, "for those who know how to use it, or you may view remotely, if suitable for your purpose. You are free to begin your day."

In class Anakron was willing to discuss current events.

"Do Altean scientists employ etheric travel?" Kessa asked him.

"Not so far as we know," Anakron replied. "The Archaean race has preferred instrumentation for its observations of the physical plane. From time to time, a theory based upon the Order's research has emerged, only to be called imaginative and fanciful. It is possible, I suppose, that some Altean research group has rediscovered the old ways."

Seerce asked, "Why is the Order not allowed an official information portal, like those in every neighborhood and wealthy residence of the land? We house a sizeable resident population and many more visit the Healing Temple." This had bothered her since the quake and the cyclone.

The look upon Anakron's deeply-lined face was familiar, the one reserved for questions he preferred not to answer. "We are tolerated to the degree that we are helpful. We heal the underclasses that they may continue their toil." He paused to see if that would satisfy her. With a wry twist of her mouth, she indicated it would not.

He chose to elaborate. "The professional class is compensated for loyalty to the Ryk with business contracts. Compliance from the military class is extracted more forcefully. That we may continue doing what we do, the Order makes no demands. We have means to discover most of what we want to know. Now let us move on to the economic diversification made possible by the terrestrial resources of Altea."

Seerce understood that Anakron was bound by his role. Subtly though he had confirmed that the Order works around Altea's duplicity. There must be reason not to record what was known about their new technology.

*

"It looks like things are well between you and Rayn," Kessa said at breakfast.

Seerce smiled and nodded. "They are."

"And Aaron has steadied himself?"

"I believe so," Seerce replied. "He does best with a challenge and his projects provide that currently." She avoided detail. "How are you and your love?"

Kessa sighed. "We see each other when we can. I wish she could be happy for this life I have chosen."

Seerce hoped her face did not betray surprise at Kessa's use of the feminine gender. "What is her name?"

Kessa smiled. "Laela. We trained together at the Healing Temple. She is a therapist there."

"Then you are in close proximity, able to spend time together."

Shrugging, Kessa rued, "Our occupations demand most of our time and energy. How does one choose between who you love and what you love?"

"I cannot say," Seerce confessed, certain that would become her dilemma at some point. "Tell me about Laela and you."

"She is practical and I am fanciful. She worries and I do not. I like adventure and she prefers to stay home. She wants more from me and I am enthralled by our mission."

"Opposites certainly attract, do they not?" Seerce remarked. "How do you cope with living apart?"

"I spend a few nights and the common day at her place. The directive here is to sleep alone beneath clear ceilings. I do that."

Seerce laughed. "You are fortunate to love someone who is not our classmate," she told her enviously.

*

It was a half moon before the community heard Tane's pronouncement on the Protos mystery. Seerce was seated customarily between her ally and her love.

"The demise of the living crystal was a natural occurrence," Tane pronounced. "The platform over which the device hovered was likely cracked in the recent quake, subjecting it to more deep Earth energy than it could withstand. When its tolerance was exceeded, it exploded."

Helped along by whatever the volcano station draws to the surface, thought Seerce. She and Aaron exchanged looks.

"Therefore we are no longer concerned for the tracking of our activities. You may venture off campus once again." He gestured to the angular object resting upon the altar. "This is an icosahedron, a crystal of twenty faces, manufactured for us in Palermo. Icos, as we shall call it, is performing beautifully. Shortly it will be installed within the Hall of Records where it will function as our new gate. Two days hence, please begin checking in and out with Icos for your etheric travels."

You first years will need Hall privileges to access the gate, Aaron telepathed to Seerce. *Then you can stop pestering me to do your research for you.* She elbowed him in the ribs. Turning to see the two snickering, Seerce noticed that Rayn grimaced before he looked away. Perhaps he resented Aaron more than he wanted her to know.

Tane invited the interested to examine Icos at the altar, dismissing the others. The first years proceeded to the classroom where they waited a bit for Anakron. He looked winded when he came in, more stooped than usual. Taking a chair, he nodded his head to Rayn, indicating he should begin his presentation.

Rayn stood to deliver his analysis of the evolution of Altean language, a rather ambitious undertaking. Gesturing and inflecting, he kept eye contact with his audience. Seerce saw the poised and confident trader he had been and the practiced performer she knew him to be.

"Absent any foreign contact for the length of the Isolationist Period," he began, "the vast resources of the Altean archipelago supplied the needs of its population. Here the deep ice age was tempered by warm currents from the southern ocean. Forests were dense, hot springs arose in places, potable water fell reliably on the windward sides of the mountainous islands, and sea life was abundant. But there were hazards to human life upon an active range of volcanoes. At first the population increased only slowly.

"It was the watchful and the clever that survived, their language constantly expanding to name and share the varied phenomena they encountered. Harnessing the energy of steam and waterfall, by mining and combining ores and crystals, they built shelters able to withstand frequent tremors. There developed a cultural preoccupation with control of the environment."

Anakron nodded enthusiastically. What an astute observation! thought Seerce.

Rayn continued, "Alteans dwelt in isolation longer than any people of Earth. Spurred to develop a recordable language to preserve their observations and their precautionary measures, their brethren up and down the archipelago benefitted, as did their progeny who built upon this momentous achievement. In a long period of peaceful existence, without civil war or invasion, the like-minded came early to their industrial age.

"Subsequent technological advances shifted their symbolic language. There came to be so many new terms, concepts, and processes that a second symbolic system was devised for the sciences. In this the color of symbols denotes degrees of emphasis and surety. A single line before or after, under or over any sci-symbol conveys past or future, proven or theoretical. In this long-lived technocracy, new symbols pour constantly into the vernacular," he told them, "such that many professionals now utilize assistive devices."

Taking one from a slender box, Rayn held it up. "This is a STEM," he told them, "an acronym for its technical description." Its fine wire half-circle he set upon his left ear, pulling forward an extendable straight wire with a tiny clear ball at its end. "The tip sees what I see," he told them, holding his left palm in front of him, "and if I held a sci-report, the transmitter would read aloud to my ear such that only I hear it. Some of these devices have tiny display windows rather than a tip, for the viewing of diagrams and graphics to assist installation and repair. I hope never to have to wear one." Carefully he retracted its viewer, removed the wire from his ear, and placed it in its cage. Turning to Kessa, he thanked her for the loan of the device.

"You get used to them," Kessa told the group. "In many sectors of Altea's world, one is dependent upon them."

Rayn finished by discussing the rates of common language acquisition among Altea's forty nations. Seerce was surprised to learn that twenty-eight had been subsumed by military occupation, largely without resistance, for the city-states of the MidTerra had little in the way of organized defense. Seven nations joined voluntarily and five suffered natural disasters, quickly aided by the Altean navy and acquired peaceably thereafter. "What influences the acquisition of common language in the Forty is the presence of the Order's schools," Rayn stated conclusively. "The Ryk expends no effort to teach its new citizens, unless one joins the military."

A long discussion followed, spilling into the noon meal, for which Anakron joined the first years. It was one of the most impactful and enjoyable days of instruction that Seerce had experienced.

/ SILENCE THE ECHO

*

"We are due a walk," said Rayn. "We have been indoors overly much." They ate a late lunch together on their day off, watching the trees of the courtyard sway with the wind.

"I should braid my hair first," Seerce told him. "You will not survive the lashing if you are anywhere near me."

Rayn laughed. "Bring your rain cape, for there are thunderclouds in the distance. I shall fetch mine and wait for you at your lift."

As they emerged from the Healing Temple, Seerce guessed, "You have found a new walking route."

"It is a short way through the neighborhood nearest the bluff, better-kept homes than what you saw the day of our air barge tour. We should plan another city excursion."

"Yes, I want to see the shops around the port, those streets you walked when you first arrived. Have you been lately?"

"No," he said, smiling. "I have another interest now." He swept his cape behind him so she might take his arm as they crossed the road. Touching the warmth of his body sent a thrill through her. Sliding her hand down his forearm, she slipped it into his. With their capes whipping in the wind and towering clouds boiling up in the southern sky, they walked the paved street nearest the bluff. Old modest homes were set wide apart and staggered, affording each a view of the ocean. Some had flower gardens, brilliant in midsummer.

Where this street curved to meet the next one, there was a tiny park of tall deciduous trees. Seerce pulled Rayn to it, then took off running to hide herself behind a huge tree trunk. When he appeared, she reached her hands around his neck, standing on tiptoe.

"May we suspend our agreement temporarily?" she asked coyly.

"That may not be acceptable," he answered, smiling.

"I wish to request the favor of your lips upon mine," she said, "if you don't mind too much."

"It is a dangerous proposition, sweet goddess," he told her, touching her chin and tipping it upward, moving his face slowly toward hers.

"You live a dangerous life," she remarked.

"I do," he admitted, kissing her delicately, once, letting the kiss linger on her lips.

"More," she said, her eyes still closed.

He kissed her firmly and longer, leaving his mouth close to hers.

"More, please," she begged.

"You have one more, madame," he said sternly, "then we resume our walk."

"Aye, aye, captain," she conceded. It was a long, tender, intimate kiss after which he held her. The branches of the old tree swayed above, dropping loose leaves all around them. She pulled back to look into his eyes. "That was rash of me," she admitted, "but I have craved your kisses for so long. Our closeness does not have to be the act of love. We know where the limits are. We can touch and keep control."

"Of late I have found myself able to reserve my desire for you, for it is but one aspect of love." He took both her hands. "I want to say what I have known since the day we met. I love you, Seerce. I love you more than I ever thought it possible for a man to love a woman."

She breathed in the humid air, endeavoring to notice every nuance of his expression and feel every nerve awakened in her, to capture this moment in her memory. "I cannot fathom from where we stand today, how we will love within this life that we have chosen. But we must find a way, for I cannot live without you. I love you with all my being."

Overhead the wind roared its approval and waves clapped in the distance. Not until lightning crackled and thunder boomed did they emerge from their enchantment to run willy-nilly down the back road to the Temple campus.

Silence the Echo

*

In the second of her presentations, Seerce illustrated historical parallels between emerging energy technology and the actions of government. Aaron had helped her with the science research by his access to the Hall of Records. The eras of waxing and waning governmental control she extrapolated from Anakron's crystal set.

"Allow me to begin with my conclusion," she requested, standing as she always did to present, two thick braids falling over her small bosom to her tiny waist, defined by a woven multicolored belt around her plain linen robe—someone too young to know the truth she was about to speak.

"The emergence of each late-age Altean technology—sonar, microwave, solar-crystalline, sonoluminescence, and dark energy conversion—correlates strongly with a peak in governmental control." She paused to let that take root in the minds of her listeners.

"Early in the evolution of these technologies, the ranks of the military expanded and distribution of information to the citizenry diminished. This stage is followed by a reduction in the people's participation in government, an increase in sanctions for crimes against it, and a falling literacy rate." All eyes were intent upon her.

"As each technology became mainstream and business found ways to profit by it, more taxes were collected and more proceeds expended for public education—in support of a more sophisticated workforce to implement and maintain the new technology.

"When literacy took hold, educated people demanded and obtained both information and representation. Military activity contracted and stability ensued. In the nadir of the cycle, Altea added to its empire by peaceful means, introducing the developed technology to emerging nations who came to depend upon it."

Now her classmates' attention was keen. Anakron sat up straight in his chair, peering intently at her. "In every instance," she continued, "after a period that lasted sometimes for centuries, that once-hailed solution to society's energy hunger began to fail a burgeoning population and Altea's expansion. New energy was required. The cycle began anew."

When Seerce finished, her classmates stood up and applauded. Anakron walked over to her and hugged her, right there in front of them. Through his lighter summer robe she could feel the prominence of his rib bones. Never had he been rotund, but he squeezed her now to a lesser abdomen.

"Which stage are we in currently?" the Chair of Exemplars asked her.

Forthrightly she told him, "The hand of the Ryk is heavy upon us. A new energy emerges."

*

Seerce boosted herself up on the high upholstered bench in front of Anakron's oversized desk. Her feet did not touch the floor, so she pulled up her robe and swung her legs playfully, feeling like a pygmy in a giant's house. Anakron smiled at her childishness, sitting his height down in his high-backed chair. "Tell me what else you know." Today he looked ancient and tired, but she noted his pleasant tone and a sparkle in his eyes.

His cramped interior space was in an area of the Temple beyond the lift for the underwater dock. She was surprised the leader of the Order did not command a more spacious and handsomely appointed office. A round crystal hovered up near the ceiling, a smaller version of the Temple Crystal. He must use it for private communication, she thought.

"I apologize, Exemplar," Seerce replied formally. "To what do you refer?"

"For the purpose of this conversation, regard me as Petrae," he requested.

She smiled, telling him, "I shall. I have missed my grandfather."

His expression turned serious. "I refer to the analysis you presented in class, researched thoroughly and presented exquisitely, altogether rather disturbing. You must believe that Altea is up to something dire. What do you know of this new technology?" he asked.

"I have seen a portion of it within the volcano power station." She telepathed to him her picture of the array of glowing tubes snaking into the throat of the mountain.

"How did you acquire the facts about Altea's earlier technologies? Such was not included in your crystal set."

"By the assistance of a colleague who has access to the Hall of Records," she replied factually. She sensed he did not wish to hear Aaron's name.

"It is possible that you and your accomplice have stepped around a few protocols," he told her nonchalantly, "and conceivable that you have happened upon something we should know. I shall see that your concerns are investigated by official means. How I have come to know this shall remain our little secret. Tell me more."

She did, informing him of the sightings of the red aurora over the western ocean, sending him her pictures of the sea barges beyond Morivay and the strangely lit construction site on the sea floor. She recounted her reasoning about the destruction of Protos. He took all this in without a trace of consternation or surprise. Trusting Petrae to do what he promised, she left his office relieved, if indeed she had told him anything he did not already know.

*

Following a strenuous session of handball, Rayn caught up with Seerce. "Allow me to serve you dinner tonight at my place," he requested. "Let us celebrate conquering history class."

"Are women allowed in the men's domicile?"

"Yes, it happens all the time. There are friendships and perhaps other sorts of relationships between priests of all persuasions," he assured her. "I have been doing my homework."

"You asked Kessa who knows all," she teased.

"I did. She is the safest source of accurate information. But just to be sure, I followed up with Barlas."

"You did not!"

"He never told us we could not visit each other. His answer yesterday was, 'Do not spend the night nor strive to make children.' I believe that is how he put it."

Seerce laughed. "Indeed we will not. However, it is necessary that I bathe first. Then I shall be over to visit."

"Second door on the right when you arrive to the fourth floor," he told her.

Rayn had set covered dishes on the low table, now pulled away from his divan. It was fare from the dining hall, but with a tablecloth, wine, and candles, it became a romantic dinner. Facing one another, they sat cross-legged on cushions, the cool stone floor insulated by a wool rug. Raising his goblet, he toasted, "To our love."

"And to your patience with me," she answered, raising her goblet, "as I run down every avenue in my quest for knowledge."

"You have been preoccupied of late. I wish I understood what consumes you."

She could not share Aaron's subjects, so she told him, "I poured too much of myself into those class projects," she admitted. "I tend to the passionate pursuit of interesting problems."

"I tend to the pursuit of your passion for me," Rayn stated, "but I know better than to interrupt you."

"I am afraid what you see is who I really am," she told him.

Thinking that over, he finally asked, "Might you be caught between two loves?"

"No," she responded definitely. "My love for you is very different than what I feel for Aaron. He is like a brother or a best friend from childhood, a catalyst for intellectual exercise, someone to argue with, a pain in my side sometimes. You," she said, taking a sip of wine, looking directly into his eyes, "ignite my insides, melt my defenses, and pull my soul into yours. You and I belong together. But we are intrinsically different. You are a linguist and a musician. I am a scientist."

"I see what happens to you when you have a mystery to investigate or a point to prove."

Seerce raised her eyebrows. "What happens?" she asked.

"You disappear into the dilemma. You eat, drink, sleep, and struggle with it until you conquer it. You disappear from life as I know it."

"Oh," she said.

"When you are done, you act like you never left."

"Oh?" she asked.

"Really, considerable time went by and I have missed you terribly," he lamented.

"I am so sorry, Rayn. Maybe I fail to balance things. I have always been independent and, I admit, selfish as well."

"I hope for more constancy," he told her.

She gave him a reassuring smile, but he was not so easily soothed. "Do you worry for Cyan taking the helm of our studies again?" she asked.

"For his surveillance of us, yes. Our time with Anakron has been so pleasant."

"According to Aaron, we shall soon have privileges in the Hall of Records so we may access Icos."

"I know nothing of the records. Is this a good thing?"

"Aaron thinks so. He can stop doing my research."

A smile broke across Rayn's face. "I felt lowly to your brilliance, as you recited all those facts and analyses."

Seerce laughed. "What did you think I was doing in the dining room with Aaron late into so many evenings?" Seeing his expression, she got up from the floor and walked behind him, sitting down on his sofa and wrapping her arms around his neck, kissing the top of his head. "Please do not worry," she told him. "I love you with all my heart and mind and soul, and if you would allow me, with my body, too."

"You make this hard on me, woman."

"I know," she said. "That is what women do."

CHAPTER 10

In the middle of the night, a few days before the autumnal equinox, Seerce was awakened by a sharp knock at her door. To her great surprise, there stood Cyan, his hair rumpled, a cloak wrapped around his nightclothes. "Would you accompany me to the Healing Temple?" he requested, his eyes solemn, the rest of his face unreadable. "Anakron has asked for you."

Half-asleep, Seerce thought she must have misunderstood him. But hurriedly she slipped her feet into sandals and threw her shawl over her nightgown. She followed Cyan as he hurried down the flights of stairs. "Exemplar, what has happened?" she begged to know.

"He took ill this evening in his apartment. Annecy insisted that he be moved to a treatment room. I was awakened by an aide knocking at my door, and I was asked to bring you with me. The rest we shall discover together."

Climbing flights of stairs in the Healing Temple, Seerce's heart beat hard for the effort and her consternation. Down a marble hallway, she saw Tane and Annecy in front of a door at the far end. As they approached, she extended her arms to Seerce, hugging her briefly to her breast. "You are the closest relative Anakron has here. Your grandmother should be informed. But first, go to him," she requested gently.

Silence the Echo

Cyan opened the door and Seerce went in alone. The room was dimly lit with a few small glowing crystals. Anakron's complexion was grey and his lips bluish. She hoped it was a trick of the light. "Petrae?" she said aloud, but he did not stir. She called his name again, taking his hand, which was cool to touch.

She heard his telepathy, though nothing of him moved. *Seerce, my body dies.*

Oh, no, no, Petrae! she told him. *You may be ill, but you may not die. I will not allow it.*

The hint of a smile pulled at the corners of his dry mouth. *You are not quite that powerful yet,* he telepathed, *though one day you might be. I have given my instruction that you are to be mentored for the position of exemplar. My spirit will ever be near you.*

She knew then that he meant to leave this life.

I go now to tell your grandmother how much I love her. Then, from another vantage point, I shall be about the business of protecting you.

With all my heart, I love you, Petrae, she told him. *Always remember.*

I love you, granddaughter, he said. With that he gasped and shuddered, then ceased to breathe.

Seerce watched but his chest did not move. She laid her hands upon his heart as she had seen her grandmother do when death arrived. Examining the serenity upon his face, she read his acceptance of transition. Hers had been the last touch to his living body, and hers was the privilege to speak on behalf of her clan their blessing of departure.

Taking a deep breath, Seerce softly recited, "Go now to the summer land, Petrae, there to rest and be refreshed. And when you are born again to Earth, may it be among those who love you, that we may love again." After a few moments her fingers began to tingle, as she had heard her grandmother describe, the last of his physical essence given to her as a signal that his spirit was on its way. Only slowly did she withdraw her hands.

Finally with her thought she opened the door, and as his

colleagues entered, she slipped out and down the stairs, through a side door into the night, to weep and walk and send her love on wings to accompany him.

*

A small trunk of Anakron's few possessions rested upon Seerce's low table. Distraught with grief, she opened it again, picking up each item to hold it tenderly. It gave her comfort to touch what he had touched, these things that were meaningful to him. Her favorite was a small ivory figure of Gaia within a velvet pouch. This she tied to her waist cord, thinking it would help her to carry something of his with her, something of their common devotion to the Lady.

Rayn walked with her to the Temple, where they sat down with Aaron. Seerce took the statuette from the pouch to cradle in her hands. More and more people filed in, priests and staff and strangers who were neither. Soon all the seats were taken and more stood in the aisles and in the foyer. Six exemplars in purple robes ringed the altar.

His body lay in the crypt beneath the Temple, placed there at sunset the day following his death. In that small ceremony, Seerce learned that Anakron was the youngest of five brothers. All but he had followed in their parents' footsteps, taking high positions in government or commerce in Altea. He was disowned by his family for his decision to join the Order of the Sun. Fellow priests and Seerce's kin were his people.

Today's ritual followed the seasons of Earth. Annecy's flowing hair was crowned by a wreath of spring flowers. She recited from Anakron's biography the interests of his childhood. Rika, who was his classmate, stooped with age herself, held a bouquet of yellow roses as she told of his student pranks and projects and his early career as an educator in North Afrikaa.

The autumn of Anakron's life was symbolized by a burnt-orange stole embroidered with gold and brown leaves, draped around Ezra's shoulders. A slender-boned Nubian with closely cropped salt-and-pepper hair and beard, he had ascended to Exemplar of Education when Anakron was elevated to chair. Ezra had visited Seerce'e academy, for he traveled the circuit of schools Anakron had. He spoke familiarly of his predecessor's accomplishments, framing these as funny stories that met with roars of laughter echoing in the Temple.

Cyan represented winter, holding in front of him a gnarled weathered branch from a fallen tree. He spoke of the changes wrought by time and the clear intention of the tree and Anakron to grow until physical life could not be lived. He spoke of the gifts of Anakron's wisdom, now imprinted upon the minds of all those he had taught and the Order he had led.

Seerce managed control of her emotions up until this point. She had even laughed aloud at some of the tales, characteristic of Petrae as she knew him. Now Cyan shocked her. "We are privileged to have in our initiate class the granddaughter of Anna, Priest of Basra. By Anakron's reckoning, this young woman was his grandchild, as much as she was his companion's."

Seerce bristled. Companion? Did he mean to imply they had been lovers? They were long-time dear friends! And while Anakron had required Seerce to say nothing of their prior relationship, here Cyan was telling the whole of the Order!

Aaron touched Seerce's arm. *Pay attention,* he said, having heard her thoughts. *Something is about to change.*

"It was Anakron's instruction that his Crystal of the Sun"—Cyan held it up for all to see—"be awarded to her at her induction, rather than interred with his body as is our custom." The pale yellow crystal worn for a lifetime at his heart had been polished to brilliance. There was a flash of light between it and the Temple Crystal hovering above the altar. People gasped.

"We look for great accomplishments from Seerce of Basra," he said solemnly, looking directly at her. Tears crawled down her cheeks, but she made not a sound.

Cyan seems to think your fate is sealed, Aaron told her, *but you are a free woman, free to choose your path.*

Seerce turned to look at Aaron, his lower lip trembling as though he would weep with her. Tears filled Rayn's eyes.

Two of Anakron's favorite poems were recited by Tane and Nova. The ceremony ended with a chant for the autumnal equinox, occurring today, light and dark in equal measure before the world turned toward the chill of winter.

*

Class was canceled for ten days, the initiates allowed to go home while the Council of Exemplars attended to the election of Anakron's successor.

"Come home with me," Aaron asked of Seerce at the morning meal.

"I cannot," she replied. "My family will hold our own ceremony of remembrance. I must support my grandmother." Seerce ached to think of the length of time it had taken Petraea to recover from the deaths of her two sons after the tragedy in Tunise. What would losing Anakron do to the matriarch? Not that the two of them saw so much of each other, but their mutual devotion evidenced such a deep bond.

"Were they lovers?" Aaron asked.

"Maybe as a child one does not know these things," Seerce replied. "Anakron was in and out of our compound all my life, staying a few days, then gone for two moons. My father seemed to harbor some resentment toward him, which I never understood. When Mother was our trade ambassador, she and Anakron met for meals whenever he passed through Tunise. She was very fond of him." She shrugged her shoulders, adding, "I thought Anakron came to see me."

Aaron chuckled. Returning this exchange to his purpose, he said, "Perhaps another time you would allow me to show you Eyre."

"Thank you for your invitation," Seerce responded, wondering why he brought this up now. "I would like to visit your part of the world."

"I do not mean just to visit," he said.

"What do you mean?" she asked.

There was a look of hard resignation in his eyes. "They will offer a role, Seerce, but not the one that is meant for you." With that, he stood up and leaned over to kiss her cheek. "May Gaia protect you on your journey and provide comfort to you and your family." He took his dishes to the kitchen and walked out.

"Enjoy your time at home, Aaron," she called after him.

*

Barlas tried to find Seerce passage to Basra via hydrofoil. All the big ships to Tunise had already sold their fares. The warming climes of the MidTerra were prime destinations for the equinox holiday, as Altea's short summer cooled. He checked for availability on smaller boats, whereby the journey would be longer and far less comfortable on variable seas.

Seerce thought of the desert of Basra with some fondness as she packed; seldom had she found much to appreciate about sand dunes and baking heat, but going home to her family would help her. She packed lightly, for her closet at home held all she would need there. Preoccupied, she did not register the opening of her apartment door until she heard Rayn's voice calling her. "Up here," she told him, looking over the bedchamber's half wall to see that his hair was newly cut and shiny, his beard trimmed perfectly, and his lips full and luscious. The beauty of the man took her breath away, distracting her from her sorrow.

"I have obtained passage for two aboard a hydrofoil, leaving this afternoon for Antakos. There is a public air barge from there to Zanata, and on to Anteema. Perhaps we could meet your family's shipping barge there," he told her, "and get you home in a day and a half."

At some point she must have mentioned the circuit that her father's barge traveled. "Oh," she asked amusedly, "are you coming with me?"

"I cannot allow you to travel that distance unaccompanied!" he exclaimed. "An agent in the city charged me a premium, but that matters not. It is your safety that concerns me."

It was the case that Seerce had never traveled alone, until she came by boat directly from Tunise to Altea. She knew little of other ports or making connections or finding accommodations.

"It is so very kind of you to offer, Rayn," she said, coming down the stairs, her tone betraying her hesitance.

"Allow me to assist you," he pleaded. "You have been through too much of late."

"My father is a traditional man. What kind of welcome you might receive, I cannot predict. You may get turned away in Anteema with only his thanks for escorting me." She paused. "But if you get to Basra, my mother will love you," she added, smiling.

"I would be pleased to take my chances," he told her.

"Then I agree. I will tell Barlas I have passage. But let us keep our joint departure under wraps."

His expression was radiant as he kissed her lips. "Meet me at the Healing Temple's dock, the second decan after zenith."

*

The sun had just risen over the dilapidated port of Antakos when they arrived, weary and stiff, having slept little in less than comfortable seats. At a small café beyond the dock, Rayn addressed the proprietor in a local dialect, learning that the air barge had been out of service for a moon. Had she traveled alone, Seerce would not have known how to proceed. It took the morning, but Rayn was able to secure passage on a merchant ship traveling coastal waters to Imazikaan, about halfway to Tunise. They purchased a basket of food and a jug of water to take with them.

It was sunset when they were discharged to a deserted dock with directions to an inn. "Does this mean we will spend the night together?" she asked Rayn.

"If we are fortunate enough to find a room, yes," he answered matter-of-factly. "Any other activity between us is subject to mutual approval. We are yet initiates."

"I accept your terms," she replied wearily. The unknowingness of sleep called her, an ease for her heavy eyelids and her aching heart.

The better of two rooms they viewed was small and the furnishings worn. A shared lavatory was down the hall, but as yet there was no sign of other guests. Rayn pulled off the sheets and inspected the mattress for bugs. Pronouncing it acceptable, he made it up again snugly with bedding he brought.

"Do you prefer that I wear clothing?" he asked Seerce.

"Of course," she told him. Behind a screen, she changed into a summer-weight night shift, thinking she would swelter in anything heavier, sleeping with him. What he wore, she did not see, for he climbed into bed ahead of her and pulled the sheet up to his chest. She noted the muscle of his naked shoulders and arms, unseen by her until now.

By the last light through one narrow window, she slipped beneath the sheet. Rayn raised his arm so she could lay her head on his shoulder and snuggle into his side. She stretched her free arm across his haired chest, another trait he shared with Basran men.

He kissed her forehead. "If there is anything else you want from me, I am yours," he whispered. "But I am most content to hold you this way until morning."

Tucking her lower arm between them, she rested her top knee upon his thigh, feeling the silky pajamas he wore. Genuinely secure in his loving embrace, she fell asleep nearly immediately.

*

On the day following, it was midafternoon when Seerce met her father at his trading booth at the Port of Tunise. To her surprise, Narad welcomed Rayn warmly. Barlas had sent word of her travel plans via crystal to the academy in Tunise. The administrator there informed Seerce's Aunt Ena, a regent of the school. Of course, none knew of Rayn's escort, but Narad was pleased that his daughter traveled in company. *You always were a smart girl*, he told her, his arm around her shoulder. She smiled to herself.

Narad took great interest in Rayn's former occupation, so much so that Seerce was left to sit alone on the deck of the family's air barge as they sailed home to Basra. Taking in the clear evening sky of the desert, she watched as the sun set behind the Aures Mountains and the stars began to emerge. A crescent moon rose in the east and Jupiter with it, a good omen.

Rayn was shown every aspect of the ordinary industrial barge, and given full report of the current challenges of doing business under Altean rule. Generally a man of few words, Narad then launched into an explanation of the family's horticultural operation, spurred by Rayn's genuine display of interest.

In just over two decans, with the stars ablaze in the cool desert night, they arrived to Orion compound. By the barge's flood lights, Rayn watched incredulously as the petals of the landing bay's lid pushed up through the sand, dispersing it, and opening to the dock below ground. As Narad busied himself landing the craft, Seerce had a chance to tell Rayn of the shifting sand that buried the bay daily. The compound was entirely underground, except for solar crystals that rose up at dawn to drink in the energy that fed the growing operation and powered their living quarters. "Those descend in the evening," she told him, "so as not to be struck by the incoming barge. We travel at night, else the heat of the day would spoil our produce."

The welcome dinner was attended by twelve residents of the compound and Uncle Sirdar, Aunt Ena's partner. Seerce seated herself next to her elderly grandmother, who seemed subdued but looked well. Across the table, Josef and Loren, her young twin brothers, took chairs to either side of Rayn. He had bought them small wooden flutes from a Tunisian market stall, these placed alongside their plates by order of their father, irritated by piercing tuneless notes echoing off the stone walls. The boys peppered Rayn with questions about sailing, after Narad boasted of his accomplishments. Fortunately dinner was ready soon after their arrival, saving Rayn a tour of the subterranean gardens.

Seerce telepathed her picture of Rayn to her blind mother, seated on her other side. The two were engaged in a private exchange about his looks, their relationship, and how the matriarch fared. Everyone else had to listen to Narad and Sirdar argue the merits of purchasing a sheep ranch outside Anteema. Basran women from several of the compounds were weavers. Narad was convinced of a high profit in wool craft, Sirdar equally sure Altean taxes upon the raw wool and the finished goods would eat up all proceeds.

He loves you, Portia telepathed privately to Seerce. Her mother was the picture of an upright sleeping beauty, her flaxen hair carefully plaited by one of the women and wrapped in a coil at the top of her head, a hint of color at her cheeks in an alabaster complexion, and a smile that was warm and impish. Seerce wished she could see the ice blue of Portia's eyes, but she kept them closed rather than subject others to the way her blind eyes wandered.

Do not make me blush at the dinner table, Mama, Seerce begged.

How much do you love him? she wanted to know.

With all my heart and so much more than I had known I might feel for a man. There was no point in keeping the truth from her mother. Portia's perceptions were never fooled.

Have you asked him for his manhood? It is your privilege as a woman.

No, Mama. I am sorely tempted, but such violates the rules for initiates until we are inducted.

Even if you are home?

Mama! Seerce exclaimed. *What would Papa say about that?*

He would say that your role as eldest is to take a partner who assists Basra's livelihood and provides us with grandchildren. Your father would say you have come to your senses.

Seerce chortled to herself, disguising this as a little cough behind her hand. Rayn looked to her from across the table, smiling enchantingly. Seerce telepathed that picture to Portia.

Practice the ritual to prevent ovulation, daughter, Portia advised.

I have since you taught me, though there has never been need till now.

There is more you need to know about the ways of men. I shall explain before you leave here.

*

Has your grandfather spoken to you of Tara? Petraea asked, as she combed the tangles from Seerce's washed hair, twirling long strands around her bony fingers, setting the waves in spirals. In the dry air of the caverns, her tresses could be tamed.

No, Seerce responded. *Who is she?*

The two were alone in the ceremonial chamber of the compound where Khubradan was held. A tall and wide six-sided crystal at center emitted the spring-green light of healing. Fused layers of sandstone, limestone, and grey slate, fractured and tipped, made uneven stripes through the circular space. Glassy patches of feldspar and granite reflected like green stars, while porous lava punctuated the magical mosaic with dark voids.

Seerce sat on a low stool before her grandmother's upholstered chair. A pillow was tucked behind Petraea's back. She was thinner than Seerce remembered and old age eroded her height, though she appeared spry and healthy. Sun spots had multiplied over her olive face, giving her the appearance of a wizened leopard with a lion's mane, for her wiry white hair stood straight out from the sides and crown of her head.

Petraea corrected her. *Tara is a place, not a person. He speaks of it as a plane between Earth lives for those of the Order who continue the work.*

Seerce noted her use of the present tense, asking, *Is this a place you know?*

It gets more difficult to differentiate between what I have learned on my own from what your grandfather has shown me at one time or another. I have incorporated much of his understanding of the universe.

Then you travel etherically?

Why, yes, of course, child.

Did your grandmother teach you?

Yes, but Seah's skills were rudimentary compared to Petrae's. He preferred that you learn from the Order.

Turning herself around to face her grandmother, Seerce asked, *Did you love him?*

More than life itself, she replied, tears gathering, her brown irises veiled by silvery cataracts. *But we are not long parted.*

Seerce reached for her bony hands. *As he drew his last breath, he told me he was on his way to see you.*

He came, she replied. *Something roused me from sleep and I woke to see him sitting on my cot. Often he came to me, but this time was different. The etheric body takes a lavender tint when it loses its connection to the physical. I knew he had left his person behind.*

The constriction tightened in Seerce's throat, the lump ever present since his death, her sorrow stuck where she could not swallow it. But in her grandmother's countenance she saw peaceful resignation. Around her frail shoulders Petraea wore the ceremonial stole that she had woven for Anakron many years ago. It was the first of the items she lifted from the trunk that Seerce brought home to her.

He asked me if I wished to go with him, Petraea continued.

Seerce calmed the panic that rose in her. *Will you follow him?* she asked, hoping she could reconcile herself to the answer.

Not yet, child. He has his tasks there and we have ours here. Now turn around and let me finish your hair.

Seerce did, dabbing at her eyes with her sleeve.

He is never far from you, Petraea told her. *If you speak to him, he hears you. If you ask his guidance, he gives it. There is much to be done, lest we lose the place of people upon Earth.*

Alea Carroll

*

The ceremony of remembrance was a party aboard the air barge, emptied out and scrubbed clean, set with folding tables and lined with benches, as the family did for celebrations. Some of their kin had come from Sarmatia, the largest of Basra's compounds, those who had known Petrae by his presence at various clan events. It was he who presided over the rites and interment of Seerce's uncles, for her grandmother was overwhelmed with the loss of two sons.

Attendees wore wool capes and caps, for the desert cooled drastically at night. The barge hovered near a huge bonfire of sweet-smelling pinewood that Narad hauled from Anteema. Dinner was grilled on braziers and wine flowed freely. Rayn played his oud with the clan much in awe. Stories were told and the family laughed more than they cried, celebrating a man who had lived his life with benevolence and levity.

For the children, Seerce pantomimed the tale of Orion, their compound's namesake, as Petrae had done for her when she was young. Tonight the constellation was bright upon the horizon. "The Wanderer left his family to see all of Earth," she told them, lumbering around the deck and exaggerating her gestures in the firelight of the braziers. "For tales of his adventures, he was given supplies for his journey.

"His belt was made of jewels from the deepest mines of the Aures Mountains. Fashioned from the tallest tree that ever grew, his sword was a gift from the wind who heard his conversations with mountain forests as he passed overhead. Laced with spun wool, his boots were gifted by shepherds who knew his nightly journey in the days before the rivers fell. They wished they might accompany him.

"It was the goddess of the sea who wove his cloak of seaweed, for she wanted him to join her underwater adventures. But Orion kept the path of the heavens, where always he might see and never forget the wondrous beauty of Earth. 'See through the Wanderer's eyes!' That is what Petrae always told me."

Silence the Echo

The wide-eyed twins climbed into Seerce's lap and Rayn's for help in finding Orion's belt and sword in the heavens. The revelry continued until Petraea stood up with a basket of dried herbs, tied in bunches. "Now let us release Petrae's spirit to his new home." Everyone took a bundle and one by one tossed the fragrant herbs into the fire below. With their hands they brushed the essences heavenward into the star-strewn sky.

*

It was impossible to find any space or time to be alone with her love. Seerce resigned herself to sharing Rayn, pleased that her family so readily accepted him. He seemed content among them. Well-mannered and cordial, receptive and attentive, who would not admire him? But it was his genuine interest in how her people lived and what they accomplished that impressed her. She had to wonder if her proper place was here with him.

But the compound was such a small world, without sunlight or ocean waves, where fresh air might be had only after night fell. She wondered at her mother's conversion to this remote outpost, for Portia had been raised aboveground in the foothills. Thereafter she lived on the coast, minding the politics and intricacies of trade and local government, while Narad came and went between there and Basra. Now Portia seemed to thrive on running a household and advising the family business, dependent as she was upon the aid of her partner's womenfolk. Narad and the twins and the cool stone caverns seemed enough for her. Seerce detected no longing for her former life, and no anger for the circumstances that took her sight and confined her here.

Spending private moments reflecting upon her grandfather's life and his influence upon her, Seerce dreaded her return to the Temple where she would not find him. Accepting that he and her grandmother had been lovers, she wondered at her own naiveté. How could Petraea part with him? Seerce could not.

As yet she had no opportunity for a private exchange with her father. There had been few as she grew up. He was hardworking, quietly observant, not much of a talker, but now he kept a constant dialogue with Rayn, more conversation than she had witnessed him share with anyone but her mother and Sirdar. Narad's interactions with the twins were playful and physical, different than the stern paternity with which Seerce was raised. The portrait of her family had evolved and she wondered what to make of it.

*

Perhaps Rayn had told her that they would return to Altea by a more direct route. She did not recall that nor did she care. Narad escorted them to the port of Tunise before dawn, where he would unload the barge at the marketplace and sell produce to shippers. He embraced her and then Rayn as they stood huddled together in the early morning chill of the seaside, admonishing them to get back as soon as they realized where they belonged.

While they awaited their boarding call, Seerce relished the opportunity to be alone with her man, to take his hand or his arm, to steal a kiss with no interested eyes upon them. The ocean liner was to leave at the second decan.

"Will we be home tonight?" she asked, secretly wishing they had a stopover.

He laughed, saying, "You forget how far we are from Altea. We will spend the night in Majorka. Might you agree we have some catching up to do?"

She giggled, snuggling into him. They had stepped out of the breeze around the corner of a port building. He held her as though he would never let her go.

"Your family is nearly as appealing as you are," he told her.

"They might have strangled you by their affection," Seerce tittered, "my father particularly."

Rayn laughed. "Your people are much more demonstrative than mine."

"No harm done?"

"None," Rayn affirmed. "In fact, my cup is full. I have never been made so welcome anywhere, not even in the home of my birth."

Seerce kept her own thoughts for a while, warm in his embrace and upheld by his support. "Thank you," she told him. "You brought me home safely. You delighted my family. I was able to spend all the time I needed with Petraea and my mother. How can I ever repay you for your kindness?"

"Love me," he said. "There is nothing else I want or need."

*

Their room for the night was in a villa overlooking the west bay of Majorka. Rayn ordered dinner to be brought to their room, where a balcony window framed a subdued sunset. Before it, they sat down to grilled fish and baked squash, spiced lentils, freshly baked flatbread, and dried fruit. Rayn raised his goblet to Seerce's. "To you, my love," he proclaimed, "ever my love."

"It is my wish ever to be yours, with the love between Anakron and Petraea as our model. I am more hopeful we might fashion lives as priests and lovers."

"As am I," Rayn replied.

"Or perhaps you are ready to join the business of the clan?" she jested. "Did Papa offer you a position?"

"With any encouragement from you, I believe he would. Portia took me aside as you and Petraea visited. She told me love finds its way, even if a couple lives and works apart, as was your parents' experience."

"They are very different people, are they not?" Seerce asked.

"Yes, but a devoted pair they are, and apparently your grandparents were, too. I know from whence your good heart arises."

She allowed that summation to reverberate in her. Warm silence enfolded them.

Eventually she requested, "Say more of your family." His

discomfort was immediately apparent and she regretted disturbing the atmosphere.

"Like Anakron," he told her, "I did not agree with the choices of my parents. Both are from wealth and their only goal was to multiply funds. I worked for one of the family businesses until I could not live with myself. Life should be lived for a cause. Riches are not that." He took a gulp of wine and drummed his fingers on the table.

"It is not materiality which drives your father," he added, "but the provision of wholesome living for his people. He fights to keep his homeland and its traditions, in the face of geologic hardship, in the path of Altean expansion, cleverly and tirelessly. I am in awe of his devotion to your kin and their way of life."

"And yet, as I grew up," Seerce told him, "I thought Papa's cause was small compared to Anakron's worldly endeavors. Now I must rethink that assumption."

Rayn raised his glass again, saying, "My wish is to be wherever you are."

*

Seerce had taken her bath and now Rayn made his evening preparations. She slipped nude into the comfortable bed, propped up by pillows, a sheet across her legs, relaxed by the wine and impassioned by deprivation of affection. In her mother's Aurean tradition, women initiated intimacy. Seerce felt empowered by her mother's approval, having followed her instructions to prepare herself to receive him. In matriarchal culture it was unacceptable that a woman be pained by her first act of love.

Watching him emerge from the bath with a towel tied at one hip, his chest hair damp, the muscle of his shoulders and calves evident, it surprised her that he strode about the room—closing the drapes at the window, covering the serving dishes, dimming the lamps—until she realized what he was doing. She giggled. "I see how beautiful you are. Come here and let me touch you."

He turned to her, smiling. "Do you prefer the lights off?"

"No," she replied. "I prefer the towel off."

That surprised him. "I will lose the towel if you come here to me," he bargained, his eyes intent upon her.

Throwing back the sheet she swung her bare legs over the side of the bed, pausing to watch him watch her. Then she stood to face him, the volume of her curls loose around her shoulders, covering her small high breasts and palest pink nipples, and falling to her hips. Swinging the length behind her, she walked slowly around the bed, to look more closely at the statue in that corner of the room. Then she made a show of touching the fabric of the settee and rearranging its pillows, offering him more views, turning to see his eyes. Sauntering past him to the table, she drank the last of the wine from her goblet. Then, stepping lightly to him, she loosed the towel from his hips and dropped it to the floor. His male member was quite erect. She did not know how that was meant to fit within her, but warmth gathered in her pelvis, an ache and a pressure that wanted his relief.

Running her hands over his shoulders and lightly stroking his arms up and down, she played with the hair on his chest and smoothed her palms along his sides, watching his face. He bent as if to kiss her, but instead swept her from her feet, an arm under her knees, the other cradling her back. She laughed in surprise. Then he kissed her. Carrying her to the bed and placing a knee on the mattress, he set her in the center. Gently he lifted her torso to sweep her hair from beneath her, to one side.

"Is there something I might do to help?" she teased, but he did not answer right away.

Instead he straddled her legs between his knees and bent to kiss her neck. Pausing for a moment to look deeply into her eyes, responding, "Only this. You must say if I make you uncomfortable, for you are a most delicate flower. This is your night and I am your servant."

"Kiss my lips for a long time," she requested, "then you may have your way with me. Find all that I am, if that is what you wish.

Then allow me to feel you deeply within me, where you may know what you have never seen or touched."

By the expression upon Rayn's face, she knew he had never been taken by an Aurean woman.

CHAPTER 11

It was desperately dark there, the black night punctuated by cries of despair and wailing, shrieking and shouting. Terror enveloped Seerce. Where was he? Finally she saw his longish hair in the dim light of the torch he carried. Planting it in the ground, bending down to someone, his face disappeared in shadow. Though she called and called to him, he did not hear her. Stones and boards fell near him. There must be more tremors. Seeing a timber swing in his direction, she yelled, "Get away from the building, Aaron!"

Awakened by her own scream, his name was upon her lips. Seerce's eyes opened to an unfamiliar room, a crevice of light above a heavily draped window. She did not know where she was. A warm hand touched her arm. She screamed again, tearing off the covers, bounding naked from the bed.

Rayn's voice pleaded with her, "You had a nightmare, love, a bad one. Come back to me. Let me hold you."

She stayed where she was, clinging to the wall, her heart pounding. He spoke again softly, telling her they were in Majorka, going home today. "You are safe," he told her. "I am here with you."

In her mind's eye was the ruin of what must have been Aaron's village in Eyre, reduced to heaps of debris, dimly lit by a few lanterns in a few hands. People were pinned and gravely injured. Somehow he stopped their pain or helped them die, because the writhing and the screams ceased, one after another.

Rayn came to her with her bath robe and draped it around her shoulders. She began to weep, not fully parted from the vision. He took her into his arms. "Show me," he requested.

She closed her eyes and called up the scenes, sending them to him one by one. "You dream most vividly," he judged.

"This is not a dream, Rayn! Surely there has been a terrible quake in Eyre! Aaron is home. He is caught in it. He is endangered!"

"Tell me, what do you think we can do?" His tone was gentle and soothing. She reached her arms around his waist, resting her wet face against his chest. The pleasures of their lovemaking came flooding back to her, while his tentative embrace conveyed his bewilderment.

"I am so sorry," she told him. "What a shock I have given you."

"It is no matter. You are sure this was Aaron's village?" he asked.

"Quite," she told him. "Something called me there as I slept, just as I was called to my mother's side in Tunise when the sea wave overtook the port."

"What calls you?"

"I do not know if it is spirit or relationship or the injured Earth. He did not hear me, intent as he was upon relieving suffering."

"Before long we must board the ship. What do you wish to do?"

"We had best go," she answered. "Missing our passage does not help him. I will try to think of something that does."

*

On a high-speed hydrofoil a short time later, Seerce realized that day would just be dawning in Eyre to the west. The wind picked up as they headed out into the open sea, but the ship remained stable, skimming over high swells. Rayn tried to purchase the use of a cabin, but all were taken. They settled for mid-row seats in a quieter section. Draping her shawl over her head and eyes, she leaned against his shoulder as if to sleep. Eventually she settled enough to launch her remote vision.

In the light of dawn and with relief, Seerce spied men loading wagons of supplies from a building yet standing. They worked swiftly, sending off wheeled carts with a pony and a rider as soon as the contents were secured with rope or fishnet. In places the ground was slushy and in others white-covered, particularly up into higher inland hills. It must be snow, which Seerce had never seen before.

A long line of villagers trudged up a muddy path, some with babies tied to their chests or toddlers on their shoulders. Where were they going? Seerce took her vision above the village for a bird's-eye view. Those hills were craggy and the snaking line moving toward them looked to be two hundred people. To the west, over the vast tumbling sea of grey, there was a dark line across the water, not so far away. Moving up higher, she saw parallel dark lines behind it. What made stripes across the ocean?

Looking down, Seerce watched the last of the riders pull away. Willing her vision to hover over him, she telepathed, *Aaron, please, open to me!* His expression remained determined. So she telepathed her picture of him flapping his arms on the day he coaxed her out on the pinnacle. Puzzlement crossed his eyes. *Aaron,* she repeated, *I am traveling with you by remote vision.*

By the Goddess, Seerce! Yes, I hear your thoughts. There has been a terrible quake. How did you know to come?

As I slept I saw you with your torch searching the rubble. Where do your people go?

To our hunting camp up in the hills. We must leave the village. That much shaking may cause a tidal wave. I studied the phenomenon after you told me about Tunise.

Is that what those dark lines are, off a ways in the ocean?

Show me, he requested. She sent him the picture. *Dear Gaia! We have little time!* He shouted to the rider ahead of him, and that man shouted to the next. The ponies ran faster, catching up to the people, who stepped aside to let them pass and then scurried more quickly up the trail.

Seerce watched from on high now, seeing that the first dark line was a huge upwelling, the parallels maintaining their chase behind it. *Is it low tide now?* she asked Aaron.

No, he responded, *it should be mid-tide.*

The water moves out of the bay, she reported.

Look directly west, Seerce, and give me that view. She did, reckoning the direction by the sun. *Now directly south,* he requested. *Better for us the waves are westerly. That coast is steep and rough. Perhaps it will break the surge. I must unhitch this cart and race ahead to tell my people. Keep sending me your pictures, Seerce.*

*

That evening, Cyan's knock on her apartment door awoke her. Seerce had not intended to fall asleep on her divan, only to rest. She patted her cheeks, trying to gather her wits as she followed him to his office. She and Rayn had agreed that she would report her visions without mention of him. He tarried in a neighborhood beyond the Healing Temple so they would not be seen returning together.

Seated before Cyan's desk were Tane and Rika. A small round crystal, like the one Seerce had seen in Anakron's office, hovered at eye level. Within it was a graphic of the Ocean of Atlas. She recognized the coast of Eyre peeking out from the ice sheet that covered the northern portion of the sea. The coastal tract on which Aaron's people lived was narrow. Cyan pulled a chair to the side of his desk and motioned Seerce to it. He took his own seat.

Rika's faded red and greying hair was twisted into a bun on the top of her head and tied with a colorful scarf, her face tan and wrinkled by the sun of Zanata. She wore a white wool robe, though Altean weather was not overly cool yet. A gaudy knit shawl of turquoise and pink wrapped her broad Archaean shoulders.

"My condolences for your great loss," Rika conveyed kindly to Seerce. "How is your grandmother?"

"She fares well, Exemplar," Seerce responded formally, "trusting that Anakron continues his work on the next plane. Please accept my sympathy for the loss of your lifelong friend." Seerce acknowledged what was surely Rika's deep sorrow. The elder's eyes misted. She reached over to pat Seerce's hand.

"Now," Rika said, "in the curious fashion that fate toys with us, I find myself elected to fill his great shoes as chair. Perhaps it is fate that draws you and me together."

Not knowing what Rika implied, Seerce responded simply, "Congratulations, madame." It pleased her to know the Order would be led by this good woman.

"Nova's group was immediately aware of a deep quake at the top of the mid-ocean ridge. The staff sent data to us here." Somehow she changed the view in the crystal. "A fracture occurred on the ocean floor beneath the ice, in an area of spectacular volcanic activity. Seismic waves in the area were typical, not the odd curvature we saw farther south. How did you become aware of the disaster?"

Seerce recounted waking with the vision, her remote viewing at Eyre's dawn, and what Aaron accomplished for his clan.

"You and Aaron are closely connected," Rika said. It was a statement, not a question.

With Cyan's eyes upon her, Seerce responded, "We are good friends, perhaps like you and my grandfather. We respect each other's gifts and we care deeply for Earth."

Rika gave her a knowing look. "Deep bonds form in these initiate classes. You see another example in these priests," she said, motioning to the two Mu. Tane smiled. Cyan only blinked.

"Madame, I wish to tell you about the waves. I tracked them from a high view, while Aaron urged his people to the tops of hills."

"Please do. But first, child, how many were saved?"

"All but those trapped under the buildings. There was nothing to be done for the gravely injured, but assist them to die painlessly. Aaron did that by torchlight. I do not know how many."

Rika sighed. "Are you able to place pictures in crystals?"

"Yes, madame," Seerce responded.

"Then hold this," Rika said, taking a slender indigo crystal from her pocket and placing it in Seerce's left hand. "Project what you observed into this and those scenes will appear in the round one."

Seerce closed her eyes, transmitting all she had seen in Eyre. The exemplars watched the hovering crystal, where her eyewitness account was recorded, to be studied and preserved in the permanent report of the event.

"Cyan," Rika requested with some authority, "come time for internships, I wish to have Seerce with me. Aaron may have his choice of science departments. These are two of the most gifted we have met since you and Tane joined us."

Seerce smiled at her and Rika smiled back. Anakron must have told her of their extracurricular observations, else why would she move so quickly to take the two of them under her wing?

*

"It is my privilege to introduce you to the Hall of Records," Cyan told the first years. "Most subjects will be made available to you today. Follow me," he requested.

They gathered at the lift for the women's domicile. "One at a time, place your hand here," Cyan directed, indicating a slight mark at the corner of the adjacent wall. "A door will open for you at my instruction. Next time you come, the lock will recognize your vibration and allow you to pass. Jair, please demonstrate." The wall seemed to dissolve and he stepped through to a hall. "Wait for us," Cyan requested as the wall seemed to solidify. Each followed suit, the exemplar going last.

The tunnel on the other side was like every other tunnel, with light walls, stone squares for the floor, and motion-sensing sconces. Inclining somewhat and veering to the left, it ended in another unadorned wall. "Here you must call the lift by the embedded crystal, approximately here," Cyan showed them, touching the wall on his right. "Simply focus your attention in this direction. Seerce, if you would, please."

She ordered the lift telepathically. An unseen door slid open and all stepped in. "You need only say or telepath 'Hall,'" Cyan advised. When upward motion ceased, the door opened to a large windowless room. To the left was a clear view of the Temple Crystal in its resting place near the top of the dome. It seemed that the floor of the Hall of Records was level with the base of the dome. Seerce had noticed from the Temple floor what she thought might be a catwalk up here, but it was always in shadow.

"This is the mezzanine level. Come look," the exemplar beckoned.

A scene from a dream! Kessa telepathed to Seerce.

Yes! she agreed.

The half-walled catwalk was wide enough that a fair crowd might gather there, perhaps three people deep, to face the Crystal at eye level if it had something to show them. Seerce had an impression of priests standing here in that fashion, those in front able to rest their arms on the short wall. The Crystal was huge before them, sparkling with its inner flashes of color. This close she saw that each oval window of the dome was embedded with a slender, double-pointed quartz crystal, each glowing brightly in the light of day.

When she looked back to the Hall, she did not see it. Rayn was nearby, so she tugged on his sleeve. *Where is the Hall?* she asked.

Turning, he exclaimed, *I do not know!*

Cyan telepathed to both, *Give the others a moment to realize this.*

"Another security measure," Cyan told the initiates, his quiet voice amplified by the shape of the dome. "A projection fills in the open space. Telepath 'Hall' and the wall blurs where you may step in. Tavia, please give the command and we shall follow you."

Once inside, the students looked back to the Temple Crystal in the dome, as clearly as they had seen it upon departing the lift. The projection operated in one direction only.

Cyan called their attention to the records. In the greater part of the space, six narrow tables were arranged as spokes of a wheel, cushioned benches along their lengths. At opposite ends stood tall and broad pastel-colored crystals, six-sided, pointed at their tops, resting in substantial metallic holders upon the floor. "Subject matter is by color. However, you need only stand near a table to recognize that section's contents. There is a flow of information between each crystal pair. You will sense the appropriate place along the table to access what you seek.

"In the rose section is the history of human presence upon Earth, beginning with the Mu oral traditions, recounted by the founders of the Order. Detailed records of Altean civilization are here, as well as observations and histories of indigenous peoples encountered by our priests.

"The science archives are mint green and include all the Order's work in all the subjects we study, as well the proceedings of past and current science committees. All subjects related to education are in the sky-blue section, including charters, methods, and preparatory coursework for instructors, and a record of all attendees. Education committee work is recorded here. The lavender pair keeps the history and progress of the Order, treatises on its Central Tenets, and administrative records.

"Yellow houses the esoteric teachings of the Mu and all records of the Cenon project. Biographies of every priest ever ordained are in the orange section, as well their life achievement summaries added after their deaths. Access to these two sections is withheld until your induction. Next year you will prepare your genealogies and incarnational histories under supervision. These will be entered into the records when you make your vows."

Cyan indicated the lavatory on one side of the lift and the Exemplars' Conference Room on the other. "Wander the rows now and find for yourself how subjects appear in your mind. Sit down for what interests you. Select your topics and subtopics telepathically. Meanwhile, I shall tend to other business in the conference room. Come in if you require my assistance."

The initiates were wide-eyed. Seerce told Rayn incredulously, *This is much more than I ever imagined it might be.* Slowly she walked each section. Between the mint crystals she stopped to request geothermal energy and sensed a pull to her left. Moving slowly down the row, options appeared in her mind's eye, like the content lists in her study crystals. When her choice topped the roster, she sat down to perceive a more specific menu. Making her way through subtopics to "volcano," she chose "dormant." Transmission commenced and she found the information astonishingly clear, but not what she sought.

Starting over, she tried "geothermal energy systems" and chose "locations." A map indicated installations up and down the archipelago. Those on Altea's mainland were situated at hot springs. At another time she would delve further, though surely Aaron had. She got up to walk along the orange and yellow rows, where she perceived nothing at all.

Moving on to the education section, she located her personal records, dates of academy entry and graduation, courses completed, achievements and honors. Hearing the lift open, she looked up to see Tane steering Rika toward the students, who he introduced. Rika smiled and waved at Seerce. Shortly the five were requested to wait on the catwalk for their privileges to be granted singly. Seerce was last.

When she joined the three exemplars at the center of the room, defined by the innermost of the pastel crystals, she saw at her feet a circular mosaic portraying the phases of the moon. She was directed to stand upon the new moon. Each exemplar held an indigo crystal.

Seerce was given a clear quartz crystal of that same slender shape, longer than those they used routinely. "Hold this with both hands," Rika directed, "left hand above right at the level of your heart." She intoned, "Today we record the energetic signature of

Seerce of Basra, initiate of the Order of the Sun. From this day forward, she may enter and depart freely this Sacred Hall, utilizing what she learns here only for good. Seerce, you may accept this oath by touching the point of your crystal to your forehead."

She did. The exemplars stepped forward to touch their crystals lightly and momentarily to the top of her head. Taking a silver case from the table behind him, Tane opened it so Seerce could deposit her Hall crystal within its velvet lining. "No other crystal will record here and yours cannot be read by anyone else. Congratulations," he told her, smiling.

"Thank you, Exemplar," she responded.

"Upon our next journey, I shall introduce you to Icos," Cyan told her, gesturing to the multisided crystal suspended in an alcove. "You may depart by the lift now and you are dismissed from class."

"Blessings upon you, daughter of Basra," Rika told her, smiling. Seerce bowed her head and took her leave. Wishing Anakron had lived to conduct this ceremony, she touched his statuette in the pouch at her waist. Surely his spirit was here with her.

The others waited near the lift in the women's domicile. "We decided on a group hug to finish the ceremony," Kessa told her. Holding their cases of silver, their arms around each other, the five squeezed in close.

*

Rayn and Seerce took lunch to her apartment. Wind-driven rain spattered her windows, clearing periodically, only to speckle and fog and drip again. "Come to me, love," Rayn requested as he set down his plate and mug. "I crave your touch and the feel of your skin and the taste of your lips and all you shared with me."

She allowed him to kiss her and stepped back. "I have complicated our lives tremendously, Rayn. It was wrong of me."

He stayed where he was, watching her pick up her plate and sit down with it. "For the gift of your love and your beautiful body, I accept no apology."

"You should," she replied. "I started it."

"As is the custom of both your matriarchal peoples."

"But you and I may never know such pleasure here, where there are glass ceilings, self-clearing windows, and remote eyes upon us."

"Perhaps in our soaking tubs, then," he suggested.

She laughed, choking on the bite in her mouth. Recovering herself, she sputtered, "That had not occurred to me."

Rayn sat down so close as to press his robed thigh to hers. "There are dense woods close by and rooms to rent in these neighborhoods. Why there are even treatment tables in the clinics that may be heated, elevated, or inclined."

"Stop, Rayn." She giggled. "I am trying to tell you that…"

"What are you trying to say, love?"

"That I love you with all I am, that I am so sorry for the shock I gave you the morning we left Majorka. Ever shall I be grateful for your escort home and back. But I must confess that I am bewildered after all that has transpired. This morning I would have told you I am not certain we belong here. But now I have seen the Hall and I am certain once more. Do you think Cyan knows somehow of our union?"

"If he does, he will act only after careful consideration."

*

"Our losses of late trouble us," Cyan acknowledged to nine students, absent Aaron. "I offer you a perspective on death, which perhaps you have not considered. What I tell you today shall be made that much clearer, once you have achieved the conscious separation of your etheric self from your physical body.

"Death is a blind spot, for our physical senses cannot detect the whereabouts of our departed. We forget to wonder where an infant's spirit dwelt before its birth, aware only of its projection into the physical world we know. Death and birth are transformations of energy to and from another existence.

"Unbound by time, our inner senses are aware of looming personal disaster and death's approach. They endeavor to prepare us. The ego, of course, finds it difficult to acknowledge such. It may struggle up to the body's final breath only to realize it does not expire, but takes its place alongside other independent egos of its Greater Mind. No longer housed in a body, it draws upon energy previously unavailable to it, its lifetime of learning still intact. Conversely, a newborn drawing its first breath begins utilizing the type of energy that will sustain its life in this plane."

Seerce remembered the finality of Aaron's goodbye on the day he went home. Some part of him seemed to know he would not be coming back to the Temple.

Cyan continued, "Anakron was aware that his physical life neared its end. But he was determined to finish history class with the first years, as he had for the second years last summer. His efforts to find you and educate you were lifelong, and he would not leave his work undone."

Seerce blinked back tears as did others at the table. Cyan retained his neutrality.

"Etheric travel is a partial conversion of one's intrinsic energy into another form. A portion of your essence transfers itself elsewhere in the spacious present. As we have discussed, this occurs naturally as you sleep. It is no great feat of magic to move your etheros, just a bit challenging to get your waking brain to allow such.

"Our current subject is for the most part a self-study course. Your new crystals are filled with exercises for you to try. You shall come to know your emotions as the outer range of your inner senses. You must *feel* your way out of your body, because you cannot force your way out.

"Moving your etheros takes practice and you will build upon these basic steps later, during your internships and throughout your career with the Order. These exercises are akin to imagining or daydreaming, intuiting or creating. You may think you do nothing at all, but in fact you teach your conscious mind to recognize what your inner senses perceive.

"Again we shall meet mornings, perhaps just briefly to share experiences. If you wish, you may see me for individual consultation. Be satisfied with subtle progress. No two of us accomplish etheric travel the same way and seldom quickly.

"I invite your return to handball at the usual time, where you may bounce away the inevitable frustrations. Tane and I have been away from the game as long as you, so you may find us easy targets."

Handball was just one more reason for Seerce to miss Aaron.

*

Sootchie's skills had improved greatly, and Seerce told him so following a game she refereed between him and Kessa.

"If you are challenging me, I accept," he teased.

"You are on," she told him. Kessa refereed.

Seerce was finding there were benefits to restraining her competitive nature, to offering a tip here and there, to helping Jair perfect his serve and Isla her backhand. Occasionally she played a soft game with Rayn, who simply could not direct the ball strategically. If she stood in the middle of her court and never moved, she could return every shot. She aimed her returns to every part of his court, though she held back on her vicious shots. He ran, he met the ball, he returned it to where she stood. But she liked watching his beautiful body in that close-fitting uniform, so she contented herself with that—if no one else would play her.

Sootchie worked hard, losing by just one point to Seerce. "Next time," he warned.

"I am sure of it," she told him.

"Would you meet a few of us for dinner in just a while?" he asked. "The science-minded are overdue for a chat."

"I would like that, yes," she answered. She bid Rayn farewell and went home to change clothes.

In a corner of the dining hall, before the platters arrived to the buffet, four huddled over tea. "I have yet to find any value in

Cyan's course," Sootchie opined. "Maybe it does something for Cenonites, but I see no application for the rest of us. How subtle or imaginary is a quake or a hurricane or the rising sea?"

Seerce smiled at his name for Cenon devotees. She had several intriguing experiences with Cyan's exercises, only a few of which she shared in class. As she waited to hear other thoughts, she saw something interesting in the way Tavia's eyes met Sootchie's across the table. It was more than a friendly look. Seerce wondered where she had been lately, not to notice another pair in the making.

Always oblivious, Jair responded, "I spend my time in the Hall, studying what matters to the real world. I asked a couple of Tane's physicists about 'etherica.' They had never heard of such nonsense." He grinned while the others laughed out loud.

"I dare you to use your new term in class!" Seerce exclaimed.

"You might get away with it," Jair told her. "Cyan would have me on the next boat home."

Tavia thought the inner sense that allowed total cognition of a concept might come in handy. "But all of us do that anyway sometimes, do we not? You have had those experiences where something incomprehensible suddenly comes into focus."

The others nodded.

"Cognition of the essence of living tissue intrigues me," Seerce admitted. "If that means looking under someone's armor, knowing who someone truly is, and whether she or he is trustworthy, that could prove valuable. But Sootchie is right. All of this better serves Cenonites, who do not know whether their adoring pupils of the future will thank them or eat them." Peals of laughter rang from their corner. Finally they got up to serve themselves dinner.

Rayn came in later and sat down with a group of musicians. He finished about the same time as the science group. Following Seerce out, he walked her up the stairs to her apartment. "Come in and keep me company," she invited. Quickly they were embroiled in passion. "I have something for you," Rayn told her, leaning in to kiss her deeply.

"What would that be?" she asked.

"It requires demonstration," he replied, taking her hands and pulling her to standing. Directing the lights off, she led him upstairs to her bed. Cold rain beat furiously on the pyramidal ceiling, chilling the chamber, but quickly she knew only his heat around and within her.

*

"There is an ancient gate by which you may travel to and from other realms, a natural intersection of planes known to the Mu." Cyan sat among the initiates in the front row of the Temple. At viewing height, the Crystal portrayed the two continents to the west of the Ocean of Atlas and the isthmus that connected them. In the common language, the northernmost was known as Kairn, much of it ice-covered as Europa was. "Alteans call the southern continent Ketru," Cyan explained, "shortened from its Mu designation, which is unpronounceable by the Archaean tongue.

"The arrow in the graphic points to the approximate location of a mountain cave, inland from where the isthmus meets Ketru. In this region dwelt the salt people and from them the Mu learned of the Bridge between Worlds. They attributed it to Persa, their own goddess of passages. We call it the Gate of Persa."

Jair asked a bit indignantly, "Has Icos proven insufficient for the Order's needs?" By his question Seerce knew Jair's pride of family.

Cyan replied, "No. We do have need of alternatives in times such as these. Now if you will project your remote vision to Icos first, we will record your energy signatures and I shall specify our destination. Hence, you need only remember Persa to take yourself directly there. Relax now in the manner most familiar to you. At our destination, endeavor to exercise your inner senses."

The students arrived simultaneously with Cyan into the heart of the cave. A broad crystal totem stood at center, aglow in silver-blue light, this incredible structure appearing to arise from beneath the black obsidian floor to pierce an irregular rock ceiling. The colors of the travelers' subtle bodies showed dimly as they arranged themselves to encircle the mythological creatures, perched one atop the other. It was impossible to determine the breadth and shape of the cave, for its boundaries shimmered in some areas and lost themselves to darkness in others.

Cyan told them, *I shall introduce you to the gate with the required incantation.* What Seerce perceived was a song of sorts, with more vibration than sound. She felt it more than heard it, like the wind blowing through her being or the deepest tones of stringed instruments. It seemed that another dimension opened, her mental picture that of random staircases. The experience struck a chord in some distant memory, but Seerce did not know when or how she might have known this place. When Cyan finished, the totem seemed to shift a bit, swelling and swaying before it resettled itself. A period of stillness ensued.

Finally Cyan telepathed, *You are acquainted and accepted.*

Kessa asked, *Was it a Mu language you spoke?*

No, Cyan replied. *I utilized a prayer of the Tamtha, the original people here, in their ancient language. I was fortunate to have been Tamthan in another existence, recalling the incantation when I worked on my biography as an initiate.*

From here you may travel anywhere, to be drawn back in a timely manner. Simply telepath your instruction to the gate.

Upon returning their awareness to the Temple, the exemplar suggested they fetch tea and bring their mugs to the classroom. He accompanied them, all the students a bit dazed, in need of a short walk through the brisk morning air. Soon a discussion commenced at the oval table.

"What would one see if one explored the perimeter of the cave?" asked Sootchie.

"Take your awareness and go back to find out," Cyan suggested. "Each will have an individual impression."

"I felt many souls in that place," Ell stated. "Did others of you perceive them?" No one else had.

Seerce did her best to describe the sensations evoked by the incantation. "The feel of the wind, yes," Isla agreed, "but I heard a symphony of strange instruments."

"And notes in scales beyond my physical hearing," Rayn added.

"Colors streamed through me," Tavia commented, "such as I have never seen with my physical eyes."

Tuura confessed, "I went right on through the gate to the other side. It is wild back there!"

"Be more specific," Cyan requested.

"Yes, sir, I will try. Tane once showed us an electron's world in a holographic projection. That is what I saw through the gate, light and speed and color and sparks. I thought to myself, 'No! I want to see order!' Everything slowed and formed itself into a pretty scene, the one I picture when I need to calm down. All those random specks settled themselves immediately. It was magical! I would have stayed, but the gate drew me back."

Cyan almost smiled.

"I heard and saw nothing unusual," Jair admitted, "but that crystal tower is astonishing!"

Seerce found herself much in awe of Cyan. Peculiar he was, but a master of esoterica, able to salvage the lost wisdom of the ancients. She wondered at his clear recall of a chant in a long-dead language, from a prior life and as a student! How clear was the mirror of his soul to reflect such detail, and how astute he had been to grasp his purpose so early in this life.

CHAPTER 12

For the upset in her sitting room, this drizzly day in the middle of autumn might have spawned a summer hurricane. Seerce sat wrapped in a blanket on her divan, hugging a pillow, blotting her eyes with a kerchief. Rayn paced before her windows. She had not known how angry he could be. She was merely devastated. Cyan had announced their internships, to span three moons. Rayn's linguistic skills were destined for Misr, and Seerce was assigned to help Rika set up a science task force.

"We are not the only ones, Rayn! Kessa leaves for Tibisay without her lover. Half of Afrikaa will separate Tavia and Sootchie."

"This is purposive and cruel!" he stormed. "We have not yet completed our first year, while the second years intern for the first time!"

"The world changes," Seerce replied softly, "and with it the Order. Earth is restless. Quakes rattle the spine of the ocean again." As yet Altea had not felt them, but the sword was at their throats. "The Temple is vulnerable and what it guards is irreplaceable. The plan must be readied to move the records. You will be a part of that, Rayn! You are crucial to it. Consider it an honor to help develop a universal symbolic language." She forced herself to be positive.

"I am honored by your presence at my side!" he protested.

"I cannot assist Rika from Misr. My work is here."

Accusingly, he queried, "The work you want to do?"

"The work I was born to do," she answered evenly. "Who else can deliver what each of us brings? Anakron gathered us here in the nick of time, each of us fitting so well with particular of the Order's needs. Do you think this is coincidence? Have you no sense of his foresight? Or your part in preserving wisdom?"

Rayn stopped pacing and hung his head. "You know that I do," he answered sullenly. "But how can I leave you here with the islands endangered? Do you understand what you mean to me, Seerce?"

"I know what you mean to me," she told him, "and I will suffer the loss of your presence and the joy you give me every day. We can meet by remote vision. We are fortunate in that regard. Three moons are not so long. We have been in Altea already half the year and time has flown. We will be together again. Think of my grandmother and Anakron, of my parents. Look at what they accomplished in their lives apart and together. Love survives time and separation."

He came to her and pulled her up from the divan. Hugging her tightly, he whispered, "We must arrange to speak daily. I cannot live without you."

*

In the midst of her dream, there was only tranquility, no worry, no fear. She stood before an exquisite slate fireplace, watching the marvelous silver mobile suspended before it, as it caught the last daylight, its tiny planets and stars twisting and turning by the currents of her breath. The intoxicating scent of lilacs emanated from a vase upon a marble-topped table behind her. Through double doors, Anakron entered this beautiful parlor from a broad foyer with a curved staircase of polished wood. He carried a tray. *Join me, child*, he telepathed. *We have much to say to one another.*

Seerce sat down on a deep plush sofa, rightly sized for Anakron's long legs, her small person swallowed by its proportions. So she arranged pillows at one end and reclined with her slippered feet upon the cushions, sipping delicious tea and nibbling nutmeats and dried fruits. By his thought, Anakron ignited the fire. Now all the intriguing shapes of the mobile spun and danced in warm currents, showing bronze and gold, sending reflections of firelight across the dimming room. They laughed and talked late into the evening.

Why had she grieved? Anakron lived. He had only been away on the business of the Order. Her heart lightened and she began to tell him all that transpired in his absence, going home to Basra, the quake in Eyre, her appointment to Rika's committee, and her love for Rayn. Instantly she knew her error in revealing the affair, but he had no reaction. He told her of his pursuits, seeking agreement among various groups within and outside the Order. But the fire changed into Cyan's face, displaying all the displeasure and disgust that Anakron's had not.

Seerce awoke trembling, Rayn asleep next to her. From a dream so real, Anakron's presence so comforting and Cyan's judgment so terrifying, she had fallen back into her waking life.

*

"It is impossible for the chair to know all, Seerce." She was in Rika's office next to the one that had been Anakron's. The furnishings must have come from storage, for they were a mixed set of period pieces arranged haphazardly. "That is why we get into a little trouble around here now and again. Help me keep the pulse of this committee. I need facts and an accurate portrayal of the players' engagement in this effort. From my new vantage point, I see the exemplars hold tightly to their departments and their habits, as I did hold mine. But we have never had such pressing need to come together."

Rika looked up to the ceiling, formulating her thoughts. "Please understand this. I care nothing for the difference between our stations in the Order. I care for truth in the manner that your grandfather did. You will meet resistance because you are young and because you are his protégé. But eventually you may take a significant role, for our oceanic challenges shall be paramount for decades to come. It is my job to steer this crew of captains in a proper direction and I want you to help me choose that direction. Keep looking and digging. You have all my support."

Seerce took her recording crystal to the Hall of Records. There was a long roster of subjects with which she needed familiarity. Rayn and Tavia met with Cyan behind the closed door of the Exemplars' Conference Room. She hoped that word of their tasks and projects would ignite a spark in Rayn, for he was deeply downcast.

Beginning with committee reports from Geology, Climatology, and Physics, Seerce searched for the subjects of their current studies. She was engrossed when Rayn emerged wearing the mask of a trader, completely unreadable. He made his way to the lavatory without noticing her. She got up to intercept him when he came out.

"Lunch?" she asked.

"How delightful that would be, but we are not finished. We meet by crystal with the staff in Misr. Our meal will be brought here. I shall find you later." Quickly he went back to business. Seerce ate with Kessa, who was inconsolable at leaving her lover.

*

"I will help you pack," Seerce offered, as they scooped up dinner that evening.

"Most of it is done," Rayn told her, looking exhausted. "Let us sleep early and I will finish in the morning. At present I cannot think straight." They carried covered plates to his apartment, where he sat down heavily on his sofa, saying, "Cyan will travel with us."

"Why would he wait until now to say so?"

"He enjoys the element of surprise," Rayn commented sardonically. "It adds to his control of every situation."

"How long will he stay in Misr?" He had learned from Tavia that staff quarters in that small outpost were limited. What if he had to share a room with Cyan?

"He does not say. Better to keep us guessing," he replied, reaching for his mug.

"Your news is concerning, but you are not much affected by it. Do I read you correctly?"

"You do." Rayn sighed. "I have decided I must be my own best friend during this trial, endeavor to do the job before me, and return to your arms."

Clinging sorrow characterized their last hours together. They could not escape their looming loss long enough to pleasure one another, nor to sleep restfully, so they lay entwined dozing, grateful that the sun had yet to rise.

Rayn declined to have her walk with him to the dock at the Healing Temple. When the time came to go, he fastened around Seerce's neck a fine silver chain with a tiny rose quartz crystal, telling her he had infused it with his love and all his memories of their time together. "Wear it, please, until we are rejoined, so you do not forget me."

She tied at his wrist a finely woven bracelet, such as the men of Basra wore, this one portraying the dunes and the mountains, a crescent moon and the stars of the desert night. One of her aunts had crafted it to Seerce's specifications while they were in Basra. "Remember to whom you belong," she told him. "My heart goes with you."

*

The first meeting of Oceanus, as the task force came to be known, daunted Seerce. She sat at the exemplars' conference table with Rika and Tane, watching department heads wrangle with each other through the crystal. She preferred her naive view of the

Order's leadership, the way Anakron had portrayed it: "Seldom do we have serious differences and generally we operate as one mind." What she saw here was far from that.

The chair employed her folksy humor to coerce each speaker back to the objective of the meeting: Determine the charter for Oceanus. Acknowledging the tremendous responsibilities each shouldered, Rika allowed them to appoint trusted aides rather than commit themselves to the press of this new business. Tane named a high-ranking associate to represent him, but Damon and Nova would not. How was an initiate to prompt any priest, let alone a busy exemplar, to complete committee work by deadline? Seerce's role, as Rika now explained it, was to track assignments, organize summaries, and distribute information to the departments. Obviously Nova resented Oceanus, arguing that the instability of the ocean floor was clearly within Geology's purview. Seerce's head ached for the worries before her.

It took all day, but finally a charter was adopted. "With haste and by the utmost interdepartmental cooperation, determine what affects the Ocean of Atlas. Strive to give the earliest possible warnings to preserve life, safety, and the assets of the Order." It seemed to Seerce they missed what ought to be the primary objective, to identify and mitigate what disturbed the body of Earth.

She discussed this with Rika afterward. "Patience, my child," the chair requested. "You will learn to be satisfied with small increments of progress. You have supporters here. Nova will not be one of them, but that has nothing to do with you."

*

Seerce missed the familiar routine of class and conversation, shared tribulations and laughter. Kessa's biting humor and wise counsel were absent from breakfast. Lunch became a singular affair, for Seerce seldom saw Jair or Ell, her only classmates to remain on campus. She tried to conjure Anakron's ghost and

Aaron's opinions on her new subjects, all the while aching for her lover.

Their contacts by remote vision were hit and miss. For four days, Rayn shared bunks on boats or rooms in hostels with Cyan, which must have been excruciating for him. The communal quarters in Misr violated his considerable need for privacy, for they were much like those at the academies with several beds to a room.

In Misr the sun rose four decans earlier than it did in Altea. When she could send her remote vision, Rayn was in sessions, and when he could find a place to remain undisturbed, she was asleep. Seerce proposed they establish a regular time to meet each day, even if she stayed up late or he came to her as she worked in the Hall of Records. He would not commit to that, citing Cyan's continuing presence. She had to be satisfied knowing he would return.

It was fortunate she had so much to do. By her research she could forget for a while how lonely she was. Going to bed early, she relived all that Rayn imbued into the rose crystal, trying to feel his body against hers, hoping to conjure dreams of him. She worried that something was amiss.

One clear, cold night when she could not sleep, she dressed and cloaked and went out for a walk on the perimeter path. Examining at length the portents of the stars and planets, not nearly as bright in coastal humidity as they were in the still, dry air of Basra, she saw that Orion was an upright figure in the mid-latitudinal sky. The Wanderer with his belt and sword traveled onward, ever running alone, as Seerce feared she would have to do.

*

"We need a fourth for doubles this afternoon," Seerce told Cyan, "if you care to join Ell, Jair, and me." Absent for an entire moon, his return surprised her, for she thought Rayn would have been overjoyed to tell her of his departure from Misr.

Silence the Echo

The chair had realized Seerce's need for a place to organize all that she tracked, so she assigned her a small office next to Cyan's. He was helpful to her, arranging for furnishings and choosing art for her walls, all borrowed from storage. Attesting that Rayn and Tavia gave their work their all, he seemed pleased with their progress.

"I accept," Cyan replied. "How long since you have played?"

"As long as you have been gone," Seerce admitted. "I run in the afternoons and knock some balls around the gym sometimes, but we three students work different schedules."

"Then we are equally disadvantaged. There is no gym in Misr, where things are rather rudimentary."

When she and he arrived to the gym in their sports attire, an unfamiliar woman stood with Jair and Ell. Immediately, Seerce perceived Cyan's trepidation.

"Who is that?" she asked him quietly.

"Her name is Sava," he replied. "I thought her return from Tibisay had been postponed."

"Hey," Seerce hollered to Jair and Ell, "you brought a fourth and I brought a fourth. That is teamwork!"

In a hushed voice, she observed, "You do not seem pleased."

"No," Cyan said. "Once we were close."

Such a personal revelation greatly surprised Seerce. "Allow me to give you some advice, Exemplar," she told him. Of late she had come to realize that exemplars were no more perfect than the general population. "Make it look like you are having the time of your life. Show her you have moved on." His expression was uncertain. "I will help you," she offered, beaming him one of her dazzling smiles as they approached the others.

She introduced herself to this stunning woman of such unusual coloring: light caramel skin, flowing brunette hair tied at the nape of her neck, and exquisite sky-blue eyes. She looked worried as they approached. Surely she was a priest, for she emanated a strong presence and an upright character.

"Cyan is so out of shape," Seerce told the three, assuming

license to tease their professor. "Let me have first dibs and whatever is left of him you can take."

Jair caught her humor, replying, "I make you that deal! He is known for slaughtering me."

"That will not happen today and perhaps no time soon," Seerce deadpanned. "Ell, show the exemplar some mercy, in light of his age and time away from the game."

The corners of Cyan's mouth twitched. "Let me know when I may respond," he stated, "because some present have privileges to lose."

"No talk just yet, Exemplar," Seerce commanded, "not until I best you." Genuine shock crossed his features. Seerce turned her attention to Sava's confusion, asking in a friendly manner, "How long have you played?"

"Ell has coached me for exactly a half moon," she responded. "Perhaps I should find another sport." The initiates laughed.

"No, no, no," Seerce said kindly. "We are easy on beginners. You just have to grow a thick skin. Most of the combat is in the dialogue."

"And we are done talking now," said Ell. "Go get him, Seerce."

Cyan walked to the opposite court with her, shaking his head. "You have reduced me to mincemeat. Now what do you want me to do?"

"Try to smear me all over this court! If you pretend the ball is your old relationship, it could be a pretty good game."

He laughed. She had not known he could. Seerce walked back to the serving line and smacked the ball hard with her paddle. Cyan, still chuckling, nearly missed the rebound. She telepathed, *You had best pay attention or she will follow you around forever.*

He threw back a ruthless shot, which Seerce nearly missed. She waited for the ball to return and bounced it off the ceiling, nearly striking Cyan. He jumped out of the way, and then dived to return the bounce.

I think you are too easy on her, Seerce told him as she fired off another hard shot.

Cyan angled his return to a point far from where Seerce stood. She scrambled and smacked it against the nearest wall. *Hey,* she said, *do you want to lose this woman or not? Show her who is boss.*

He cracked the ball against the ceiling. Unwittingly, Seerce held her paddle at such an angle that the rebound was sent directly to Cyan's head.

"Duck!" she hollered. He dropped his paddle and fell full body on his stomach to the floor, just in time to avoid the hit. Then he rolled over on his back, laughing.

Seerce dropped to her knees in hysterics, pounding her paddle on the floor. She could hear Ell howling and Jair's belly laugh. In a fit of giggles, she sat down cross-legged on the gym floor. Finally, Cyan got himself up and walked over to her, stopping twice to bend over in laughter. When he came to her, she reached both her hands to him. He pulled her up and hugged her to him for just a moment.

"The exemplar is up for grabs!" she hollered to the others.

*

Climbing into bed late that evening, Seerce sent her remote vision to the dining room in Misr, thinking that it must be early morning there. Rayn was alone at a small table. *Have you forgotten about me, Rayn?* she telepathed. He looked up and smiled. She kept her image dim, so the few in the room would not notice her.

No, he answered. *How could I ever forget you?*

Cyan is back here at the Temple. You might have warned me.

Is he bothering you? he queried suspiciously. His expression changed entirely, to one of bitterness verging on hatred.

Not at all, she replied. *He seems more relaxed than I have known him to be.*

Of course he is, there with you when I am not.

I am surprised you did not share what must surely be great relief for his departure.

In fact, I did not know he had left. I assumed he met with others in the community. How do you fare at the Temple?

I am lonely. I miss your kisses and your affection, your eyes and your smile and your love. I worry about you. He agreed then to meet her daily by remote vision, in a vacant chamber beneath Leo. She would rise at dawn to see him at his midday break. Admitting then that the Misr staff was friendly and they liked his oud-playing, she thought there might be more to enjoy there than he mentioned.

*

After another grueling Oceanus meeting, the exemplar and the initiate spoke as friends over lunch in the dining room. Not often had Seerce seen Cyan there, so when he invited her to sit down, she did. "I know what it means to have to step up to high expectations," he told her, "which I say as a veteran of the road you now travel. I have reservations about this role you have assumed."

He shared some personal history about his upbringing in a remote clan, where his spiritual gifts were recognized early and trained by local priests. Like her, he was young when he arrived to the Temple of Altea.

"May I ask you more about my role?"

"Certainly," he replied.

"Is it you or Rika who oversees my work? Which office shall I be called to, when I have offended an exemplar or made some equally egregious error?"

Cyan grinned, giving those minor smile lines some exercise. "During your internship, Rika is your superior. When she gives you direction, follow it or challenge her, for she is most reasonable. If you ask my advice on any matter, I will give you my opinion. But I desire no authority over your work and I have made this point to Rika. At times I will be faculty for your studies, but that comes and goes with the schedule and will end altogether at your induction. We are colleagues. Know that I hold tightly any matter you entrust to me."

"But you have great advantages, sir," she told him. "You know too many of my secrets."

Cyan startled.

"I believe you call them limbic influences," she reminded him.

"Oh, yes," he said, resettling his features to neutrality, "that is a better term. Your forthright manner ever surprises me and your laughter brings light to a dark world. I shall enjoy our friendship."

When he smiled, when his severe demeanor softened, she could almost conceive of such a thing.

*

Seerce sat with a crystal full of romantic tales, a going-away gift from her Aunt Ena when she left Basra. "Even priests need love," Ena had told her. "Console yourself with these until you find your man."

Her man was absent when she took her vision to Leo this morning. Too miffed to go look for him and too angry to go back to sleep, these stories were her only escape on a common day when the sea roared beyond her windows and rain swept by in sheets. She was restless.

Twice already she had taken her vision to Eyre, nosing around the snow-covered rubble, looking for Aaron. Women and children were huddled around cooking fires in a few communal buildings, the men absent. On the second attempt, Seerce found him asleep in a bunkhouse at the hunting camp, in a heavy coat, its furry hood encasing his head, boots still on his feet, and his face a picture of exhaustion. Every bunk was taken by a man looking similarly.

She wanted his company to check the status of the ocean floor site. It concerned her that she had yet to find any report of its observation by any science researcher. She would rather not visit there alone, eerie as it was, but now that seemed her only option. Soon her remote vision hovered over what had quickly grown to be a vast complex.

The barges and the drillers were gone. The perimeter of the site was marked now by light standards anchored to the ocean floor, topped by those strange amber globes. Piercing spotlights up and down the standards were trained upon six round turrets, equally spaced in a broad circle just inside the site's perimeter. She assumed these had been prefabricated and dropped into place over the drilling sites. One was topped by a light-colored dome of similar material. Thick, high circular walls characterized the others, which were uncapped. In diminished light beyond the perimeter were heaps of rock cores that the drillers had extracted, random piles dumped here and there.

Passing her vision through the walls of the domed structure, she saw a glow at its lowest level. Moving downward, she encountered a mixed stone and concrete platform with sheen to it, beneath it one set of five glowing tubes positioned at center, descending straight down. This array was much like what she had seen in the volcano station.

Emerging from other sections of the platform were singular tubes of an opaque material, each one set at a different angle. These did not glow, but descended into tunnels drilled at different trajectories.

Returning her vision home, Seerce deposited her pictures into a new crystal. Whether or not anyone took her observations seriously, she would keep her own record. Someday Aaron might be interested.

*

Along with her duties, Seerce researched her personal interests, specifically the geologic disasters that preceded Altea's acquisition of five city-states. This was one of Rayn's revelations in his history presentation. She found that Geology attributed all these events—a river flood, three earthquakes, and a tidal wave—to the shifting weight of Europa's glaciers as they retreated.

Carefully she examined the reports of the tidal wave over Tunise, which Aaron had studied. It was the event that destroyed the port and many buildings and homes along the coast, killing seventy-three people and maiming many others, Seerce's uncles and her mother among the casualties. Judged to be a local event, the likely cause was a dip-slip fault in the floor of the MidTerra Sea, not far beyond the Bay of Tunise. The earthquake was minor, scarcely noticeable on land. But the sudden fall of one part of the fault generated a wave in the direction of the port, high enough to swamp one-story buildings of mudbrick and wood along flat beaches.

The rest of the story Seerce knew personally. Navy ships arrived within a half moon to take charge of the port. Within three moons, new docks were constructed and more substantial buildings erected, soon occupied by military personnel. The flag of Altea was raised over the city and taxes were collected from all port traffic, the citizenry unable to do anything about that.

Seerce found nothing about the refitting of Altea's volcano power station. The most recent Physics records indicated it was yet a conversion facility for the dark energy of the night sky, though the eye of the dome had been closed for years.

Frustrated, she went in search of Rika, only to find Sava in that office, now tastefully arranged and decorated. "Hello, Seerce," she heard in a friendly tone from the woman who once loved Cyan, or maybe it was vice versa.

"Good morning, Sava. Has Rika's office moved? I want to make an appointment to see her."

"Away on business in Zanata, she will return five days hence."

"She will miss the Oceanus meeting?" Seerce questioned.

"No. She will attend from there and you will see her on the crystal."

"But I need to speak with her privately."

"I will arrange that for you. I am her number two."

"Her what?"

"Her assistant. That is what the Order calls the right hand to each exemplar. Barlas assisted Anakron, but on his own he has too many responsibilities. Rika prefers her own sidekick."

Seerce laughed. "That sounds like something she would say."

"I was Cyan's number two in Tibisay."

That cast a different spin on Cyan's love life, thought Seerce.

"I enjoy serving Rika," Sava stated, her tone implying that she had not enjoyed serving Cyan. "You are an accomplished athlete," she commented.

Seerce smiled. "Thank you."

"May I make a collegial suggestion? Mind your parameters around Cyan, for he imagines certain things. I will contact Rika about your appointment and let you know." She sat down to her desk and pulled open a drawer.

Seerce left, wondering about Cyan's imagination all the way back to the Hall of Records. Sava found her there a short time later. "Rika is available now," she told Seerce. "Come with me." In the Exemplars' Conference Room, she called up Rika's face in the crystal and took a seat at the table, as did Seerce.

"Good morning, madame. This regards my observation of yesterday," the student told the chair. Seerce expected a private conversation.

"You may speak freely before Sava. Just be sure the conference room door is closed," Rika advised.

"It is, madame," Sava told her.

Seerce described in detail the progress she had seen at the ocean floor complex. Rika's eyes grew large. Sava's expression was unreadable, an asset for a number two. "We must proceed cautiously," judged Rika. "The last thing we want is the Ryk to think we are interested in their experiments. I do not care to meet the Autark's guard in the middle of the night. Let me see what I can do about setting up a small research team at the Temple, one that reports only to me." They said their goodbyes and the crystal dimmed.

"You have her ear," said Sava, "as you should with news like that. Say none of this to anyone."

Seerce stood up, replying, "Indeed I shall not. I thank you for your tip regarding Cyan."

Silence the Echo

*

As rain pattered against the odd angles of the pyramidal ceiling above her bed, Seerce had to wonder at the events that had caught her in a tangle of relationships at the top of the Order. Hers was a singular place to be. And her ever-changing perspective on Cyan needed another revision—but not tonight.

Directing the lights off, she felt Rayn's presence and then heard his telepathy. *You did not meet me today,* he said.

You did not meet me yesterday, she replied.

I thought the common day was excluded from our plan.

Am I less important to you on the common day?

He disregarded that. *I apologize for disappointing you. The community went on a boat trip up the River Iteru.*

I woke to chimes before dawn when I should have slept until noon.

Sleep now. I will meet you here at this time tomorrow. Then he was gone. She was too tired to care.

*

Sometimes one needs to disappear from one's life. If Rika was gone and Cyan was not her supervisor, Seerce decided to take a hike, requesting of the cook the favor of packing her a lunch. "Sunny day," said the withered brown elder, Jonna. "Two lunch?" she asked in her broken Altean, holding up two fingers.

"Just one," Seerce replied with one finger.

"That pretty man, where he?"

It embarrassed Seerce to think even the cook knew Rayn and her as a couple. Gesturing with her hands, she replied, "He is far away in Afrikaa. He will return soon."

Jonna smiled around her mostly missing teeth. "I like him. Tea?"

Seerce nodded yes. Jonna gave her a bottle with a lid, saying, "You do. Tea stay warm." Taking the container to the pot in the dining room, Seerce filled it, surprised the bottle remained cool to the touch.

"Magic," Jonna said, bringing a small woven basket and taking the bottle to tuck it in just so.

Seerce giggled and gave her a hug to thank her. Donning the warm wool cape that she carried over her arm, she stopped by Admin to check out with Ell. "This looks bad, does it not, leaving in the middle of the day?"

"Your secret is safe with me as long as you are back by sundown. Barlas went to the city."

"I accept your terms," she replied. Chuckling, Ell returned to his task.

Heading up the trail along the seawall, Seerce took a bench seat overlooking the waves. Fuzzy clouds wandered lazily across a pale sky. By the low angle of the sun in early winter, the water reflected more grey than blue. Brisk air scoured Seerce's lungs, oxygenating her brain and clearing her thinking of its weary fog. She had to face what had roamed the outskirts of her awareness since Rayn left—in all this time he had shared nothing heartfelt or personal.

Their brief conversations by remote view never became what she hoped they would be—the sustenance that kept her going. He said little of his work or colleagues, challenges or insights, joys or sorrows. Craving more of his companionship, she had suggested the two might, on a common day, view the coastline of the MidTerra or tour more of Majorka or visit the Port of Hammas where he was born. Always he declined, citing a pressing task or the risk of breaking some supposed rule.

Taking the thermos from her basket, she sipped carefully at its heat, trying to think through the whys and wherefores rationally. She was done with her meal of pickled vegetables and egg salad wrapped in flatbread before it occurred to her that remote visioning was an emotionless venture, not a means of carrying on a relationship. The portion of telepathy that rode along was rudimentary and two-dimensional, nothing akin to what one knows and feels in the presence of flesh and blood. Never had it been advertised as anything other than a tool of observation, just a baby step along the way to launching one's etheric self. Unfortunately, it was their only sure method at this point in their training.

Taking this into account, she understood better what Cyan tried to impart in his lessons on etheric travel. While her science-minded friends dismissed the relevance of his pronouncements, Seerce recognized that Cenon observers would get nowhere perceiving as little of their subjects as she did of Rayn. Yet here she was blaming him for his emotional distance, when unpracticed faculties were the likely issue. She wondered if he felt similarly frustrated.

But soon all of this would be behind them. Seeing the nearly-full moon high in the day lit sky, she hung all her hopes upon the new moon, when he would return to her.

CHAPTER 13

Seerce had scarcely slept in anticipation of Rayn's arrival. When she could wait no longer, she went to his apartment where her knock went unanswered. Maybe his boat was delayed or he had fallen heavily asleep. As she turned to leave, she heard his door open. Spinning around she greeted him, "Welcome home, my love!"

"Allow me a little time," he requested, hiding himself behind the door. "I will come to your place."

She was taken aback. They had been apart for three moons. Even if he just walked in, or just stepped out of the bath, even if he was exhausted by the long journey, could he not take her in his arms? Every night that she slept alone she had imagined their joyous reunion.

Returning home chagrined, she tried to distract herself with the power of the waves crashing against the seawall, on a dark day when the Circle of Stones was scarcely distinguishable from the leaden sky. Instinctively her fingers went to the pink crystal at her breastbone. Well she knew every detail of his affection and his passion, all their declarations of love, their hopes and promises and dreams of a life together. She lapsed into these.

It was some long while before Rayn arrived, nicely dressed

in street clothes, carrying a heavy coat over his arm, his face unreadable. "If you wish to go for a walk," Seerce said, "I shall fetch my cape."

"Maybe we could talk here," he suggested.

She took his coat to hang on the hook behind the door. When she reached for him, he seemed to withdraw. "May I fix you tea?" she asked politely.

"No, thank you," he said. "I have had my fill. I do have an appointment in town." Seemingly he meant this to be a short conversation. She proceeded to her divan and sat down. He took one of her chairs. In the grey light, his face looked thinner. Gone was the radiance of his complexion and his eyes were dull. Yes, his hair was long, and he was prideful of his looks, but was that his priority, the reason he must leave her now?

"First," he said, his smile artificial, "my congratulations on your accomplishments with Oceanus. You will go far in the Order. The mission should be your first priority. I see that now. I must allow you to do what you are called to do."

She was stunned by the subject and the chill in his voice. "Has something changed between us, Rayn?" she asked uncertainly.

He looked down, as if to recall something he had rehearsed. "I cannot stand in your way," he answered. "Your place is here and mine is in Misr."

"We have more than a year of study left!" Seerce protested. "You and I have known all along that we will sometimes be apart. Now we are together." The floor seemed to drop from beneath her and the ceiling to spin. Shaking herself, she took a deep breath, trying to reckon the differences between the Rayn who loved her and the man sitting in her chair. She could not.

"It is wrong to take your attention from what matters. We have our parts to play. I have come to realize that."

"I can work hard and love you, honor your pursuits and exercise mine! That is what I have done since we met and in your absence. I can do it forever!"

To her great shock, he stood up. "I must be going," he said.

"Oh, no," she responded emphatically, "you must not! Sit down and tell me what is wrong. What happened to you in Misr? Were you taken ill? I love you, Rayn. We are joined. We are to be priests and lovers, like Anakron and Petraea. Have you forgotten?"

He did not sit down but moved to the window to look out. "I have had time to think this through," he said, his back to her. "My perspective is different now. There is great urgency to the work beneath Leo and there are few to do it. I see myself going back soon, perhaps never to return here. Dark days come. If we are to preserve wisdom, everyone among us must work to capacity. You know this." He turned to face her, but he seemed to look through her. "I tell you nothing that you have not said to me. I believe you. That is what has changed."

"Do you love someone else?" she asked incredulously. "One of the priests or the staff or the craftspeople, someone from your past? You are a poet, Rayn, a musician, a lover! You were much more committed to those pursuits than the priesthood."

"You insult me, Seerce!" he retorted. "You are not the only one with a calling for your work."

"I am sorry," she said, recognizing the walls around him but not the prisoner within. "I mean no disrespect. But the Rayn I knew would never say these things."

"You do not know me. That is evident. Now you must excuse me." He strode to the door.

"May I hug you, at least?" she asked, as she got up to follow him. He assented, but there was no warmth to the perfunctory embrace. He took his coat and opened the door. Sinking down to the cold marble floor before her legs gave way, Seerce hugged her knees to her chest and dissolved into racking sobs.

*

"I think he drinks too much," Kessa told Seerce. She was back from Tibisay and a night of reunion with Laela. "He would not want you to know." They ate dinner in Kessa's apartment. This followed rigorous handball and a long soaking bath, the beginning of Seerce's daily post-Rayn ritual. "His color is unhealthy, his skin has lost its turgor, and the circles are deep beneath his eyes—classic signs of too much ethanol and too few nutrients."

"He had to have fallen for someone else. He was so cold to me."

"He drank when he was younger, and quite a bit from what he has told you. Likely he could not cope with your separation and his old habit found him in Misr."

Seerce had no familiarity with this subject. "People choose wine over love?"

"Astonishing, is it not?" her friend replied. "For some it is a lifelong problem, one often seen at the Healing Temple."

"What can I do, Kessa?"

"Wait for him to come to his senses," she replied.

"I sit at the classroom table with him! What am I to do with my heartache? Every time I see him, I will fall apart."

"Sit on his side of the table, but up front, close to the presenter. Do not look back."

*

The next morning Seerce waited for Tavia to come to breakfast. After some friendly chat, she asked what she and Rayn accomplished in Misr.

"I rarely saw him," her classmate replied. "You know Rayn. He likes to be on his own."

"Did he not have something to do with what you carved?"

The question seemed to surprise her. "No," she said, "it is too early for that. He worked with a couple priests and a local shaman on developing a symbolic language anyone could interpret. My uncle and I met with them once, early on, but they have much work ahead of them. We are a long way from knowing what to carve within the chambers. I assisted two Cenon researchers."

"Oh," Seerce said.

"Rayn did not tell you any of this?" she asked politely.

"He has scarcely said a word," Seerce replied.

Tavia shrugged. "He seemed to want no company at all, the way he had been when we first arrived here. I assumed he was heartsick over your separation."

*

Seerce still wore the rose quartz pendant. At night she fell asleep with the crystal between her fingertips, hoping to reach him in dreams or live again some scene from their love affair, to know the feel of her hand in his, the warmth of his body pressed to hers. Sometimes she dreamt of Anakron or her family, and there were long sagas about people she had never met in places she had never been. Sometimes she seemed to be in Eyre with Aaron. But never did she find Rayn in dreams. It was when she walked into class every morning that the nightmare began anew, his body present and his spirit untouchable by any of her faculties.

Though the duties of her internship had been handed off to Sava, lightening her burden, Seerce struggled to drag herself through each day. As she removed a few personal possessions from her office one afternoon, Cyan came by full of concern. She acknowledged only that grief for Anakron's death had caught up with her.

"Perhaps you should go home for a time. I can arrange a leave for you."

"No, thank you," Seerce replied. She could not say to her family that she and Rayn were no more. "I prefer to be here learning."

"Perhaps you would accept a suggestion to help you disregard your pain. Easily you overcame a fear of water. A similar intervention would give you power over your current situation."

"You are kind," she told him, struggling to keep her composure. "I will consider your offer." Fortunately he did not linger. She closed the door by her thought and fell apart at the desk.

Silence the Echo

*

Their new subject was observations and probabilities. Seerce arrived early each day to be sure she was in the seat closest to Tane, this time facing the windows. As Kessa recommended, she never looked toward the back of the table. At dismissal, she lingered till everyone left, then made a mad dash up the stairs to her apartment.

"Long have we known that the presence of an observer influences the outcome of experiments," Tane began. "Likewise, as you travel etherically, there is potential to influence the situation you investigate. If you intervene, you add to potential outcomes for that situation. So let us begin with what is commonly called 'the observer effect.'"

Reflexively, Seerce reached for her crystal on the table to be sure it was recording. In so doing, her eyes met Rayn's ever so briefly, for unbeknownst to her, he had taken a seat across the table and back one chair. In that moment, the room chilled and a mist formed. Tane's voice became intermittent. "The type of measurement…whether atomic or electromagnetic…strive to… creating effects upon…"

Was that pity on Rayn's face?

"Sensorium…to our minds…employ caution." Tane's voice floated away altogether.

Or was that sorrow in his eyes?

The classroom seemed to recede from view. Maybe she got up and left. Seerce found herself in her apartment.

Keeping busy should banish her devastation, right? Physics in the morning, study in the afternoon, handball, dinner, more study, sleep. Do all that again tomorrow. But she had stopped sleeping. She could not focus. What she could do was what she did now, sit on her divan wrapped in a blanket, sip hot tea, and empathize with the sky as it cried its myriad of tears. She could dissect every nuance of every thought she and Rayn had ever sent to one another, stacking clues into neat piles of evidence for any argument she wished to make about why he dropped her.

He was a womanizer. His history supported that. Weak, unreliable, a reed blowing in the wind, incapable of commitment to anyone. A loner happy with his oud and his solitude and his spirits in a carafe. Having accepted her maidenhood, he was finished with her.

Alternately, she judged herself for failing him. She knew how happy he had been in Basra. He would have gone home with her forever, if she had asked this of him. She was selfish, bent on her own accomplishments, never quite willing to relinquish Aaron, and he knew it. She seduced him, breaking the intimacy rule for students, turning from her true purpose, and bringing about this horrible situation. It was delusion to think that they would ever balance being priests and lovers.

The wheel of blame and consequences spun in her mind. Occasionally she would doze off into a light sleep that only partially relieved her. She lay upon the cushions and washed herself away in the rivulets of rain that ran down the windows of her grey world, succumbing to a fog that hid her from her life and losses.

*

Voices startled her awake. Kessa and a young woman she had never met came into view as Seerce struggled to orient herself. Her head ached dully, but the pain in her heart was much worse. She closed her eyes again.

"Seerce!" Kessa shouted. "You need to sit up and eat something. You look awful. You missed class altogether today."

"I did?" she asked weakly.

"Hi, honey. I am Laela. We brought you soup. Obviously, you are in a bad way."

Seerce peered out of one eye to see bright copper hair cascading in loose waves over Laela's shoulders. Such rich coloring, she thought. Murmuring, she replied, "I am not hungry."

"Well, we have a choice for you then, dearie," Kessa pronounced. "Eat something or we will arrange a room for you at the Healing Temple. That is why Laela came with me. If you need that, you shall have it."

"No, please, I will try to eat."

They helped her sit up, rearranging her pillows and blankets around and over her. Laela collected the empty mugs from her low table, taking them to the kitchenette and running water to wash them. "Can you balance the tray on your lap or do you want me to feed you?" Kessa asked.

"I am not a baby."

"I beg to differ, sweet girl. You are a big, neglected baby in need of some tender loving care."

Laela returned with a warm wet cloth and washed Seerce's hands and face. "I diagnose a broken heart," she said, "worst case I have seen in a while." Seerce cracked a smile in spite of herself. "You are a pretty baby, too. Fear not, there are a million men who want you, and likely quite a few women, if you gave them a chance."

Seerce had not laughed for an eternity, but a titter escaped her. "I should try women."

"We have friends," said Kessa.

"We will get you through this," Laela said assuringly. "Everyone loses at love one time or another, but the first time is always the worst. You had not grieved your grandfather's passing before this happened."

Seerce put her spoon in her bowl and started to cry.

"There is nothing wrong with tears," Laela soothed, taking a soft kerchief from her pocket and handing it to Seerce. "You need to cry buckets."

"I do not want to hurt like this," she whispered, dabbing at her cheeks.

The two women sat down in the chairs. Laela told her softly, "There is help for your hurt. But you still have to reckon with your losses. It is a process and it takes a long time, maybe a year to heal so much grief."

"I do not have a year," Seerce moaned. "I have to study and work hard to graduate with Kessa next spring."

Her classmate addressed her sternly. "The only one who expects you to do all that is you. You need help with your circumstance and you have options. Laela can arrange for a healer to see you. Cyan would give you a suggestion, something to help you think and concentrate. You might go home for a while. Maybe you need to do all three."

Sure that Kessa had spoken with Cyan, Seerce replied angrily, "Whose side are you on?"

Raising her voice, Kessa emphasized, "Yours! You need help. All of us want to help!"

Seerce thought this through, as best her muddled mind could. She stated truthfully, "I do not know what I should do."

"Sleep on it," Laela suggested.

If only I could sleep, thought Seerce.

"Meet me for breakfast in the morning and tell me what you choose," Kessa directed.

"Or else what?" Seerce shot back.

"Cyan will call you to his office and send you home."

The women waited silently while Seerce finished spooning the soup. Laela took the bowl and bid her the light of healing. Kessa kissed her on her forehead, saying sweetly, "See you in the morning."

*

She did not really see Rayn around the campus anymore. By whatever spell Cyan had cast, Seerce scarcely noticed him, even in class. "It is quite strange," she told Kessa one morning, "like looking right through him." She found she could compartmentalize her grief during the course of her long days. It never left her, but temporarily it could be disregarded. She cried herself to sleep most nights, but at least she slept—for long periods, actually, which Laela assured her was normal and helpful.

The rose pendant bothered her. She did not want it on her person or within sight or reach. There were moments when she thought to fling it into the cold sea, but not all of her was ready to part with it or him. So she removed the crystalline tales of romance from their small rosewood box and set the pendant inside, proceeding to bury it beneath extra blankets in her closet. Laela said that was a proper ritual, if it brought her peace. She warned Seerce about the part of anger in grief, eventually to rear its ugly head. "It may be prolonged," she warned. "Give some thought to how you will discharge your rage, because you are likely to experience a double dose. Strenuous exercise helps."

Seerce had no energy for handball. She ate dinner alone in her apartment and went to bed early.

*

Following Tane's subject, the initiates were treated to Rika's history of the Order of the Sun. The chair was incredulous to find that neither the first years nor the second years knew the origins of the Cenon Project. So she spent a session filling them in, bundled up in a winter robe, a shabby wool coat, and a heavy shawl over her head, all in clashing colors.

"This is a story," she remarked, "still told in the halls of the University. Two hundred years ago, Cenon and Maoran were initiates like yourselves, but rivals from the day they met. Both excelled in physics. Both were Mu, Cenon with some creative ideas about studying the future of civilization, and Maoran convinced that the enhancement of Earth's subtle energy fields was a planet-friendly method to power society."

Seerce's ears perked up.

Rika continued, "As Cenon worked on his biography, he endeavored to identify his own future lives, documenting several in considerable detail. Intrigued by this innovation, his professor requested other students under his supervision to attempt the same. Several were successful. Later the Council of Exemplars accepted Cenon's proposal to study all future lives reported by initiates over a twenty-year period, allowing him to collect data from volunteer subjects among priests of the Order as they sought their future lives.

"Meanwhile, Maoran delved deeply into his examination of what the early Mu called 'the wind through Earth.' He proved that electromagnetic energy moves constantly through the body of the planet. His radical proposal was to amplify that energy and use naturally-occurring properties to broadcast it from one place to another."

Thank you, Rika, for these clues, thought Seerce.

"After Maoran's presentation at a University conference, Cenon took the podium to deliver his harsh rebuttal. Calling his rival's proposed technology an assault upon the planet, Cenon cited his own research: Future times bear no resemblance to that of the present or the past. His resounding conclusion was that humankind would shortly be trapped in a long period of primitivity, never to regain the advanced state of Altean civilization. This, he asserted, would be the result of implementing Maoran's technology."

Seerce was stunned. Sootchie reacted, saying, "There was no reason in those early stages to allege cause and effect! Those were two passionate physicists espousing unrelated theories!"

"But their arguments split the Order in two," Rika explained. "To some degree the divide persists even today."

It was bold of the chair to be so candid, thought Seerce, herself a witness to some sort of sharp division among the leadership of Oceanus.

Tuura spoke. "We know Cenon's research became the cornerstone of the Cenon project. What happened with Maoran's?"

Rika seemed to choose her words carefully. "This scrapping back and forth, debates during conferences, confrontations in the halls of academia, all this went on for another decade. Until one day Maoran, his associates, and all of their research disappeared from the Physics department in Zanata."

"Disappeared?" chorused several voices.

"Yes," Rika confirmed, "surfacing later as a department of research and development within the Altean Energy Authority. Whereas once there had been certain cooperative ventures between scientists of the Order and the Ryk, there have been none since. Unfortunately that divide persists. You should be aware."

After class Sootchie and Seerce went directly to the Hall of Records. "I will search the history of the Mu," he proposed, "if you will look in the physics files for kemic energy. I believe that is what early Altean scientists called the wind through Earth."

Seerce replied, "I have always wondered how the magnetism of the core rises through solid layers to become the magnetic poles and the atmosphere's protective shield."

"Let us find out," Sootchie told her. Busy at their task for two decans, both deposited information into their slender Hall crystals. Over dinner they compared notes.

Sootchie explained, "The old legends speak of forces which flow from the shadowed side of the planet to the sunlit side, toward the equator at night and toward the magnetic poles during the day. The Mu used it to propel their boats when their sails were windless."

"So they encountered it as a force within or over the seas," Seerce ventured. "I learned that early Altean scientists were able to measure low-voltage current traveling through land masses. Kemic energy was sufficient in places to create what they called 'Earth batteries.' They knew it to be directional with diurnal characteristics, having a daily cycle as you describe."

"What is an Earth battery?" asked Sootchie.

Seerce told him, "A pair of electrodes made of dissimilar metals, for instance, one of iron and the other copper. These are buried in the soil or immersed in the sea. Placed far apart, they tap kemic energy, which is low voltage. Aaron had mentioned once that the air barges are powered by enhancing a natural current. This must be what he meant.

"What do you know of the crystalline properties of Earth's mantle?" Seerce inquired. "Might a pressured and heated state allow for the transmission of electromagnetic energy?" She wished with all her might she could tell Sootchie about the undersea complex.

He replied, "I know that when atoms of magnesium oxide are forced together under high pressure, some of them collapse, freeing electrons to move through its crystalline structure. Mag oxide has similar properties to iron oxide and silicates, which make up Earth's crust and mantle. It is reasonable to think it is the mantle which moves natural energy upward. How else would kemic energy arise?"

"My thinking exactly," Seerce told him. It was not too far-fetched, she realized, to harvest energy from deeper Earth, nor to transmit it through the mantle. "Maoran was on to something."

"What a loss to the Order, a mind like that," rued Sootchie. "I wonder what Altea made of his research?"

Seerce had to leave that rhetorical question to hang in the air.

*

There were few assignments for Rika's class. More time on her hands added to Seerce's growing restlessness. As her tears dried up, irritability took root. She jogged in the cold rain and slammed balls around the handball courts alone, missing Aaron desperately.

If ever he returned to his studies, it would be no time soon. His clan would struggle to build anything in the dead of winter, needing all their fight to find food and stay warm. At best he might return next year, after a season of rebuilding, to make up his work and perhaps take his vows with her class. One early afternoon she sent her remote vision to Eyre. It might make a difference to him that she and Rayn were no more.

The snow was deep, with just a few paths cleared by shovels and manual labor, as she observed groups of people doing. Men walked baskets of fish up the steep trail from the pier. Smoke from chimney fires hung over rooftops. A few new dwellings had been erected since Seerce's last visit, windowless, likely for lack of materials.

From a ramshackle hut she noticed several young men emerge, followed by a girl with long fiery-red hair. Seerce moved her vision in closer, to see her reach for the arm of one of the men, these two hurrying away down a path of icy boot prints, around a snowdrift, out of sight from those on the stoop of the hut. Wavy auburn hair spilled from beneath the man's dark felt hat. Seerce redirected her vision to face the two. The low brim kept his eyes in shadow, but the smile she knew as he stopped to take the girl in his arms and kiss her tenderly. They stayed wrapped up in each other's arms until she took off running and laughing, slipping repeatedly, managing not to fall. He chased after her until she gave herself up and rejoined him in a more passionate embrace.

Seerce did not want to know where they went or what they did. She closed her remote vision and opened her eyes to her sitting room. Getting up, she sat back down and burst into tears.

*

Standing in front of his desk, Seerce told Cyan emphatically, "I am going home, as soon as Barlas finds me passage!" Furious that he had failed to coax Aaron back to the Temple, if indeed he had tried, it was Cyan who ruined her life by sending Rayn away for so long. She blamed all the exemplars for the schism that bound the Oceanus investigation. With Anakron dead she had no defender and no purpose here.

In Basra she had a role to fulfill. Her grandmother deserved rest in her old age and Seerce had best take it on before Petraea departed. She should be helping her mother with daily life, restoring her father's faith in her, and being a big sister to her brothers. The stone enclave of Orion would embrace her once again and there she would be safe and loved.

Looking profoundly dismayed, Cyan answered, "I approve your request, of course. But I much prefer that you stay. Tell me what I can do."

"Nothing!" she shouted, storming out.

Orion was a pleasant cocoon. Here turmoil was absent. Life was routine, with none of the obstacles that loomed at the Temple. Plenty of mindless work needed doing, picking and packing, sweeping and hosing, loading pallets aboard the air barge and taking them off when Papa and Sirdar came home.

Seerce took the assignments no one wanted and the most physical of the chores: scrubbing down the kitchen, cleaning out the storage rooms, sweeping up buckets of sand that trickled into the landing bay. One of the more exacting tasks was hand-pollination, for there were no insects belowground, nor was there disease, crop failure, or damage from weather. Yields were high, for long had the clan experimented to maximize their harvests.

Horticulture was accomplished in wide chambers with high ceilings, hewn from bedrock after the rivers fell. Orion compound was situated along one, cisterns and pumps providing water for the growing operation and daily needs of the residents. Substituting for daylight were glowing crystals suspended horizontally from high ceilings, powered by the solar array at the surface. Fans made breezes that rustled date palms and trellised vines. Each chamber maintained an ideal temperature and humidity for the garden it housed.

As a small child, Seerce had hid herself between pots of bushes and beneath tables of hydroponic troughs. She pulled her favorite purple carrots for dinner and plucked ripe berries that stained her fingers. Her aunts let her pick baobab and black plums and sour tamarind, if they were ripe, but ube was her favorite. In the afternoon, overhead sprayers in the subtropical garden made rain showers, through which she would run.

Now as she set up to pollinate cucumbers in the vegetable garden, Seerce recalled her first lesson on the subject, laughing out loud. Cousin Shad had tried to pass off his most tedious chore to her. Several years older than she, he was not a patient teacher, but they had an alliance of sorts as the youngest in the compound.

Showing her the differences between male and female flowers, he ignored her comments about female superiority. As he demonstrated that there was enough pollen in any one male flower to accommodate three females, she had wrinkled her nose in disgust, saying to him, *That is typical male behavior, is it not?* He had reached over to smear his flower's pollen down the length of Seerce's nose. So she picked up a nozzle and sprayed him until he was soaked. The ensuing water fight dashed all the hopes of male flowers that day.

*

The matriarch judged that her granddaughter would need at least two years of apprenticeship, including midwifery, before she was ready to assume duties of the clan's priesthood. Seerce cringed. Seeing that, Petraea suggested, *For now, just be my granddaughter. We will take up the rest eventually.*

Angry then with Petraea, Seerce stormed off to the temperate garden and threw a couple of cracked clay pots against a stone wall. She rather liked the effect, so she went in search of all the broken and chipped pots and trays, stacked in and around all the gardens, and destroyed them in like manner. The shards she pummeled with a mallet and crumbs she swept up and dumped down the disposal chutes, where detritus found its way to a compost pit. Briefly she felt better.

While the women prepared the evening meal, Seerce went aboveground at sunset to sweep shifting sand from the platform around Orion's escape hatch. If her father was away trading, she carried up chairs so she and her mother might breathe fresh air after dinner, before the desert cooled too drastically. Sitting with cups of mulled wine, together they examined the depths of their lives and loves and losses, while Seerce watched the evening star emerge, followed by the wide swath of the galaxy and moonlight frosting the crests of the dunes.

Portia had suffered a few failed romances, too. One evening, Seerce asked how she had come to accept her confinement, when she had lived so freely in Tunise and accomplished so much on behalf of the region's farmers. She considered the question carefully. In moments like this, she forgot to close her eyes, turning her absent gaze toward Seerce, as if she could see her. One lid drooped. One eye appeared to focus while the other wandered. It seemed her mother both saw her and looked past her.

"While all of you kept my body alive, my spirit roamed. I remember closed doors along a hallway, a brilliant light at one end and a dark abyss at the other. Not immediately did I realize those doors could be opened. At first I floated toward the light, but I sensed finality there, beautiful and hypnotic though it was. So I crept back to the abyss and peered over its edge, afraid of falling, looking for a way through a tangle of brambles in darkness, trying to judge how far down I would have to go to escape. I could not tell.

"I chastised myself, Seerce, for being away when you were young, envious that Aunt Ena cared for you and taught you your lessons. Suddenly a door opened and I saw you at the kitchen table here in Orion, puzzling over something in your study crystal. I sat down to listen to all the little things you would have told me had I been here with you, everything a daughter says to her mother."

"Mama, I sat with you part of every day when you were motionless on your cot. Your healer instructed us to tell you everything we would if you were conscious. Maybe you heard me!" Seerce marveled.

"I am sure I did," Portia replied. "In my vision, I kissed your cheek and you handed me one of your crystals, telling me it would light the darkness. I went out with it and that door closed behind me. A different door opened as I thought of each of you: your father, Petraea, my sister, Ena, and Anakron. Each of you gave me something for my journey.

"Eventually I felt brave enough to go down the narrow path into the abyss, with your crystal beacon and a rope, sturdy shoes, a scythe, a cloak, all the things each of you gave me. Hope was Anakron's gift. I found my way back, child. When I awoke, it was

215

acceptable to me that my eyes could not see, for certainly my spirit did. I had everything I needed."

*

Seerce chased her little brothers through the halls of the compound, playing hide-and-seek with them in the gardens, and tickling whomever she could catch. Miniatures of their father, one would never guess that fair Portia was their mother. Josef was all boy while Loren was quieter and introspective, reminding Seerce of Petraea. At bedtime she would tell them something of the greatest city on Earth, sending them her pictures of the neighborhoods, the Autark's palace, and the roiling sea. She found the crystal she had read over and over as a child about the legends of the Mu. Those tales captivated the boys.

Her father asked her nothing, but as she helped him scrub the deck of the barge one day, he remarked: *A man who believed in himself would never walk away from the woman you are. Rayn does not see himself as your equal.*

How do you know this, Papa?

He spoke only of you, never of his own pursuits.

But he is a gifted man, Seerce countered. *You saw him play his instrument. He speaks more languages than I knew there were.*

All that and more counts as long as he knows his own worth. That is something a man must teach himself. It is nothing you can do for him. Narad stepped off the barge, never speaking on that subject again.

On another evening, not long after Seerce went to bed, Narad came to her door. *Come with me, daughter,* he beckoned. *The sky has changed and we do not know what to make of it.*

She donned her robe and slippers, following him to the landing bay. Its petals were open and a strange red light reflected in the windows of the barge's helm. They had just arrived home from Tunise, and Sirdar remained at the controls. As her father had done when she was a child, he took her hand to climb the few steps to the deck. *Take her up,* he told Sirdar. With a small vibration, the air barge rose to clear the bay. Her uncle set it to hover and came out to join them. In the northeastern sky there hung a shimmering curtain of red.

What is it, Seerce? Papa asked.

The aurora, Papa, the light of the goddess of dawn. It has shown itself lately around Altea, but from an odd direction. When the sun erupts with energy, its emanations are caught in the magnetic field that surrounds Earth. It is unusual to see the lights at Altea's latitude and I have never heard an account of its appearance this close to the equator, although tonight it shows in its proper direction.

We have lived long lives here, Sirdar commented, *our kindred before us. No one speaks of this. Something Altea does, I suppose?*

Seerce replied, *That is my opinion.*

Sailors speak of odd metallic spires in places along the coastline, he added. *No one knows what they do.*

Seerce inquired, *Where, Uncle?*

Majorka, Palermo, Pylos, he replied. *None along the southern shores yet.*

Is it dangerous, this red light? Narad asked.

Of itself, no, Seerce replied. *The red glow is caused by electrons interacting with oxygen high up in the atmosphere. In the northern realms near the magnetic pole, the light shows green or blue, where energy interacts with oxygen lower in the atmosphere or with nitrogen. Something changes the magnetosphere.* She stopped at that. They watched awhile longer until the curtains parted and the red glow faded away.

It was late before Seerce fell asleep. During Khubradan she had been seeing visions, seas of rage washing over ports and buildings crumbling in quakes. She discussed these with Petraea, who gave her a cryptic comment: *The degree of difficulty is equivalent to the necessity of your task.*

When the crystal in her bedchamber began to glow with the artificial light of dawn, Seerce awoke from a dream of Anakron, his message quite clear: "That you seem to walk alone is illusion, for I walk with you."

When Seerce made her announcement, it surprised no one. Upon the next new moon, she would return to the Temple.

CHAPTER 14

Cyan met Seerce's boat at the Port of Altea. He seemed altogether a different person, animated and smiling. She had rehearsed her formal request for readmission, but there was no opportunity to deliver it. He recounted lecture topics he had covered in her absence, reciting her classmates' questions verbatim, his responses, and a summary of each group discussion. He made a point of telling her that Sava's Oceanus summaries were far less comprehensive than those Seerce once provided. The second years had taken their vows in her absence. Tuura and Isla remained with Cenon, Ell with Administration, and Sootchie with Geology in Zanata. No mention was made of Aaron.

A solitary ride on a water taxi would have provided Seerce an opportunity to revel in the vistas of sea and sky and mountain, to regard her future as a priest of the Order, to recommit herself to Temple life. But Cyan chattered on, saying her classmates missed her opinions and her telling expressions, and he missed her competitive handball.

They were close to the Healing Temple before Cyan registered Seerce's silence. Then his mask of neutrality took his features. "We must plan for catching up your studies."

"Perhaps tomorrow, Exemplar?" she requested. "I left Tunise early yesterday and slept poorly last night on the ship. It has been a long two days."

"Of course," he replied. "I will expect you in class tomorrow and in my office at the seventh decan."

"Thank you, sir, for your kind attention to my return," she replied, taking her travel bag from him at Barlas's office. "I wish you a pleasant evening." With that, she proceeded alone to her apartment.

*

Cyan added two regular private sessions with him, in addition to regular consultation for beginning work on her biography. Seerce succeeded handily at the assigned exercises for envisioning other of her existences in Earth's plane. Perhaps by her active imagination, scenarios showed themselves readily. Soon she began to experience the odd duality of being both viewer and subject, as in a lucid dream, when one knows she dreams even as she participates in the drama.

Placing in her response crystal a vivid recollection of a male incarnation, she had experienced particularly strong feelings and urges foreign to her as a female. Cyan took great interest in this report. "Where on the planet were you, standing in warm turquoise water, spearing fish?" he asked.

"I have no idea," she told him. "I have never heard such a place described, nor have I viewed in crystals such splendid environs. It must have been a tropical locale. I felt crunchy seashells in the sand beneath my calloused feet, the balance of a bamboo spear in my hand as the water lapped about me, the slippery scales of the fish I tossed toward the beach. All of it I perceived so intensely, as though this me"—she gestured with a sweep of her hand down the length of her person—"experienced it."

"It may have been in the time of the Mu," Cyan ventured. "Say more about what you saw."

"The beach was crescent-shaped, of fine pale sand sparkling in the sun. Beyond was dense foliage, some with broad bright flowers, an occasional tall tree trunk with spiked leaves spilling from its top. A narrow path led through the entanglement to our dwelling. The passage was familiar to me, as we traveled it daily to gather food."

"Was someone with you?" Cyan asked.

"My woman," Seerce said, her face growing hot, "my companion. When I looked back to shore, where she cleaned the fish that I threw her way, I knew affection for her. She crouched in shallow water, gutting and rinsing them, tossing them into baskets, one for each of us to carry. When she missed, I teased her. When I threw too far, she scolded me. We laughed."

"You loved her," Cyan stated.

Seerce did recognize a profound love in the heart of that man for that woman, perhaps in the way Rayn had loved her, a male kind of love, more physical, more lustful, and more protective. The subtleties were hers to treasure, nothing to be shared with Cyan. "Yes," she responded.

"Describe her, please."

Why did this vision of hers intrigue him so? She closed her eyes to recall the woman more clearly. "Her arms were muscular, for she knew lifting and heavy work. She was slender with an appealing figure, near the age I am now."

A woven hat had shielded her eyes and thick, ebony hair hung in braids over her bare breasts, her nipples wide and dark-colored. Full lips were coated with something that made them shine in the sunlight, her teeth large and perfect, and her smile radiant. She sang to herself and smiled shyly when she caught her mate's eye. But Seerce voiced none of that.

"Her color was richly brown and there was a glow to her complexion. It was as though the sun lived in her. That is what I would tell her, that is what I thought when I looked upon her." Seerce opened her eyes.

"And how did you see your male self?"

"His skin was a deeper shade than hers, his hands broad and his arms sinewy as he plunged for fish and pulled them from the spear's point. I do not think he knew his own face. Perhaps he had never seen it."

"What did these people do after fishing?" Cyan asked.

Annoyed by his prying, Seerce told him, "I was so amazed to be male that I came out of the experience!"

There was sensuality to the silken water as it lapped about his upper thighs. His loin cloth rhythmically draped and released his male member as he lunged and stood, bent and straightened, stroked by the water. Watching the dipping of his lover's breasts in and out of the sea caused him to remember the taste of her salty skin. He wanted to take her now, here in the shallow water, as he had that morning when they awoke. But he should be gentle with her for they were newly joined. He applied his ferocity to the fish.

Cyan looked disappointed. "Endeavor to take yourself forward in that life. Discover what you can about that relationship, children you may have had, and what you learned."

"Why?" Seerce asked defiantly. "The assignment is to *identify* other existences, is it not? This glimpse is a stunning discovery for me, to know that I have been male, lived primitively, supremely content with my life, as simple as it was."

"Surely you want to know more about your maleness and how it influences your female being. Spirit is androgynous, of course, for duality is an experience of this dimension. But it is one of the unique advantages of physicality, to know both."

"What do you know of your feminine influence?" she questioned.

"There was at least one experience as a woman." He did not elaborate.

"Were you also required to identify all your past and future incarnations for your biography?"

"I endeavored," he replied evasively, "as we all do. Greater Mind allows access to what benefits us and shields us from the rest. It is doubtful any of us see all the paths our souls take."

"Why, Exemplar?"

"It is the Greater Mind which incorporates lessons learned. We are not that."

"Then why conduct this investigation at all?" she challenged. "There might be good reasons not to know some of our existences."

"To wear the Crystal of the Sun, Seerce, you must understand the true purpose of your current life, where your tendencies are rooted, the threads that weave your relationships, and why you are the way you are. Priests must acknowledge our influences and lay to rest any that interfere with our work."

"What is it, Exemplar, that I must confirm for you? You dig for something you want me to reveal."

She knew she touched a nerve. He turned his gaze away from her. "This process is for your betterment and nothing to do with me. That will be all for today."

*

"You are hard on him," Kessa judged. She and Seerce were early to class the next day. "Cyan has one foot in a realm beyond ours. He wants to impart what he knows before he crosses the boundary one last time."

"Did he tell you that?" Seerce sniggered.

"No, but that is what the staff in Tibisay said of him. He has evolved differently and is probably quite lonely. One of a kind, I imagine."

"I think he wants to see himself somewhere in my other lives, hoping he has some deep and ancient connection to me."

"Maybe he owes you something," Kessa remarked, "or vice versa."

"I doubt it."

"You cannot see what you will not."

Seerce disregarded that, asking, "Have you male incarnations?"

"Yes. Soldier, bandit, sailor, farmer, husband, son, father, but I have not found another life as a woman."

"Maybe you are female for the first time."

"Perhaps. I should ask Cyan about that."

"If you take over my extra sessions, Kessa, you may ask him hundreds of questions on every subject."

"I do not need to see *that* much of him."

"Neither do I," said Seerce, laughing just as Cyan came through the classroom door. His hair was tousled and there was a distracted look about him, most unusual. Once Jair and Tavia came in, Cyan began. Rayn was absent, but Seerce had no concern for that.

"As you seek to know other incarnations," he told them, "consider your most conflicted relationships. Animosity may be rooted in another existence. A struggle between you remains a stumbling block for one or both. For example, a cruel partner may, in another life, take a parental role with you. As a child, one perhaps has little choice but to submit, but in adulthood you may be able to forge a different sort of relationship. Or, you might choose to rebel against every authority figure, as your Greater Mind digs deeply into the differences between controlling and being controlled.

"If in some life you abandoned someone, you may be abandoned in another, to learn that dichotomy. Two may often come together, out of love or out of hate, trading roles as husband and wife, brother and sister, teacher and student. Contention persists until there is forgiveness and release." As he spoke, his eyes went to the window, for the drapes were open to a courtyard in bloom.

"Endeavor to remember that the ones you see in your visions are aspects of your Greater Self. They are not you, but rather part of a constellation, like cousins perhaps, but sometimes little more than strangers. Look from the perspective of lessons learned and move on to accomplish what you as your present self has come to do. You are dismissed early to examine a conflicted relationship. I shall be in my office this afternoon if you require assistance."

Seerce went to get her light cloak, for as yet there was a nip in the morning air of spring. The sun promised a pleasant afternoon. Along the seawall to the north she would consider this latest assignment. But for two fishers perched on boulders along the way, the area was deserted. Stepping carefully from rock to rock down a wide portion of the seawall, Seerce found a sunny perch sheltered from the southerly breeze. The tide was out and the waves lapped gently below. Two shades of blue filled her vision, one still, the other in perpetual motion.

Her thoughts came to Aaron, their up-and-down relationship a blend of competitive siblings and shipmates thrown together on a perilous journey. Something about him was as comfortable as her slippers. He grated on her nerves, of course, the way he assumed that she was his, provoking defense of her precious autonomy. But he was also the genius by whom she learned the secrets of their times. Seeing him with that redhead had caused her the only jealousy she had ever tasted.

Taking her cloak from her shoulders, for it was warm enough on these dark rocks, she rolled it up and placed it between her head and the boulder behind her. Leaning back, Seerce summoned insight into what rooted their connection. Breathing evenly and slowly for quite a while, waiting for pictures to come to her mind, she saw nothing and felt nothing. By the tangles between them, she expected to find history. No one else read her thoughts, thank the Goddess. Surely that alone represented a soul-level connection.

Perhaps she tried too hard. She stood up and stretched, then sat down and repeated the exercise, this time holding her father in mind. Seerce was much more like her mother, but Papa was hardly a foe. Their battles were about leaving Basra, when she wanted to visit her mother at the port, attend school there, or study in Altea. But never had she doubted his devotion to her. Immediately a vision assembled itself.

Silence the Echo

Here was a young girl on the verge of adolescence, lanky, dirty, picking berries along a river bank. Hungry, she ate as many as she dropped into the sling tied at her shoulder, her fingers purple and sticky. Crouching at a little creek she rinsed her hands. The peaceful sounds of leaves stirring in the breeze and the muted tumble of a river were shattered by an animal's roar. The girl heard the screams of a young child and the snapping and breaking of branches. Turning toward the sounds, she saw a young boy crash through the underbrush, running so fast that he tripped at the last and went over the bank into the rock-strewn river. A black bear emerged at the very spot, two cubs close behind her. While the little ones clambered up a tree, their mother patrolled the bank.

Without hesitation, the girl emptied her cache of berries onto the bank, hoping Mama Bear would stop for the snack. Returning quickly to the little creek, she waded in barefoot, making her way carefully over slick gravel out into the river, where the rush was fast and cold and numbing. Carefully she moved from rock to rock toward the center.

The boy had managed to wrap his arms around a small boulder. She called to him and waved. He seemed to acknowledge her with a nod of his head. Slowly she moved around and over snags, testing for the strength of submerged debris. Finding a loose, slender tree branch of a useful length, she tied her sling to the thick end and waded nearer to the child, working to keep her balance in the oncoming current, extending the branch to him. He slipped his head and one arm through the pelt to hold the branch tightly. Bleeding from cuts and scratches, the cold river must have stung him terribly.

Guiding him toward her, she was finally able to pull him up under his arms, landing him on her hip. He shivered violently, his fingers and lips blue-tinged, clinging to her, eyes wild with fear. She untied the precious pelt and rung it out. Carefully she walked him over river rock using the branch as a staff to keep her balance. Setting him down on a log, she wrapped and tied the pelt around a bleeding gash in his upper thigh. Then she rubbed his arms and chest and back briskly.

After they rested briefly, she told him, "You have to climb now. You are too heavy to carry." She did not know if he understood her language, so she pulled him to his feet, keeping hold of one hand. Clinging to roots and rock outcroppings, they scaled the bank opposite where both had been previously. As they reached the top, the scene evaporated.

Seerce was awestruck. Again it was that odd experience of being herself and this young girl, the watcher and the subject. The river felt like icy shards poking her flesh, the child slippery and heavy. In a flash of insight and with deep certainty, she recognized her father's spirit in that little boy.

Now she understood why Narad objected so strongly to her leaving Basra. This time around he wanted only to protect her from a dangerous world.

*

It was easy to trace the bonds of love. Both Seerce and her great-great-grandmother Seah had been priests of the Order in early Altean times, when the scattered islands were a contiguous continent, when the duty of priests was to observe the night sky from stone circles, keep the calendar, and celebrate the cycles of Earth. Cyan told her that her rank at induction would reflect her prior service to the Order, meeting one of the requirements for elevation to exemplar.

"You must have served the Order previously," she gathered.

"I was twice a Mu priest, so I was accorded credit," Cyan affirmed. "Tell me, is it Seah's voice you have sometimes heard?"

"It is," Seerce replied, quite sure of it.

"You are fortunate to retain such a strong connection."

"I am fortunate in many ways. I wonder if Anakron's spirit knew us both in that life. Perhaps that is why he and I came together this time."

"You must do your own work to identify your connections to Anakron," he replied, "if indeed you have any."

"He is my grandfather, Cyan."

"He was your grandmother's paramour."

His reaction puzzled her. Likely he envied the rich life Petrae lived. Poor thing, she thought, ever subject to his odd personality.

*

Just prior to the summer solstice, as she endeavored to finish her biography, this much was apparent—it was difficult to pinpoint where and when in Earth's history other of her existences occurred. Seerce wondered if Priest Cenon's suppositions were any more than his own delusions. She dared share this heresy only with Jair as they ate dinner. "Either Cenonites know something we do not or they decline to admit the obvious," she pronounced.

"It is fortunate you and I pursue science. I just have to scratch my head about this biography business." Jair had struggled mightily to turn up two incarnations with very little detail. "Now we have to look at one of our deaths. Gruesome," he judged.

This was the last of the incarnational exercises to be accomplished. Cyan had given them a procedure that morning, if anyone wished to attempt it alone. He recommended his assistance in a private session, of course, which Seerce was loath to do.

"I shall help you, if you like," she volunteered. "I was raised to see death as part of life. The departures I have attended have been peaceful transitions."

Jair accepted. "You save me a torturous encounter with Cyan. Your place?"

"Yes. Then we shall brew some exquisite tea I brought from home, to celebrate our lives among the living."

Reclining on Seerce's divan, a vision came slowly to Jair. Afterward he recounted watching an elder man sleep, aware that this aspect was dreaming, though Jair also experienced the dream. The spirit of this elder's wife, who had predeceased him, begged him to stay with her and a group of souls who seemed familiar. Jair reported, "He simply chose not to go back to his body."

"That was an easy way out!" Seerce exclaimed, relieved for her squeamish friend.

"Not scary at all," he agreed, "just a change of focus, like looking through another facet of a prism. Where he went, his new place in the universe…there are no words to describe it. But willingly he left his body behind."

"My grandmother says it is much easier to die than to be born," Seerce told him. Jair moved to a chair and she reclined on the divan with a blanket over her, for she tended to shiver in trance states, not because she was cold, but due to a sensitive nervous system, a trait common to empaths.

"Do you want me to say anything?" Jair asked her.

"No," Seerce replied. "I shall give myself the instruction. Just call my name if I am out too long." She moved readily into the experience, to the same jungle island she had seen before, but this time near a hut built on stilts. Largely open to the air, its roof was woven of dry fronds tied with reeds. The young man she had once been chipped a shiny black stone with a larger rock, crafting a new spear tip. Periodically he stood up from the shade where he squatted to examine the edges in sunlight. His woman was up in the hut, working a basket with strips of bark, singing softly. Heavy with child, her sarong was tied beneath swollen breasts over the top of her bulging abdomen.

He stood up once more only to feel something rip his chest. The stones fell from his hands as he grabbed at the arrow that pierced him. As he fell backward, a circle of blackness closed rapidly around his vision. Distantly he heard his woman scream, as he seemed to drift up and out the top of his head. Hovering over a now-silent scene, his spirit saw her wailing over his body, pressing at the gushing wound with her sarong.

From a trail that led to the island's interior, there emerged a painted man, a chieftain's son with a bow in his hand. He grabbed the naked woman by her hair and forced her up that trail ahead of him. Seerce opened her eyes to the present, stunned. Jair knelt beside her. "Are you all right?" he asked with concern. "You cried out."

It was not the view of death that disturbed her, for she had given herself the instruction to watch with detachment. She perceived no pain. What concerned her was the welfare of the woman and her unborn child. Somehow Seerce knew the painted man made their two lives a living hell. The soul of the murderer she did not recognize, but she knew with certainty the spirit of the woman was an aspect of Rayn.

Jair and she had their celebratory tea. She told him only that she witnessed a sudden parting from what may have been a Mu existence. Never did Jair ask questions of a personal nature. They spoke instead of the red aurora she had seen over the MidTerra. Confirming that it was unknown in his homeland, he promised to look remotely around Palermo for an Altean-built spire, as mentioned by Seerce's uncle.

A little later, as she climbed into bed, Seerce reconsidered her vision. Had their love survived, she might have told Rayn. Finally Cyan had explained his absence from class. He had gone back to Misr to assist a crucial phase in the development of pictographic symbols. A priest there took responsibility for supervising his biography.

*

Seerce was days late returning from the summer solstice holiday in Basra, the four remaining initiates allowed to go home. Serial storms dealt significant blows to Altea, before rolling into the MidTerra Sea and disrupting marine traffic. But the interlude at home was pleasant, assisting her grandmother with the rituals and grounding herself in her people's devotion to the old ways.

Petraea counseled Seerce regarding her vision of death. "It is part of a pattern between your spirit and Rayn's, and though you think he is gone from you, I doubt that is the case. The universe went to great lengths to draw you together this time from homelands far removed. You created a life between you then, so your separation from him and the child must be mended. The bond between you is significant."

Seerce did not know how she should feel about that. "What of the murderer?" she asked.

"The extinguishing of any flame invites a life of woe. You will come to see the killer for who he truly is, one who has no power over you." The matter remained between Seerce and her grandmother, for she did not record it in her biography.

*

Later in the summer, Rika took ill and Cyan stepped in to perform her duties. The four students were reassigned to their former internships, but Kessa would remain with the Cenon group at the Temple. She was greatly relieved.

"Does Oceanus actually need me?" Seerce asked Cyan. "I am sure Sava and Kieran have done a fine job without me." Kieran had worked for Rika in Zanata; he had become her designated researcher at the Temple.

"Believe me," said Cyan, "they will be happy to see you."

They did welcome her warmly, pleased to part with responsibility for committee reports and ruffled feathers.

"Nova is obtuse," Sava stated.

"We are observers, not children to be scolded," Kieran complained.

Seerce was impressed by the excellent logs Sava kept of surface conditions and shoreline measurements. Kieran's command of climatology was apparent in his analyses of oceanic-atmospheric relationships, but Seerce could find no observations of the complex on the ocean floor. She hoped these existed in someone's private possession, but asking Rika would have to wait, for she was too ill to receive visitors.

Little had been done to compare recent findings between the science departments. Seerce caught up that work, resuming her attendance at Oceanus proceedings. Cyan's presence in Rika's place enforced a rather orderly calm, making these more perfunctory and less raucous than she had known them. Nova was on her best behavior, but absent was the scientific debate from which Seerce had learned so much.

In a class meeting that Tavia and Rayn joined by crystal from Misr, Cyan told the five, "Your final tasks as candidates for the priesthood will be in three parts: an interview with Rika, an oral exam with Tane, and an exercise by which I shall evaluate your skills as an independent etheric traveler. All will be conducted individually where you are stationed." He put off scheduling the tests, however, awaiting Rika's recovery. Cyan shouldered the responsibility for leading the Order.

Absent any close oversight, Seerce took liberties with her role, visiting the undersea complex regularly, looking for clues to the strange technology being installed. A large round hub stood at center, topped by a huge dome, with odd tubular hallways connecting it to each domed turret. Small submersible vessels ferried technicians to the site and docked beneath the hub. She was there often enough to recognize that no one stayed longer than two decans and they had to wear breathing masks within the pressurized structures. Everything she observed she deposited in her private crystal.

Spending much of her time in the Hall of Records, Seerce delved into research regarding the mantle of Earth. Peridotite was the dominant rock of the upper mantle, dense and coarse-grained, formed by the cooling and solidification of magma. It consisted primarily of the minerals olivine and pyroxene, both prone to crystallization under heat and pressure. Olivine became the yellow-green crystal known as peridot, while pyroxene was dark grey, found occasionally on Earth's surface embedded in volcanic glass. Garnet was another common crystal, though its color was subject to the presence of iron, zinc, manganese, or aluminum. Estimates varied according to the era of the research, but the mantle was no less than sixty percent crystalline.

It was in midwinter that Cyan scheduled Seerce's final evaluations. By projection he accompanied her to the Gate of Persa. "I shall wait here," he said, directing the totem to take Seerce's spirit to an undisclosed location.

There she saw a tower of rooms and floors shifting, constantly rearranging itself. Multiple occupants were visible through vivid swirling colors. Seerce reminded herself that this was another dimension and she would not understand it. She need only find the means to accomplish the task Cyan had given her.

A loud boom in the otherwise silent vision frightened her. Intuiting the distraction as communication, she imagined producing an equally loud shriek. Visible waves of sound rolled away from her in all directions. Then the scene cleared and an image of her mother materialized. Portia held in one hand a large glowing emerald, so beautiful and alluring that Seerce felt she could not resist it, even as Portia sought to place it in her hand. But Cyan's instruction was to bring back a red jewel. *Change this to a ruby,* she requested of the image, *and I shall accept it.*

The jewel changed shape and form endlessly as Seerce watched in fascination, but it never turned red. Other beings appeared with items to show her and tales to impart via language she understood only partially. But all of this was unrelated to her task. She began to feel the gate tugging on her spirit. I must create the ruby, she thought.

Holding out her palm, she envisioned a red jewel of many facets, sparkling in the fog of color and light. She watched as molecules assembled themselves into a crystalline structure, deepest red and brilliant. Closing her hand around it, she fell forward into the mist. Momentarily her etheric self floated before the glowing totem of the gate. In one gauzy hand of her etheric body she held the ruby and in the other the emerald first offered by her mother. *Well done,* she heard Cyan say, though she could not see him. *You remembered your purpose, accomplished what was requested of you, and even obtained that which you desired. You are the creatrix of your universe.*

Silence the Echo

*

Rika remained in confinement at the Healing Temple, on an upper floor in a small room with a view of the southern ocean. Seerce was seated at a viewing window in the hall outside, seeing Rika propped up in bed beneath a skylight. Within this room she breathed a treated atmosphere fortified with oxygen. A glowing pad covered her chest, infusing a wavelength of healing light into her lung tissue. Her face was swollen and her lips pursed. There was effort to her breathing. But her eyes glowed with copper fire and her lively spirit.

Seerce! she exclaimed. *You cut your hair!*

Yes, Exemplar. Kessa insisted upon the shearing of my locks. Now shoulder-length, the curl arranged itself pleasingly. *I rather enjoy being regarded as an adult.* Seerce giggled. *Of lesser height than all you Alteans, but an adult, nevertheless.*

Laughing, Rika choked and then coughed spasmodically. A gowned healer wearing a face shield entered the chamber, standing by until she regained her breath. Then he gave her a sip from a cup.

No more jokes, Rika telepathed. *I am a wreck.*

I tax your rest, madame, Seerce told her. *Allow me to return later when you feel better.*

No, no, the elder insisted. *There is nothing to be gained by waiting. I know your character and I know your lineage. There is nothing you need to prove to me. I want only to know what you have learned of Altea's installations.*

The volcano station has not changed. Upon the ocean floor, the physical plant is complete and now its technical installation proceeds. I regret that I have determined nothing of its functionality.

What will you present to Tane in your final interview with him?

Frankly she told her, *He has posed a strange question, madame, and I have not decided how to approach it.*

Reveal to him your research and your observations. You need the physics team to help you.

I shall worry that my ordination is at risk.
The security of the Order is at risk if this problem is left to fester. I take responsibility for the directive I give you.

I will prepare my presentation accordingly, she replied, hoping Rika lived to defend that directive.

*

Seerce had never been to Tane's office. His looked like an exemplar's office should, she supposed, furnished in a contemporary style, with two upholstered chairs before his desk and a round table with simpler seating for a small meeting. His window faced east, looking out beyond greenery to the Healing Temple. A mobile of the solar system was suspended there, the planets and their moons spinning in minor air currents. Not a speck of dust upon it, his desk was inlaid with calculators and instruments, his communication crystal hovering up near the ceiling. Framed renderings of novae, galaxies, and glowing stellar clouds were placed precisely upon the walls. His surroundings embodied the order of creation.

Tane poured two steaming cups of tea from a side bar, setting one before the chair he meant for Seerce to take. As he placed his own cup and seated himself behind his desk, he repeated the exam question with no prelude. "What is your place in the universe?"

She took a moment to center herself with a slow, deep breath. "I am a messenger," she replied, "a portion of an entity that exists in multiple dimensions and is by its nature an explorer. My Greater Self is of a group of souls affiliated with the spirit of the planet upon which we dwell."

Tane set down his cup and sat upright in his chair.

"This is my message: A disruptive force has been set in motion by governors of the dominant civilization. Deep Earth energy surfaces beneath the dormant volcano of this island and at the south central floor of the Ocean of Atlas."

The exemplar's pupils widened and his dark eyes grew darker. An errant shock of hair fell over his forehead. He left it untouched.

SILENCE THE ECHO

"I have examined the frequency of geologic harbingers over the past three centuries. Evidence indicates a growing imbalance, which threatens the stability of Earth's crust." She took a crystal from a pouch at her waist and handed it to Tane. It was a duplicate of her own, made by Jair in the physics lab. "You may wish to review my observations and analyses."

She looked directly at his eyes. "You are a specialist in energy physics. My place in the universe is at your service, that we may counter this threat."

He was silent for a time, never taking his eyes from hers. "Congratulations," he said finally and simply. "You have passed the physics portion of your exam. I shall consider your submission and call you back here for further discussion."

*

In the Hall of Records, on the day of her induction, Seerce stood upon the full moon. "Every requirement has been met," Rika whispered, leaning on her cane, wheezing.

"The biography of Seerce of Basra has been recorded in this Hall," Cyan stated.

"We present you with the symbol of the Order of the Sun," Tane told her, "and welcome you to our number." He lifted the fine gold chain over her neatly confined hair, which Laela had smoothed and pinned in a twist at the back of her head. She touched the pale yellow rays of the Crystal of the Sun and closed her eyes, whereby she saw Anakron very clearly in her mind, beaming.

Is he here? Rika asked her privately.

Yes! she exclaimed.

Rika smiled, and Tane gave this pronouncement:

It is conferred upon Seerce of Basra,
a facet of the light and a navigator of the dimensions,
an incarnation of Niamh of Altea, Seventh Observer,
the title of Tenth Messenger of

the Order of the Sun.
Know her by the crystal she wears,
that of her predecessor,
Anakron of Altea, Ninth Messenger,
who attested at the decan
of his departure from this realm
that his spirit guides hers
in all its endeavors upon Earth.

Tears of joy welled in Seerce's eyes.

Rika told her that responsibility for Oceanus would be assumed by the Physics department and Tane would now supervise their work. This seemed to amuse him. Cyan's face was lit by his broadest smile ever. The three offered her hearty congratulations.

For all the twists and turns since Seerce had arrived at the Temple of Altea, it seemed to her now that she had plotted her course correctly.

PART II

CHAPTER 15

Despite the extra duties that Cyan performed during Rika's frequent absences, he made it a point to intercept Seerce daily. She would look up from her research in the Hall to see him emerge from the lift, sure to greet her personally with some minor news or question, sitting down for a short while to look up something in the records or taking his business to the conference room, leaving the door open and sitting where he could see her. She learned to take her meals at various times or arrange for company among her friends. Failing that, she would dash into the dining hall to fill a plate and hurry to her apartment. But often she found the roster of handball matches rearranged to reflect him as her next opponent.

Stepping out to the patio one day between the thunderstorms of springtime, Seerce escaped the close quarters of the Physics department. The atmosphere there was a bit intense at times, with the addition of the Oceanus three and Jair, though often he was away on the business of perfecting the crystal communication system. The four tenured physicists carried on with their projects and research, huddling, speaking technically in hushed voices and sometimes loudly in heated arguments, paying little heed to their new colleagues.

Breathing fresh air, she watched a new batch of cumulus clouds boil up in the southwestern sky. Hearing the patio door open behind her, she knew who had followed her out. Shortly Cyan stood with her. "Have you been to the Rose Theater in Altea?" he inquired.

"I have not," she admitted. "Which group is going?" Lately she had learned that resident priests with common interests sometimes went to events in the city.

He seemed to hesitate before replying, "I have reservations for two, front row balcony seats for *Isidra and Eliane*."

Seerce knew of this popular production, featuring a Majorkan troupe and elaborate sets, a story from Mu mythology retold in modernity. Kessa and Laela had been twice and planned to return. She would be thrilled to go with anyone but Cyan. Shading her eyes, she pondered how to respond, noticing a nervous look upon his face. To her immense relief, Sava emerged from the dining room carrying two mugs.

"Your tea grows cold," she said to Seerce, handing her one. "Good afternoon, Exemplar," she greeted Cyan. He scarcely acknowledged her. Sava planted herself in front of Seerce, sipping at her beverage, nonplussed.

"You are so very kind," Seerce told her. Turning back to Cyan, she said, "If you advise me of the date, I shall consult my calendar of commitments."

"The evening prior to the next full moon," he responded. "I do apologize. I failed to recognize that you two were engaged."

"No apology is necessary, Exemplar," Seerce replied, "but Sava and I do have a pressing deadline to our new supervisor. Thank you for the invitation. I shall send you word." With that the women went inside.

Hurrying to the lift, trying not to spill their tea, the two stepped in. "How did you know I needed saving?" asked Seerce.

Sava stated flatly, "He follows you around salivating."

Laughing at that apt description, Seerce begged, "Tell me how to stop this! He grows only more persistent."

"You ended his obsession with me, for which I shall be forever grateful—but let us *not* wish him upon another woman. I thought I would have to leave the Order to lose him. The day you strolled into the gym together it was plain to see he had moved on."

"How bad was it, Sava?"

"As though his shadow chased my own," she replied. "Not only will he seek your presence, but he will turn your allies against you, trying to make himself your only option."

That gave Seerce chills.

"Keep your distance," she urged. "Give him no opening. Be perpetually busy when he seeks you out."

A day or so later, when Cyan happened upon her in the hall outside Physics, Seerce realized a prior engagement for the proposed date, declining with regret his invitation. His expression changed not at all. He simply walked away.

*

By summer, Rika had stepped down from the Council of Exemplars and returned to Zanata to convalesce in the warm climate. Cyan was elected Chair of the Order, with the happy result that he ceased to follow Seerce around the campus. Mostly he missed handball. But within a month he dissolved the Oceanus task force. No more would the three be meeting with the heads of the science departments. This was a great disappointment to them.

Tane's number two, Shahana, had always represented him, attending dutifully, listening politely, and delivering her superior's lukewarm pronouncements. When Rika wanted more, she sought that privately from Tane. Cyan wanted less. Seerce feared their measuring, monitoring, and analyses would be buried and voiceless in the Physics Department.

Tane assured the three that the Council of Exemplars valued their ongoing research. "By your efforts," he told them, "Oceanus has been legitimized as a subdepartment. Be proud of what you have accomplished." He asked Seerce to continue sending pertinent findings and periodic summaries to Climatology and Geology. "You know staff in those departments. They will help you as needed. Let me know if they do not."

It was not long after this that Tane, once again, sat down with the three. He was required, he said, to enforce the strict rule of the council: All of the Order's researchers were prohibited from observing within Altean facilities.

Seerce doubted that Kieran and Sava had ever violated this supposed policy, about which she had never been told. The message was for her—no longer did she have the sanction Rika had given her to investigate on her own.

Profoundly disappointed by this restriction, Seerce thought to go in search of Aaron. Perhaps he would agree to keep watch for her.

*

On the next common day, Seerce hiked up to the thundering bay that Aaron had once showed her. How lovely it would have been to have a companion. But Kessa and Layla stayed busy with their city friends. Jair was in Zanata. Ell liked this trail, but lately he kept company with a young Afrikaan man among the healers. As she walked, Seerce could not help but remember the feel of her hand in Aaron's as she stopped at the glorious waterfall and tread across the creaky wooden bridge, eventually finding her way out of the thicket, following the roar of the waves.

It was a long list, all that she hoped to impart to Aaron if she found him in Eyre. So often she thought of him and never stopped missing him. She wanted him to know her pride in achieving the priesthood and her joy in wearing Anakron's pendant, but most importantly her worry for the Order's disinterest in Altea's new energy. Of course she would temper her bid for his assistance according to his circumstances. Had he never thought to send his remote vision to her at the Temple? Did he never think of her?

Clambering over and around the boulders of the rocky shore, Seerce moved past the tumult, finding a flatter little beach to the north where the waves kept a softer rhythm. Sitting down on the warm sand with her back against a sea-tossed log, bravely she took her etheric body to Eyre, knowing that whatever she found there she would feel deeply. Already trepidation came upon her.

Arriving immediately to the vicinity of that same ramshackle farmhouse she had seen before, the summer view revealed a flagstone path in front and a garden plot off to one side, where vines bearing pea pods climbed trellises and leafy greens sprouted in rows. A sturdy, sunlit porch now fronted the west side of the tiny house, where both the door and window were open to the breeze. Moving in closely, Seerce saw a side view of Aaron, sitting on a homemade chair, his long auburn hair tied back with a woven cord. He whittled points at the ends of thick wooden stakes, idly rocking a baby cradle with his foot.

Seerce kept reins on her emotions, determined to make contact with him, calling him by telepathy. Bravely she set her etheric body before him and this infant with sprigs of auburn hair and blue eyes, moving its fisted hands and arms in the jerky and random fashion of a newborn, squirming under a light blanket. Showing herself brightly in her signature violet light, Seerce called, *Aaron! Aaron look at me! I stand in front of you!*

Over and over she called him, as the infant frightened and wailed. Into the room came the flame-haired lass, untying the closure of her gown, lifting the child and putting it to her breast. Aaron stood to kiss his lady's neck, saying something to her in his native tongue.

Out he went to the garden with an armful of stakes. Seerce followed him, circling him, beseeching him. But he did not seem to notice her. How could this be?

Rejoining her body, she sat motionless on the sand with the ebb and flow of the surf in sunlight, the breeze blowing her hair, aware of none of it. She waited long for resignation to set in, as the sun declined and her stomach wanted dinner, finally realizing she would have to race the fall of darkness back to the Temple.

Silence the Echo

*

By example, the Oceanus three learned the physicists' rigorous methods of questioning, testing, and analyzing, and the habit of challenging each other's work. Kieran devoted himself to what spawned violent weather, while Sava focused her attention upon the retreat of the ice sheets and the rising sea levels along the coasts of the Altean Nations. Seerce compared Geology's data on recent earthquakes with the historic record. To help her track appearances of the aurora, she enlisted observers from the Order's academies, science instructors primarily.

Seeking to know more of Maoran, Seerce looked for his biography in the Hall of Records. To her surprise she could not find it. Cenon's she found easily, along with his lifetime achievements. In the education section was the roster of names for his initiate class, but Maoran was not among them. There were transcripts of Cenon's conference presentations at the university, but none for his rival. All traces of Maoran had been purged. She wondered who had the authority to do such a thing and when it had been done.

Seerce applied herself to her research, hoping that ultimately her efforts would turn the political tide at the council's level. She ran off her frustrations playing handball, but not every day, and she met up with her few remaining classmates when they were available. Occasionally she attended a lecture or performance on the campus or in the city, with colleagues or kindly resident priests. But no one enjoined her as Aaron had, and she doubted she would ever love anyone as much as Rayn.

She could not dwell on the past. It was paramount that the place of people on Earth be preserved. Wearing Anakron's pendant was her constant reminder. Seerce came to know the truth of her grandmother's pronouncement: 'The degree of difficulty is equivalent to the necessity of your task.'

*

A year passed before the Oceanus findings began to show anomalies in two areas: surrounding the main island of Altea and in the broad vicinity of the ocean floor complex. Seerce finally revealed to Kieran and Sava her private observations of the two energy facilities.

"Why have you kept this from us?" Kieran demanded.

"Tane reviewed my analyses before I took my vows. I was told to keep those to myself. Because you did not know of them, your data has been collected and evaluated with total objectivity."

"But your data may not be that!" he countered. His navy blue eyes darkened in defiance and color rose in his neck. Kieran was passionate about scientific method, an idealist prone to an occasional outburst. With his elbows on the lab table in the initiate classroom, which the three now utilized, he placed his head in his hands, longish black hair spilling over them.

"I beg your pardon!" Seerce spat back at him. "I analyze what is garnered by Geology and science instructors. Beyond my own sightings of the aurora, I have nothing to do with its collection!"

Sava stepped in. "Who else in the Order knows about these energy plants?" she asked.

"I told Rika shortly after she was appointed chair," stated Seerce. "I do not know when the Council of Exemplars was told. But I have never found any record of an official observation."

"You defied the exemplars?" Kieran questioned, looking up, his expression softening.

"I followed Rika's directive," Seerce stated flatly. "You worked for her, Kieran. You know she set science above politics."

Sava told them pointedly, "Now we have strong correlations between data streams, analyzed independently by three of us, pointing to the same two suspicious locations. Let us take the evidence to Tane and see if we can get an exception to this rule on spying."

*

Silence the Echo

Swarms of minor tremors and appearances of the aurora occurred every three or four moons. The trio suspected activity at one or both of the energy stations, perhaps test cycles. The council never responded to their request for an exemption from policy. Then a moderately severe earthquake, centered closer to the mainland than any had been in centuries, cracked the exterior of the Temple dome. Finally the council reconsidered its stance.

"The original directive stands," Tane told the three. "But the exemplars now differentiate between Altean facilities and those of private businesses with which the Ryk contracts. You may observe at contractor sites and aboard their ships. You may not observe at any office of Altean government, nor inside the volcano station, nor within the walls of the ocean complex."

Seerce recognized a compromise; some on the council wanted free observation and some wanted nothing changed. She wondered which position Tane had taken. Of course, he did not say.

"Who are the contractors?" Kieran asked him.

"You have the means to find out," Tane replied.

That afternoon, Seerce and Sava visited the Gate of Persa, then moved etherically into one of the utilitarian shuttles parked beneath the hub of the ocean floor complex. Eventually, the hatch opened and three technicians entered, waiting for a time before they removed the respirators that covered their noses and mouths. Then the vehicle was quickly out and away. The male pilot attended to the craft and the other two, male and female, donned headgear from their workbags. It seemed they both heard and saw information, for they spoke softly but not with each other, and their eyes moved as though each watched something. Perhaps they made reports.

After a time, the devices were returned to their bags. With the pilot they discussed the air locks in the tubular hallways. Seerce gathered that they tested a system designed to isolate pressure abnormalities. She described for Sava how the hallways appeared to ripple with fluctuations in pressure, made of some manufactured material that allowed such flex.

Through two wedge-shaped windows at the front of the shuttle, the priests watched the color of the water change from deepest purple to aqua, and then to lighter greenish-blue. The oncoming rush slowed and the windows darkened again as they moved beneath a structure where other shuttles were parked. Presumably they had come under the hull of a large ship at the surface.

The cabin lights blinked, the instrumentation went dark, and the hatch opened outward. *We have arrived somewhere,* Sava remarked.

I hope we can discover whose ship this is, Seerce replied.

They followed the crew into a lift, and when the door opened on another deck, the technicians scattered. Moving to hover above the vessel, the priests oriented themselves to its location in the Ocean of Atlas. *The pilot set a northeast heading from the energy plant,* Sava reported. Noting the position of the sun, Seerce would later calculate the latitude and longitude of the ship. Symbols affixed to its sides indicated its name: *Amymone.*

It looked to be a converted industrial barge. Nearly three hundred people were aboard, all in civilian attire. The upper deck housed work spaces and meeting rooms. Cabins and recreational facilities occupied the second deck. Below that were storerooms of test equipment, spare parts, provisions, and a cafeteria. *It looks like this crew is on long-term assignment,* Seerce remarked.

Wandering separately into conversations and gatherings, offices and labs, eventually the women met up again. *They focus upon the physical plant,* Seerce told Sava, *not the energy operation.*

A company called Aldus Lever owns this vessel, Sava reported. *I found the ship's license posted outside the captain's office. We must pay a visit to their building in Altea.*

*

When Seerce and Sava walked in the next morning, all the physicists were in the lab of the initiate's classroom. Kieran looked like he had been up all night, his eyes bleary and his beard stubbly. Jair stepped back so the two women could see what had the group's attention. On the lab table was a hologram portraying the complex on the ocean floor. Kieran had combined his exterior observations into a depiction. Looking up to acknowledge his teammates, he told them, "I heard the name of this complex aboard a submarine that circles it. The contractors call it 'Echo.' There was talk of an upcoming test cycle. Whereas they have been powering up one tower, the next time it will be a pair. I cannot say how a submarine controls the towers remotely. What kind of signal moves that reliably through deep ocean water?"

"Narrow beams of sonar," answered Tane.

"They intend brief ignitions and shutdowns," Kieran reported, "which is concerning when one considers doubling the side effects of prior tests. What did you ladies find?" Kieran asked.

"Nothing so noteworthy!" Sava exclaimed. She gave a quick description of the *Amymone* and named the contractor.

"How is that ship propelled?" Jade inquired. She and Jair took more interest in the work of Oceanus than the others. Close to Seerce's height, she was a slender Nubian with short-cropped kinky hair and a sweet smile. Often the two reminded their colleagues of great strides made by small people.

"We did not check power sources," Seerce answered.

"Maybe our superior would allow me to go back with you," Jade ventured.

Tane nodded his approval. "If *Amymone* is at sea for long periods, as you surmise," Jade explained, "it must draw its energy from Echo. Something has to power that huge ship and all those shuttle trips."

"Whose submarine is it, Kieran?" Sava asked.

"I apologize," he said, "I forgot to look for its license."

"Was the crew uniformed navy?" Tane inquired.

"No, sir," Kieran replied.

"No harm done, then," the exemplar told him. "I am sure you will go back. Well done, Oceanus. What say you, physicists?"

They gave a cheer for their colleagues.

*

Jade became energy consultant to the Oceanus team. In their first meeting together, she provided a tutorial regarding sonar transmission. "Surely there are transducers in Echo's towers," she told them, "devices that convert one form of energy to another. Electrical, solar, chemical, and thermal energy may be changed by various means to sonar, which is acoustic energy."

She explained that Altea had long ago placed transducers at the shoreline along its maritime routes. "This is what makes the Ryk so successful as shipper and conqueror. Unlimited energy is available to sea traffic, so long as your rig is licensed and your usage fees are paid. Otherwise you and your mates may expect to row your boat." The three laughed.

Jade continued, "In the deep ocean, sound waves are subject to scatter as they bounce off schools of fish, large marine animals, and pockets of warmer or cooler water. Utilizing low-frequency sound waves and projecting narrow beams minimizes the scatter effect. At the receiving end, a filtering device sorts for the presence of the required signal, because water transmits all kinds of noise."

Sava surmised, "Sonar generated from land would lose its punch before it reached these ships, out here in the middle of nowhere."

"Since people cannot stay in the depths for long, it makes sense to monitor and control Echo from ships," Kieran reasoned.

"But Echo is overbuilt for transmission to a few vessels," Seerce remarked. "What other energy might it broadcast?"

"The ocean floor is its only other medium," Jade replied. "We know that infrasound surfaces from deeper layers, of very low frequencies. From eruptions and tremors we have learned that seismic energy travels predictably but differently through the crust and mantle. To my knowledge, the purposeful transmission of energy through Earth has been utilized only in the air barge systems, for short distances and shallowly. The Ryk is up to something unprecedented."

Silence the Echo

*

Early in their third year working together, Tane confessed to Seerce his initial reluctance to accept a climatologist, a Cenon staffer, and Anakron's granddaughter to his department. He had agreed to Rika's request in deference to his friend Cyan, who was at that time intent upon winning Seerce's heart.

"What?" she cried out loud, nearly spitting out the last mouthful of her iced fruit juice.

Seerce and Tane were in Zanata, he to present research and she to meet with her contacts in Climatology and Geology. Late in the afternoon on a hot day they sat in a tavern with a group of academics. Ceiling fans did little to counter the heat and the company bored them thoroughly. She and Tane carried on a telepathic dialogue, which had lapsed into his best effort to shock her. It was a side of him she had not known. Perhaps he had downed too many mugs of chilled ale.

He looked at her mystified. *Do you mean to tell me you had no idea of his intentions?*

I mean that after acquiring my title, I limited my contact with him to group activities and official business. Do you know how much time I was required to spend with that man before I graduated?

Yes, I do, Tane replied mirthfully. *I was the sounding board for his plotting.*

Seerce was aghast. *What advice did you give him?*

I suggested that he play with older children.

With a spoon she lifted an ice cube from her goblet and fired it slingshot style in the direction of Tane's head. The table erupted in laughter as he slid down in his seat to escape impact. Standing up, she told him aloud, "I believe I need another drink," and went to make her request of the tavern keeper.

While she waited for juices to be squeezed and stirred, she mulled over Exemplar Damon's private request of her that morning. A beefy man with a booming voice, she found his physical size intimidating as she met him personally for the first time. From meetings by crystal, she knew his pale round face, his receding hairline, and more reserve than she witnessed today.

To her great surprise, Damon suggested that Oceanus join his Climatology department in Zanata. He reasoned that her team needed immediate access to unfiltered data, sent to the University from the Order's schools all around the MidTerra. Collegially she agreed to bring up the matter with Tane, though truly she hated this miserable climate. Lately, Seerce had come to appreciate their association with the physicists. She wondered why Damon thought she had any leverage at all in moving Oceanus.

Cradling a chilled and filled goblet in both hands, Seerce was intercepted by Tane and directed to a table for two beneath a fan. Setting her drink down, she pressed her cool palms to her perspiring face. Now that they were alone, she introduced her subject, saying, "I wish Rika could have tolerated Altea's climate. She had connections Oceanus needs to other Earth science communities."

Tane stated, "Damon is much better connected than Rika ever was. I know he wants Oceanus in his fold. It is not the best idea, Seerce."

"Why not?" she inquired, squelching her own misgivings, thinking that in his tipsy state Tane might reveal more than he generally did. "Damon has been a supporter of Oceanus since the beginning, a counterbalance for Nova's ongoing resistance," she added. "He is invested in our work."

"As am I. The three of you are dedicated researchers. Cyan has an alternate proposal in mind." Tane paused. "He wants to elevate you to exemplar."

Seerce's mouth fell open. "I have not even three years as a priest! What would I contribute to leading the Order?"

"Oceanus has bearing upon the Order's direction. Cyan wants you and your efforts where he is. As for tenure, Tuura became Exemplar of Cenon with equivalent experience. This has precedent."

Seerce countered, "Tuura is a gifted etheric traveler, devoted to Cenon, and the right person to deal with the chieftains in Misr."

"You are a gifted scientist, devoted to Oceanus, and perhaps the only one who can handle the associated politics."

Seerce thought of Anakron's last words, his instruction that she be mentored for the position of exemplar. But certainly this was too soon. She told him, "Cyan's personal interest in me is what drives this."

Tane admitted, "He knows there is too much power differential between a priest and the chair."

"But the chair is superior to the other exemplars, is he not?"

"Technically, the chair is a voice for the group, with no more authority than any of us."

"You are a peculiar sort of friend to him," Seerce judged.

"I have the distinction of being his only friend," Tane replied, draining what remained of his ale. "Regardless, I am obligated to uphold the good of the Order. I provide you with supportive counsel, my duty as your superior. I am telling you to be careful." With that he took his leave.

*

Over six months, Cyan conducted Seerce's instruction for the role of exemplar, as she continued her work for Oceanus. She found nothing concerning about his behavior. Of course she knew he was a master of timing and a most patient man. He would reveal himself after the title was bestowed. But she opted not to worry, thinking herself capable of keeping her boundaries and a professional relationship with him. This was her opportunity to influence the exemplars, to gain Oceanus the freedom to investigate Echo's technology directly.

In a joint ceremony Seerce would be named Exemplar of Oceanus, the eighth member of the council, while a man she had never met would become the ninth. His name was Jory and he would assume another new title, Exemplar of Colonies.

On this day before her installation, Tane arranged to take Seerce to dinner in the city. A bouquet of flowers from the chair adorned her desk in the new Oceanus suite, remodeled from the initiate's classroom, Cyan's former office, and the little room Seerce utilized as an intern. Oceanus was granted two more research positions.

From her new private office, Seerce looked out to a closer seawall. The men's domicile was gone, battered repeatedly by storms and floods. After its foundation shifted, the council had it dismantled block by block, selling the pure white limestone for a small fortune. The Circle of Stones was reconstructed between the High Temple and the Healing Temple, for the west gardens and the south-facing patio were now under water. From the remaining domicile, which now housed both men and women, the unobstructed sea view was framed by bracing on the inside of smaller windows, defense against the winds of severe storms. Today at summer's end the ocean undulated gently beneath a clear sky.

Seerce returned her attention to crystal reports from her staff, which now included Jade as physicist and a geologist, Cesar. Sava was her number two and Kieran her lead researcher. His most recent summary concerned her, so she went to find him. His office door was open, but blackout drapes were drawn and he sat in darkness before a full-color hologram on his desk. Seerce's staff required current technology and she was pleased to authorize purchases via the generous budget made available to her.

"Those were dire tidings you left me, Kieran. Do you want to borrow one of Tane's people for the analysis?"

"Please, madame," he replied. "Jair is my first choice."

"I am not 'madame' yet," Seerce replied lightly, "not until tomorrow." It was Cyan's requirement that the rank and file address exemplars as sir or madame. "For the favor," she suggested, "you might allow Tane to beat you once on the handball court."

Kieran grinned, saying, "If that is what it takes."

Despite assurances that the crystal in her office was secure, Seerce held no personal conversations by it. Instead she walked over to Tane's office.

"I come to beg Jair's attention to our latest concerns. Would he run an analysis of surface magnetic flows for us?"

"You know he would do anything for you," Tane answered.

"We owe you," Seerce admitted.

"Yes, you do," he agreed.

"When should I be ready?" she asked.

He responded with a question. "Have you been to the establishment called Coast?"

"I have not," she replied, "but I know to dress up."

"I reserved a table on the outdoor patio, so bring a wrap. A water taxi will pick us up at the dock next door at the decan before sunset."

"Tane!" she exclaimed. "That is much too extravagant for a congratulatory gift."

"I think not," he replied. "You are the first Exemplar of Oceanus and the singular highlight of my constrained existence. Let us have a riot of an evening." To her shock, he stood to kiss her cheek, then sat back down to his work.

*

Seerce relived the press of his lips to her face a hundred times as she dressed. How long had it been since anyone had showed her affection? Donning a flowing and somewhat revealing gown that she had worn to concert performances with Kessa and Laela, she settled upon a silver brooch for her wrap and a glittery half-circle comb to hold back her curls in the breeze along the shore. Her dress was the iridescent turquoise of a summer sky just after sunset, the wrap a pale tint of the same color in coarse silk. Did he mean to flirt with her?

They were fast becoming friends, she supposed, sharing the secret of her evolving circumstances, seeking his advice as she set up her own department, one ever dependent upon collaboration with his. She was freer with her humor now, taking license with Tane as he did with her. Teasing him about his lectures, he admitted that he enjoyed performing his one-man shows, taking little notice of the students, except, of course, Jair. Teaching, he told her, was its own brand of perversity.

He came to her door dressed handsomely in light grey formal wear, narrow trousers of fine fabric and a silver-buttoned waistcoat to match, his white silk shirt of a subtle pattern with wide sleeves gathered at the shoulders and the cuffs. The two in their finery attempted to escape unnoticed through the tunnel. But here was Jair coming toward them.

Stopping in his tracks, he emitted a low whistle of admiration. "The Autark must be hosting a ball. I missed that invitation."

"And you missed seeing us leave," Tane instructed.

"Indeed I have, sir," Jair replied. "I hope you and our lady have a splendid time of it."

Easily they laughed and conversed as the taxi sped along Altea's shoreline. The evening breeze stayed warm as wispy clouds gathered around the volcano and the sun dipped behind it on the eve of the equinox.

As the two were seated outdoors, Seerce removed her wrap. It seemed that Tane admired her close-fitting dress. Even if all of this was just pretend, she enjoyed his attention. That he was older than she added to the enchantment. Tonight he looked the part of a courtier, his carriage regal, his smile constant, and his eyes flirtatious. They told stories and laughed more through the gourmet courses.

Coming to the subject of community living, they agreed how difficult it was to nurture a relationship in such close quarters.

Seerce told him, "I tried and failed."

"I gave up when I came here," Tane admitted. "In Zanata the staff lived off campus. One's liaisons were less likely to be known by one's students or colleagues."

"How many of your students fell for you?" Seerce inquired.

"Not as many as I wished." He chuckled. "I returned the favor once and it cost me more commotion than I care to have. And you?"

"And me, what? My love interest was exactly one classmate. I am sure you know the story."

"How would I?"

"Even if you were oblivious, surely Cyan made mention of it."

Deepening his voice and looking professorial, Tane panned, "My attention was on physics."

Seerce giggled.

"Cyan discussed only you among the initiates," Tane told her. "Allow me to quote you something: 'I recall her childlike presentation at dinner on the day she arrived. Her stature was petite, her unbound hair long enough to sit upon and wild, like a street urchin's, but hers was spun gold. Overly large and light-colored eyes and the palest of lips, set in the creamiest of complexions, all causing me to wonder from which ethereal realm she had emerged, this embodiment of innocence.'"

Seerce burst out laughing, having to cover her mouth with her napkin. "I doubt that you could invent such a speech, but why do you bother to remember such balderdash?"

Tane shrugged. "We were both curious as to who Anakron's granddaughter might be. It is highly unusual for any priest's offspring to present as an initiate. We had to wonder at the life our fearless leader led while in service around the MidTerra."

Seerce clarified, "I am not of his bloodline."

"That much came to light. But there was more that impressed Cyan: 'The effect upon those around her was remarkable, the men unable to take their eyes from her. When she looked to one, it was as though an enchantment fell upon him. In snatches I heard an unfamiliar accent and pauses as she searched for proper common words. Yet her voice was strong and self-assured, pleasing, rhythmic, and interspersed with laughter that rang in peals of bells, bringing color to her cheekbones. She was mesmerizing in a way I have never known. I could not disregard her.'"

Now the two lost their decorum altogether, Tane hooting and Seerce in hysterics, attracting the attention of other diners and the wait staff on the patio. "Truly," he told her as he recovered himself, "you are going to have to watch it. The spell was never broken."

"Cyan and his illusions! Poetry may be his calling," she remarked. "How does he do as chair?"

"He is quite practical, actually, good with finances, careful to keep a neutral position for council discussions, and able to facilitate compromise. The rest you shall find for yourself. I will enjoy hearing your perspective."

They sipped their dessert wine in silence and perhaps regret, about to return to their cloistered lives on the other end of the island. Rhetorically, Seerce mused, "Living as we do, who can one trust with one's secrets?"

"You," Tane responded.

In candlelight she sought his eyes. "I know you as my instructor, my superior, and a brilliant physicist," she told him, "all of which impresses me. But I know not who you truly are."

"Then I shall have to make amends," he promised.

In the taxi Tane held Seerce's hand, and as they approached her apartment door, he suggested they step inside to say goodbye. He kissed her long. She responded hungrily, a long-extinguished flame reignited. Dare she hope that her loneliness might be banished?

CHAPTER 16

Tuura and Annecy waited for Seerce at the lift, where she was hugged and warmly welcomed. At the center of the Hall of Records, in their purple robes and wearing their Crystals of the Sun, seven exemplars witnessed the vows Seerce and Jory made to uphold the Order and preserve wisdom.

The council was scheduled to meet for six days. Headway had to be made on a plan to move the seat of the Order. Climatology had forecast the inundation of the High Temple within fifteen to twenty-five years. In a prior vote, three exemplars had supported Misr as the site of the new Temple, while the other three favored Zanata. The chair might have cast the deciding vote, but instead he waited for the installation of the new exemplars.

As Seerce listened it became apparent that the crux of the matter was not so much destination as finite resources. Maintenance and repair of the Order's weather-damaged academies, many of them situated in older sections of MidTerra ports, had risen exponentially. Moving the most vulnerable to higher ground had taken priority. What remained in the coffers had to be spent judiciously.

Jory upended the conversation by proposing Tibisay as the site of the new Temple. A ruggedly handsome man, suntanned and sandy-haired, he spoke boldly and persuasively. "Natural resources are plentiful and labor inexpensive there. Altean expatriates build new homes and businesses. Situated in foothills, there are fertile soils in the valleys, beautiful lakes, and a pleasant climate. Tibisay meets survival criteria of higher elevation and distance from Altea."

Damon and Nova spoke in his support. These two, Seerce knew, stood to lose autonomy if the Temple administration relocated to Zanata.

Upon questioning, Jory admitted that the Order would have to purchase land. But the academy there was well-attended and many parents were pillars of the new community. He was already engaged in pricing property and its development for the council's consideration, and he was confident of generous contributions from supporters.

Tane justified his rather fervent plea to keep the four science departments together. His passionate delivery was new to Seerce's picture of him. When he finished speaking his eyes were full of fire.

During a break that afternoon, Tane walked Seerce back to the domicile, inviting her to accompany him to his third-floor apartment, the last down a long hall. "The trek is rather conspicuous," he admitted, "but Cyan's apartment is on the second floor."

Seerce raised her eyebrows. "Am I to make a habit of seeing you here?" she asked.

"I hope so," he replied and when his door closed behind them, he took her in his arms and kissed her soundly. Then he led her by the hand to sit down with him on his sofa. "You make me a happy man," he told her.

"And you make me a nervous woman!" she exclaimed. "What about this do you think Cyan will disregard?"

"Probably none of it, but council is one thing and we are another."

"Oh, I see."

"You need not accept."

"I would like to accept. I just need a plan."

Tane leaned over to kiss her again. "Where did you learn this fine art?"

When she could speak, she countered, "I want to know the same from you."

"Perhaps we should leave those secrets in the past."

"As I remember, Exemplar, there is only the spacious present."

He laughed. Placing her hand over his mouth she prevented another kiss. "We have a meeting to attend." He kissed the palm at his lips so she dropped it.

Telling her, "The best excuse for a late arrival is an urgent matter in your department," his mouth covered hers before she could respond.

"And what shall your excuse be?" she managed to ask.

"An angelic visitation," he replied.

*

Several times Jory asked Seerce to dine with him. Finally, on the third day of deliberations, she invited him to lunch with her in the Oceanus suite. Introducing him to her staff, she learned that he and Sava were already acquainted, both having worked in Tibisay.

Seerce and Jory sat down to a meal delivered by kitchen staff. Closing her conference room door by her thought, she told him, "It was daring of you to lobby the council your first day on the job," she told him. "I admire that."

"Thank you," he replied. A big man, he ate voraciously for a time. "You are close to Tane and Cyan," he pronounced.

It was a true statement by an astute observer. "They were my professors," she responded. "I grew up with them."

Surely he wanted more detail, but he let that drop, saying, "I grew up with Damon and Ezra."

"I know so little of them. Tell me," she encouraged, seeking to size him up before she divulged anything at all.

He responded with a sunny smile across his bronzed face that must know outdoor work. By the copper flecks in his hazel eyes, she was convinced of a mixed heritage, certainly some Archaean ancestry. Light hair and an aquiline nose suggested Aurean blood. "Ezra was the headmaster of my academy. He knows my family, my faults, and my determination. It was he who managed my acceptance to the College of Earth Sciences in Makaria. Damon was one of my professors there, and later, dean of that school. We stayed in touch through my time as a construction superintendent for the Order's new facilities. He posted me on talented graduates for hire, those who could solve real-world problems. It humbles me to sit at their table."

"What kind of people are they?" she inquired.

"Highly intelligent and supremely ethical, as dedicated to Gaia as your Mu friends. Ezra has a gift for drawing the best from people, invested as he is in the worth of each soul. Damon works as persistently in the greater community. He has some magical ability to get everyone rowing in his direction, folding other leaders into his vision. He is a master crafter of shared progress."

"What gifts they are," Seerce marveled.

"Make Damon your friend. He has powerful contacts in Altea's world and access to information the Order would not otherwise know. A legion of scientists and engineers are disgusted with the Energy Authority. Many insiders have left. Some may be willing to help your cause."

Thereby he acknowledged Seerce's dilemma. Votes from Jory, Damon, and Tane would help an effort to change the policy on spying in Altean facilities. But a piece of Cyan's advice came to her mind: "These are powerfully persuasive people and you will need every fiber of your fine intellect to separate what is true from what is advertised. Consider everything and commit to nothing until you are entirely sure." To Jory she replied neutrally, "I appreciate that tip."

"Your turn," he said, finishing up his plate as she began to eat.

"Shall I send for more food?" she inquired.

"No, no," he responded. "I am satisfied. Out on sites one eats quickly and hurries to the next task. It is my habit." He watched her eat until she chose to address his question about her relationships. A teaspoon of truth would not stave off his curiosity.

"They were the first Mu I had ever met and it has taken me some time to appreciate their cool exteriors." Jory's interested expression did not change nor did his eyes move from hers. "They were incredible instructors, and I have since come to appreciate their skills in running tightly knit and productive departments."

"But what kind of people are they?" he pressed, asking exactly what she had inquired of him.

"They are rather private, somewhat aloof, but terribly competitive, particularly at handball. Do you play?"

"I do not know the game," he responded.

"Both enjoy theater. Tane has a dry sense of humor. Cyan is shy, difficult to read, and more aware of all that goes on than any of us ever suspect."

Now he looked at her curiously.

"Both are invested in my success," she told him confidently. "I was given a difficult task as a student, at which I succeeded. They have supported my ambitions since."

"Except they will not let you solve this little mystery on the ocean floor."

Seerce was taken aback. "They speak only of council decisions, not personal votes."

"You and I both know what a problem this is, Seerce."

"Then you and I understand," she countered, "that we are going to move that vote."

"Thank you for sharing your position on the matter. Please consider me a friend and ally," he urged.

It seemed to Seerce that Jory's interest was more personal than that.

*

On the fifth day of their marathon meeting, Cyan took a different approach to the question of where to move the Temple; he asked the exemplars to determine the best location for their own departments. Tane came to Seerce's office late in the afternoon to question her vote. "Look at logistics," she suggested. "It makes some sense to move my department to Tibisay. It is closest to the great ocean we study."

"How close do you have to be when your observers travel remotely or etherically?" he questioned. "It is far more important to station Physics and Oceanus together. We have been together more than three years. We have joint projects."

"Then bring your group to the shores of Lake Macabo, which I am told is beautiful. The climate is temperate. One cannot say that of Zanata, and Misr is a political nightmare."

"The science departments belong together," he stated once again.

"The Order cannot afford to house all of us under the same roof, Tane. If we split up, we may be incorporated into existing sites with less costly additions. That seems the only reasonable route. Anyway, this is a long-term plan. We are not leaving tomorrow. Likely we are not leaving for years and years."

"I think you are falling under the pretty boy's spell."

"I already have, Tane," Seerce replied. "You are a beautiful man."

"Jory never takes his eyes from you."

"I have no control of that and you have no worries."

*

A discussion ensued at dinner about the older port cities of the MidTerra Sea. Jory told the exemplars that aging wharfs and piers were damaged beyond repair, the sea creeping ever inland, flooding the old town centers. "Altean contractors experiment with modular docks and floating buildings, to be anchored temporarily and moved later. Smaller ports have been deserted."

Tuura asked, "What happens to the derelict structures? In these storms they must not fare well."

"They do not," Jory affirmed. "The debris that washes away is a hazard to maritime traffic. A new division of the navy is charged with cleaning up the detritus."

Damon shook his head, saying, "The cost of running the Altean Nations must be exorbitant and yet there is official silence regarding these Earth changes. How irresponsible can the Ryk be?"

"Sufficiently to operate energy facilities that disturb Earth!" Seerce asserted. "Is there nothing we can do about those?"

There was shocked silence around the dinner table. Cyan cast his disapproving gaze upon her, saying quietly, "We are not subversives or rebels, Seerce, we are priests."

Swiftly she responded, "With due respect for the position of the chair, I pose this question: Are we not obligated to act for the preservation of the planet that hosts us?"

"Gaia will choose the outcome of this struggle," Cyan told her. "No subset of humanity has power over the conscious and willful Earth. Civilizations come and go. She preserves Herself."

Tane gave Seerce a sharp look across the table. *What are you trying to accomplish this evening?* he asked her privately. She ignored him.

Damon spoke again. "There are a number of factions working quietly at what Seerce suggests," he said. "We might consider lending our expertise."

Too late Seerce realized why Damon wanted Oceanus in his fold—she and her team might have been helpful to these factions. She wished he had been more direct with her when she saw him in Zanata. But looking back to Cyan, she understood why he was not.

Seerce knew who her allies would be. There were too few to sway the vote of the council.

*

"I would like to spend more time with you," Jory told her as they ate breakfast in a corner of the dining hall. It was his last full day in Altea.

Seerce nodded and smiled.

"Keep all your secrets," he added. "Just tell me this. Are you committed to someone?"

"I am not."

"Level with me, please," he requested.

"Jory, I welcome getting to know you. Certainly our alliance is important to me. However, I am bound by various degrees to others. I am not as free here as you may be in Tibisay."

"That is a good reason for you to visit," he offered, smiling.

"I intend to survey what may become my department's home," she told him. "But it is newly my department and I have many tasks ahead of that one."

"Our door is always open," he assured her, "and if you would like an escort, I will come fetch you."

That afternoon, the council agreed upon a plan for the eventual move from Altea. Physics and the Temple administration would take residence in Zanata. Cenon would divide its staff between Misr and Tibisay. The healers would decentralize to the Order's largest temple communities, while maintaining a small presence in Altea for the benefit of the poor. Seerce recommended that the decision for her small department be subject to space available at the time of the move. The compromise was approved unanimously. Cleverly, she managed to stay in the good graces of all concerned.

*

It was nearly a moon thereafter when Cyan invited Seerce to lunch in his apartment, saying that he wished to discuss finer points of the Temple's emergency evacuation plan, particularly the security of records kept in her department. She had consulted her staff and prepared recommendations. As they sat down, Cyan had little to say, so she launched into her proposal.

He interrupted her, saying, "Something about you has changed of late. What is it? You must tell me."

Forthrightly she responded, "I am learning I must sometimes set aside personal loyalties to make good choices for Oceanus and for the Order."

If he registered her response, he gave no indication. Turning away from her, he faced the window. As sunlight peeked through a break in the clouds, something glinted from its ledge. Seerce notice a small bronze statue of Lady Gaia, the wreath upon her head studded with tiny diamonds. This symbol of Her presence served to embolden Seerce.

"Cyan, perhaps it is timely to address what underlies your concern." She had decided some time back what to say when this moment arrived. "I do hope you will find the abiding love you seek, but surely by now you recognize that I am not that woman. Ever will I be grateful for all that you have taught me. I do prefer to believe that I earned my promotion, that in me you saw potential for leadership. Surely you know my perspective is different from yours, but I am equally devoted to Gaia, to the Order, and the preservation of wisdom."

Seerce watched his shoulders sag. Some moments went by before he stated, "I would like to be alone."

"Of course," she told him. "You know where to find me when you have more to say."

Picking up lunch from the dining room, Seerce returned to her office to read through a list of government contractors that Damon had sent her. After only a few bites, she took the list to Kieran, telling him, "We might find good information snooping around these companies."

"I think we might," he agreed. "I accept the task."

"Not you alone, Kieran," she clarified. "We shall divide these up. Sava can take the military contractors. Coming from a navy family, she understands that world. Select two or three, and Cesar and Jade and I shall divide up the rest."

"I have a personal interest in Control Star," Kieran told her. "My father was an engineer there."

"Do you think he has information he would share?" Seerce asked.

A drastic change in Kieran's demeanor was apparent. "No, madame. He died testing the installation of one of their systems."

Through the years she and Kieran had worked together, never had he spoken of this. "Deeply I regret your loss," she conveyed. "Allow me to assign Control Star to someone else."

"I prefer to keep it," he said, his eyes hard upon her.

Something told her she should overrule him, but she did not.

*

Cyan failed to show for morning meditation in the Temple, which Seerce had attended regularly since preparing for her exemplar role. He did not answer the knock at his apartment door, so Tane and Seerce let themselves in. He lay upon his sofa, staring at the ceiling.

"Cyan?" she called tentatively. "Tane is here with me."

He did not move.

"I will stay with him," Tane offered.

"I shall be in my office after breakfast. May I bring you a plate?"

"No," Tane replied. "First I will try a Mu method. If need be, I shall obtain Annecy's assistance."

Seerce ate alone, thinking through what she might have done differently all these years, with or for Cyan. He lived so singularly. She had done little to fill that void because, as she reminded herself, he misinterpreted friendliness for the love he sought. There was no good explanation for chemistry between people. Her whole being had vibrated at the same wavelength as Rayn's. Tane's affection, his humor, and his looks called her, but lately his political stance gave her pause.

It was after lunch when Tane came to her office. "He was in a healing trance. I waited for its conclusion, then we had a talk. I think he needs to go home for a moon or so."

Seerce could not remember that Cyan had ever taken a leave. Occasionally he was away on the Order's business, but never for pleasure. "A rest is well-deserved," she replied, "but how will we run this operation without him?"

"How would he run it in a state of paralysis?" Tane asked sharply. "Think of him, not you."

"Maybe I caused some of this, Tane, unable to be who he wishes me to be. What am I supposed to do, pretend that I love him? Is that what I owe him for making me exemplar?"

"Certainly not!"

"I think I have done a fine job of walking a long tightrope. What do you think he makes of *our* little flirtation? Do you suppose you have any hand in this?"

"Both of us do!" he replied angrily.

Coolly she agreed, "Yes, that is how I see it."

"If he takes my advice, we will manage while he is gone. But I must leave for Palermo rather immediately. The crystal network across the MidTerra is down intermittently. I suspect it has to do with some Energy Authority project. Tuura just left for Misr to deal with the chieftains. You and Annecy will be the only exemplars in residence. Essentially, that leaves you in charge until I get back."

*

Seerce arose early the next day and went to the Temple. The first to arrive, she drew down the Crystal by her thought and watched dawn's light sparkle across its face. Eyes closed, she withdrew to her place of peace. Others came in to conduct their own attuning, but she was only vaguely aware. She invited Anakron's guidance, for surely she needed it.

Returning her awareness to the Temple and fluttering her eyes open, she saw that Tane was on her left and Cyan on her right. She waited quietly for the two to rouse, then they walked together to Cyan's office.

"Tane advises me to go home," he said quietly, "but I am too exhausted to travel to the other side of the world. I shall go instead to a house of retreat in Majorka. The island is on Tane's way to Palermo, so I shall leave with him and Jair tomorrow, to return, Goddess willing, by the next new moon." His expression was mask-like. To Seerce he felt wooden, as though much of his life force had left him.

"I appreciate that you will assist the Order in my absence. I trust you implicitly." He made no eye contact with either one, instead looking between them. "I will make a work list for you, if you will kindly return here at the third decan after midday. That is all," he said.

Seerce and Tane stood. "Will you take your meal with us?" she asked Cyan.

"I have no appetite," he said.

"Call us, please, if we may help," Seerce urged him.

She followed Tane around the corner to his office. "He is not fully present in his body," she said.

"It is his defense against pain. He does what he can."

"What do you think of his plan?"

"He has to wean himself from you, Seerce. It is going to take time. Since the day you arrived, he has made you his answer to everything. I hope he stays gone long enough."

"I am pleased you will travel with him," she said. "I fear he would not be safe on his own."

"Agreed," Tane said.

"What are we going to do, Tane?" she asked worriedly.

"Have breakfast," he replied. "Everything looks better on a full stomach."

*

Cyan had prepared a crystal for each of them. Seerce touched hers to her forehead and skimmed the list. It was extensive.

"I have no expectation that you will address all of this," Cyan stated. "I simply leave you the status of current subjects. As you do in your departments, prioritize and accomplish what you can. The crisis of the moment takes the better part of one's time." He was a bit more animated, but the circles beneath his eyes had darkened.

"Shall we hold council meetings as scheduled?" Seerce asked.

"Yes," Cyan said. "With travel as dangerous as it becomes this time of year, I suggest holding them by crystal. Ell will set that up for you."

"Give us your best advice for leading," Tane requested.

"Take care of each other," Cyan said. "Love runs this place. Tane, I will see you in the morning. Seerce, would you stay?"

"Of course," she replied.

Come find me when you are finished, Tane telepathed to Seerce. He went out.

She looked into the eyes of her mentor, concerned for his well-being. No one deserved such devastation.

"In Majorka I shall enter into a process to unburden my soul," he told her. Looking down, he added. "There is one transgression that bothers me more than any other and it is what I must confess to you." He paused, glancing up to Seerce once, fleetingly. "When you were an initiate, at about the time that you and your class began your internships, I instructed Rayn to stay strictly away from you, threatening his expulsion if he did not."

Horror welled up from the pit of her stomach. She covered her mouth with her hands.

Cyan would not meet her eyes, but continued speaking. "He did as he was told. Never again did I perceive his energy around you. I used my office to manipulate for what I wanted most."

Dropping her hands, silently and slowly Seerce shook her head, protesting silently, *No, no, no!*

"I am justly rewarded, never to obtain your love. That is precisely what I deserve."

Tears crawled down her cheeks.

"Whatever path your relationship might have taken, it had no chance. You continue to seek its replacement, but not with me.

I vow to you that never again will I interfere with the course of your life. Whatever decisions you make, you have my blessing. I do hereby stop preventing you from loving who you wish." He appeared most ashamed, looking up to add, "I am deeply sorry."

She had to escape his presence! As she bolted for the door, he directed it to open. Her feet took her to the Temple, blessedly empty of others. Kneeling on the cold stone floor at the altar, she laid one hand against its cool marble face and held Anakron's Crystal of the Sun with the other. Bowing her head, she sobbed, long-buried sorrow unleashed in torrents.

The myth of the life she had imagined, the role she had been prompted to take, the deepest love she had known, and all her dreams of what she could do by her recent appointment, all of it came crashing down around her. What was she to believe in now? A million jumbled thoughts and remembrances flooded her mind, washing her high hopes for love and life into the abyss of this betrayal.

Eventually she quieted. The heaving in her chest diminished to a shudder and tears slowed to a trickle. Shivering from shock and cold, she got to her feet only slowly, her legs rubbery from kneeling so long. Leaning over the altar, she reached across to touch the chimes. Their reverberations brought her back to the world where she would have to live, one greatly altered by that confession.

As she turned to leave she saw Tane in a doorway to the foyer. He strode quickly to her and wrapped his arm around her waist to support her. "I will take you home," he said.

There she changed into nightclothes and donned her robe, though it was early still. She washed her swollen face with cold water. There was nothing she could say or do, so she laid down on her bed and shut her eyes, hearing the door close downstairs as Tane let himself out.

Seerce thought of the loving relationships of her childhood, with all her family and kin, Anakron, and her friends at school. She had grown up to believe that she was meant to be loved, that love upheld life, and that Gaia's great love allowed for human existence. It was terribly disturbing to her that in this place of holiness, in such tumultuous times as these, Cyan spent his gifts manipulating for the love of a woman—Sava, Seerce, who next?

It made no sense that he would crumble with her understated acknowledgment of his game. Surely he revealed his betrayal to hurt her further, to throw her off balance, to cause her to fail in handling his great responsibilities in his absence. He could have appointed Annecy to manage the Order, the veteran in the temple next door. Not only devious, he was vindictive.

Seerce regretted having to undertake this new examination of her circumstances. As of tomorrow, she would have temporary charge of the Temple, with nothing to rely upon but her own counsel, ever to remain on guard. An era of naiveté had just slammed to a close.

*

Later in the evening Tane called to Seerce from the hallway outside her apartment. She opened her door by her thought and he came in with a laden tray to set on her low table.

"How are you feeling?" he asked.

It surprised her that he knew those words. "I feel nothing," she replied. Surely her earlier display had shocked him, her raw emotion foreign to his nature and his culture. Rarely had she seen him angry or frustrated, and then only momentarily. She doubted he had ever shed a tear.

Tane served her. Her stomach settled some with spoonsful of soup. The warmth of tea helped. With his heaping plate, he sat down on the other end of the divan. Placing her hot bowl on the table, she changed her position to sit cross-legged facing him. He turned toward her and continued eating.

"May I recount for you exactly what was said after you left us?"

"Please," he replied.

She recited that verbatim. He set down his plate. She watched his face. It took him a while to conduct his analysis, his expression scarcely affected. "I paid no attention to the romances of the initiates. I was aware of how very young you were and surprised when it was decided that you would staff Oceanus. Cyan's demeanor changed when you took the office next to his. I figured he was up to something. I was busy building the crystal network between school sites." He paused and then grinned. "It was a few years before I noticed the woman you became."

Seerce rolled her eyes and sighed.

"Do you understand that he was obsessed with you?" Tane asked.

"I suppose I do now. What professor manipulates his students' lives to the degree he has mine? But what did I know then? I thought his interest in me was that of a mentor. Aaron and Rayn both warned me. They saw it. I did not."

"Explain to me the breakdown in the Temple."

"By the Goddess, Tane!" she exclaimed. "Are you impervious? Cyan's exact words were, 'I will stop preventing you from loving who you wish.' I have lost so much that will never be restored, beginning and ending with the love of my life! What has he done to Rayn by his cruelty? Cyan leads us. I will never trust him, never believe him, and never tolerate his presence anywhere near me. The world I have known these last five years collapsed around me today!"

He was quiet for a long time, staring into nothingness. Then he looked directly at her. "I will state the most obvious first: We have an Order to run. We live in a dangerous world. Leadership from the exemplars is expected and required. We dare not dissolve into factions over misjudgments and lost love affairs.

"Secondly, you cannot change the past, but make Cyan responsible for his sins. Leave him to his own misery. Well he deserves it.

"Lastly, tell me if you want me to cancel my trip. Jair will get Cyan to his destination with or without me. There is plenty for both of us to do here. I offer this as your colleague and for the good of the Order." He looked away. "But there is something else I want to say."

Seerce saw his face crumple in sorrow or pain or by something that frightened him. But he took a deep breath and rearranged his expression to placidity. How did the Mu do this?

"Allow me to hold you," he requested.

He stood up and pulled her up by her hand. Leading her around the table, he took her in his arms and cradled her, saying softly, "It tore my soul to see you hurt. I recognize that your heart is tender, that you love your work and believe in your colleagues, that you always do more than your best. It slays me to think what he has done to you by his selfishness. The Cyan I thought I knew would never do such a thing."

By now Seerce was empty of tears, hollowed out by sorrow, adrift in uncertain seas, numb. She let Tane support her. She felt the heat of his body and his wish to comfort her and his physical desire for her. But she was far from trusting anyone now. "I will handle things here," she told him. "Go fix the network. Communication is vital to the Order."

CHAPTER 17

The following day was a blur of subjects from Cyan's list and notifications to the exemplars, one by one, of his leave and Seerce's charge. Damon recommended that she suspend unnecessary travel beginning two days hence, for a series of heavy storms were poised to roll over Altea and into the mouth of the MidTerra. When she called Jory, he offered to come back to assist her. She declined politely, citing the weather forecast.

At midday she walked over to the Administrator's office, Ell's position since Barlas's death a few moons ago. Together they crafted a formal announcement for campus residents and the headmasters and deans of the Order's schools. Ell agreed to track down Ezra and Tuura in their travels to inform them. Graciously he accepted several other tasks from Cyan's list.

On her return Seerce picked up lunch from the kitchen to eat hurriedly in her office. Requiring background on some of Cyan's subjects, she told Sava, "I will be in the Hall this afternoon. Please forward my calls to the Exemplars' Conference Room."

Sava replied, "I will distract you only if it is important."

Reviewing the storm and earthquake protocols first, praying that neither occurred while Tane and Cyan were gone, Seerce then checked recent department summaries to familiarize herself with current issues.

Long after the staff had gone home, she returned to her office with dinner and sat to read a report Sava had left on her desk. Climatology researchers had interviewed a number of community members in Eyre, including a local priest called Aaron who kept records of ocean sightings. Seerce's heart skipped a beat.

She went on to read an account of the fieldwork. Fishers described slithering bubbles bursting at the surface, with a smell like rotten eggs. Some had seen clouds of vapor erupt from the deep sea. Preliminary analyses showed the bubbles were largely methane gas. Frozen water crystals in the depths held molecules of methane hydrate in stasis. If the ocean depths were warming, there was potentially a massive amount of it yet to be released. Implications for the atmosphere were unknown. A task force of researchers would be convened.

The crystal above her head brightened with a call coming in. "What happened to Cyan?" demanded Tuura with no preface. "Is he ill?"

"No," Seerce replied, "but he is exhausted. None of us can remember when he last took a break. He should be back in a moon, weather permitting."

"How did you happen to take the mantle?" Tuura asked, in her ever-direct style.

"Tane left to try to fix the crystal network," Seerce replied.

"Good news, because I have had a terrible time getting this crystal in Misr to call you. Our situation here deteriorates. The chieftains jockey for control of the air barges."

"Is the Order's business with them settled?" Seerce asked.

"For the moment. I have had to dress up like one of their kept women and attend too many of their banquets. I have grooves in my tongue from biting it. But they agreed that the Order will keep control of Leo."

"Until Altea wants it," Seerce surmised.

"You know we will lose that fight," Tuura rued. "We need to move the Hall of Records and seal off the lower chambers sooner than we planned. Put me on the council agenda to discuss that at our next meeting."

"I will. What else can I do?" Seerce asked.

"Pray for safe passage," Tuura requested. "I intend to return to the Temple. Rayn and his negotiating skills shall accompany me, as it is not safe to travel alone. I will try to call you from Tunise when we get there." The crystal dimmed.

Both their names came up only decans after Cyan had left the Temple. But Seerce could not allow herself to think of Rayn or Aaron right now. There was too much that needed doing.

*

It was several days before Seerce thought to look up Cyan's biography in the Hall of Records. Her rational mind required an explanation for his neurosis.

Raised by elder relatives and later placed in a boarding school, he grew up on remote islands in the southern ocean of the other hemisphere. His mother died when he was an infant and he had no siblings. Thereafter his father went out to sea with a fishing fleet, never to be seen again.

All of Cyan's successes were scholarly. Teachers looked out for him, taking him home to their families on holidays. Priests ensured that he was among a small Mu contingent accepted to study with the Order of the Sun. His childhood must have been lonely. No wonder his devotion to Gaia and the ancient ways.

Seerce moved to his record of incarnations. He identified two lives as priests, another as a mother of ten children. In mid-Altean times, he died as a young man, leaving behind a woman he loved deeply. He described her at length. In his Tamthan existence, to which he alluded at the Gate of Persa, he practiced magical shamanism.

Concluding that his desperation to be loved drove his obsessions, Seerce closed the file. From Sava she knew of his relentless pursuit when they were classmates and when they were assigned together to the Cenon project. His approach to Seerce was more sophisticated and manipulative. If he did not conquer his tendencies, what might he do when he returned to the Temple?

*

"Madame, Jair is on your crystal waiting for you." Sava was in the foyer of the Temple as Seerce emerged from morning meditation.

"From where does he call?" Seerce asked.

"Palermo," she responded.

"Is Tane with him?"

"He did not say, only that it is urgent he speak with you."

Seerce's heart leapt in her chest. Running across puddles in pelting rain, the women were dripping when they reached the other building. The storms that Damon forecast swept over Altea. "Stay with me, Sava," Seerce requested, going into her office and drawing down her crystal.

Jair asked, "When does the next Echo test start?"

"Fourteen days from now," she answered. "What concerns you?"

"Something has been constructed here, some kind of array built into a rocky promontory on the northeast end of the bay. It is not easy to see. The bulk of it seems to be underground."

"Were you able to view the hidden portion?" Seerce asked.

"Yes. It may be a transducer of some kind, but I cannot figure what it detects or converts. Palermo uses nothing more sophisticated than hypersound and solar power. The navy's marine transducer is at the opposite end of the bay. Tell Kieran there is a Control Star vessel in a stationary position beyond the bay. I cannot imagine what business it has around here."

"We will investigate, Jair," Seerce assured him. "You and Tane have your hands full with network issues."

"We do. He is in town arranging our passage to Sardinia. We will spend two days here with my father and then take him with us to temples in this area of the MidTerra."

"Would you let me know," Seerce requested, "as you reach each destination?"

"I shall try. I am amazed I got through to you at all." The crystal dimmed.

"Altea invests some time and expense there," Sava pronounced. "That is worrisome."

Seerce agreed. "Palermo is a simple farming community and rather remote. What would the Ryk want with it?"

*

Several days of intensive observation commenced with an emergency meeting between the science exemplars and Seerce's staff. Shahana attended in Tane's place. Fortunately, the crystal connection to Zanata remained intact. Seerce requested that questions be held until her staff finished a brief presentation.

Kieran displayed on the crystal his latest image of the Echo complex, saying, "As we usually see prior to a test sequence, there are submersibles coming and going frequently between the contractor ships and Echo." Showing a schematic of the positions of four ships in the vicinity, he told the exemplars, "Two of these we know well, *Amymone* and *Tethys*. New lately are two military ships. The *Rhode* is a typical navy frigate in a stationary position west of Morivay. A new hybrid navy submarine called *Ceto* is conducting sweeps all the way around Echo."

Demonstrating her compliance with council policy, Seerce stated, "We have not boarded the military vessels, but we hear it discussed aboard *Tethys* that the upcoming test cycle will include an attempt to control earthquakes. This is the first time we have known Altea to be interested in the side effects of this energy.

"Kieran," she requested, "please show us Palermo so the exemplars may understand the situation there." A map appeared in the crystal, featuring the small port situated on a northern MidTerra peninsula.

Cesar took up the narrative. "East of the village are foothills fronting an active volcano. There have been occasional minor eruptions in the last several centuries. However, it is far enough away to pose no threat to the town.

"The peninsula is forested, but where it has been cleared, the volcanic soil is rich and productive. The marine climate is warmer and calmer than Altea's. Construction here is largely one- and two-story wood buildings, inland from the bay and up into nearby hills. The Order has a temple and school situated on one of these." A rendering of that campus appeared.

Seerce told them, "Several days ago, Tane and one of his staff were in Palermo to assess network difficulties. They discovered an array along the coast and a contractor's ship nearby."

Sava reported her observations. "Madame and sir," she began most politely, "there is a navy armada in the area east of Majorka, towing portable docks and heavy machinery on barges. One of the ships is a military hospital and another carries food. The entourage heads east in the direction of Palermo."

"We have only ten days to find out whether our observations add up to a problem," Seerce stated. "I remind you that the Order's crystal supply is manufactured in Palermo, and the central relay for the regional network is in our temple there. My staff and I wish to conduct a thorough survey of the area, but we need more observers to accomplish that. May we borrow as many of yours as you can spare?"

The meeting concluded with an agreement to reassign a total of six observers to Oceanus, beginning the following day at noon in that part of the world.

*

Waiting for Sava, Seerce peered out between the braces across her office window, recalling a statement that Damon had made in the last council meeting, that the Ryk had launched an energy industry on half-truths and hope that problems of safety would eventually be solved. When she came in, Sava closed the door behind her.

"I wish to offer a service, madame, should you require it. There is an esoteric practice of the Mu by which one is able to project one's physical body through time and space. I employed it when I was with Cenon."

Seerce had to think that through for a moment. "Are you saying that a physical body may project itself in the manner that we send our etheric bodies?" she asked incredulously. "And you have done this?"

"Yes and yes," Sava said, sitting down. "Cyan trained me. It was a useful skill when we visited future Olmekah priests. Often it was necessary to get in and out quickly. They were a motley crew."

Seerce laughed. "When we were students, Cyan led Rayn and me on a journey to a decaying Olmekah pyramid. Rayn was convinced that I had been kidnapped in some prior visit there. Cyan intimated they had other uses for me and would have killed Rayn."

"That sounds like the Olmekah," Sava said. "After your experience, Cyan took them off the list of teachable civilizations."

"Truly?" Seerce asked.

"Yes," Sava said. "I was greatly relieved."

"Does one use a gate for this physical projection?" Seerce asked, concerned for leaving tracks.

"No. You attend to your physical needs where you go, so you do not require a gate to call you back. But you are subject to your new environment. If endangered there, you need your wits about you in order to project home. There are historic accounts of priests who failed to return."

"I see," Seerce replied. "How does this skill of yours aid our situation?"

"Say that the array in Palermo could be caused to malfunction." She raised her hands and wiggled her fingers. "I have these weapons."

"Can you travel with tools?"

Sava laughed. "No. We deconstruct and reconstruct our bodies, but we have no power over inanimate objects. Generally one investigates remotely to assess a situation, then drops in physically to accomplish a particular task."

"Does everyone in Cenon do this, Sava?"

"To my knowledge, I was the only one Cyan trained and I needed his prior approval to teleport. Usually we made those visits together."

What other way would Cyan have it? thought Seerce. Special favors bought him more control. "Would you teach me, Sava?"

"Yes, madame. That is why I bring it up."

"Please do not call me madame. You and I have known each other for years. Call me by my name."

"You deserve the title. You earned it."

"You and I both know why I have this job."

"Stop it, please. You lead us admirably. Are there others who should be trained?"

"I will think about that. For now, let us keep this between you and me." Seerce smiled, saying, "You give me hope."

*

Ell called Seerce by crystal that afternoon. "Exemplar Jory wishes to speak with you, madame. Are you available?"

"I am," she responded.

Momentarily, Jory's face was before her. "Seerce, your days must be more than full. Let me assist. How can you possibly handle the affairs of the Order and these Echo tests on your own?"

He and Damon must have spoken. Seerce looked out to a downpour, hearing the crash of heavy waves against the seawall. "Unless you are a whale, Jory, you would not get here. But you are kind to offer. We have incredible staff doing everything possible."

"Is Tane back yet?" he asked.

"No. He may be in Sardinia now, but the network interference continues. These storms will roll over the MidTerra. I do not expect him any time soon."

"Please, Seerce, let me help," Jory persisted.

"Might you be able to find among the expatriates in Tibisay someone who knows how Echo extracts and transmits energy? Restricted as we are, Oceanus makes no headway on those questions. We have to know why its operation causes earthquakes."

He hesitated. "It will take me a while to find an appropriate contact."

"That is how you can help, in the biggest way, without endangering yourself."

"I will do my best. Tell me how you fare."

"I am sleep-deprived and due to a meeting. How are you?"

"Looking forward to your visit," he said, grinning.

"As am I," she fibbed, dimming the crystal and heading down the hall. Jade had something to show her.

"Please have a seat, madame," Jade invited. "I have studied your early observations of Echo, in which you describe glowing tubes emerging from a fabricated block in the only tower that was operational at the time." On her desk she laid a diagram, hand drawn on a sheet of velum. "Looking similar to this?" she questioned.

"Roughly," Seerce told her. "Separate light sources spiral through those tubes as though they were strung along a coiled wire."

"Those may be heat-converting wafers. Heat is the only constant energy at the depths. Metallic wafers wrapped around an iron wire or bar might produce an electric current. I shall go looking for manufacturer's specifications. There are several companies that make such transducers."

*

As the test cycle approached, the Oceanus staff met daily. Today, around Kieran's desk, they viewed the image he constructed from Jade's description of the Palermo array. She had determined that it was a passive relay station, but how deeply it was drilled she could not say. "Thick iron bars descend into rock beneath it. Crossbars of a metal alloy are attached to the pole that extends vertically above the array. It communicates with ships by microwaves through the air."

"It sends no pulses through Earth?" Cesar clarified.

"No," Jade replied. "The iron below ground may detect energy, or even attract it, perhaps in the manner that a lightning rod draws an electrical charge."

"We need to find the party responsible for its design and manufacture, if we are going to understand it any better," Kieran said. "Control Star did not build it. They just monitor it."

Seerce informed her group that their borrowed contingent of observers had found no other arrays and no new power stations along the coasts in the MidTerra's north central region She had asked that team to move their search inland.

*

For several days there had been intermittent minor vibrations, like low rumbles of thunder in the distance. Cesar spoke loudly from the hallway, "It is safe to go to your observations. These are not tremors." Their observation lounge was a dim inner room at the back of the Oceanus suite. Comfortable lounges were arranged in a circle around a small table with a rack of chimes, to rouse observers if there was a quake.

Sava heard mention at a contractor meeting about a transmission of mixed energy wavelengths beneath the volcano. Jade reasoned that such a strategy might serve to deflect or cancel damaging transmissions from Echo, perhaps a protective measure for Altea's mainland. Sava wished to investigate further, so Seerce took her watch at the Control Star vessel, *Andromeda*, outside the Bay of Palermo. Agreeably, Exemplar Annecy took charge of the Order's affairs.

Reclining in the observation lounge, Seerce transferred her etheric self directly to *Andromeda*'s communications hub, fore on the uppermost deck. No longer did she or her staff record every journey with Icos, a ridiculous requirement when routinely they

Valid through 10/31/2019

Buy 1 Fresh Baked Cookie Get 1 FREE

Mix or match any flavor.
Try our limited time only
Cookie Monster's Everything Cookie*

To redeem: Present this coupon in the Cafḭ.

D4R9D9L

Buy 1 Fresh Baked Cookie Get 1 Free:
Valid for Fresh Baked cookies only.
1 redemption per coupon.
*While supplies last.
Ask Cafe cashier for details.

Return Policy

With a sales receipt or Barnes & Noble.com packing slip, a full refund in the original form of payment will be issued from any Barnes & Noble Booksellers store for returns of new and unread books, and unopened and undamaged music CDs, DVDs, vinyl records, electronics, toys/games and audio books made within 30 days of purchase from a Barnes & Noble Booksellers store or Barnes & Noble.com with the below exceptions:

Undamaged NOOKs purchased from any Barnes & Noble Booksellers store or from Barnes & Noble.com may be returned within 14 days when accompanied with a sales receipt or with a Barnes & Noble.com packing slip or may be exchanged within 30 days with a gift receipt.

A store credit for the purchase price will be issued (i) when a gift receipt is presented within 30 days of purchase, (ii) for all textbooks returns and exchanges, or (iii) when the original tender is PayPal.

Items purchased as part of a Buy One Get One or Buy Two, Get Third Free offer are available for exchange only, unless all items purchased as part of the offer are returned, in which case such items are available for a refund (in 30 days). Exchanges of the items sold at no cost are available only for items of equal or lesser value than the original cost of such item.

Opened music CDs, DVDs, vinyl records, electronics, toys/games, and audio books may not be returned, and can be exchanged only for the same product and only if defective. NOOKs purchased from other retailers or sellers are returnable only to the retailer or seller from which they were purchased pursuant to such retailer's or seller's return policy. Magazines, newspapers, eBooks, digital downloads, and used books are not returnable or exchangeable. Defective NOOKs may be exchanged at the store in accordance with the applicable warranty.

Returns or exchanges will not be permitted (i) after 30 days or without receipt or (ii) for product not carried by Barnes & Noble.com, (iii) for purchases made with a check less than 7 days prior to the date of return.

Policy on receipt may appear in two sections.

came and went from observations every decan or so. When she last saw Sootchie in Zanata, he assured her that Geology observers never utilized the gates.

Seerce listened as two crewmen discussed prior assignments with the navy, while she examined their instrumentation, about which she had been briefed. The monitor for the Palermo array showed no activity.

Locating the captain of the vessel in a meeting with civilian crew, Seerce positioned her invisible self opposite him. He discussed sailing on to Ruda once their business in Palermo was finished. She knew of that port, where the River Iteru emptied into the MidTerra Sea, the lower portion of the same river that flowed past the Monument of Leo. She gathered that *Andromeda* would aid military communications as a new navy base was established at Ruda.

This was most alarming! Altea must intend to take Ruda under its flag. It would meet no resistance from such a small port. Then the navy would have easy access to Misr, a dire development for moving the Hall of Records, for every ship coming into Ruda would be searched and taxed on the value of its cargo. Perfectly matched pairs of pastel crystals were stunning antiquities. Whether or not their contents were recognized, they were worth a fortune as fantastic pieces of natural sculpture, and most likely they would be seized. Seerce knew that the overland routes to Misr were made treacherous by warring chieftains, demanding payment for safe passage across their fragmented territories. Before long there would be no safe way to get the records to Leo.

The conversation among the crew revealed no time frame for *Andromeda*'s reassignment. Though she stayed through the meeting, she heard nothing else noteworthy.

*

Deeply worried, Seerce tossed and turned that night, unable to surrender to the solace of sleep. Long after midnight, the thrum

Silence the Echo

of a steady rain on the pyramidal ceiling finally entranced her conscious mind. A cool ocean breeze touched her face as she crossed into her dream world.

Off in the distance was a small boat, the only occupant standing in silhouette before a setting sun. Alone on a beach, she watched the little craft draw near. The stance of the man was familiar, his long hair blowing loose in the breeze. She watched to see where he would come ashore and set off in that direction. Something about him called to her.

The wind picked up and she pulled her shawl close around her, as the little skiff caught on a sandbar not far from shore. Stepping into shallow water with a lantern and a coil of rope over his shoulder, the sailor pulled the narrow vessel up on the beach, tying it to a rock. Though darkness would shortly fall, she must know who ventured so far across the open water alone.

He picked his way over the logs and stones and rivulets. When he saw her, he raised his lantern to his face. "Aaron!" she cried out in surprise. The sound of her own voice woke her.

His message echoed in her mind, *Stay with me!* But the dreamscape evaporated.

Hoping that somehow he still heard her, Seerce begged him over and over, *Come back to the Temple, Aaron, please! We need your help!*

*

Early on the first morning of the Echo test sequence, the Oceanus team and physicists Shahana and Ari informed Exemplar Annecy of the plan for the day. Seerce would monitor *Andromeda*. Kieran managed the technical observations, as he always did, and Ari would keep night watch. The others had posts aboard contractor ships and outside the volcano substation, from which they would return briefly to provide updates. That annoying low vibration restarted shortly after dawn.

Projecting to *Andromeda*, Seerce found a different technician in the communication hub. As she moved in close to read 'Ensign

Ruzar' in Altean symbols on his pin, he looked around nervously, swatting the air in front of his face as though a mosquito buzzed around him. When she moved behind him, he turned around to look through her invisibility. It seemed that he sensed a presence—she supposed some of the untrained could. Moving out to the narrow hall, she endeavored not to disturb his routine.

Whereas it was midmorning in Altea, it was early afternoon in Palermo's vicinity. Seerce took her vision far above the ship to find the position of the Altean armada. Yet on track for Palermo, now it was less than a half day away. Perhaps *Andromeda* would attach itself to this flotilla on its way to Ruda.

As she returned to the ship, she heard a voice speak clearly. "Ruzar here. We have signatures from the spire." The captain and his first officer hurried through the narrow hall into the small lab. Their voices were excited, their heads bowed toward the console, alive with tracings. Stepping to a window and looking toward shore, the captain's expression indicated that something was amiss.

Seerce took her vision above the ship once again, to view Palermo hanging on the hills above its broad bay. Narrow columns of dust or smoke rose from numerous places. Too far away to see detail, she moved instantly over the center of town. Structures began to sway and roofs to twist, but at this height she perceived only muffled sound. People ran from buildings. Docks along the bay pulled apart and fell into choppy water. She could not understand what she was seeing.

Soon there was a deafening sound, like a roar from deep inside Earth. The ground rolled in waves. Destruction played out in terrifying slow motion. As structures collapsed, billows of debris rose into the sky, wind blending the dust clouds and obscuring her vision. Finally the roar ceased and muffled screams replaced it. Sensations of transmitted terror buffeted Seerce like shock waves.

From Kieran's map she knew the approximate location of Palermo's temple, so she moved there, descending through swirls of airborne particles. Where she thought the campus would be was a silent field of debris. These had been simple framed buildings. Now they were heaps of rubble. If she had known the whereabouts of Jair's father's business, she would have gone there. But if a temple and a school were reduced to this, likely she would find nothing. Overwhelmed, Seerce willed herself back to Oceanus.

Upon reuniting her inner senses with her physical body, a wave of nausea nearly sickened her. By sheer will she quelled it, waiting a few moments before she sat up, trying not to disturb her staff in the recliners around her. Responsible to record what she witnessed for later analysis, she went directly to her office to deposit her recall directly into her communication crystal. Then she summoned Annecy.

Within a decan, all test activity ceased, along with the odd vibration. Seerce steeled herself to inform her staff as they returned. Kieran transferred her eyewitness scenes to the conference room crystal for those who wanted to watch. She had to leave the room.

By the destruction of the relay in Palermo, the Order's entire crystal network failed. Seerce and Annecy composed a brief communiqué to other members of the council, which Ell would deliver one by one, requesting their etheric presences the following day at noon in Altea.

The community gathered at sunset in the Temple, where Annecy conducted a brief ceremony to honor the souls parted from life that day.

Seerce and her staff believed they could have prevented this carnage, if only they had been allowed to observe within Altean ships, facilities, and the offices of the Energy Authority.

CHAPTER 18

As acting chair, Seerce gave her report to the Council of Exemplars, most of them in etheric form, all present but Cyan. Telling them calmly and factually of the dreadful events in Palermo, the immediate arrival of an Altean rescue armada to its shores, and the flag of the Ryk now flying over the destruction, Seerce imparted just how dire their situation had become. She recounted the navy's plan for the Port of Ruda, as she had heard it aboard the Control Star ship. Tuura reported on the unrest in Misr.

Unanimously, it was agreed that the Administrator would seek valuation of the Temple's art and antiquities. Funds would be needed to transfer the Hall of Records to Misr, which had to be accomplished in short order. Tane agreed to return as soon as possible to manage the packing of the precious crystals, leaving Jair and his father to build a new communication relay center in the Sardinian temple.

Seerce stated, "I urge the council to lift its ban on observations within Altean facilities. Too many have died and my staff fears more murderous destruction, as we rely on blind luck and hit-and-miss sources of information. Individual Altean contractors have only pieces of Echo's puzzle. Unless we learn the master plan, we are left with guesswork. The council needs a fuller picture if it is to preserve the records, protect the Order's members, and aid the communities we serve."

"Well you know the arguments for and against, so I suspend debate on the matter. Please vote your conscience now. Who is in favor of suspending the council's ban? Say your name to cast your vote." Damon, Ezra, and Jory joined Seerce.

"Who is in favor of keeping the council's ban as it is?" she asked. Those votes came from Nova, Annecy, Tuura, and Tane.

With all the neutrality she could muster, Seerce announced, "The vote is tied. Therefore the council's rule stands. Plan to meet here again, etherically or personally, every three days hence at zenith of the sun in Altea," Seerce told them. "This meeting is adjourned."

She returned to her office, unsurprised. Fighting her own fury, particularly with Tane, it was late in the afternoon before she acquired the presence to tell her staff in an exemplary manner.

*

Coming late to the dining hall on a subsequent evening, Seerce saw Rayn sitting alone at a corner table. In the midst of recent travails, she had forgotten about his return with Tuura. She noted a few white threads in his longish hair and beard. Walking over with her plate, she asked if she might join him. Clearly she interrupted his reverie. It took him a moment to recover his social graces.

"I would be delighted," he said. By his tone and the set of his jaw, she knew that was not the case. She seated herself and began to eat as an awkward silence ensued.

"I understand your journey was harrowing," she said finally. "Tuura will be ever grateful for your company." He made no comment, so she asked about the progress at Leo. Shrugging, he said it moved along slowly. When she inquired about Tavia's work his eyes brightened a bit.

"She has finished the innermost chamber that will house the records," he answered.

"I would love to see her work," Seerce said.

"Visit. You will be amazed by her artistry." But he did not offer a tour.

She tried to engage him in discussing his project. "Tell me of this pictorial language," she requested, but he did not answer. "Rayn," she encouraged, "I want only to know that you are well and happy." He looked away. Surely he would avoid her as long as he remained at the Temple. Realizing that she might never have another opportunity, she decided to take her chances.

"There is something I must tell you, Rayn. I recently learned the truth about what happened years ago. Cyan confessed to me that he threatened you with expulsion to keep you from me. I wish I had known. I could never fathom what happened to your love for me."

He stood up. "I cannot discuss this with you. Please excuse me."

Seerce touched his arm as he picked up his plate. "Cyan is not here. He is in Majorka. He has no power over you, no matter where he is."

Leaving his plate, Rayn walked out the patio door into darkness and driving rain.

*

Seerce heard Tane's telepathy in her mind and then his image shimmered before her. Reading through valuations of the major artwork, she was still in her office at midnight. *I have reached Majorka,* he told her.

By Damon's report, she knew the weather had deteriorated again.

Are you safe? she asked.

Yes, he told her, *though leaving here will be delayed until the seas calm. You look exhausted.*

I do not sleep. I see Palermo crumble over and over again. Annecy has her methods. Ask.

Seerce waved her hand at him dismissively.

Cyan seems better, he told her.

Unless Cyan will do more than stand by while civilization perishes, he is not better, she snapped.

I will leave you now, Tane said. *Try to rest.*

*

Jory located an informant. This middle-aged scientist was a relative to one of his staff and recently arrived in Tibisay. She had once been a researcher with the Energy Authority, and more recently a consultant to a contractor. In etheric form, Seerce observed the meeting between the two, unbeknownst to the guest.

"The Order lost staff and students in Palermo, and many of their family members," Jory told her sadly. "How might we ensure the safety of our temples and schools?"

The woman fought back tears. "A dear cousin of mine perished there," she said. "I, too, grieve."

Jory offered kind condolences. "What has happened to Earth that such destruction occurs so frequently?" he asked. "Our university wants to focus its research properly."

"You have heard, I suppose, of the EA's ocean floor facility?"

Jory nodded that he had.

"They intend to utilize the heat of the depths as a perpetual energy source," she said. "Within deeply-tunneled conduits, heat is converted to electromagnetic current along an alloy chain, that portion of the system a massive generator with no moving parts. Some of the energy feeds the facility, and more is broadcast as ocean sonar. But largely it is intended to supply power stations around the MidTerra.

"The EA tests for wavelengths to send through the mantle, where pressure has compressed free water into the crystalline structure of rock. More water may be hidden in the mantle than is contained in the oceans of Earth. Water conducts acoustic energy and crystals conduct current."

"How would energy be directed with any precision through the mantle?" Jory asked incredulously.

"Transmission channels were drilled at various angles. There are limitations imposed by the curvature of Earth, but the upper mantle is thick enough to accommodate straight-line transmission as far as the eastern shores of the MidTerra."

Seerce was shocked. Oceanus had no such information.

"Is energy stored at the plant?" asked Jory.

"Enough for redundant systems," the woman answered. "Excess current is returned to the depths unconverted, where it is thought to disperse without effect. Have you seen the aurora at the mid-latitudes?"

"No," Jory replied.

"It occurs with the test cycles. Natural systems of Earth are affected, to what degree and with what result, we do not know."

Now Jory pressed her. "There are those who think the destruction of Palermo was purposeful."

The scientist measured her response carefully. "Clearly these methods have consequences. That is what concerns those who have left the industry." She changed the subject, for she had need of Jory's connections with a mining enterprise in Tibisay, as she tried to secure a position.

*

Cyan called a council meeting the day after his return to the Temple. Seerce had left him a detailed summary of what was accomplished in his absence. If her initiatives disturbed him, he gave no indication. Tane, Tuura, and Annecy were at the table with Seerce, the other four present etherically.

"I recognize the extraordinary efforts each of you made in my absence," Cyan stated. "I am grateful to the Exemplar of Oceanus for her capable leadership during an especially difficult time. Her summary illustrates her courage in confronting many issues. I am humbled to be among you once again."

Seerce distrusted everything about this man, disturbed to be in the same room as he.

"We must prioritize our most pressing tasks," Cyan continued. "Many are interrelated. Give me your best advice now, one at a time. We shall craft a method to address the most significant issues. Keep in mind that the Order is not this Temple nor your departments, but a voice through time for the Spirit of Gaia. Let us align our every decision accordingly."

As each spoke, options were distilled into tinctures of bitter medicine. The immediate liquidation of the Temple's salable assets was approved. Jory was directed to exercise his option for two floors of apartments in a new building in Tibisay. A cap was placed on expenditures for the crystal network, for the Order's members had the option to meet etherically, as they had through the millennia of their existence. A budget was set for the transfer of the records and a power source for the chambers of Leo.

Other difficult questions awaited plans: Which endangered academies should be closed to protect lives? Should the Order decentralize so that local decisions could be made quickly? If the contingent in Misr had to be evacuated, where would they go? Assignments were made and the council agreed to gather every half moon until pressing questions were resolved.

The sorrow in that room was palpable. It was one thing to reckon with a set of budgetary choices. It was quite another to close temples and schools, move the records, and disrupt the stability that had been for so long the hallmark of the Order.

*

Tane sent Shahana to rig a temporary crystal relay to the University of Zanata. While there she was able to reconnect a few schools along the north coast of Afrikaa, including the Academy of Tunise.

It was early one morning when the headmaster of Seerce's former school reached her by crystal. At her request, he had summoned her aunt and uncle, Ena and Sirdar of Tunise. Benefactors to his school, he knew them well. Their faces appeared in the crystal.

"Seerce!" Ena exclaimed. "We came as quickly as we could."

"It is wonderful to see you both," Seerce replied. "I have an urgent request for assistance, if you would kindly share this with my father. A group of us from the Temple of Altea will arrive to Tunise seven days hence, with people and freight to send on to Ruda. We need his help to arrange safe transport." Small ports beyond Tunise could not accommodate the Order's submarine.

Seerce explained what was required in the least revealing terms possible, including transport for three priests. "This is highly valuable cargo," she emphasized, "consisting of approximately twenty large and heavy crates. We require a trustworthy crew and a capable vessel to meet a river barge in Ruda." Tavia was making those arrangements with her family.

"Your father and I will locate the best we can find," Sirdar assured her.

Ena added, "No doubt your family will come to greet you. All of us will be so delighted to see you."

"Please convey to my parents that it will be but a brief stop in Tunise, perhaps only a day. Thank you for helping us."

"Safe travels," Ena wished her.

"Gaia's light upon your task," Sirdar added.

"My love to both of you," Seerce told them. Then she thanked the headmaster for his assistance.

"Do not hesitate to call on us, Exemplar," he responded formally, "whenever we may be of service."

*

Tane and Seerce had just sat down to tea in her apartment when there was a knock on her door. She opened it to Ell. "Madame, and sir," he added, acknowledging Tane's presence, "there is a visitor in my office. Seerce, I bring his urgent request to see you."

"Who is this?" she asked, surprised.

"Aaron of Eyre."

Her heart leapt, her prayers answered.

I shall accompany you, Tane offered privately.

I will see him alone, she responded. "How is he, Ell?"

"I would say he is the same Aaron we knew, a few years older like all of us. He requests hospitality, but I do not know if we permit such." Ell was a stickler for protocol and there was none for this situation.

"Take me to him," she requested. Turning to Tane, she asked him to convey to the council that an urgent matter required her attention. His displeasure was apparent.

Aaron looked much as she had seen him in her dream, his hair longer than hers and wild, his beard unshaven for days, dressed in heavy well-worn clothing. An old travel bag was set alongside his wet boots. Those emerald eyes were as striking as the day she met him.

"Seerce!" he exclaimed, standing up. "It has been far too long."

"Welcome, Aaron! Ell has a private space where we may meet. Come with me." He picked up his bag and boots and followed her to a little room down the hall. She closed the door behind them. "I saw you in a dream and begged you to come. You heard me!" she exclaimed. "Am I allowed to hug you?"

He laughed. "You had best hug me! It has been a harrowing journey over the worst of seas."

"Thank the Goddess you are safe!" She threw her arms around him and squeezed him tight, disregarding his need for a bath.

"Am I allowed to kiss you?" he asked.

"Quickly, yes," she replied. "I am on a break from a council meeting and must return."

It surprised her that he kissed her lips, which he had never done, though lightly. Then he looked quizzically into her eyes. "Are you in trouble?" he asked.

"Routinely," she giggled. "I am the most errant of the crew. Are you hungry?"

"I am starving," he told her, "without a hot meal for too long."

"Ell will order you food and tea. Stay here and I will be back as soon as I can. If Cyan comes first, justify your stay by whatever reason you care to give. He is chair now." She hugged him again, flung the door open, and ran back to Ell with her request to feed their guest.

Nova was speaking by crystal when Seerce tiptoed into the council meeting. Taking her chair, she telepathed Cyan privately, *I must see you at your first opportunity.*

Cyan nodded slightly to her. He allowed the discussion to reach its natural conclusion, then told the council, "My apologies to all. There is a matter that requires my attention, so let us adjourn for the day."

Uninvited by Seerce, Tane followed her out to meet Cyan on the catwalk. "I understand we have a surprise," said the chair.

"Aaron of Eyre is in Ell's office requesting hospitality," Seerce replied, glancing at Tane's unreadable expression. "I recommend we give it."

"Aaron failed to complete his studies," Cyan stated. "He has no standing here."

"May I remind you, sir, we need to buy some time to get the records to Misr. Surely both of you recall that Aaron was the finest technical observer among the ten initiates you trained. Please!" she implored. "Recognize that Gaia assists us."

"I must ascertain just what kind of priest Aaron has become," Cyan stated.

"One who assists our Climatology observers in his homeland," she asserted. "I shall await your decision in my office."

Cyan signaled the wall to let him pass.

Seerce turned to Tane. "Have you nothing at all to say, no support you can lend me?" she questioned.

"You do well on your own," he responded, before he crossed through the projection.

She wondered what it was that Cyan held over Tane's head. Obviously, he was right back at his friend's side.

*

At a joint meeting of Physics and Oceanus, Seerce introduced Aaron as priest of Eyre, her classmate and friend. "Independently, Aaron has obtained information that we have not. You may share freely with him what we know." She introduced her staff.

Warmly, Aaron told Tane, "It is good to see you, Exemplar." He was met with only a nod.

"Please, Aaron," Seerce requested, "summarize your perspective on that which concerns us all."

Looking at her curiously, he requested, "May we pause to align our energies to focus upon the Spirit of Gaia?" He closed his eyes to draw deep, even breaths. Those around the table straightened their spines and followed suit. Calm settled in the room. Then he spoke.

"Echo is what Altea intends to be its prime and inexhaustible energy source for the future. The prototype was built into the volcano beneath the dome thirty years ago. One consequence has been the destabilization of the upper portions of this island, basalt and gabbro rock particularly. Peridotite forms the roots of the underwater mountain range. That is a mantle rock suitable for insulating the energy carried by deep conduits. But the higher rock deteriorates."

Turning back to Seerce, Aaron asked, "Do you remember when you and I first viewed the interior of the volcano station? It was one of our remote sightings as initiates."

"Yes," she answered. How astute he was to portray their secretive act as a sanctioned foray, indicating just how long he and Seerce had been concerned about this errant energy. "The stone surrounding the conduits crumbled. It seemed to me that something changed the rock at a molecular level."

"Weaker portions of this volcano are subject to catastrophic collapse," Aaron stated. "Echo tests aggravate the stress. The Order may need to leave Altea." Seerce knew this was what he had told Cyan last evening. His stay at the Temple was approved for the length of a moon, but he was restricted from the Hall of Records.

Now staff members shifted in their seats, understandably concerned, unaware as yet of contingency plans agreed upon by the exemplars. Tane glanced at Seerce.

"A host of ethical scientists and capable EA leaders have been dismissed over the years for speaking the truth about this energy. Some of them plot to destroy Echo. Do you feel tremors during the test cycles?"

"Yes, often," Kieran answered.

"The EA experiments with the broadcast of protective wavelengths through the volcano system," Jade told Aaron.

"Are you aware of the navy's involvement?" Aaron asked.

Sava answered, "Two navy vessels are stationed near Echo, and we know the militia increased its presence at the volcano during this last test cycle. If I may speak freely, madame," she requested of Seerce, who nodded her approval, "we believe the military had a hand in the disaster at Palermo."

"What happened there?" Aaron asked.

Tell him, please, Seerce telepathed to Sava. Aaron's eyes remained on Seerce as Sava gave the summary.

I am sorry you had to witness this, he told Seerce privately. "I had no idea," he said aloud. "I was aboard fishing boats, trying to get here to warn you."

Tane finally spoke. "So we have a bungling bureaucracy, an endangered mainland, and plotting conspirators. Have you more dismal news, Aaron?"

"Only this," he replied. "The Autark and his entourage have left the palace for Majorka. I trust they know something we do not."

"Obviously we must work quickly," Seerce concluded. "Kieran, please orient our colleague to the department and take him with you on observations. Accept our deepest gratitude, Aaron. You risked your life to warn us."

Silence the Echo

*

"Has Cenon revised its forecast for the demise of civilization?" Seerce asked this of Kessa as they lingered over tea. She had not seen much of her since she had moved into Laela's apartment, happily giving up her Temple residence when campus housing was in short supply.

"My, we are cheery this morning," her friend remarked.

"Altea's recklessness destabilizes the volcano."

"It would not be a bad thing for the Ryk to go away."

"But if it fell, think of the water that mountain would displace!" Seerce exclaimed. "The greatest of all waves would drown all the seaports, even at a distance. What does Cenon have to say lately about the terminal event?"

"There is no vision from on high for a grand ending, my dear. The change may be slow and pervasive, like the floods and storms, consuming resources until people migrate inland or starve or both. All Cenon can do is look here and look there and follow intriguing leads. Human population is greatly diminished in the near future. But no one has seen the end." Kessa asked gently, "Is it your survival that concerns you?"

"No," Seerce replied. "It is having done too little to prevent the passing of all that is good."

*

It was moving day for the Hall of Records. Before the crystals were crated, Seerce had found and deposited information she needed to her Hall crystal. On the way to and from Tunise, she intended to study the Mu practice of teleportation. She went to say goodbye to Aaron, who greeted her joyfully.

"Is it allowable to entertain a beautiful woman in my room?" he asked.

"Yes," Seerce replied, "any beautiful woman you choose."

"Then please, lady, take my most comfortable chair." He motioned toward the one and only wooden chair in a tiny room on the third floor of the Administration building. He sat down on the narrow bed.

"Just so you know, the exemplars do have a plan for abandoning the Temple," she told him. "The details have not been announced to the staff."

"Ever will you have a home in Eyre," Aaron told her. "Come back with me."

"That might be awkward. You have a woman and child, do you not?"

He looked at her askance. "No, I do not."

"Who is the flame-haired girl I have seen with you in Eyre, when I have tried to get your attention?"

Aaron drilled into her eyes. "Did you allow Cyan to plant some crazy suggestion in your mind? There is no one with red hair in Eyre! I have no child. The only woman I ever loved sits here with me."

"Oh, my Goddess!" she exclaimed.

"Seerce, I warned you not to let him hypnotize you! Whatever he did kept me from getting through to you. So many times I have sought you by remote vision, but you would not hear me. Lately I tried to find you in dream states. Finally your spirit called back to me."

Cyan had not confessed this! "I recognize now that he is every bit as sinister as you thought him to be," Seerce told him. "But all the while you have kept watch on Echo?"

"Yes, because Altea can take everything from us in the blink of an eye. I saw it in Eyre and you saw it in Palermo."

Seerce bowed her head. Tears welled unbidden. She stood and took a step toward him, needing someone to uphold her in her grief. He rose and took her into his arms, saying nothing. "Aaron, only you understand how difficult it is to bear what I have seen." She pulled back gently, just far enough to look into his eyes. Switching to telepathy, she told him, *I have a proposal, something we might do together.*

Tell me, he said, releasing her reluctantly.

She described what she knew of Mu teleportation. *Will you*

study this with me? If we can project our physical selves, we can disrupt their tests, potentially even disable Echo.

Aaron sat down on the bed, his eyes wide. *I have never heard of teleportation!* he exclaimed. *Who does this?*

To my knowledge, only Cyan and Sava. He trained her some years ago. Covertly she will coach us when I return from Tunise. Might you stay with us more than a moon, if need be?

My brothers have watch over Eyre. They know of a beautiful woman here that I wish to bring home. If I am delayed, they will tell me to be more persuasive.

Seerce laughed. "I will return in a couple days," she said, leaning over to kiss Aaron's cheek. "Be good while I am gone."

*

Traveling eastward through the depths, there was nothing to see through the submarine's tiny oval windows. Crates were stowed where seats had been removed. Tane slept on a bench seat in the rear, for he had been up all night. Perhaps fifteen were aboard, including healers bound for Palermo.

Seerce sat alone to begin her study of particular Mu teachings. She had found clues to teleportation scattered among a range of subjects: the structure of the universe, the nature of consciousness, and the attributes of subtle inner senses. Depositing her interpretations into a recording crystal for Aaron, often she paused to search for explanations of Mu terms and underlying concepts, adding these as she went along.

The Mu held that consciousness assembled the atoms and molecules of the corporeal being. Therefore, consciousness was capable of disassembling and reassembling these elsewhere. Physical manifestation was first imagined and then constructed. Time and space were nothing more than camouflage accepted by the physical brain. The inner senses were unconstrained by camouflage.

Seerce realized that she had come to accept these truths. Once she was convinced that she could move her inner vision outside her physical body, she was able to view remotely. When Cyan led her etheric body on tours, she learned that her inner senses were capable of travel to any place, in any time frame. Her brain's panic might be quelled with a reminder of the deeper and larger framework of her existence. As she was trained, so she had come to accept that indeed she was a multidimensional being in a multidimensional universe.

For the act of teleportation, one first must be convinced that such a feat is possible. Acceptance of the idea must precede the attempt. The ego must be assured of its safety. Only fear prevented success.

Seerce looked up to see Rayn walking in her direction from the front of the vessel. He went with Tane and Shahana for the same reason he had accompanied Tuura—to interpret and negotiate, if need arose. She was sure he would slip by, pretending not to see her, portraying himself deep in thought. If he had wished to speak further with her, surely he would have by now. Her Hall crystal was at her forehead when he stopped at her row of seats.

I see that you are busy, madame, he telepathed formally. *Perhaps you would allow me a few moments later when you are free.* He glanced away as Seerce met his eyes, but then he pulled his nervous gaze back to her.

Just for a moment, she recalled how she had loved to look at him, when his eyes revealed his fascination with her, when his smile or his touch ignited her passion. She had to stop herself, for she knew not what her face portrayed. *Rayn,* she greeted him with a smile, *please sit down. There need be no formality between us.*

He seated himself opposite her. *I have intended for too long to apologize for my regrettable behavior, when last we met in the dining hall. It was wrong between priests, unforgivable between two who loved each other as we have.*

She was most surprised by this.

He continued, *I did not realize how tightly I had bound that portion of my life. I tried to forget, to pretend none of it happened. I was unprepared for you to break open that buried vault.*

I meant only to relieve long-held pain, not to revive it. Forgive me, she beseeched.

Aaron and I have spoken, he said. *All of us suffered by Cyan's manipulations.*

I loved you, Rayn, with every fiber of my being. I could not imagine what changed so much while you were gone to Misr.

He hesitated. *That needs apology, too. Following Cyan's threat, I convinced myself that you desired visibility and rank, that he offered you those and you agreed to his terms. I am so very sorry, Seerce, to have made such assumptions.*

I accept your apology because you give it, but really, there is no need. Each of us had to reckon somehow with what befell us. They looked at each other and then looked away.

Do you still think about what might have been? he asked her.

Sometimes I do, Seerce admitted. *But always I have thought I belonged at the Temple. You seem to be happier far from there.*

You are correct, he agreed.

So I do not know how we would have maintained our love long-term. One of us would have been away or one of us would have been out of place.

The choice should have been our own. We might have worked it out. A look of wistfulness crossed his face. *Like Anakron and your grandmother.*

Seerce sighed. *But there is no going back. I fear for your safety in Misr. We do not know what Altea intends there.*

If they want to build and expand, we can count on our connections with Tavia's family.

The Ryk wants only to conquer, Rayn! Seerce responded with vehemence. *They stop at nothing to impose their will upon any populace.*

I doubt we have a choice anymore. All of us will have to live with the greater power or leave for a corner of Earth that Altea does not want.

She was a fighter and he preferred compromise, as true now as it had been in their past. *I am grateful for this sharing,* she said. *One never knows which conversation will be the last.*

Rayn startled.

I consider moving Oceanus to Tibisay, she explained, *on the other side of the world. I may never see you again.*

Then, please, may I embrace you while I might? he requested. The two stood up and held each other. Neither stirred for a long time.

I must let you get back to your work, he said finally.

I hope we have another time around the wheel, Rayn, another life to live the love we knew. It was bold to say but heartfelt.

Let us agree that we will. He touched her face and then he left her. She watched him walk to his seat in the back, on the other side of the aisle. Sitting down, he leaned forward and covered his face with his hands.

Seerce took her seat and allowed the river to escape from behind the dam that broke periodically now, crying silently.

CHAPTER 19

Arriving in the port of Tunise near midnight local time, the submarine was easily berthed, but disembarking was impossible. The side hatch could not be utilized here. The pilot tried to rig a gangway from the upper hatch, but the surf was heavy and the vessel bobbed high in the water. No port staff arrived to assist. The passengers stretched out on the floor or tried to sleep in their seats.

Tane awoke during this commotion. He and Seerce went to the galley on the lower deck, where he ate a dinner packed by the Temple cooks. "This is worrisome for getting our cargo off-loaded," he remarked. "I had not anticipated lifting crates through the upper hatch."

"If we can get ashore and find my father, you will have experienced hands and proper equipment," Seerce told him.

"Likely it will be sunrise before we see any help from the port. That bench seat is fairly comfortable if you want to rest. I will assist the pilot if there is something I can do."

Though it would be early evening in Altea, Seerce was exhausted. Too much sitting, concentrated study, and a flood of emotions had taken their toll. Maybe the gentle rocking of the vessel would put her to sleep.

*

Seerce awoke to her father standing over her. She sat up, exclaiming, *Papa, you came to rescue us!*

Yes, my daughter, he said. *We did not find you at the hotel, and this is the only submarine at port. I assumed you were on it. I caused those lazy port hands to bring their portable gangway.*

She swept her hair back from her face. *Sit down with me for a moment. I need to collect myself. Did Mama come with you?* she asked.

Yes, yes, of course, and the twins, Narad replied. *Your grandmother stayed home. She hopes you will visit.*

Much as I want to see her, we have pressing issues. Looking to the front of the ship, she saw no one. *Did everyone get off already?*

Yes, they are having breakfast. I needed to size up this cargo of yours, so I told them I would wake the sleeping empress when I was done.

I am an exemplar, Papa, she corrected, giggling. *Thank you for all you do,* she told him, kissing him on the cheek. *I know your great love for Altean priests and their problems.*

I do this for you alone, he assured her. *I was surprised to find Rayn in this company.*

He will handle the transfer of the cargo at Ruda.

Then he can help us with the transfer to the boat I have arranged. Shall I make it hard on him?

No, Papa, please! The past is behind us. We need to leave it there.

*

The morning was a blur of logistics, hellos and goodbyes, hugs and good wishes. The healers were on a boat to Palermo by early afternoon. Those remaining had a late lunch at a café with Seerce's family. Then Rayn, Shahana, and Tane joined Narad and Sirdar to assist the cargo transfer, the twins along to watch. Their exhausted pilot took a hotel room and slept.

Silence the Echo

Rayn has aged some, Portia noted. Seerce had relayed telepathic pictures to her as they ate. Josef and Loren remembered him fondly, seating themselves near him and pestering him with questions, which he seemed to enjoy.

I agree, Seerce replied. *The pressure on those in Misr must be great. Fresh air and exercise may be lacking.*

He regrets that he did not fight for you, her mother discerned. *Your lives would be so much happier.*

Portia and her perceptions! *But he did not, Mama, and so much has transpired since.*

You have long lives ahead of you. There is no reason that you cannot be together, if you choose. Think about it. He is.

Seerce could not think about it. She had obligations to fulfill.

*

Both the hired boat and the submarine would launch at dawn. Out on the wharf, Seerce hugged her colleagues in turn.

I will miss your uncommon sense, she conveyed to Shahana. *Keep these men in line.*

Tane thanked Narad on behalf of the Order, then he turned to Seerce. *I will be in touch,* he told her.

I hope so. Thank you for taking this great responsibility.

Rayn embraced her tightly and a bit long. *Let us not forget our promise to each other,* he said.

Never will I, she replied. *Please let me know when you are safe in Misr.*

I shall, he vowed.

Narad stepped forward to take Rayn's hand and wish him safe passage. Rayn took both of Portia's outstretched hands and she pulled him into a hug. Seerce saw his tears as he turned to follow the others up the gangway.

Narad assured Seerce, *The captain is an old friend, the boat is reliable, and the weather is favorable for a two-day journey. It is not the fastest vessel, but a fishing boat draws little attention. For security in times like these, it was the best choice we had. Perhaps now you will tell your mother and me what else concerns you.*

That the Order will have to leave Altea, she replied, *sooner than we are ready.*

Come home, daughter! Narad exclaimed. *Bring your friends with you. There is nothing you can do to change anything at all about the Ryk.*

Seerce expected this. *We must try to understand what they do to Earth.*

To what end? he asked pointedly. *You will not stop them. You are not a navy, just priests.*

Papa, my staff and I feel for the planet as you feel for our homeland. We fight for it.

Narad replied, *I fight for my daughter's life.*

Portia interjected, *You are welcome home, child, you and whoever you choose to bring with you, at any time. We can leave it at that.* She reached for Narad with one hand and Seerce took the other. They walked to where the submarine was docked on the other side of the port.

Before she climbed aboard, Seerce told her parents, *Know how very much I love you. I will get home as soon as I can.*

*

Traveling westward faster than the sun, Seerce was among her staff in her own department at midday in Altea. Aaron's face betrayed his delight in seeing her. *You will have to tone that down some,* she telepathed. *People will talk.*

"Cyan asked to meet with all of us as soon as you are ready," Sava told her.

"Do you know why?" Seerce asked.

"We had a moderate quake here yesterday. The epicenter was near Morivay."

At the southern tip of the archipelago, Seerce thought, not far from Echo. "Of course," she responded. "Now is fine, if he is available."

Seerce sat down at the conference table with a cup of tea. She was responsible for Tane's team for as long as they were without their superior and his number two. Setting up the Hall of Records would be a painstaking process. Installing the power source for the chambers required more time and effort. They might be gone several moons, maybe longer. With another test cycle looming, she was doubly appreciative for Aaron's presence.

Cyan came quickly to sit down with Oceanus, the two remaining physicists, and Aaron. He told the group that Exemplar Jory had been traveling by boat near Morivay yesterday, on his way to Altea. "He has yet to arrive," the chair stated. "Geology observed giant waves in the area following the quake. They suspect that a flank of the undersea mountain range gave way. Ell is viewing remotely in Morivay and in Piaroa, where Jory's boat originated. We have no other information."

Seerce's stomach knotted.

"There is damage to campus buildings," Cyan continued, "cracks in stone walls above and below ground level. Skylights fell in the Healing Temple. Panes of glass are broken in Admin. Pantry shelves fell. None of our staff was injured beyond bruises and a broken toe. We are fortunate, indeed."

"Older structures in Altea collapsed," Aaron reported. "The cooks say two hundred or more are dead and many more injured, per official news."

Seerce set aside her shock to report the successful transfer in Tunise. With one hand she held her Crystal of the Sun, twisting its gold chain idly with the other. Jory is dead, she thought. What other way could it be? Who would take responsibility for Tibisay?

"Madame," she heard Kieran say, "we have other updates, if you have finished yours."

"I apologize," she responded, rousing herself from her tangled thoughts. "I have nothing to add." Aaron's eyes were upon her. She picked up her cup, trying to drink in more disturbing news about the Autark's entourage taking residence in Majorka.

Sava signaled Kieran with a look. He concluded with a final

recommendation that Ari assume night watch for both Oceanus and Physics. "Madame and sir, there is too much at stake to leave the departments uncovered."

"Ari, does this meet with your agreement?" Seerce asked.

"Yes, madame," he replied.

"Thank you," said Seerce. "We shall give you report at change of shift." Standing to signal the end of the meeting, she said to Cyan, "We appreciate, sir, that you keep us informed," remaining where she was until she was sure he had gone. Then she led Aaron, Kieran and Sava into her office and closed the door behind the best and brightest on her team. Lowering her voice to a whisper, she said, "We must end this savagery! Sava has a means that she will teach us."

*

The conspirators met later in the gym. Aaron had obtained sports attire from the storeroom. Dressed for handball, they sat on mats in the center of the gym with paddles and balls. For as long as they remained uninterrupted, their workout would consist of practicing teleportation. Seerce presented Aaron with the study crystal she created for him, in violation of several protocols, and gave Kieran a duplicate that Sava made in the physics lab.

Beginning with a demonstration, the others watched in amazement as Sava disappeared from their circle to materialize instantaneously in a corner of the gym. For good measure she teleported to the other corners. Walking over to join her cross-legged associates, she sat down, saying, "Now for some background.

"Naturally, we project ourselves with a body image," Sava told them. "As you know, you may adjust your projections, making them bright or dim, colored or invisible. The difference with teleporting is that your dense body accompanies your etheric self.

"Your boundless spirit erected your physical being in the first place. It certainly knows, therefore, how to move its creation through imaginary space and time. Teleportation is a motion of consciousness, not a heavy-lifting exercise.

"Your several bodies are chemically and electromagnetically connected, so one will not be lost from the other. It is helpful, though, to send your etheric body first, to scout where you intend your person to be. A mind picture and a safety assessment are calming to your ego.

"Let us begin. First, project your etheric self somewhere in this room and take in a view different than what you see now with physical eyes. Study that view in great detail. Then return to your physical body and open your eyes."

Seerce chose the west door of the gym, open to a storage room, moving her etheric body under its frame. She studied the four seated in the middle, her person among them, indeed a strange experience to look upon herself. Noting how they were positioned in relation to each other, where their hands rested, and the varied colors of their hair, she committed the picture to memory. Then she returned her knowing to her physical body.

When the attention of all was present, Sava requested, "Now enter into your stillness by your own method. Imagine with all your might that you have successfully moved your physical body to the same spot your etheric was a few moments ago. Stay within this exercise with your eyes closed until I speak again."

Seerce followed these directions carefully. Easily she saw in her mind's eye the current view of all of them on their mats. But that was incorrect, she thought. If indeed she had moved her physical body, she would not see herself in the circle. She repeated the exercise again, from start to finish. Now her small frame was absent from her view and momentarily, so was Aaron!

Eventually she heard Sava's voice from a distance saying, "Now you may open your eyes."

Seerce did and here was her physical body beneath the west doorway of the gym! Aaron was cross-legged on top of a wooden chest near the closets. In the middle of the room were Kieran and Sava. Seerce shrieked and Aaron whooped. They ran for each other, colliding midway in a bear hug.

Kieran stood up, disbelieving his eyes. "Are they fooling me?" he asked Sava.

"No," she answered. "I watched them disappear and reappear, Seerce first, then Aaron. They are truly strange. No one accomplishes this on a first try."

*

Waking to what she thought was the sound of driving rain on her pyramidal ceiling, Seerce realized a sharp rap on her door. She donned her robe and went downstairs, opening the door to Kessa in soaking clothes, with dripping hair, as though she had just come in from the storm. "You are a sight, my friend, and in the middle of the night?" She motioned her in. "Let me fetch towels."

"I just heard about Jory," said Kessa sadly. "I have been at my parents' for several days, helping them pack up their household."

"What will this mean for your move to Tibisay?" Seerce asked, having learned a while back that Kessa and Laela had been reassigned together.

"We will go. My parents will take the healers with them on the boat they hired to move their worldly possessions. They do not seem to mind if Laela and I tag along," she joked feebly, handing her wet coat to Seerce, then wrapping a towel around her head.

"Your parents are going to Tibisay? I had no idea."

"I have been trying to convince them that all is not well here. If they had any lingering doubts, this last earthquake convinced them."

"Oh, Kessa, I so regret losing Jory! What a fine person and a powerful force for good." Seerce had just begun to process what it meant to lose one of her few allies on the council, to have to find someone as capable as he to be Exemplar of Colonies. Spreading another towel on one of her chairs, she invited, "Sit here. May I make you something hot?"

Kessa declined.

"Do you want to stay the night with me?"

"No. Laela left something she wants in her office. I will meet her in the dining hall shortly and we will go home. Who knows what we will face in Tibisay?" she rued.

"So much has happened here, Kessa! I cannot seem to get past a challenge before two more find me."

"Tuura said Rayn was here and I saw Aaron myself. How are things between you three?" she asked.

"Rayn is on his way back to Tibisay with Tane and the records. Aaron assists my group with observations. Give me your shoes so I can dry them."

"But your personal universe has shifted," Kessa declared. "I feel it. Level with me, sister. It may be a long time before we see each other again."

Kessa had always read her well. "It will only disillusion you, my friend."

"Our world comes apart. What would shock me anymore?"

"Likely this," Seerce said, sitting in the other chair to share a brief version of Cyan's methods for separating her from Rayn and Aaron.

Kessa's color changed and her eyes narrowed. "Do you not suppose that Cyan recognized the role that was yours to play?" she asked, with a flavor of malice that caught Seerce off guard. "In the beginning, when either of those two might have pulled you from the Temple? Was it not his responsibility to see that you applied yourself to the Order's challenges? Be grateful he took an interest in you! Without him you would not be exemplar. You would not even be priest. How dare you be so ungrateful for all he has done for you?"

"Kessa!" Seerce exclaimed, truly shocked. "He destroyed what he himself called a capable trio for the Order's efforts! Who knows what we might have accomplished together, had he not been so intent upon eliminating his competition! He did not want me for the mission, he wanted me for himself!"

"I will give you this, Seerce," Kessa spat back. "Your ego is well-fortified. Your perceptions are skewed, but it is quite clear on whose behalf you act and it is always your own." She stood up. "I would have preferred not to know this of you." Picking up her shoes with one hand, she took her coat in the other and went out the door.

Seerce sat quietly with her hands folded in her lap. How well Cyan had controlled Kessa's perception of him, she thought, recalling her frank admiration for him and how she always defended him. It pained Seerce to think so, but he might even have enlisted Kessa's services to monitor her relationships with 'the boys.' Her classmate was fortunate if she had suffered nothing else by Cyan's wiles.

Climbing into bed, she recalled something Sava had told her years ago: 'He will turn your friends against you, trying to make himself your only option.'

*

The conspirators held their next practice session in the music hall of the Healing Temple, attempting moves between there and adjacent practice rooms. By the third session, as they transferred between the Temple floor and the empty Hall of Records, Kieran had his first success, cheered noisily by his colleagues behind the closed door of the Exemplars' Conference Room.

Aaron quizzed Sava about the teleportation of material items. Could they borrow gear from Echo contractors and bring it back to Oceanus for examination?

"The Mu had no such devices, so we have no guidance on the matter," Sava told him. "Personally I am reluctant to mix the electromagnetic properties of instruments with my own being. Routinely, though, I have teleported with my Crystal of the Sun. Something about natural crystals likens to our own physical properties. Perhaps we can examine the contractors' equipment when their technicians are absent, and record what we learn in memory crystals that we carry on our persons."

Sava recommended that in their next session they practice

sudden departures, their only defense if they found themselves in the wrong place at the wrong time.

*

Tane's etheric body appeared to Seerce in her apartment that night. As she rinsed her tea cup, she heard his voice in her mind. Then his image glistened before her. *We have arrived in Ruda, safe so far,* he told her.

I am relieved! Are you yet aboard the fishing boat?

Yes, he said. *It is dawn here and Tavia's uncle is due this morning with his river barge.*

Are there signs of a military approach? she asked.

Maybe, Tane said. *Shahana spotted three navy vessels traveling together, but they are at least two days from here. Along our route we saw no boats bearing Altean symbols and none here in Ruda. Rayn is out walking the port to be sure.*

Seerce told him of the quake near Morivay and the presumption of Jory's death.

This is terrible news, Tane responded. *He was our best hope in Tibisay and a good man.*

Jade found an energy substation on the Palermo peninsula, Tane, in the foothills of the volcano. It is largely underground, situated along a river.

How close to operational is it?

She could not tell. A subterranean reservoir has been constructed. We guess that it performs a cooling function, or maybe quantities of water are required to convert what Echo transmits. There are banks of transducers, but no human presence. Perhaps it awaits the resolution of Echo's problems.

Tane told her, *I will get the coordinates from Jade later. After we transfer our cargo to the river barge, Shahana and I will take a look. We hope to get the crystals beneath Leo in the next two or three days. Sleep well.*

As his etheric body faded away, Seerce realized what she had just admitted: Her staff conducted observations in and around a new Altean facility, in violation of the council's directive. Yet Tane agreed to make his own assessment. Perhaps he could step away from Cyan.

*

Kieran and Aaron focused their attention on the function of control panels within Echo's hub, trying to figure how one of its vital systems might be shut down. Oceanus had considerable information about how contractor vessels controlled Echo. But they had yet to observe human hands on the facility's instrumentation.

When they noticed technical gear left in a submersible or an empty lab aboard ships, one of the two teleported in and held those devices in their flesh-and-blood hands. Kieran easily grasped the purpose of these and Aaron captured schematics with his technical memory. What they learned they recorded in memory crystals carried in their pockets.

Seerce reviewed their activity summaries daily, endeavoring to understand each small piece of the technological puzzle. Today the cold distracted her concentration. Her office window bowed against its braces with the ferocity of a gale. She shivered despite her wool robe and a long knit scarf wrapped over her head and around her shoulders.

Drawing down her crystal, she called Ell. "Do you have a stack of blankets somewhere? I have observers out of body who will return to frozen corpses."

Ell chuckled. "I will find some and bring them shortly." When he arrived, the two of them tiptoed around the observation lounge, carefully covering each with two blankets as they lay quietly. Seerce thanked him, observing his departure. Then she went to Kieran at his desk, so engrossed in his task he would not know if he was cold. From behind him Seerce draped wool around his shoulders. Eventually he acknowledged her.

"I have a model of Echo's console," he said, switching on his imager. Upon his desk appeared a miniature, portraying status screens and gauges. "We have discovered that it is voice controlled," he told her.

"Is it voice specific?" Seerce asked.

"Yes. There is a sequence in the headsets for adding one's voice to the security system. We would have to cause *Amymone* and *Tethys* to disregard the alarms that Echo sends for each newly registered voice."

"That could be challenging."

"It is purposefully complicated. If, for instance, we wanted to disrupt the pressure pump system, we would have to gain voice control of the panel, then disable the redundant system, which broadcasts its own alarms. But we will find a way," Kieran told her, ever determined.

*

Seerce and Sava observed project meetings at contractors' offices. If they heard or saw something pertinent to their quest, they teleported to those locations at night after those staffs went home. Opening drawers and cabinets, laying out renderings on tables, looking through specifications and switching on viewers, they sought information about Echo's systems.

One evening, the two women came for details regarding the air locks in Echo's tubular hallways. Unfortunately, several people worked late at the Aldus Lever building in Altea. The chief engineer's office was the most likely place to find what they sought, but he showed no sign of departing.

How loud can you holler? Seerce was in etheric form, asking Sava who was physically present. They were on the third floor of the building, currently dark and unoccupied, having this conversation in a lavatory.

It has been a while, but I can work up a bloodcurdling scream, Sava replied. *I had four older brothers.*

Do that near the half wall on this floor, Seerce suggested. The offices bordered an open atrium, extending through four floors to skylights in the roof. *Then meet me in the storage room on the second level. Hopefully the chief will rush out his door and up the stairs to aid a damsel in distress. I will keep watch.*

What fun! Sava laughed. *Now?*

Now, Seerce told her. Sava left the lavatory and Seerce moved to hover invisibly in the atrium, watching as Sava hid her person in the shadow of a column. *No one can see you,* Seerce confirmed.

Sava emitted a high-pitched, earsplitting, terrifying shriek that might have woken the dead. Fifteen people tore out of their offices and labs. The chief engineer was among the first to arrive on the third floor. Seerce watched uniformed guards take two stairs at a time from the ground floor.

Teleporting into the second floor storage room, Sava rubbed her throat. *It's a good thing we speak telepathically,* she said. *I may have damaged my vocal cords.*

You are a true banshee! The coast is clear. Head for the chief's office and take all the conceptual drawings from beneath his drafting table. I will warn you of any trouble.

Where do you want them? Sava asked.

Two doors down in the sequencing lab, Seerce told her. *No one is in there tonight. We should have enough time to see if what we want is in that stack. If we have to run, leave the goods there. It will be just one more mystery in the haunting of Aldus Lever.*

Sava tittered then disappeared.

They found two velum diagrams that would aid their cause. Sava rolled these up and inserted them into a tubular sleeve that she took from the lab. Opening a window, she dropped the tube into the bushes below. Meanwhile, Seerce summoned Aaron, who teleported to the grounds. The women watched as he moved in shadow to recover the bundle and conceal it under his long, dark winter cloak. Sava teleported back to Oceanus.

Seerce kept watch for his safety as Aaron made his way to the Temple via the air barge system. In the darkness he looked like every other night-shift worker, arousing no one's interest.

Over glasses of wine in their conference room, the two

women recounted their tale to Aaron and Kieran, minus a display of Sava's vocal prowess.

*

On the following day, Kieran watched a technician place a headset, such as many of them used, in a compartment near Echo's console. In the same location was a cache of respirators. After the submersibles left for the day, Aaron and Kieran teleported to Echo. They had no difficulty donning and activating respirators, as they had seen the technicians do. Seerce kept etheric watch over them while Sava floated through the facility, familiarizing herself.

The men examined the headset. Schematics appeared serially on the tiny screen at the end of the flexible stem. Kieran had learned some verbal commands to use with the device. Aaron recorded in a crystal the prompts that opened to promising subjects. Several times he took the device to study the schema it displayed, projecting what he saw into his memory crystal.

Kieran replaced the headgear where he had found it. The respirators they dropped into a waste disposal. By that foray they obtained much of what they needed to know to execute a shutdown of Echo's pressure pump systems.

*

Three days passed without word from either Tane or Rayn. But Seerce knew if she saw the crated crystals in the chambers below Leo, their mission had succeeded. Early in the evening she reclined in the Oceanus observation lounge and projected etherically to the new Hall of Records.

It was the middle of the night in Misr and no one was present. The empty central chamber glowed with the luminescence of its ceiling, its wall carvings indistinct in dim light. Seerce floated through the surrounding chambers. In one of these, stone-cutting tools were laid on slabs across heavy wood boxes. In the next she found crates like those in which the crystals had been packed. One long box had been opened, its lid resting against the stone wall. Enough of the wool packing had been pulled aside to reveal a mint-green pillar! She counted the unopened crates. All they shipped was here! Relief washed over her.

CHAPTER 20

When the four conspirators met over dinner, Aaron told how he had gained brief access to *Amymone*'s interface with Echo, via a broad control panel in the converted barge's communication hub. The sole technician on duty had stepped away from his post to use the lavatory. Aaron teleported in and manually extended the expiration date for an instruction to disregard pressure alarms, something done routinely for technicians as they conducted tests at Echo. He planned to do the same later this evening aboard *Tethys*. If successful, the four were set to proceed the following night with their plan of sabotage.

Kieran demonstrated with his imager the instructions he and Aaron would give to the hub's console. Their first task was to delay start-up of the redundant pump system. Sava had researched design specifications for that system, enabling this breakthrough.

I will plant a false high-pressure reading for a section of one of the tubular hallways, Kieran told Sava and Seerce, telepathing to be sure their colleagues did not hear. *Aaron will disable the automatic closure of the air lock doors in that section. The system will respond by continuing to decrease the pressure in that hallway.*

Sava explained, *When the pressure reaches its low limit, the system will detect a failure and call for start-up of the redundant pressure system. We shall ensure that it is unable to respond. When the primary system sends out alarms, those alarms will not be registered aboard the ships.*

So a breach will occur in that tubular hallway, Seerce predicted, *because external pressure will quickly exceed internal pressure. Do you expect the resulting implosion to displace a large volume of seawater?*

The collapse of the hallway will have only a local effect, Kieran assured her. *We have no idea what kind of force might be generated by sea water entering the two operational towers. It may be a whimper or it may be a bang.*

How will you work around the alarm for new users at Echo's console? Seerce questioned.

We each have a favorite tech whose voices we will imitate, Aaron told her. *We have practiced successfully with headsets.*

Kieran grinned.

Well done! commented Sava.

But Aaron's assertion impressed Seerce as something less than truthful. She chose not to question him before his colleagues, intending to confront him privately. Never had she known Aaron to bend the truth. But first she had a task to accomplish.

Going up to knock on Cyan's apartment door, Seerce carried tidings that would not wait. "I apologize, Exemplar, for disturbing you," she said formally. He welcomed her inside, inviting her to join him for a glass of wine.

"No, thank you," she replied, "for I am on duty. I saw that the records arrived to Leo. Do you know if our people are safe?"

"They are," he confirmed. "Tane appeared to me earlier. It is late now on the continent, so it was my plan to inform the exemplars in the morning. There must be more on your mind. You are nervous. Have a chair with me at the table."

She accepted, saying, "We expect an energy transmission to be sent from Echo to a new power station on the Palermo peninsula, within the next several days."

Concern settled at the bridge of Cyan's nose, knitting together his thick eyebrows.

"Given the unpredictability of such," she said, "it is my strong recommendation that the community leave before this test sequence commences. The mid-ocean ridge and the volcano are already stressed. The community should not be here for another serious quake."

He peered intently at her. "Tane said the same to me earlier."

"Oceanus has considerable activity to monitor," Seerce told him. "Four of us wish to remain here through the test period."

There was a flicker in Cyan's concentrated gaze. "How do you propose to escape if the island shakes badly or is washed over by waves?"

"We will do what we can," she answered, "as will our healers who stay behind. I can be in touch with status reports and make myself available to plan next steps with the council."

His features hardened. "Depending upon what you have wrought, Exemplar, there may be no call for you to do such. You have a duty to bring all your initiatives to council debate. It seems you have allowed Aaron of Eyre to take control of your faculties. I despair to think what you permit, unsanctioned by the council."

The repressed rage in Seerce's gut finally burst out. Fury flashed like lightning through her mind. "Is that what you feared years ago, Cyan? *Aaron's* control of my mind?"

His stare was icy.

She shouted at him, "You prevented me from hearing him all these years!" Her volume caused him to flinch. Slowing to measure every word, still she shouted, "It was *you* who planted the illusion of his lover in Eyre, and prevented me from hearing him when he came looking for me! You have consequences of your own to face, Exemplar! May you find as much misery as you have caused me and those I love!"

The corners of his mouth twitched and his person trembled. Seerce surprised herself by her ability to unhinge a little piece of his self-control.

"You have no place in the Order," Cyan pronounced quietly, but with venom. "Surrender your Crystal of the Sun."

Seerce jumped to her feet with a hand over her pendant. Reducing the tenor of her voice to match his, it dripped with hatred. "Damn you, Cyan! This pendant hung at my grandfather's heart for his long life of service to Gaia. His love touches my heart where it lies upon my breast. You may not take this from me. You cannot twist love and make it your own!"

Moving quickly to his door, it would not open for her. He had locked it with his mind.

She disappeared.

*

Toward midnight Sava made up the sofa in her apartment as a bed for Seerce, saying, "You need not have told him that we are staying. As he boards the submarine would be sufficient notice."

"He knows I can teleport, Sava! He will blame you."

"That does not worry me. Sleep," she encouraged.

But Seerce did not sleep. What had Cyan intended to do to her, after locking her in his apartment?

*

Oceanus staff spent the morning roaming the ships and the energy sites. Most fortunately, Kieran was present etherically at Echo's hub when a technician removed the headgear that he and Aaron had used, replacing it with a different set. A uniformed navy officer stood by as she did so.

In Seerce's office, behind a closed door, the four discussed this development. *We cannot proceed if the shutdown sequences in that new headgear have been altered,* Kieran stated.

Did she work the console? Aaron asked.

No, Kieran replied. *But as those two left, another tech arrived with another officer. He gave voice commands to the control panel, checking the pump system. Then he went to the pump room to examine the equipment, with the officer on his heels.*

Silence the Echo

It is regrettable that they took back the headgear that you handled, Sava worried.

Seerce questioned whether other saboteurs had made their way to Echo, planting their own disruptions.

If saboteurs are operating at cross-purposes, Sava reasoned, *the consequences may be more disastrous than the EA's foolhardy tests.*

I had been thinking we were quite invincible, Kieran admitted, *given our ability to teleport. But there are variables beyond our control.*

Aaron challenged all of them. *We have been over and over these procedures! We know Echo's systems now, how they are connected, the redundancies, the fail-safe measures. Waiting introduces more variables! We are in early enough to shut Echo down now, to prevent more destruction. That is our goal, is it not?*

Of course it is, Seerce responded neutrally, determined to stay out of a tussle with Aaron. *But the EA is nowhere near making Echo fully functional. More time buys us better information.*

We have done an admirable job in the last moon, learning their technology, Sava stated. *But we have done nothing to discover what other conspirators do. We might devote effort to that.*

Aaron steamed. If Kieran had anything else to say, he did not, caught between his superior and his colleague. The bond between those two was apparent. Seerce appreciated Sava's cool head, for she always stayed above the fray.

Cancel what we planned to do tonight, Seerce directed. *We have one more night ahead of this test cycle. Let us be sure of ourselves before we take action.* With that, she dismissed them.

*

In the middle of the afternoon, Cyan came to address the Oceanus staff and the two physicists. Seerce called the observers back with a ring of the chimes. Sava poured Cyan a cup of tea and left him to sit alone in their conference room. Seerce entered only after the others had filed in, taking the seat opposite Cyan and nearest the open door. Sava was on one side of her and Aaron on the other. Seerce had told him what transpired in Cyan's apartment last night.

The chair stated, "Aaron, you may be excused, as this concerns Temple staff."

He did not move nor did he take his eyes from Cyan.

"As a member of my staff, Exemplar, Aaron will hear what you have to say," Seerce stated. "Please proceed with your business." No one at the table moved an eyelash.

Cyan looked directly to Seerce, saying, "The community will evacuate the Temple as a safety precaution. Please board the emergency transport at one decan prior to midnight tonight, with one large or two small travel bags. Our destination is a private port in Maribu on the west coast of Afrikaa. Further plans depend upon how the campus fares during this test cycle."

The staff listened without obvious concern.

"Our hosts require an accurate head count," stated Cyan. "Please place a hand upon the table to signify that you will travel with us." All hands disappeared beneath the table.

"Perhaps I have not made my point entirely clear. If you elect to stay, it is at your own considerable risk."

"Exemplar," Jade inquired, "will the kitchen remain open?" she asked.

"Yes," Cyan replied.

"Will utilities be functional?" Cesar asked.

"Yes, unless catastrophe damages them." Momentarily there was silence. "If you change your minds," Cyan concluded, "notify Ell by sunset." He stood, so all of them stood. Hurrying out, he made no eye contact with Seerce.

As staff left the room to resume their duties, Seerce thanked each one for their dedication. She had not expected such a response. Their commitment in the face of personal danger amazed her.

The conspirators remained and Kieran closed the conference room door, saying, "With your permission, madame, Aaron and

I will take night shift beginning at midnight. After we finish up a few details, may we be excused to sleep?"

"Yes," Seerce replied. "Sava and I will see to the observations this evening." It did not surprise her that Aaron and Kieran wanted to gather the most up-to-date information for tomorrow's decision.

Sava followed Seerce to her office, saying, "You have done the right thing, calling a halt until we can be more certain of success."

"I appreciate your objectivity," Seerce told her.

"Aaron was not happy about it."

"No. He can be hot-headed."

"I have found him gentlemanly and professional throughout his time with us."

"He has those qualities, too. But he is ever passionate about his cause and it is to take Echo down."

Sava commented, "A worthy goal, I believe."

"And difficult beyond measure," Seerce responded. "I am afraid he sees solutions where none exist. We may come many times to the brink of a plan's execution, only to find reason not to do it."

While Seerce reviewed the day's reports, her remaining staff was out monitoring the vessels that controlled Echo, the volcano station, and the new energy facility near Palermo. It was nearly midnight when Sava returned, just ahead of Aaron and Kieran coming on duty. The four sat down for report. "The ships' control rooms are busy long after day shift," Sava told them.

"Anything noteworthy in the dialogue?" Kieran questioned.

"No," Sava answered, "but I observed a number of practice sequences in each vessel's control room, as though they are less than sure of themselves."

"The stakes are higher this time," Seerce judged. "They had best not destroy their target."

"What about the military vessels?" asked Aaron.

"Same story, but with a single officer on duty at those stations," Sava responded, "people known to us." Kieran and Aaron glanced at each other.

Seerce told them, "Cesar covered at the volcano this evening. The usual contingent was present. Jade found lights on within the new power station, but no human presence."

"Then let us assume our shift," Kieran suggested, "and you ladies can get some sleep."

Before she turned in, Seerce sent her remote vision to Cyan's apartment and the underwater dock, assuring herself that he and the submarine were gone. Tremendously relieved, she climbed into bed and listened to silence. Breathing evenly, she relaxed into the cocoon of her thick quilt and drifted away.

*

Waking sometime later to pressure in her inner ear, perhaps infrasound, Seerce's ceiling portrayed that dawn had yet to break. Getting up, she wrapped her bath robe around her, seeing the red aurora across the western sky as she descended her stairs. The closer she came to the windows, the better she heard heavy swells against the seawall. But the light standards on the grounds showed the trees were perfectly still. There was no wind and yet waves crashed. This was not a good sign.

Donning shoes, she headed down to Oceanus. Sava was already there and Cesar, too. They wore unusual clothing, grey-and-yellow coveralls, exactly alike. "Where are Kieran and Aaron?" she asked.

"They are not here," Sava answered.

"The waves kick up," stated Seerce. "Has there been a disturbance along the mid-ocean ridge?"

"I will call Geology, if you like," Sava offered, "but we have felt no tremors."

"But you have seen the aurora?" Seerce questioned.

"We often see it around test time," Cesar said.

But not this close to dawn, Seerce knew. "I have pressure against my eardrums," she told them.

"Likely another protective measure has been instituted at the volcano," Cesar surmised.

"We will keep watch until Kieran and Aaron return," Sava told her. "Sleep if you like."

Something was amiss here. Whatever these two knew, they were not sharing it. "You know where I am if you need me," Seerce responded. Disturbed, she paced in her apartment. She disliked doubting her staff. She hoped Aaron had not been so bold as to act independently. Worse would be Kieran's complicity. Never had she considered they might take matters into their own hands. But she should have, reminding herself wryly that, as of late, she operated under no one's authority but her own.

Reclining on her divan, Seerce tried to steady her nerves and slow her breathing. The pressure in her ears eased, but now the waves pounded. Closing her eyes, she willed the calm that allowed her etheric body to escape its moorings. Her intended destination was Echo's hub, where she suspected she would find her night watchmen. But she perceived only blackness and wild turbulence there. A terrible roar enveloped her. She returned to her body to try again. It was precisely the same experience, but this time she stayed with it. There is nothing to fear, she told herself. I am in etheric form. Simply rise up. The darkness and the chaos around her seemed endless. Faster, faster, she willed. Finally she broke the surface of the great ocean, moving up higher still.

The moon was absent. In places, the water reflected the red aurora. She heard the slap of great waves falling hard, the surf bubbling and thrashing. There is no Echo, she realized, only this maelstrom.

Seerce moved to hover above *Amymone*. There was cloud cover there, no aurora, but the ship's lights showed that it tossed atop a wild sea. Likely the crew was engaged in survival measures, their instrumentation useless in such turbulence. She would learn nothing here.

Perhaps aboard *Tethys*, she thought. By its depth or its distance from Echo, the submarine was steady as she willed her essence into its communication hub. The small space was packed with people, alive with adrenaline and rapid-fire conversation.

Two technicians at the console watched blank screens, their red-faced and horrified superiors crowded in around them, most in nightclothes. Whatever happened must have been unexpected, because confusion reigned here. From their mouths Seerce heard "catastrophic failure" and "massive implosion" and "vanished."

*

"I have never been so furious with you or so happy to see you!" Seerce took one of Aaron's wrists with both of her hands and pulled him into her office as Kieran scurried away. The sun had risen to reveal a restless ocean and a strange mist in the air. "Sit!" she ordered him. "Explain!"

"It is over, Seerce! Echo is no more, just the way we planned it!" He was so jubilant he could scarcely contain himself.

She applied emphasis to her stern response. "I cannot believe you and Kieran would strike out on your own, place yourselves in grave peril, and in the event of your failure, endanger all of us!"

He replied coolly, "This was a precisely executed mission, meticulously planned over years. Your objection was irrelevant."

"Who planned this meticulously for years?" she demanded.

"A contingent of ethical scientists and concerned citizens. Of course I am not at liberty to name the living, but among the departed you knew Anakron, Barlas, and Jory. Had you steered clear of Cyan's influence, you might have been one of us." Aaron shook his head disappointedly, saying, "You would have been such an asset to our cause.

"But I give you credit for some terrific assistance here in the final stages—a safe base of operation and fine recruits among your staff and Tane's. Teleportation made certain logistics more manageable. Thank you." That familiar bemused expression settled upon his face.

"Whoa, Aaron! Start back at when you arrived here a moon ago. Already you were involved in a conspiracy?" Seerce questioned, sitting down hard in the other chair.

"I have been since Anakron's death," he replied. "It has been a long, arduous project, but eventually we placed operatives aboard all those ships, people who piloted the submersibles, worked the control stations, and figured out how to silence Echo's perpetual energy system. What was buried in the ocean floor would have radiated through the mantle of Earth for centuries to come, with or without the complex above it. The mission was much more difficult than imploding a tubular hallway."

"Then why did you bother with Oceanus and me?" Seerce asked.

"Because when finally I got through to you, you begged me to come. But we could not risk bringing you into our plans at the final stage, never sure what Cyan learned from you or what he would do with information. I will tell you that Echo's technology was far more complex than Oceanus knew. Only the minds who crafted it could figure how to destroy the most harmful part of it."

He paused, adding in a serious tone, "You should not be here when Cyan returns. Would you like to come home with me?"

Seerce laughed long and loudly at the thought. "You really know how to charm a girl—taking her staff and implying that she is a simpleton! No, thank you. I am going home to Basra to be priest of my people."

Grinning, Aaron told her, "Do come to visit Eyre. If you teleport in, surely I will see and hear you. Now I must be going." He got up and leaned over to kiss the top of her head. Then he went out the door.

Seerce sat dumbfounded, reeling with these revelations. It was some while before she noticed that her desk had been cleared, empty now of her report crystals and a stack of velum diagrams she had been studying. Going out to survey the offices, she found no one present. All their instruments were gone—Kieran's imager, Jade's calculators and reference crystals, the tools and paraphernalia that Cesar kept. Always pristinely organized, Sava's shelves and drawers were empty and the department files gone.

They were quick to dispose of all the evidence, thought Seerce, saving her the trouble. Upon his return, Cyan would find nothing and learn nothing.

*

After a meager breakfast of tea and biscuits left over from dinner last evening, Seerce soaked in a hot bath, concluding that she was a poor judge of character and a bigger fool. She failed to account for strong personal motivations among those she trusted most, when well she knew what those were. Kieran avenged his father's death at the hands of Control Star. Sava defied Cyan, divulging his teleportation secrets. Aaron punished Altea for his mother's death and the earthquake in Eyre. And he offered all her staff the perfect antidote for their guilt and angst over the destruction of Palermo—a well-orchestrated conspiracy to destroy Echo. That he could steal all of them from under her nose—why was she surprised? Regardless, Echo was no more. She should rejoice.

Donning casual clothes, Seerce left her hair up in a knot at the back of her head. There were only a few items to go home with her, defined by what she might wear on her person. She tucked her Crystal of the Sun inside her dress, Ena's crystalline collection of romances in one pocket, and her Hall crystal in the other. Intending to teleport to Orion's ceremonial chamber, she hoped to shock no one by her sudden appearance.

Digging for the rose quartz necklace buried in her closet, Seerce thought she heard Rayn's voice calling her name. Not his telepathy—his voice.

She got up to look over the half wall to her sitting room and there he was, standing by the window in flesh and blood, looking the way he had years ago when they loved each other—dressed in a beautiful set of clothes, his beard trimmed short and his hair newly styled. She tried not to trip as she stepped down the stairs.

"I hope I have not frightened you," he said.

"You have not. I am pleased to see you. How did you get here?"

"I teleported."

Seerce laughed. "I thought that was a clandestine practice of the Mu."

"Perhaps it is. I was taught by an elder Mu priest."

"Shall I make us tea?" she offered.

"Maybe you would allow me to hold you instead," he suggested. "I have thought of nothing else since I left you in Tunise."

She went to his outstretched arms and reached her hands up around his neck. But she resisted his pull at the small of her back, saying, "Please, let me look into your eyes and find that you are real." The gold petals bordering his richly brown irises sparkled, even in the subdued light of a winter day. A more welcome sight there could not be. "You made it safely to Misr. I appreciate that you have come to let me know."

He studied her face before he replied. "Your work here is done," he said finally, "and I am finished in Misr."

"I do not understand."

"Let me explain it this way." Now she allowed him to pull her close. He tipped her chin up with one finger, placing his mouth tenderly on hers, the way he used to do, sweetly and briefly, letting the kiss linger.

"More," she said, her eyes still closed.

He kissed her longer this time, and then pulled back just a little.

"More," she repeated.

"You have one more, madame," he told her commandingly, "then we are going home to Basra."

Acknowledgements

For those who helped me birth *Silence the Echo,* please accept my heartfelt gratitude for your generous participation in this chapter of my life!

Kyra Freestar at Tandem Editing in Seattle, who saw my vision for this story and provided professional direction for its telling.

Brad Luke, patient and intuitive artist, he captured in the cover art the essence of my story with magical clarity.

Tim O'Neil, inspiring friend, cheerleader for my efforts, and realtor extraordinaire.

Jared Files, author of *Elementals: The Seven Spheres.* Published at age 21, he is my shining example and my listening ear for the agony and ecstasy.

Melissa Jentzsch, photographer and fellow near-death survivor, capturer of my true self in the portrait she made for me.

These generous people read versions of my manuscript, making helpful suggestions and buoying me with their encouragement: Cristi Zimmerman, Trisha Newell, Jamie Zimmerman, Megan Allyn, Merewyn Lynn, Don Williams, Terry Williams, and Ryan Luke.

Finally, I wish to thank my beloved spirit guide, Anakron, for helping me tell our story. May humankind be reminded of the sanctity of Earth and our obligation to live lightly upon Her body.

Blessed be,

Alea Carroll

Alea Carroll has taught country dance in bars, worked in hospitals as a social worker, and managed family support programs. A passionate community volunteer, she has served on Boards of Directors for nonprofit agencies and as a city planning commissioner.

During a medical procedure at the age of 37, Alea had a near-death experience. Aware that she was outside her body, she felt only profound peace, even as she seemed to accelerate through a dark tunnel toward a brilliant light. Reentering her life without fear of death, she became an advocate for hospice services and a counselor for dying patients and their families.

Since childhood Alea has studied astrology. Utilizing dream states, meditation, and age-regression hypnotherapy, she has uncovered a number of prior lives. *Silence the Echo* was inspired by one of these.

A native of Phoenix, Arizona, Alea moved to Washington State three decades ago. Currently she lives on the Olympic Peninsula, writing in the midst of its enchanting coasts, mountains and rain forests. Her two sons are software engineers in the Seattle area, one an accomplished musician, the other a talented artist.

For more information about the author, visit her website at www.aleacarroll.com.

CPSIA information can be obtained
at www.ICGtesting.com
Printed in the USA
FSHW010509110919
61910FS